Books by Georgia Bockoven

The Year Everything Changed

Things Remembered

Another Summer

Disguised Blessing

The Beach House

An Unspoken Promise

Far from Home

Alone in a Crowd

Moments

The Way It Should Have Been

A Marriage of Convenience

The year everything changed

GEORGIA BOCKOVEN

wm

WILLIAM MORROW
An Imprint of HarperCollins*Publishers*

THE YEAR EVERYTHING CHANGED. Copyright © 2011 by Georgia Bockoven. All rights reserved. Printed in the United States of America. No part of this book may be used or reproduced in any manner whatsoever without written permission except in the case of brief quotations embodied in critical articles and reviews. For information address HarperCollins Publishers, 10 East 53rd Street, New York, NY 10022.

HarperCollins books may be purchased for educational, business, or sales promotional use. For information please write: Special Markets Department, HarperCollins Publishers, 10 East 53rd Street, New York, NY 10022.

FIRST EDITION

Designed by Diahann Sturge

Library of Congress Cataloging-in-Publication Data has been applied for.

ISBN 978-0-06-206932-0

11 12 13 14 15   OV/RRD   10 9 8 7 6 5 4 3 2

This one's for John—my husband, my best friend.

Prologue

October 2011

Elizabeth stepped deeper into the late evening shadows of an eighty-foot-tall heritage oak, the advertising symbol for a cemetery nearly as old as the tree itself. Here was where the elite, the historic, the movers and shakers of Sacramento, California, were buried. With park-like grounds, stately mausoleums, and subdued but elegantly expensive granite headstones, it was plain that those without significant means need not apply to have a loved one buried in such august company. The rules governing the who and how were strict and inflexible, if not always openly admitted. At one time Elizabeth would have obeyed these rules unquestioningly; she was not the same woman she'd been a decade ago.

She'd come early for this final farewell, wanting to be alone with her thoughts before the others arrived. Memories were a poor substitute for what had been a deep and ever-expanding friendship, but they were all she had left. How long would it be before she stopped automatically reaching for the phone to call and share something she knew would make them both laugh, or maybe even make them feel a little wistful? When would the shards of loss develop rounded edges?

A flickering movement near an azalea caught her eye. It was one of the orange-and-black monarch butterflies that drifted through the valley each year on their way to winter over in a eucalyptus grove on the coast. There they would rest and sleep and mate and four months later take off again to begin an eighteen-hundred-mile migration, returning, four generations later, to the same grove to begin the cycle anew.

Elizabeth had read that, in theory, a time traveler could change the future by accidentally altering the path of a single butterfly. Was that what had happened to them? Was that how . . . *why* . . . the fabric of their lives had come apart eleven years ago and then been resewn in a pattern none of them would have recognized just a season before?

Time travelers and butterflies were ideas Elizabeth would have laughed at once. Now she wasn't so sure. Something, be it butterflies or destiny or simple inevitability, had led to the year everything changed. It was also how she had wound up in the middle of a cemetery where she was about to do something that could land her in jail.

One

Lucy

March 2000

Lucy Hargreaves stood in the doorway of the cherry wood–paneled study and stared at the only man she'd ever truly loved. For twenty years she'd gone to bed alone, questioning her decision not to tell him, and awakened the next morning knowing her silence was the only way to keep him in her life. Where women were concerned—and there had been more than she cared to think about—there was no middle ground with Jessie Reed; it was sex or friendship.

The sex would have been good. Better than good—the kind she'd dreamed about when she was a young girl and then tried to forget when reality turned out to be more Marvel Comics than Shakespeare sonnet.

The day Jessie Reed walked into her law office she was thirty-nine and looking for a way to forget she was about to turn forty. He was new to Sacramento, fresh from his second divorce, and the only things separating him from the homeless men who drifted through the Greyhound bus depot she passed on her way to work every morning were his intelligence and a single-minded drive to rebuild his fortune. He did so with a cunning and fearlessness that bordered on fanaticism, treating free time as an enemy, recreation as a mortal sin.

Now, with his head propped against the wing of the leather chair, his thick silver hair long over his ears, his eyes shuttered and unresponsive, he looked vulnerable—a word as alien in any description of Jessie Reed as indecisive.

He opened his eyes and, without blinking, looked directly into Lucy's. "You're late," he said, a note of irritation accentuating his soft Oklahoma drawl.

"The meeting ran longer than I expected."

He straightened, ran a hand through his flattened hair, and motioned impatiently for her to join him. "So, what did you find out?" he asked.

She'd never lied to him. Not even in the small social ways friends used to dance around the truth. But this was different. He'd never asked her to be a party to something she was convinced was this misguided. He could have months more to live, even a year if he defied the odds with cancer the way he'd defied the odds with every other aspect of his life. But it still wouldn't be enough time to do what he wanted. Not nearly enough.

"Nothing yet," she finally said. If not an out-and-out lie, it was certainly its kissing cousin.

"This is takin' too long. Hire another investigator." He shifted in the chair. "Hell, there are people who advertise on talk shows that they guarantee they can find anyone in a week."

"When did you start watching talk shows?"

"That's not the point."

"I know it's not the point, but I still want to know why you're wasting your time watching—" Could she have asked a more stupid question? Neither of them had anticipated how quickly or seamlessly he could divest himself of his various businesses or how empty his life would become without their distractions.

Three and a half months ago, on Thanksgiving day, Jessie had gone into the hospital to die, wryly disappointed that he would not see a new century arrive with all its wild predictions of computer crashes and meltdowns. He left a week later, his cancer seemingly in remission, something no one had thought possible. Grimly accepting that he would not die the quick death his doctors had predicted, he appeared at her office two days later and handed her a copy of the will that he'd had drawn up by another attorney. When he'd first told her that he'd gone somewhere else she had been confused and hurt, but careful not to let either reaction show.

Going through the papers, she'd skimmed the details. Convinced she'd gotten it wrong, she'd gone back to read more carefully. Finished, she sat back in her chair and stared at the man she'd thought she knew, too stunned at the revelations to say anything for a long, long time.

"Talk shows are like doing research," Jessie said. "I've discovered there's a whole world out there I knew nothing about. It's time I learned. I think I've even figured out the appeal. It's like watchin' people who've been in a train wreck jump out the windows so they can steal what fell on the track. You can't believe what you're seein', and you feel guilty because you're lookin', but you can't close your eyes or turn away."

"So I've heard. I just never thought I'd be hearing it from you."

"Don't judge me too harshly, Lucy," he said, giving her a chastising smile. "It stops me from thinking too much. Gives me something to do."

"You mean something other than what I've already suggested?"

He eyed her, curious, then said, "I don't remember what you suggested."

Her heart broke a little at the admission. Jessie was sixty-four when they met but could have passed for midforties, his mind quicker and sharper than anyone she'd known before or since. He was tall and lean and had the look of a man who'd made his living on horseback. When he smiled, it started with a slow tug on the left side of his mouth, and when he was particularly caught up in the moment the smile would end with a wink. He'd had her five minutes into their first conversation. From that day she had measured every man she met by a new standard.

"Visit the charities you named in your will," she gently reminded him. "Give them a chance to thank you in person."

"Why would I want to do that?"

"Because it will make them feel good."

"Not as good as the check will."

"That's not the point. Let me arrange one meeting. If you don't like it, then you don't have to—"

Jessie leaned forward, placing his hand against his side as if he could hold in the pain. "No."

"All right. What about a trip? Nothing long or strenuous, just a day or two." She stopped to think. "The Golden Gate Bridge wrapped in fog . . . Lake Tahoe . . . wine country. My brother still works for Opus. I could arrange a private tour."

Jessie smiled wryly. "Did you ever play that game where you were supposed to say what you would do if you knew you only had a month to live?" He wiped his hand across his face, stopping to rest his elbow on the chair arm and prop his chin on his fist. "The answers come so easy when it doesn't matter. Now everything just seems a waste of time. All my life I traveled for the experience and the memories. What good are either now?"

"I could take some time off." The small catch in her voice kept it from sounding as casual as she'd intended. "We could go together." His gaze pierced her shell.

"Don't go getting all maudlin on me, Lucy. I've led a good life, lived it on my terms for the most part, and had a lot longer to do it than most. I'm not complaining, just looking for a good exit line."

"How can I help?"

"You're doin' it. I just need you to do it a little faster."

"Is there no way I can talk you out of this?" She understood his need to try to set things right with his daughters before he died, daughters Lucy hadn't known existed three months ago. What she couldn't make him understand was that it wasn't possible. He needed forgiveness; they needed answers and a target for a lifetime of pain. She was the child of divorce and emotional abandonment; she understood what Jessie's daughters had gone through, what they were still going through. In their anger they would break his heart and consider it their right. If Jessie had another twenty years it still might not be enough time.

"There's nothing you can say that could get me to change my mind," he said softly. "I know you believe I'm doing this because somewhere in the back of my mind I think they're going to come runnin' into my arms callin' me Daddy, but nothing could be further from the truth. I'm doing it because I can't face dying without trying one last time to tell them I'm not the total son of a bitch they have every right to believe I am. I might have walked away, but I never forgot them."

He braced his hands against the chair arms and pushed himself into a standing position. It wasn't that the cancer had made him appear his true age as much as it provided benchmarks for his disintegration. "When I decided to do this, I told myself it was for them, to give them what little peace of mind I could while I still could and damn the consequences to myself. I wish that were true, Lucy. With everything I have I wish I were that selfless." Unflinchingly, his gaze met hers. "I'm doing this for me. It's the only way *I* can have any peace."

He went to the desk, opened a drawer, and took out a sheet of paper. "I found the address I had for Elizabeth when I tried to get in touch with her a few years back."

Lucy took the paper. Fifteen years ago Jessie found his oldest daughter living in Fresno and called her. She'd refused to have anything to do with him. She told him she would get a restraining order if he ever tried to see her. His letters were returned unopened. After a year he stopped trying.

When they'd gone over the information the detective would need to find Jessie's four daughters, Lucy asked if Elizabeth was the only one he'd ever tried to contact. She simply couldn't believe the man she knew would abandon his children the way her father had abandoned her. Jessie had hesitated before answering, plainly upset by the question. She'd let it go then. Now she decided to try again. "You never tried to find anyone but Elizabeth?"

He looked away from her, his gaze fixing on the bookshelves behind his desk, shelves that held the treasures and trash gathered during a lifetime of incredible wealth and abject poverty. There were first editions of Hemingway and Twain, arrowheads he'd found on his family farm in Oklahoma, a spent bullet discovered in a plowed field in Gettysburg.

One shelf stood out from the rest, the one he stared at now. Centered, propped on a wooden stand, was a small, hinged box. Inside was a Purple Heart medal attached to a tattered and faded purple-and-white ribbon, the bronze relief worn nearly featureless. Years ago Lucy had started to ask about the medal when the look in Jessie's eyes stopped her. She'd never tried again.

"A while back I heard through an old business partner in Mexico that Christina was back in the States going to college in Arizona," Jessie said. "After what happened with Elizabeth, I was—" He faltered. "Let's just say I was hesitant to contact her outright, so I went to Tucson to see a play she was in."

"And?" Lucy prompted.

"I didn't recognize her. I had to look at the program to figure out who she was. She was three or maybe four years old the last time I saw her. How foolish I was, going there thinking I'd find the little girl I remembered. And how was she supposed to know me?" He shrugged, physically reinforcing his decision. "Still . . . I tried. Stupid thing to do, but I stayed around for that thing they have afterwards where the audience can talk to the actors. I watched her for a long time before I finally came up with something to say that wouldn't scare the bejesus out of her. I asked her if she had inherited her talent, and she answered without a hint of question or curiosity about who I might be. I tried to come up with a reason to tell her who I was. . . ." He let out a deep sigh, then finished with a sad smile.

"And the other two? Ginger and Rachel?"

"I never tried to find them. Well, not beyond a time or two when they were kids. Considering the circumstances, I knew there was no way they would want to see me once they were grown." When she didn't comment, he added, "Say what's on your mind, Lucy."

After twenty years, she finally understood Jessie's single-minded, consuming need to build his empire. It had nothing to do with money or success. He'd filled his days to escape the ghosts and guilt that consumed him now. "There's no way I can talk you out of this?"

He shook his head. "This is something I have to do."

Resigned, she said, "Then I'll see what I can do to light a fire under the detective."

"Double his fee."

"I don't think—"

"*Do it*, Lucy." Modifying his tone, he added, "I believe in new beginnings, Lucy. I wouldn't be where I am without them." He gave her a smile followed by a wink. "This time circumstance is even on my side. Something special should mark the beginning of a new century, don't you think? Something memorable. There has to be a reason I got to stick around to see it."

Two

Ginger

Feeling equally hurt and pissed off, Ginger Reynolds went from the living room to the upstairs bedroom extinguishing a hundred dollars' worth of pumpkin pie–scented candles. Willowy streams of black smoke rose to the ceiling creating a cloud to match her mood.

Anticipating a hefty increase in her car insurance to cover her latest run-in with a concrete pole, she'd hesitated about spending money on something as frivolous as candles. But it had been so long since she and Marc had shared anything fun and foolish that she'd dipped into her savings, something that threatened to move from developing pattern to dangerous habit in the year since she'd moved from Kansas City to San Jose, California.

Even if it turned out the article in *Cosmo* was wrong about pumpkin pie topping the list of erotic smells for men, Marc still would have been pleased. He liked it when she tried new things; it meant she was thinking about him, planning, working to keep their relationship fresh.

But what good was it for her to plan and buy and prepare for a special evening when Marc called at the last minute to say he wouldn't be there?

She stepped into the bathroom and pinched the wicks on the votives around the tub. Emergencies were one thing, but tonight's excuse wasn't even close. He had to have known for weeks that his daughter had a piano recital. His wife left him reminders everywhere—his pager, his voice mail, his steering wheel, the bathroom mirror. She treated him like a child, just one of the reasons on a long list that had made him leave her again a year and a half ago.

For six months.

That was one month longer than the first time three years ago when Ginger had met him at a friend's house and foolishly assumed his divorce was past the planning stage. Marc Osborne was everything she'd convinced herself she would never find in a man—tender, sexy, intelligent, attentive. Most compelling of all, he was someone who admired her mind over her body. He'd actually managed to focus on her eyes, not her chest, while they were talking and had made her laugh—genuinely, not the practiced laugh she used to make men feel clever and funny when they weren't. He asked about her work and her dreams and where she wanted to be ten years from that night. He was as different from the last man she'd invested her time and heart in as a pencil is from a computer. She was hopelessly in love an hour into their conversation.

She fell hard, too hard not to compromise, not to admire him for what he was doing, when he decided he owed it to his five-year-old son and eight-year-old daughter to return to his marriage and stay until he could make them understand he was leaving their mother, not them. What was supposed to take months had, with an insidious, irrefutable logic, turned into years. Ultimatums produced promises that were invariably sacrificed on the altar of good intentions.

Ginger opened the walk-in closet and stepped out of the three-inch, sling-back heels Marc encouraged her to wear because he thought they made her legs look sexy. She lifted her skirt and removed the black lace underwear she'd put on solely for him to remove.

Damn him. He knew she'd planned something special tonight. She'd skipped lunch to drive to Los Gatos to buy the Lou Pevre cheese he loved and had even splurged on a bottle of Merlot that the wine expert at Late Harvest had pulled from his private stock when she asked for something extra special.

It was their anniversary, or what was passing for it this year. They'd missed the actual date by three weeks because of Marc's sister's surgery and then a marketing crisis that required an un-planned trip to the home office in Kansas City.

What was it that drew her to men who loved her but couldn't or wouldn't take the final step? At twenty-three she'd molded her-self into everything Bruce had said he wanted in a woman, and six months after they broke up he'd married someone completely opposite. Tom insisted she was perfect just the way she was, yet as soon as they moved in together he started cheating on her.

She wasn't rowing the boat alone. Nothing happened to her that hadn't happened to her girlfriends, or at least the ones who remained single. There were a few seemingly happy marriages along the way, but when kids entered the picture, likely as not, single friends left. Time together became as scarce as divorced men who said they wanted more children with a second wife.

The phone rang. Her heart did a funny skipping dance in breath-stealing certainty that Marc had found a way to be with her after all. He loved surprising her, and she'd somehow let him think she loved being surprised. She dove across the bed and grabbed the receiver. "Hi," she said, her voice low and sexy and happy.

After a moment's hesitation, a woman's voice came on the line. "Something tells me you were expecting someone else."

"Mom—hi." She tried but couldn't hide the disappointment. "Are you okay?"

"Of course I'm okay." When Ginger sold her house and left her job and friends in Kansas City to follow Marc to California, the arguments between her and her mother, Delores, had left them on the verge of estrangement. To stem the blood and try to heal the wound, Marc became off limits.

Succeeding at a breezy tone, Ginger asked, "What's up?"

"Your father wants to know if you got your car fixed."

She and her father weren't one generation apart, they were two. In his early forties when she was born, he communicated with her the way his father had communicated with him, through the women in the family. If he had a question or wanted Ginger to know something, her mother linked them.

"Not yet," Ginger admitted.

A hand over the mouthpiece muffled what came next. "She says 'not yet,' Jerome."

Ginger waited.

"Your father says it's important for you to get the work done as soon as possible. Just tonight on the news they said there was another car like yours that caught fire. The whole family died. Six of them. It was terrible the way those—"

"I'll call first thing in the morning."

"That's what you said last time."

She rolled onto her back and covered her eyes with her hand. "I'm writing myself a note right now." She understood the nagging and tolerated it because it was the only way her parents knew to tell her they loved her. She'd been raised in an undemonstrative household where touching was as rare as buried treasure on a desert island.

"Did I tell you Billy's coming home for your dad's birthday?"

A dozen times. "Yes, Mom, you told me. Remember, I said I'd see if I could get a couple of days off and come too?"

"A week would be nice."

"That's not going to happen. I don't get a vacation with this job until I've been here a full year. The best I can do is try to get a Friday and Monday off and make it a long weekend."

"If that's the best you can do, then it's the best you can do."

"Mom, I really have to go. I'm meeting someone in a few minutes."

"Someone?" she asked.

"A girlfriend."

After an awkward, strained silence, Delores tried humor. "Does this girlfriend have a brother?"

"As a matter of fact, she does," Ginger answered, her patience strained to breaking. "But he's gay."

Without missing a beat, Delores said, "I understand there are places people like that can go now to be cured."

Ginger was speechless. And then she laughed. "I love you, Mom. I'll call in a couple of days when I have more time to talk."

"Don't forget about the car."

"I won't. Bye." For a long time she sat on the edge of the bed and stared unseeing at the parking lot behind her condo. She hadn't just wanted Marc there, she'd needed him. And not just for the sex. Cut off from her friends in Kansas City, who'd tried to talk her out of following Marc to California, and slow to make new friends in California, she was achingly lonely and desperately missed having someone to talk to and confide in. The women she liked whom she'd met at work and at the gym all had lives and loves and careers that left them too busy for anything beyond a cup of coffee or occasional lunch. Friendships, at least the kind Ginger longed for, required time and nurturing. It was something she'd never say aloud, not to Marc, not to anyone. Lonely people were needy people and needy people were pathetic.

She was running out of time. No matter how hard she worked at the gym, her breasts weren't as high or as firm as they'd once been, and no matter how religiously she applied creams and lotions and makeup, the lines at the corners of her eyes seemed to grow deeper every time she looked in the mirror. She was showing her age. Not in the careless way the women pushing strollers and hauling kids back and forth to school and music lessons and base-ball practice were, but in a more frightening, trying-too-hard-not-to-let-it-happen way.

In four years she would be forty. The thought made her sick to her stomach. She'd be able to get away with claiming thirty-six, just as she was able to claim thirty-two now without raising eyebrows. But even thirty-six was old to the men who were her peers. When they reached forty and decided it was time to grow up, they went looking for sweet young things who were easily impressed with money and experience and who wouldn't have to spend a fortune at a fertility clinic to get pregnant.

Ginger's stomach rumbled, reminding her she'd skipped lunch. She was hungry. A dangerous kind of hungry. The kind that fed her soul over her body. If she didn't get out of there she was go-ing to do something stupid, something to feed the 300-pound woman who lived inside her 112-pound body, a woman she had to battle every minute of every day.

Ignoring both the real and imagined hunger, Ginger changed into her sweats and running shoes and headed downstairs. She'd pinned her house key to her pocket and was leaning against the door to stretch her calves when the doorbell rang. This time she refused to get excited, to even consider the possibility it might be Marc.

It wasn't.

"Sorry to disturb you at dinnertime," the condo manager said, running a hand over his bald pate. "The wife forgot to remind me that this came for you today, and I thought it might be impor-tant." He handed her a FedEx overnight envelope.

Ginger looked at the return address. A law office—in Sacra-mento. She didn't know anyone in Sacramento.

"Hope it's not bad news," the manager said.

"What? Oh, no, I'm sure it's not. The company I work for has connections in Sacramento. Someone must have sent this here by mistake."

Still, he didn't leave. "I would've brought it sooner, but it's the wife's birthday, and to be honest, we both forgot about it until now."

Ginger smiled. "No problem. Please wish her happy birthday for me."

"I'll do that."

She went back inside and tossed the envelope on the sofa. If she didn't get to the track soon, she'd have to share it with the guys from the local freestyle wrestling club and wade through the testosterone lying around like towels in a locker room. She was almost to the door again when curiosity proved stronger than self-interest. It wasn't every day a lawyer sent her something. As a matter of fact, she couldn't remember ever receiving anything from a lawyer.

She sat on the sofa and propped her feet on the coffee table, making a quick mental note to look for a new pair of running shoes the next time she was at the mall.

"Nice . . . ," she said aloud as she pulled out two velum envelopes. One was from the attorney's office, the other from a travel agency. She opened the one from the attorney first.

Dear Ms. Reynolds:

I'm writing to you on behalf of your biological father, Jessie Patrick Reed. I regret to inform you that Mr. Reed is dying. He has expressed a desire to meet you, and in light of the finite time left him, I'm sure you will understand the urgency involved. He has asked me to tell you that he understands why you might feel a meeting is not in your best interest, but he is prepared to do whatever necessary to encourage you to rethink your position.

Plainly the letter wasn't hers. Ginger felt an odd mixture of relief and disappointment. A sad indication of how uneventful her life had become.

> *To facilitate your travel to Sacramento, I am enclosing a round-trip airline ticket and have arranged for a car and driver to meet you when you arrive. It is not necessary to confirm. If you have any questions, please feel free to call me at any time.*
>
> > *Regards,*
> > *Lucy Hargreaves*

Ginger refolded the letter and put it on top of her briefcase. She'd call from work in the morning and let the attorney know she had the wrong Ginger Reynolds.

Ginger ran her laps in a bemused fog, caught up in thoughts about the woman in the letter, wondering who she was and how they had come to have the same name. She was still thinking about her when she returned home to a ringing telephone.

She picked up in the kitchen.

"I was beginning to worry," Marc said at her hello.

She glanced at the message light and saw it blinking. "I was at the park." They used to run together before time became too precious to spend on something so ordinary. "Is the recital over already?"

He groaned. "Not even close. We're on the first page of the program, and Jenny doesn't appear until the third. I slipped out to call you. I needed to hear your voice and find out if you were okay."

She leaned against the counter eyeing the clock. Eight-thirty. There would be no surprise visit that night. What an idiot she was to have allowed herself that thread of hope. "I'm fine." She fought to hide her disappointment. "You must be proud of Jenny. They always save the best for last."

"And you always know what to say to make me feel better. You're an incredible woman. I must have done something wonderful in some past life to have you in my life now." He paused. His voice dropped to a low, pained whisper. "I really am sorry, Ginger. I know how much tonight meant to you."

She melted a little. Not as much as if he'd said how much tonight had meant to them both, but enough to keep her going until she saw him again. "We'll have other anniversaries."

"I don't deserve you."

No, he didn't. But he would one day. "I received the strangest letter today. From an attorney in Sacramento. She's—"

"You're going to have to tell me about it some other time, hon. I need to get back before Judy comes looking for me. Remind me tomorrow, okay?"

"It's not important."

"Sure it is. You wouldn't have said something if it wasn't. Now, I want you to go upstairs and take a nice long bath and feel sorry for me that I'm stuck here and not there with you."

He would forget about the letter, and she would let him because reminding him would be something Judy would do, and Ginger worked harder at being Judy Osborne's opposite than she worked at anything else in their relationship. "I'm headed that way now."

She said good-bye but held on to the phone. It was nine-thirty in Denver. Her father would be in bed, but her mother seldom joined him before midnight. Deciding the letter was a rare opportunity to include her mother in something that had happened in her life that had nothing to do with Marc, Ginger dialed the number.

Before Ginger could get to the reason she'd called, she had to convince Delores she was okay and not laying the groundwork for devastating news by calling so late. "Mom, really, there's nothing to worry about. I just wanted to tell you about this weird letter that came today."

"Someone is stalking you?"

Ginger laughed. "Not even close."

"I was just reading an article about how vulnerable single women are, how men zero in on them and—"

"I don't have a stalker, Mom. The letter is from an attorney who represents this man who thinks he's my father."

A thick silence filled the line. Ginger waited. "Mom?" she prompted.

Several more seconds passed before Delores answered. "I'm here."

"Don't you think that's funny?"

"What else does the letter say?"

This was not the reaction Ginger had expected. "He's dying and wants to see me. Well, not me, his daughter."

"Did they give you his name?"

She reached for the letter. "James Reed—no, not James, Jessie."

Another long silence followed. "What are you going to do?"

Puzzled, Ginger was beginning to wish she hadn't called. This was supposed to be fun, not an inquisition. "I guess I'll call and let the attorney know she has the wrong person so she can keep looking."

"You don't have to call. It's not your responsibility. She can figure it out for herself when she doesn't hear from you."

"The guy is dying, Mom. I'd feel bad if I was the reason he didn't find his daughter in time."

"Don't get involved in this, Ginger." It wasn't a suggestion, it was an order. "Just throw the letter away and forget about it."

"I have to return the ticket, or at least let them know I won't be using it."

"Ticket?"

"This guy is so desperate to see his daughter, he sent a plane ticket from San Jose to Sacramento. I could drive there faster and with a lot less hassle."

"Then send it back with a note. Just don't call."

"Why? What possible difference could it make?"

"It's for your own protection. I've read about people who run scams like this. When they find someone who—"

"Mom, it's just a letter sent to the wrong person. You're making way too big a thing out of it. If I'd known it was going to upset you like this, I never would have told you about it."

"I know about these things. I read more than you do."

"All I'm going to do is call the attorney and tell her that she has the wrong person."

"*Damn it, Ginger. Just this once would you please not argue with me and do what I say?*"

Ginger blinked. Her mother rarely raised her voice, and she never swore. Something wasn't right, and it had nothing to do with stalkers and scam artists. "Okay. If it means that much to you, I'll just return the ticket."

"Thank you." Delores's relief was almost palpable.

"I'm going to hang up and take a shower." Before Delores could question her abrupt departure, Ginger added, "I went running before I called and I stink."

"I love you, Ginger."

"I love you too, Mom," she said automatically.

"I mean it. I really do love you, Ginger. More than I could ever tell you. I don't know what I would do if anything ever happened to you."

"Would you please stop worrying about me? And stop reading those articles."

"Go take your shower."

Ginger said good-bye, grabbed a plum from the counter, and headed upstairs. The plum was sour, but she ate it anyway, calling it dinner, saving calories for the weekend, when she planned to talk Marc into taking her to the spa in Sonoma that she'd read about in the Sunday newspaper.

She was in the shower and laying the groundwork she'd use to convince Marc to take off for the weekend when her mother's voice intruded into her thoughts. *Damn it, Ginger. Just this once, do what I say.*

Why just this once? What made this letter so important?

The answer came on a wave of stunning logic too painful to be believed, too obvious to be denied. Still, she fought knowing. She couldn't say the words, not to herself, and certainly not out loud.

She was wrong. She had to be. All her life she'd been told that her dark blue eyes were just like her Aunt Louisa's, that she had inherited her father's temper, that she should take calcium supplements because Reynolds women were prone to osteoporosis. She was related to John Quincy Adams on her great-grandmother's side of the family. Her mother wouldn't lie to her about something like that.

She finished washing the shampoo out of her hair, taking her time, telling herself that it was the plum making her sick to her stomach. As soon as she was out of the shower she would call her mother back, and they would laugh over Ginger believing, even for a second, that she wasn't Delores and Jerome's child, that Billy wasn't her brother, that she wasn't really related to John Quincy Adams.

Ginger told herself that it was late in Denver and therefore not an indication of panic if she skipped her normal after-shower beauty routine and called as soon as she dried off. She called from the bedroom. "Hi, it's me." She didn't know what to say next. After a long pause, she added, "I was just thinking about that letter."

"I figured as much," Delores said.

She clung to one last hope, giving her mother one last chance to tell her she was wrong. "Why did it upset you so much?"

"I'm tired. I've had a long day."

"It was more than that. Please . . . just tell me. Is it true?" She almost choked on what came next. "Is this man my father?"

"Your father is right here in this house with me."

For an instant, the space of a heartbeat, all was right with her world again. But something—a need for clarity or conclusion—pushed her toward one last question. "But is he my biological father?"

"It doesn't matter."

A chill traveled Ginger's spine. "It's true then?" she asked, her voice little more than a whisper. "I'm adopted?"

"It doesn't matter," Delores repeated.

"You're wrong."

"Why?"

"Because it means everything about me is a lie." Ginger stood, walked the room, and then pressed herself into a corner.

"I understand why you're upset. But once—"

"How could you lie to me all these years?" Quick, fierce anger kept the pain from overwhelming her. "I trusted you."

"We had to promise we would never tell, not you, not anyone. It was a condition of the adoption."

"That's bullshit. It might have mattered back then, but not after thirty-six years. What could they possibly do to you now?"

"I thought about telling you. But then I would—"

"Who is she?"

"She's gone, Ginger. She died when you were seven."

"Then who *was* she?"

Delores didn't answer.

"What possible difference could it make if you told me now?"

"Barbara Winston."

She recognized the name but didn't know why. "Who—" And then it clicked. "The singer?" Not just any singer, an angelic beauty, an icon who had guaranteed her place in music history by dying in a plane crash with her band on her way to perform her nominated song at the Academy Awards.

"Yes."

"And this man, this Jessie Reed, is he my father?"

"Yes."

Slowly the information that her father was alive sunk in. "He agreed to the adoption? So that means he didn't want me either?"

"All we knew about him was his name and that he was aware of what was happening. The lawyer told us he'd signed a paper promising he would never try to contact you."

"Well, he changed his mind."

"What are you going to do?"

"I don't know."

"Don't go. You'll regret it if you do."

Thirty-six years and her mother still hadn't figured out that the one sure way to get her to do something was to tell her not to.

Three

Christina

Christina Alvarado sat on a cracked leather sofa in the living room of the two-bedroom bungalow she shared with Randy Larson, her feet propped on the piece of painted plywood that passed for a coffee table. Her hand at the back of her neck, her index finger twirling a strand of bright pink hair that her beauty-school drop-out girlfriend had convinced her was the perfect way to welcome a new century, she slowly reread the letter delivered by courier only minutes earlier.

Randy stood in the arched doorway that led to the kitchen, a can of tomato sauce in one hand, a pot in the other. "So, what's it say?"

"My father's dying." She struggled to make sense out of something that made none. "He wants to see me."

"Enrique's dying?"

"My real father—Jessie Reed."

"I thought he was dead already."

"He is—he was. At least that's what my mother told me." Her father couldn't be alive. Second comings were the providence of Jesus Christ—not Christina Alvarado's father.

"Why would Carmen lie about something like that?"

Carmen treated truth like a too-tight shoe, either stretched to fit or tossed. Christina opened a second envelope and unfolded an airline ticket to Sacramento, California. "Who knows why my mother does anything."

"Call her and ask."

"She's not talking to me."

"Now what?"

"I told her I couldn't come home for her birthday."

"Did you tell her why—that you'd be in rehearsal?"

Randy was missing the point. A father rising from the dead took precedence over a petulant mother. "She said it's only community theater and that I had no business taking on the assistant director job when I knew it would interfere with my promise to her."

"Maybe if you told her you'd be there if she sent money to pay the rent?"

"Like that's even a possibility." Christina had Enrique to thank for paying her way through school in the States, even though it was more self-serving than philanthropy. Separating mother and daughter brought him the peaceful household he longed for. To her mother money was like a cold, something you shared accidentally.

"There's got to be someone else you could ask about your father."

He'd been a forbidden topic when she was growing up. What little she knew came from a cousin. "My Uncle Mario was in business with him. That's how he met my mother."

"Yeah? What kind of business?"

"Strawberries."

Randy laughed. "Your uncle was a farmer? I thought he was some big wheeler-dealer in the import-export business."

"He found the growers in Mexico and my dad found the buyers in the States. They were the first ones to figure out the demand and made a killing until the market became glutted and collapsed."

"And that's why your mother dumped him?"

"I think it was more that she hated living in San Diego. When he refused to move back to Mexico, she went without him." Now Christina questioned even that family lore. "At least that was what I was told."

"More likely she left when the money did."

She glared at him. "Why do you do that?"

"What?"

"Slam my mother. You don't even know her."

"I know how she treats you."

"Maybe she has her reasons."

"Like she needs a reason to be a bitch where you're concerned."

"Too far," she warned.

Randy put the can and pot on the table, grabbed one of the mismatched chairs from the table, and straddled it. "So, what are you going to do?"

"I don't know." Her father was alive. She should be happy, ec-static. When she was a child, this was the man she'd gone to in her dreams when she needed to feel loved, worthy. Why wasn't she excited? Why wasn't she eager to see him again?

Because, if he was alive, it meant that he'd abandoned her on purpose. The man she'd loved and missed all these years would never do that to her.

"I don't know what I'm going to do," she answered.

"What do you *want* to do?" he tried again.

"Direct a Steven Spielberg film," she shot back. She put her feet on the floor and leaned forward. "How the hell do I know what I want to do about something like this when I can't make up my mind whether to junk my car or get the transmission fixed?"

"Junk it."

She'd have more confidence in his answer if he weren't balancing the money she'd use on the car against money they could use on the film. The tighter their finances, the more protective Randy became of *Illegal Alien*.

Christina examined the airline ticket that had come with the letter. "Whoever this guy is"—she couldn't accept he was really her father—"he must be serious about wanting to see me. The ticket's first-class."

"Ticket?" Randy crossed the room and sat next to her, plucking the paper from her hand and studying it. "Holy shit. Is that really what it costs to fly first-class from Tucson to Sacramento?"

"Apparently."

"He has to be nuts to put out that kind of money when you could drive up there for a couple hundred dollars." He stared at the ticket for several more seconds, then looked at Christina, a sly smile in place. "Nuts—or rich."

"Or desperate. The attorney said he's dying. He probably thinks this is his last chance to see me."

"You gonna go?"

Her stomach did a slow roll. What if she got there and it turned out this man was her father and she did something stupid—like forgive him? "It's not a good time. Rehearsals start next week, and Harold said he'd fire my ass if I missed another shift." Harold threatened to fire his waitresses on an ongoing, rotating basis, but Randy didn't know that. He only knew that if she lost her job, he might be forced to find one.

"Shit—it's not like he's asking you to move in with him and call him Daddy. Think about it. Wouldn't you rather be sorry you went than regret you didn't?"

"Why do you care?"

"Self-protection." He gave her an unconvincing smile. "I don't want to have to listen to you whining that you should have gone after it's too late."

"I have to think about it."

He took the letter and read it. "It says here that he's paying for a car and hotel, too. If you want, I could go with you. We could trade that first-class ticket for two economy and probably have money left over." After several seconds he flashed her a conspiratorial smile. "Or . . . you could turn this in and we could use the money for *Illegal Alien*."

Their independent film, a documentary—*Illegal Alien*—had consumed every dime and dollar she'd managed to earn, beg, and borrow for the year and a half she'd known him and was still months from being completed. To help him, Christina had gone from the relative comfort of Enrique's monthly stipend during the five years it had taken her to earn her degree at the University of Arizona to working two part-time jobs and living on the edge of poverty.

She was twenty-six years old, and it was getting harder and harder to maintain the fantasy that her big break would come when the film started winning awards. She either got to L.A. in the next year or settled for growing old in Tucson directing community theater productions and staring in underpaid, late-night used-car commercials.

"If I turn in the ticket"—could she get a refund on something she hadn't bought herself even if her name was on it?—"how would I get to Sacramento if I decided to go later?"

"Put up a notice at school and see if anyone is headed that way?"

"Why not UPS? A little bubble wrap, a couple of Power Bars, I'd be set. And if you had me delivered to the office, we might be able to get a refund on the limo, too."

"Look, all I'm saying—"

"I know what you're saying. And I know what you were thinking—but there's no way in hell I'm going to hitch a ride with some pervert so you have money to go back to Texas for a couple of pickup shots."

"All I need is a couple of days, a week at the outside."

"Then get off your ass and get a job. If those extra shots are that important, it seems to me that you would be willing to flip burgers for a month to pay for them." They could be having a playback of the argument they'd had a dozen times already. She didn't think the shots were necessary, Randy believed they were crucial. She liked mean and lean, he liked long and lingering.

He put his arm around her shoulder and drew her into his side. "Think about it, Christina," he said, effectively ignoring her outburst. "With that kind of money not only could we get the scenes we need, we could get some more footage of that cop in Phoenix."

Randy wouldn't leave Tucson until *Illegal Alien* was in the can, and she'd stupidly promised she wouldn't go without him even though they could finish the editing as easily in L.A. as in Tucson. She grounded him. She was his inspiration, his drive to succeed. Besides, he loved her. And if she was into believing everything she was told, she might as well buy into the line that thong underwear was comfortable.

She was his meal ticket, pure and simple. She knew it, and she put up with it because she wanted the film finished even more than he did. Not only had she worked on it as hard and long as Randy, she'd contributed every spare dime she'd earned and all the Christmas and birthday money her mother sent every year because it was too complicated to send actual presents from Mexico to Arizona.

"Why don't I call the airline." Before she could say anything, he added, "Just to see if they'd let you exchange this for coach and what kind of refund you'd get."

Bottom line—whether it was first-class or on a bus, she would go. She had some questions for Jessie Reed. Starting with where the hell he'd been the last twenty-three years.

That night was the best sex they'd had in weeks. Randy was high on the possibility they'd be back to work on *Illegal Alien* and as solicitous of Christina as he'd been after she'd agreed to pay all the household bills with a second job so he could put all his time into the final edits. He'd prepared dinner, put candles and flowers he'd filched from the neighbor's yard on the table, and even in-sisted on doing the dishes himself while she studied the director's notes for her upcoming play.

Later, spent from their sexual gymnastics, Randy put his arm around her and held her close, her head on his shoulder, his chin nestled in her hair. "What kind of memories do you have about your dad?"

Although sated and languid and seduced by their intimacy, she hesitated in answering. Her memories of her father were like her dreams of flying, intensely private and vulnerable. Awake, she knew she couldn't hop into the air and flap her arms and disap-pear into a cloud, but knowing this did nothing to diminish the wonder and freedom she felt when it happened in her dreams. It was the same with her father, or at least the way it had been before today. Thinking about him was like going to a secret place where she felt special and loved. She would close her eyes and feel the warmth of reaching up to put her hand into his, see eyes that radiated joy when he looked down at her, and hear a deep and gentle voice tell her the man in the moon hadn't smiled until the day she was born. Her life changed after he disappeared. All that was special and tender and forgiving became memory, childhood armor in the hostile world she inhabited without him.

She'd gone through a time when she doubted her memories of him. At two months shy of her fourth birthday, could what she remembered be real? Was the Jessie Reed she carried in her heart someone she'd made up to make herself feel loved?

"Memories?" she repeated. "Hardly any." Facts she would share. "He and my mother divorced when I was two. That's when she moved back to Mexico to live with my grandparents. I only saw him a few times after that."

"And Carmen never talked about him?" He traced the circle of her belly button with his finger, then stopped to tug gently on her navel ring.

"Never. The little I know is all bad and came from my cousin, Ricky—my Uncle Mario's oldest boy. He hated me." She smiled. "With good reason. I was really mean to him when we were growing up. He retaliated by telling me things about my mother and father he knew would hurt me."

"Like?"

"My mother was pregnant when she met my dad. Her father had thrown her out of the house and she was living with Ricky's family. Ricky said the only reason my dad married her was because no one else would and he felt sorry for her."

"Wait a minute. I thought you said Jessie was your real father."

"She lost that baby. I was born a year later, after they'd moved to San Diego."

Randy propped himself up on his elbows and fixed her with a stare.

"What are you thinking?" she asked.

"That he might be richer than we think. If he made it big once . . . well, maybe he did it again. I've read about guys like him and your uncle. Having a business go belly-up doesn't faze them, they just start over. Sometimes even doing it three or four times before they hit on something that sticks."

"So?"

"So what if it's not guilt he's feeling but something else? Like not having anyone to leave his money to except some charity—or you? Maybe you shouldn't change the ticket." Randy warmed to the idea. "You might give him the wrong impression." He sat up. "You don't want him thinking you're only there because of his money."

"Like he's going to think I'm there for any other reason."

"Oh, man, this is unreal." He shook his head in wonder. "You can't even say it was luck. What are the chances your old man would still be alive and rich and ready to kick off and leave it all to you? Sweet Jesus, this could be the answer to all our prayers."

Randy either thought she didn't care how callous he sounded or he was oblivious in his excitement.

"You *are* his only kid, right?"

"As far as I know. But he could have had a dozen after me."

"Not at his age. Even if he did drop another kid or two, who cares? God, Christina, think what this could mean. Anyone who spends money the way he does has to have a lot to spend."

His excitement growing, Randy jumped up and stood in the middle of the bed, straddling her. He reached to pull her up to join him. She resisted.

"Come on, baby." He dropped to his knees and clasped her hands. "Be happy for me. For us," he quickly amended.

"This is my *father* who's dying, Randy."

He eyed her. "Like you really care. You don't even know the guy. Besides, it's gotta piss you off in a major way that he's known where you were all this time and he's never once tried to see you."

"If you had a kid living in another country and you had to deal with someone like my mother every time you wanted to see her, how hard would you try?"

"Your mom's not that bad. And you left Mexico almost eight years ago. Why wait until now to get in touch?"

"What you're really saying is that if I'd been cuter or smarter or—"

"Cut the crap, Christina. You know I think you're one of the smartest people I know. And I wouldn't be with you if you were a dog. I care what people think."

"Thanks. Can't tell you how much better that makes me feel."

He moved in closer and nuzzled her neck. "You want our movie finished just as bad as I do. What's wrong with your father helping us out? Isn't that what fathers do?" He leaned back to make eye contact. "This could be our big break, baby." She didn't say anything. "I'll dedicate the film to him—and not at the end. Right up front. I'll say we couldn't have done it without him. He'll be famous. Hell, I'll even make him an associate producer."

"I can't tell him that."

His eyes narrowed as he considered what she'd said. "Yeah, you're right. You want him to think you came because you care."

Randy wasn't going to let go. She either gave in now or spent the next month listening to the reasons she should give in. "I'll go," she finally said. "But not for the money." It was what she needed to believe; what she wanted him to believe.

Randy grabbed her and rolled across the bed, burying his hands in her black and pink hair, kissing her deeply and thoroughly. Coming up for air, he murmured, "That's my girl."

Christina listened to Randy softly snoring beside her. She was thirsty but didn't want to chance getting up and waking him. She wanted time to think about her trip to Sacramento, what she would say, how she would act.

What if it turned out her dad really was rich and what if he wanted to leave his money to her? What if it was enough money for her and Randy to get to L.A. and for her to see agents without having to squeeze in the appointments between work?

Christina glanced at the bedraggled stuffed bear sitting on a shelf beside the bed. Missing an eye and an ear, his arm hanging on by a thread, he was all she had had to remember her father by. She rolled to her side and pressed her face into her arm. Her cheeks were wet. How could she be crying and not know? A wave of aching sadness hit the shores of her heart. *Why did you leave me, Daddy? What did I do? Why wasn't I good enough?*

Four

Rachel

"Good morning, Ms. Nolan."

Instead of simply responding to the usual greeting, Rachel stopped at her assistant's desk. "So—who won?"

Maria grinned. "It isn't winning or losing that's important, it's whether the kids had a good time."

"Uh huh."

This time Maria laughed. "We did, five to four. Sidney scored three goals."

"I hope you're writing all this down," Rachel said, only half teasing. "When *Sports Illustrated* does a cover story on her in a couple of years they're going to want to know what she was like when she was ten." Rachel had caught one of Sidney's soccer games a couple of months ago at an indoor tournament where her own daughter, Cassidy, was playing. Sidney stood out from the other players the way Tiger Woods had stood out in his early years. Rachel left the tournament secretly grateful Cassidy was in a different age bracket and the two girls would never play against each other.

"I try not to think that far ahead," Maria said, following Rachel into her office.

Rachel pulled her cell phone out of her purse and put it on her desk. "Anything pressing this morning?"

"Arthur Stewart wants to know if he can reschedule your meeting for later in the week. He said he's still waiting for the reports from accounting. And there was a message from Ms. Hawthorne that she needs the actuary figures on Selman Electronics as soon as—" Maria smiled "—someone came in this morning."

"I assume you passed that one on?" Madison Insurance's home office was in Baltimore. Andrea Hawthorne was one of the long-time employees who was slow to adjust to the three-hour time difference and accept the fact that the year-and-a-half-old branch office in San Francisco wasn't being run by slackers who liked to sleep late.

"Bob is working on it."

"Good choice. Thanks." She hung her coat in the closet and dropped her purse in the bottom left-hand drawer of her desk, then opened her briefcase to retrieve the flash drive that held the confidential research she'd been working on the night before. A folded note, written on lined paper, was wrapped around the drive held in place with a smiley-face sticker.

Maria dropped the morning's mail on Rachel's desk. "Coffee?"

"Tea, please. Something decaffeinated."

Maria nodded and left, softly closing the door behind her.

Rachel opened the note.

> *Knock knock.*
> *Who's there?*
> *Isabel.*
> *Isabel who?*
> *Turn over for answer. . . .*

She did.

> *Isabel broke? I had to knock.*
> *I know, pretty bad, but it was the best I could come up*
> *with this morning. Have a good one, babe. See you*
> *tonight.*
> *Love, Jeff*

Rachel smiled and taped the note to her computer screen, where she would see it the rest of the day. By habit she moved her chair six inches to the right and with one hand logged onto her computer to check her email and with the other began sorting through the mail Maria had opened that morning and flagged according to urgency.

Outside Rachel's office window a thick fog hid all but the orange triangular peaks of the Golden Gate Bridge. The fog would dissipate by noon, leaving the bay a blanket of sequined blue. In the beginning she'd been mesmerized by the view and the ever-changing qualities of the city's landscape. Lately she'd had to remind herself to take the time to look.

Rachel skimmed the names on the email messages. Only one was unexpected. Connie Helgren. She saw Connie in passing almost every day, but the lunch-and-shopping friendship they'd had in Baltimore had become an unanticipated casualty when Connie took a lateral transfer to the new office in San Francisco and Rachel was given a promotion that put her into one of the key positions. Rachel made lunch dates with Connie and worked hard to keep them, but as often as not something came up that forced her to cancel. Then, when they did get together, the conversation was stilted and formal, with none of the quick and easy laughter and teasing that had bonded them in Baltimore.

Rachel missed their time together. Connie was the closest thing she'd had to a real girlfriend since college. Sad commentary for a woman four years short of her fortieth birthday.

Connie's note was short. She asked if they could get together for drinks after work and suggested a neighborhood bar that was a little on the seedy side but where they wouldn't have to fight a crowd or talk over a sound system. When Rachel responded, she asked if they could meet at six instead of five-thirty and was surprised with an immediate answer.

She rocked back in her chair and smiled. Why was it that she never knew how much she missed something or someone until that person or thing came back into her life? She hadn't been the one who'd let the promotion come between her and Connie, but she hadn't made any concentrated effort to help Connie get beyond it either.

Rachel arrived ten minutes early and was surprised and oddly pleased to find Connie already there waiting. She stood and waved from a booth at the back of the dimly lit room. A year ago they would have hugged. Today, by awkward, tacit agreement, a smile sufficed.

"What a great idea," Rachel said. "I'm so glad you—"

The waiter interrupted her. "What can I get you?"

Rachel glanced over to see what Connie was having. In place of the stout beer she'd always ordered on their girls' night out, she was drinking something hard. "I'll have what she's having."

"Vodka on the rocks?" the waiter supplied.

Rachel shot her friend a questioning glance. Connie used to insist vodka was a drink for closet alcoholics. "Make mine a gin and tonic. Bombay Sapphire, if you have it."

He nodded and left.

"So, have you adjusted to living in San Francisco?" Rachel asked.

Connie let out a humorless laugh. "Kind of an odd question after all this time, don't you think?"

Willing to let Connie have that one, Rachel tried again. "I've been meaning to tell you that I like your hair." She'd changed the style a while back, going from long and curly to short and sleek.

"I cut it six months ago."

Rachel sat back and crossed her legs, her knee hitting the table. She grimaced and rubbed the spot, working to hide her disappointment that renewing their friendship plainly wasn't the purpose of the meeting. A weariness settled through her, and not from the less than four hours' sleep she'd had the night before.

The waiter brought her drink and a bowl of pretzels. Rachel took a sip, judged the drink weak and made from something bottom shelf. "Okay, I can see you're upset. Let's talk about it."

"What makes you think I'm upset?"

Rachel frowned. She'd seen Connie indulge in game playing with others but never with her. "Am I wrong?"

Connie took a minute to answer. "No—but the reason isn't what you think."

"What I think is that we've neglected a friendship because we didn't know how to maintain it, and we should have done something about it months ago."

"*We?*"

Proof positive that there was nothing as unreliable as an eyewitness account—whether over an accident or a breakup. "You're right. Rehashing whatever happened won't change anything."

"I understand how awkward it was for you, how hard it was to be seen with me."

It took supreme effort to keep from shooting back an equally caustic reply. "I'm sorry if I gave you that impression. I don't know how it—"

"It doesn't matter," Connie added before Rachel could say anything more. "That's not why I'm here." She finished her drink and motioned to the waiter to bring another. "I know how hard you worked for this promotion and what it meant to you. I was there. Remember? If I hadn't been, I would have thought you'd let the money and power go to your head. But I know that inside you're the same person."

Why was Rachel having such a hard time believing Connie? The right words were all there, put together in what should have been a convincing way.

"For you being promoted was like the ugly girl in school making the cheerleading squad. You run with a different crowd when that happens. There isn't enough time for all those new friends and the old friends, too."

Kiss, kiss, kill, kill. Rachel just hadn't waited long enough. She had witnessed Connie's sarcasm turned on others but had never been the target. It hurt. "Well, now that we've gotten that out of the way, why don't you tell me why you really wanted to see me." It was almost impossible to hide her disappointment.

Connie waited for her drink. "I want you to know that this isn't easy. For a long time I've gone back and forth over whether I should say anything." She ran her fingertip around the rim of the glass, avoiding Rachel's gaze. "I know you're not going to thank me. No one likes hearing this kind of thing. But sometimes, when it's a friend and you know you're her only real friend, you have to do what's right, not what's easy."

Connie moved to the edge of her seat and leaned close. Plainly whatever she was so eager to tell wasn't a secret. A little investigation and Rachel could find out for herself. She was tempted to leave, to deny Connie the satisfaction that danced in her eyes.

"Jeff is having an affair."

The words hit hard and low and left Rachel reeling. Her salvation came from a childhood that had taught her how to mask her feelings, to keep quiet when someone expected a response, letting them fill the silence, learning more from what was said in those awkward moments than the main text.

"It's been going on for months." Connie picked up her drink.

The paper coaster stuck to the glass for several seconds, then fell onto the seat. She didn't bother retrieving it. Still Rachel said nothing. Connie added, "Everyone at work knows. They're all talking about it. Some days it's all they talk about."

"I assume I have you to thank for telling them?" Rachel immediately regretted the question. Not only had she given validity to the insane accusation, she'd given Connie the satisfaction of seeing that she cared about being the subject of gossip.

Connie glared at Rachel. "I'm not going to dignify that with an answer."

"You're telling me about this alleged affair because . . . ?" Was that really her voice? She sounded so composed, so detached.

"You're my friend," Connie insisted. "And no one else would. They're all afraid of you."

"But you're not?" Rachel said softly.

"Why should I be?" The challenge was unmistakable.

"It's all in the pecking order, Connie. After a while, if you don't move up. . . ." She shrugged. "You move out." Rachel cringed. Had she really just threatened Connie? She had to get out of there. She ran her hand over her skirt, smoothing the exquisite, silk-like wool of the Armani suit, stalling, composing herself, determined she would not let Connie see the devastation she'd come there to create. It was a small thing, but all she had at the moment. She reached for her purse. "I assume that's it?"

Clearly unexpected, the question caught Connie off guard. "You don't want to know who Jeff is seeing? How long it's been going on—or where or when they meet?"

Rachel took enough money from her wallet to cover her drink and a tip, pointedly leaving Connie to pay for her own. She stood and slipped her purse strap over her shoulder. Digging deep, she found the strength to pull off a smile. "Not nearly as much as you want to tell me."

Numbness replaced bravado on the ride home. Her driver was

accustomed to her working in silence during the forty-five-minute trip from the city to Orinda. No reason for gossip later. Nothing to tell the guys back at the limo office.

The wife being the last to know was such a cliché. One Rachel had never believed and had trouble reconciling. If that amount of self-delusion was really possible, she should be more surprised. She must have known on some level.

Until now it had been easy to find explanations for all the clues, the times she'd called his cell and had to leave a message, the fact they hardly fought anymore, his easy acceptance when she pleaded she was too tired for sex. Most damning of all, Jeff was happy. Happier than he'd been in years. She'd put it off to their private celebration that past New Year when they'd shared a bottle of obscenely expensive champagne and toasted the new century by vowing to make the rest of their years even better than the ones before.

Jeff's happiness had seemed contagious. Rachel had even noticed a change in the kids. Cassidy seemed to be outgrowing the need to dominate her brother, John, and John had stopped looking for ways to get under Cassidy's skin.

Jeff was the hands-on parent; she was the breadwinner. A stupid, old-fashioned term. She didn't win the bread her family consumed, she worked damn hard for it. They lived well because of her. Better than well. They lived in a thirty-five-hundred-square-foot home that sat on the side of a hill in one of the most prestigious communities in the Bay Area.

The money Jeff brought in from the part-time consulting work he did from home barely covered the taxes and utilities. He could earn more, he was a genius at taking an impossibly difficult architectural design and fitting an air conditioning and heating unit into that design that would actually function the way it was supposed to. But as it was, it took her income to pay the mortgage, the children's tuition at their private school, the country club membership, the retirement plan, the Range Rover, the Lexus—everything else fell on her shoulders.

How could Jeff do this to her? To them? To their family? Was he so unhappy? Why hadn't he come to her? Why hadn't he given them a chance to work things out before he threw it all away? Did she mean so little to him?

The driver pulled up to the house and started to get out to open her door. He normally carried her briefcase and whatever work she'd brought home that night, then handed them to Jeff. Lacking the patience to listen to the small talk the two men customarily exchanged, Rachel waved the driver off with, "I'm fine."

He nodded and closed her door. "Have a nice weekend."

"You, too," she answered automatically. *At least one better than mine.*

She waited for him to back out of the driveway before she climbed the dozen steps that led to the front door. Digging her key out of her purse, she paused before slipping it into the lock.

Defining moments are discoveries made in hindsight. Rarely is anyone aware when they are in the middle of a situation they know unequivocally will change their life forever. Perhaps it is hope that keeps most people from knowing, a need to believe they can manage a crisis without losing everything that is important to them. Rachel held no such illusions. The minute she walked through the door and confronted Jeff, her life would change. Everything between them that she'd taken for granted would be over.

For one brief, sorrowful moment she considered turning around and walking away. But where would she go, and to what end?

The key heavy in her hand, it took three attempts to slip it into the lock. The door finally open, she took a deep breath and went inside. Jeff met her in the hallway.

"I thought I heard you out here." He gave her a quick kiss. "You look beat. Rough day?"

She dropped her purse on the hall table, her briefcase on the floor. "Are the kids still up?"

"When you didn't call I figured you and Connie were going to make a night out of it, so I put them to bed. Cassidy has an early soccer game tomorrow." He helped her off with her coat and hung it in the closet.

Rachel watched him, trying to see him as a stranger might. At forty-two he still had all his hair, but the black was shot with gray, the mustache even more so. She'd thought him handsome when they first met, but it was his intellect and passion and caring she'd fallen in love with. And his sense of humor. He was the only one she'd ever known who could make her laugh out loud, something neither of them had done enough of for a long time.

"We have to talk," Rachel said.

"You want me to fix you something to eat first?"

She shook her head.

"Drink?"

"*No.*"

He stopped to look at her. "Sounds serious."

She'd promised herself she wouldn't cry. She blinked to clear her eyes, but it didn't work. Tears spilled over her lashes onto her cheeks. She clenched her jaw and wiped them away.

Jeff didn't react for several seconds and then, with a sigh, said simply, "You know."

She nodded.

"How?"

"Connie told me."

"I thought Connie was your friend."

"Me, too—something else I was wrong about."

"I'm sorry."

"About what?" she challenged.

"Whatever you want. Whatever you need."

"Bad timing, Jeff."

He shoved his hands in his pockets and looked down at the entrance tile. "Did Connie also tell you that it's over, that it's been over for months?"

The question threw her. "Is that supposed to matter?"

"I guess that's up to you."

She'd never hit anyone in her life, never understood the need. She did now. "How could you?"

"That's what you want? A reason?"

"Yeah, sure, lay it on me. And then I want you to tell me how you could have been so goddamned careless that you let yourself get caught."

He frowned. "I've been tearing myself up about what I've done to you, what I've done to us, and what matters to you is that someone found out?"

"If you'd been a little more discreet, we could have handled it quietly, between us." Her breath caught in a sob. "We might have worked it out. Now, I have to do something. No one respects a doormat, and if I don't have the respect of the people who work for me, I can't do my job. Without my job"—she was feeling her way through a dark tunnel of pain, grasping for handholds to guide her—"we lose everything." It was a smokescreen, words she could hide behind because the truth left her too exposed. Without Jeff . . . oh, dear God, she couldn't imagine her life without Jeff.

"I don't care."

"Obviously," she shouted.

He reached for her. She threw her arms up to ward him off. "We don't need all of this, Rachel. We got along fine on a lot less. We could again."

"And why would I want to go back there, Jeff? What's waiting for me? A solid marriage? A man who loves me? A faithful husband?"

"I know you don't want to hear this right now, but I'm going to say it anyway. I love you, Rachel. I want our marriage to work. That's all I've ever wanted. What I did was stupid, the biggest mistake I've ever made. I don't want to lose you. Not over this."

"Why, Jeff?" she said in a choked whisper. And then, shouting again, "*Why?*" If she could understand maybe it would give her something to hold on to. Even alone in the middle of an ocean, the floating seat cushion from a plane brings hope.

"Whatever I say is going to sound self-serving." He glanced at the stairs. "Do we have to do this here?"

She looked around. "Is one room better than another? Do we have one I don't know about set aside for dissolving a marriage?"

"I was lonely." He hesitated. "She needed me. You don't."

She felt as if they were in the middle of a bad movie where the wife was being accused and punished for emasculating her husband with her ambition. "That's bullshit. Of course I need you. I've always needed you."

He ran his hand over his face. "I can't do this. I can't defend something that's indefensible. It's not your fault. It's mine. It's something I'm going to have to live with."

"How noble."

"What do you want, Rachel? Name it."

She was overcome by a crushing wave of sorrow. "Yesterday."

He put his head back and stared at the ceiling. Tears escaped the corners of his eyes. "I'm sorry."

"Yeah, me, too." She moved around him and headed up the stairs to their bedroom.

He followed, standing at the doorway to watch her as she opened the closet, went inside, and came out seconds later with a suitcase. "Is that for me or you?"

She stopped and frowned. "I don't know." She didn't want to spend the night in a motel, but it didn't make sense for him to leave. She knew Cassidy had a soccer game, but not where or what time. She counted on Jeff to keep that schedule for her. John had a birthday party on Sunday, but she had no idea if the friend was a girl or boy or whether they still needed to buy a present.

He took the suitcase and put it beside the dresser. "Whatever we decide, it doesn't have to be tonight."

Rachel sat on the edge of the bed and covered her face with her hands. "How could you do this to us?" If Jeff was lonely, why hadn't he said something? She could have taken time off. She could have. . . .

He knelt in front of her and caught her hands before she could pull away. "It was a stupid mistake, Rachel. How can I make you understand that? Sandy was—"

"Sandy?" An insane feeling of relief swept through her. She didn't know anyone named Sandy. At least it wasn't a friend, someone she could look back and remember smiling and greeting her at the club or on the tennis court and feel the heat of humiliation that she had been laughing at her behind her back.

"Browning—her daughter was on Cassidy's soccer team. She moved here to be near her parents when she and her husband separated. I thought I could. . . ." He shrugged. "What I thought isn't important. The only thing that matters is what I did."

Rachel freed her hands. "Do you love her?"

"No."

"Are you still seeing her?"

"Like I said, it's been over for months. She moved back to Texas four weeks ago. She wanted her daughters to be near their father and to see if there was any chance the two of them could get back together. The separation was hard on the kids."

He might as well have hit her. "At what point did her children become more important than your own? When did you decide you were willing to sacrifice their home and their happiness to fuck Sandy?"

Jeff sighed in resignation and stood. "I'll stay in the guest room tonight."

"Say something that will make me understand. Give me that much."

"There isn't anything I can say that's going to make this any easier, Rachel. I screwed up. Pure and simple."

"Nice play on words, Jeff."

"Look—I was lonely. I had no idea how lonely until someone came along who treated me like I mattered. And, yes, I know how lame that sounds, but you wanted the truth and there it is. It just happened. It wasn't planned. I didn't set out to seduce Sandy, and she sure as hell didn't need her life more complicated than it already was."

"Did you think I would never find out, that you could keep this a secret?"

"I didn't think anything."

"That's not good enough."

"What do you want me to say? Tell me, I'll say it."

"I trusted you. I knew with every fiber of my being that no matter how rough things got between us, we would work them out, that there was no way you would ever be unfaithful to me." Pain radiated through her chest as if her heart really could break. She needed a release, to run until she stumbled in exhaustion, to cry until there were no more tears. Instead she held on to her veneer of control as if that were a lifeline. "You destroyed something I can't live without, Jeff."

"I know you're not ready to hear this, but if it takes the rest of my life, I'm going to find a way to earn your trust again. I'm not going to let this family fall apart because I did something stupid."

She looked at him long and hard. "This isn't about what you want anymore."

"I—"

She put her hand up to stop him. "No more."

* * *

A light tapping sound on the bedroom door woke Rachel. She glanced at the clock on the nightstand, stunned that she'd actually fallen asleep. It was one-thirty, and she was still in her suit. When she'd curled up and drawn the comforter over her she was sure it would only be for a few minutes.

The door opened. "Rachel?"

She sat up and ran her hand through her hair. "What?"

"Were you asleep?"

"It doesn't matter."

Jeff came across the room and held out a courier envelope. "This came for you today. It's from a lawyer in Sacramento. I thought it might be important."

She took the envelope and put it on the nightstand. Whatever it was could wait. Anything of any importance would have been sent to the office.

Jeff hesitated as if torn between staying and going. Finally, the decision made, he said, "I'll see you in the morning."

She waited until he was gone before she got out of bed and undressed. She hated Jeff for doing this to her, for becoming what she'd spent their entire marriage convincing herself he wasn't—a man like every other man she'd ever known.

Five

Elizabeth

"All I'm saying is that Stephanie is being incredibly selfish and it's up to you to tell her so. If you don't, I will."

Elizabeth's hand tightened on the telephone receiver. "Please don't do that, Mother. This is Stephanie's last summer of freedom, the last time in her life she'll be completely free of responsibilities. Let her enjoy it." Several of the girls Stephanie ran around with at Sarah Lawrence had parents with summer homes on Long Island. She'd been asked to stay before; this was the first time she'd accepted.

"No one made you get married at twenty. You could have been just as selfish."

Where had that come from? "I thought we were talking about Stephanie."

"I could tell what you were really thinking." Denise Reed liked to think she knew her daughter and was always telling her how she felt and what she thought and was rarely right about either.

Elizabeth laughed. It was either that or throw something in frustration. "Well, you're wrong. What I'm really thinking is that I have to get off the phone and finish making breakfast for Sam. I'll call you back later today." She wouldn't. She would wait a couple of days and then call with news about the next book she'd be reading for her book club or something Sam was doing or a piece of gossip about a mutual friend that would derail her mother from going after Stephanie again. Sometimes it worked, more often it didn't.

"Wait a minute before you hang up," Denise insisted. "I need a ride to the airport next week."

She was leaving on a tour of Italy with her best friend, something they'd been planning for over a year. "I thought Mabel was going to pick you up."

"We had a fight."

"Don't you think you ought to try to work things out before you leave? Three weeks is a long time to share a room with someone you're not talking to."

"This is none of your business, Elizabeth. Besides, if I wanted your advice, I'd ask. Now, can you do it or not?"

"Yes."

"Fine."

Elizabeth said good-bye and put the phone back in its cradle. She'd known it was a mistake to tell her mother that Stephanie had changed her mind about coming home. But the biggest mistake had been made a week ago when she'd shared her excitement over the special plans she'd made for her and Stephanie that summer. Telling her mother something like that was tantamount to giving the neighborhood bully a pellet gun.

Sam called from the top of the stairs. "Have you seen my glasses?"

"Look in your office." The timer sounded on the bran muffins she'd put in the oven just before her mother called. She tested one with a toothpick and reset the timer for an additional three minutes.

Sam came into the kitchen tucking the fat end of his tie through the loop at his neck. He adjusted the knot and stopped to check his collar in the glass reflection of the Wysocki cat print behind the table. "Who was that on the phone?"

"My mother."

He extracted the sports section from the newspaper, tossed the rest on the table, and leaned against the counter. "Kind of early for her. What did she want?"

"To tell me how awful Stephanie is."

"What's she done this time?"

"She's not coming home this summer."

"I thought you weren't going to tell her about that until she got back from Italy."

"Yeah, well, you know how that goes. Open mouth, insert foot." Elizabeth busied herself spooning fruit salad into one of the Jadite bowls she'd found at a garage sale.

Sam refolded the sports section. "I forgot to tell you that Stephanie called me at the office yesterday. She's out of money again and wanted me to put a thousand dollars in her account—a little spending money to get her through spring break."

"What did you tell her?" She didn't have to ask, she knew.

"That if she wanted spending money, she'd better find a job. That's what her brothers did."

For three years they'd engaged in a running battle over Stephanie's careless spending since she'd gone away to college and how much more responsible Eric and Michael had been. Sam insisted the only way she would ever learn to budget was to do without when the money they gave her each month was gone—even if the thing she had to do without was food. Elizabeth refused to let Stephanie go hungry to prove a point. "I'm assuming she talked you into *something*?"

Sam peered at Elizabeth over the top of the newspaper. "Do

you have any idea how much spending money she's gone through this year?"

He worried that Stephanie would never be independent while Elizabeth's heart ached with every step she took away from them. "It's not like we can't afford it or that it's going to go on forever. She'll be out of school in a year and earning her own money."

"We can only hope."

"That's not fair." The timer went off. She nudged him aside to take the muffins out of the oven.

"You're trying too hard, Lizzy."

"I don't know what you mean." She turned the muffin tin over and tapped the corner against the granite countertop. The muffins tumbled onto a cooling rack.

"To not be your mother. You want to give Stephanie everything Denise didn't give you. You need to find a place in the middle."

"This has nothing to do with my mother."

"It has everything to do with her. It always does." He reached for Elizabeth and pulled her into his arms. She came, reluctantly. "I'm sorry. I didn't say it to hurt you. But it's true. You spend five minutes on the phone with Denise and she's ruined your entire day. She has too much power over you." He blew on her forehead to move the hair aside before planting a kiss. "You know your mother hates Stephanie. She always has. Nothing would make her happier than to drive a wedge between you."

"She doesn't hate her." Elizabeth didn't want to believe her mother was capable of hating her own granddaughter.

"All right, maybe hate is too strong. But she sure doesn't like her."

"It's just the way she is. She shows her love differently than other people."

"I'll say."

She shot him a withering look.

"Okay, she stuck around when your dad didn't. I'll give her that." Sam started to add something, then let it go. Changing the subject to something safer, he said, "Don't forget, I'm going to be late tonight."

She had. "How late?"

"Steve seems to think we can wrap up the meeting by seven. I'm figuring we'll be lucky to get out of there by nine."

For the first five years after Sam bought his original tire store in Fresno she'd managed their bills like a Cirque du Soleil juggler. The second five years they'd scrimped to cover opening six more stores. Now, with seventeen in the chain, their financial concerns centered on paying taxes on what they earned. Stephanie might not know exactly how much money they had, but she knew it was a lot. "What about dinner?"

"I'll have Janet send out for something."

"Not pizza." His cholesterol had risen fifteen points, and the doctor had warned him he needed to control it with either diet and exercise or medication.

"Not pizza," he echoed, reaching around her to take a cup from the cupboard. "Back to Stephanie—"

"Can we do this later?"

"All I was going to say is that when she calls you to plead her case you can tell her that you talked me into matching funds. Whatever she earns—up to a grand—we'll kick in an equal amount."

Elizabeth smiled. "That's fair."

"It's more than fair, but she's not going to think so." He poured his coffee. "Did you tell her how much you were counting on having her home this summer?"

"No. What's the point? She's not going to change her mind, and it would only sound like I was trying to lay a guilt trip on her." Elizabeth put a muffin on a plate and handed it to him. She and Stephanie used to be so close. What happened that turned hour-long phone calls four or five times a week into a rushed five minutes between classes? "You're going to be late."

He set the plate on the counter. "Just tell her how you feel. I'm sure—"

"I can't."

"Why not?"

"I want her to come home because she wants to, not out of a sense of obligation." Most of all, Elizabeth didn't want to spend the summer being reminded of how much fun Stephanie was missing with her friends. For all of her wonderful qualities, Stephanie wasn't hesitant to express her unhappiness when things didn't go her way. Reluctantly, Elizabeth had finally acknowledged what Sam had been saying for years. Elizabeth was spoiled. And not the self-aware kind that came with appreciation for all she had and all she was given, but the kind of spoiled that led to a sense of entitlement that came across as more arrogant and demanding than grateful.

"What difference does it make how she gets here as long as she's here?"

"Can we just drop this? Please?"

"If that's what you really want."

"It is."

He looked at his watch. "I've got to get going. Steve's car is in the shop, and I told him I'd give him a lift." Sam snatched a muffin as he leaned over to kiss her. "Why don't you do something fun today? Go shopping. Call Kathy and see if she's free for lunch."

"I'll be fine."

"At least get out of the house."

"I am getting out of the house. I have a library meeting this afternoon."

He stuffed a banana into his pocket to go with the muffin. "If we're going to have the summer to ourselves, let's do something. Just the two of us. What about a cruise?" When she didn't respond, he tried again. "Okay, how's this? Since Stephanie doesn't want to come home to see us, we'll go to Long Island to see her. We could take in a couple of plays in the city, pop up to Boston for a little history. We could even stop by to see the boys on the way home."

"She didn't say she didn't *want* to come home." She followed him outside.

"Just that she got a better offer."

"Nice, Sam. Just what I needed."

He made a face. "I did it again, didn't I?"

"Big time."

"Sorry."

"Drive carefully." She gave him a dismissive wave.

Their normal routine was that he told her he would, she watched as he got in the car, waved good-bye when he reached the end of the driveway, and went back inside when he turned the corner. Today he tossed his briefcase into the passenger seat and came back to take her in his arms. "If Stephanie knew how much this meant to you, she'd be here."

"I'll be all right," she said, relenting enough to put her arms around him. "I just need a little time to get used to the idea."

"I know." He kissed the frown line between her eyebrows. "But that's tomorrow. Today is the shits and I'm sorry."

Not exactly what she needed, but enough to make her feel a little less alone. "Maybe something will happen and she'll decide to come home after all."

"Isn't that supposed to be my line?" he said.

"No, your line is to tell me to go shopping and buy myself something I don't need."

"Ouch." He let her go and went to the car without saying anything more.

Her guilt set in before Sam reached the end of the driveway. She would call later and apologize.

Before she went back inside, Elizabeth took a minute to glance around the yard, noting the impatiens that were thriving and the ones the snails had decimated. She checked the roses for aphids and the flower beds for weeds, the spent tulips and daffodils that needed attention and the dead branch on the birch tree. She'd gone through three gardeners in a year, each one younger and less reliable than the one before.

Complaining about laziness and lack of pride in the younger generation made her sound older than the forty-eight she reluctantly admitted to, so she rarely said anything aloud. But she thought about it a lot. At times the sense of separation she felt around her own children and their friends in ideals and standards and goals left her speechless.

Drawn by the parched look of one of the lilacs near the bird feeder, Elizabeth crossed the lawn to check the sprinkler. She was still working out the problems in the drip system Sam had installed the year before to conserve water. When they'd built the house twenty years ago Sam had designed a simple landscape for the near-acre-size lot, one that he could take care of on Saturdays with a gas edger and riding mower. Over the years she'd added shrubs and flowers, while Sam added a pool and built-in barbecue. Their yard became the showcase of the neighborhood, featured in the garden section of the *Fresno Bee* twice and visited by garden clubs every spring, and every year it became more labor-intensive.

The work hadn't mattered so much when the kids were home, when there were weekend parties and friends to enjoy and appreciate her efforts. Now, with the occasional exception of a barbecue for friends or the employees at one of the tire stores, it was she and Sam sitting outside on Sunday morning drinking coffee and reading the newspaper.

She'd given "retirement" three years, and it was driving her nuts. If she didn't find something, if she couldn't come up with a new reason for getting up every morning, she was going to go out of her mind. And take Sam with her. She knew her moods were wearing on him, and she tried to stay upbeat for his sake, but it was hard to be bouncy in lead shoes.

Elizabeth bent to check the soil around the lilac. It was dry and rock-hard. She broke off a leaf and rolled it between her finger and thumb. There was still enough moisture to save the plant with a couple of deep waterings. As she headed for the hose, she saw a Federal Express truck stop in front of the house. Seconds later a young man sprinted up the driveway, a clipboard in one hand, an overnight envelope in the other.

Elizabeth motioned to him. "Over here."

He smiled and crossed the lawn to meet her. "Great yard," he said.

"Thanks." Assuming the letter was for Sam, she was surprised when she spotted her name. She looked closer. It was from a law office in Sacramento. She didn't know anyone in Sacramento. She couldn't even remember the last time she'd been there.

He handed her the clipboard and pointed to the signature line. "Sign there, please."

She did, her curiosity growing.

She waited until the truck was gone before she looked inside and found two business-size envelopes, one unaddressed with a travel agency logo in the corner, the other from the law office and addressed to her.

She opened the one from the lawyer first.

Dear Ms. Walker:

I'm writing to you on behalf of your father, Jessie Patrick Reed. I regret to inform you that Mr. Reed is dying. He has expressed a desire to see you again,

*and in light of the finite time left him, I'm sure you will
understand the urgency involved.*

Elizabeth's structured world imploded, a star collapsing into
a black hole. The sun, the birds, the crisp morning air were no
more, in their place a phalanx of rancorous memories.

*Mr. Reed has asked me to tell you that he understands
why you might feel a meeting is not in your best interest, but he is prepared to do whatever necessary
to encourage you to change your mind. To facilitate
your travel to Sacramento I am enclosing a round-
trip airline ticket and information about the arrangements for the car and driver that will be waiting for
you when you arrive. It is not necessary to confirm. If
you have any questions, please feel free to call me at
any time.*

*Regards,
Lucy Hargreaves*

"You *bastard.*" Long-repressed pain and anger flared through
her like flames through a summer-parched forest. He was sum-
moning her as if she were supposed to care that he was dying?

"Well, I don't," she said. "As far as I'm concerned, old man, you
died a long time ago."

Six

Jessie

Jessie peered at Lucy over the top of his menu. She studied the list of Italian dishes as if she might really be considering something besides a salad. They were at Biba's, one of Sacramento's finest restaurants. The food came in reasonable portions, and the bill was rarely less than what someone who worked in fast food made in a week.

Lunch had been Lucy's idea. A good one, but not for the reason she'd tendered. He didn't need an excuse. He liked being with her. Always had, and always would, even if it meant letting her think he needed company while he waited for the meeting she'd scheduled with his daughters that afternoon.

He was ready for fireworks—more than ready, he was looking forward to it. But he was more than a little nervous, too. He had a lot to say and a nagging certainty he wouldn't be given a lot of time to say it. He'd finally reached the point in the dying process where he could feel the difference between the pain that came with the disease, which the doctor had told him was no longer in remission, and the signs that his body was shutting down. He hated being aware of such things. Most of all he hated thinking about them.

Lucy laid her menu to the side. "What are you having?"

"The lobster ravioli."

"Kind of rich, don't you think?"

He chuckled.

"Habit," Lucy said.

"Since when?"

"All right, so it's not. But maybe it should have been."

"Wouldn't have made any difference." He took a sip of the pinot noir the waiter had recommended. It slipped over his tongue with an elegant fruitiness that managed to penetrate the metallic taste of medicine in his mouth. He did love a good wine and was grateful he could still appreciate this small indulgence. "And think of all the incredible meals I would have missed."

"Kind of like skipping dessert on the *Titanic*."

This made him laugh. "Precisely."

"Still, I think I'll have the spinach and pine nut salad."

"Live a little, Lucy. For me. Just this once try the ravioli."

Long seconds passed before she picked up the menu again and replied, "I'll make you a deal."

He sat back in his chair and nodded for her to go on.

She, too, sat back. "For twenty years you've changed the subject every time I asked you about your past."

"I didn't want to bore you."

"You knew you wouldn't."

"How can you be so sure? Wouldn't you rather talk about something that matters now? Like this rumor I heard that you're thinking about retiring."

"You're doing it again, Jessie."

"So I am," he admitted.

She folded her arms across her chest. "I'll up the stakes. You know that chocolate cake you're always insisting I try?"

He'd never lacked for women in his life, but until Lucy he'd never known what it was to love one intellectually as well as emotionally. God, he was going to miss her. He glanced up and saw the waiter working his way toward them.

"Why do you want to know about my past?" It was a meaningless proposition, a means for two old friends to pass the time. Nothing he could tell her would change anything.

"Curiosity—pure and simple. I've been thinking about your girls and that they all come from different mothers. I know you've been married twice. . . ."

"It's a long story."

"I have time."

He looked at his watch. "Not that much."

"Then give me a chapter."

It was then he knew just how afraid she was that the meeting with his girls was going to turn out badly. "You want me to play your Scheherazade and spin tales for you?"

"Maybe."

"It won't work, you know."

"Indulge me."

"I'll give you twenty questions."

She smiled, satisfied. "One—why did you leave Oklahoma?"

"That's easy. It was leave or starve."

"You're going to have to do better than that if you expect me to put cream sauce in this mouth."

The waiter hovered expectantly. Jessie smiled. "You drive a hard bargain."

Lucy returned the smile before she looked at the waiter. "We'll both be having the lobster ravioli."

Jessie rarely looked back. The past put too much weight on a man's shoulders and made it harder to move through life than it needed to be. But some memories were etched in his mind like daguerreotypes. His last day in Oklahoma was one of them. Although filled with a crimson sorrow, an acorn dust, and an indigo of broken dreams, the image always came to him in stark black and white.

In his mind's eye he saw himself standing on the porch of his grandfather's farmhouse outside Guymon, Oklahoma, watching his father check the knots on the ropes he'd used to secure the family's belongings in the back of their old Ford truck. His mother stood to the side, her hand resting on the brass handle of the wardrobe that had been passed through her family from mother to daughter for six generations.

His father had promised to make room for the wardrobe—a promise he couldn't keep.

Jessie looked down at his hand. "I can still feel the splinters in the porch pillar of that old house and still remember thinking how I'd sanded and painted it just two summers before. The land, the building, the trees, the wells—everything was in ruin from two years of wind and dust. And yet all I could think about was how hard I'd worked on that damned old porch pillar. . . ."

The past took hold of Jessie. He slipped into memories of Oklahoma so vivid he wasn't sure which he gave voice to and which he only heard in his mind.

Jessie's Story

It was my birthday. September 19, 1935. I was sixteen years old. Old enough to be on my own. Older than my uncle had been when he struck out on his own, and argument enough to talk my ma and pa into letting me stay behind while they went to California to be with Pa's brother now.

No one wished me happy birthday. I figured they didn't remember, or if they did, Ma told them not to say anything. No sense in making the leaving any harder than it already was.

I was careful not to let on that I wasn't as sad as she expected I would and should be. Being on my own was an adventure I'd been living in my head for weeks, and now it was about to happen for real. I would have felt different if I'd known that they would never find my uncle and what the move would do to Pa, how all that happened to him and the rest of the family in California would drive him so deep into himself that he would stop talking two years later and stop eating the year after that.

When Pa decided it wasn't possible to add one more thing to that old truck, Ma lined everyone up to say good-bye. She made my sister, Rose, hug me, but my brother, Bobby Ray, refused. He punched me on the arm harder than I felt was right or fitting, so I hit him back. We would've been down on the ground rolling in the dirt if Grandma hadn't stepped in to pull us apart. She put her hands on my shoulders and held me there, looking at me like she knew it was for the last time.

"You got no business staying behind by yourself. There's nothing for you here. It's done with, Jessie. Leave it be and come with us to California."

Somehow she'd gotten it in her head that I was staying behind to work the farm. Pa never could tell her that it didn't belong to them anymore, that the bank had foreclosed. "I gotta try, Grandma," I said figuring it was what she needed to hear.

When it came Pa's turn to say good-bye he shook my hand like I wasn't just his boy anymore but a grown man. "You stay out of trouble, Jessie."

Ma was crying when she put her arms around me, squeezed me like it would hurt to let me go, and whispered in my ear, "If things don't work out the way you want, you come lookin' for us."

"I will."

She wasn't taking the easy answer. She grabbed hold of my wrists and looked me straight in the eye. "You promise me."

"I promise," I told her. And I meant it. Finding them in California one day was part of my plan. But I wouldn't go there because I needed something. When I arrived it would be with pockets full of money that I'd use to buy them another farm.

Ma didn't look back at me when the truck pulled out on the road, only my brother and grandmother. And then it was just Bobby Ray. He stood in the back of the truck, balancing himself on the trunks and mattresses and pots and pans, swinging both arms in the air like he was cheering for me and not mad anymore that he couldn't stay, too.

It was the last time I saw my brother. I've been back there a thousand times in my mind looking for something, wishing I could find a look or word that let him know I thought he was the best brother a kid could have and that I loved him. But I never do. Bobby Ray wasn't much for sentimentality and would've been all over me if I'd have tried something like that.

I stayed rooted to the spot like one of the dying sycamore trees out back watching until there wasn't anything to see but a long trail of dust hanging in the noon sky. When I was sure they weren't coming back for something they might have forgot, I went inside to get the suitcase that Ma and I had hidden in the front bedroom closet.

Knowing there was no way I'd ever be back, I took a last look around the place. Ma had left the sheets hanging across the ceilings, her way of catching the dust that seeped from the attic like talc through a sieve. Right up to the day she left she'd changed those sheets every morning before breakfast. She'd sweep and dust and check the rags stuffed in the cracks around the windows and under the doors while the rest of us were washing off the dirt that had settled overnight on our faces and in our ears and noses. Even with all she did, we could write our names in the dust on the edge of our plates by the time she had the eggs fried. When the winds blew, my sister washed dishes before and after we ate and we still felt the grit between our teeth with every bite.

It was my job to help with the laundry. I'd empty the wash water three or four times before it came anywhere near close to running clear, dumping it in the vegetable garden and spillin' as much as got there. Ma would hang the clothes out to dry, and I'd watch for wind so we wouldn't have to do it all over again. Sometimes it worked, most often it didn't.

She was the last one to bed and yet still got up in the middle of the night to check the sheets she'd hung over my sister's bed and the wet rags she'd given me and Bobby Ray to wear over our faces. Most mornings it wasn't the sun that woke us but someone coughing up something that looked like tobacco juice.

Right up to the end, even when he couldn't see three feet past the end of the tractor, Pa tried to work the fields. He'd have me and Bobby Ray walk the rows so he could follow, the blade digging into the dirt and half of it blowing away.

I remember sitting on the porch one night talking

*about where all that dirt was going to land when it
finally settled again. Half of Texas, Oklahoma, Kansas,
Nebraska, the Dakotas, and Missouri was floating around
in those clouds. Bobby Ray said he liked thinking it was
headed for New York to bury the men who ran the banks.*

*I wandered around the house for a long time after
everyone left like I expected to find something.*

*The mattresses were gone, but not the beds that had
held them. Closets held the "maybe" clothes—maybe it
would fit one day or maybe it could be cut down or let
out for someone else to wear. The sideboard in the dining
room still held linens, the cupboards in the kitchen the
dishes Ma had saved to buy at the five-and-dime.*

*I just kept going from room to room until finally the
quiet and the emptiness convinced me that it wasn't
home anymore, that when I left there would be no reason
to look back because nothing that counted was there
anymore.*

*It stuck in my throat that someone from the bank would
decide what was worth selling and what would be thrown
away. Once planted, the frustration took root and grew
like nothing had grown on the farm in a long, long time.
My anger against the wind and the drought and the dust,
the unfairness of Ma leaving her wardrobe, of Pa leaving
his pride, of everything I couldn't do anything about had a
name—the Guymon First National Trust Bank.*

*Knowing what I had to do, what had become the only
thing I could do, I took my suitcase out on the porch and
spent the next hour hoisting the wardrobe back into the
house. I waited around until sunset watching a coil of
dust gather on the horizon. Panic-stricken birds raced
the cloud, the weaker ones falling out of the sky, dying
from sheer exhaustion.*

When the worst of the dust and wind came through, rabbits and coyotes and all manner of wild things died of suffocation, some in their dens, some looking for a place to hide, some just lying down and giving in.

I swore I wasn't going to be one of them. I was sixteen years old, and I wasn't going to let anyone or anything stop me from going and doing and seeing and succeeding. Nothing was going to hold me back or hold me down.

The air turned still before it kicked up a spit of dust. Just enough wind to do what I had in mind. I went into the kitchen and pulled the matches from the drawer beside the old wood-burning stove. The clothes in the closets caught quick and burned hot, and I had to race to reach the other bedrooms. Before I bolted for the front door I stood in the middle of the living room and felt the power of what I'd done, the heat burning my face and drying the first tears I'd shed since I was five and saw my grandpa gored to death by a bull.

Outside I watched just long enough to be sure the wind would finish what I'd started, then turned my back and headed for Oklahoma City.

"Now I understand why you feel the way you do about banks," Lucy said.

Her words snapped Jessie back into the world that was coming to an end instead of just beginning. "I got carried away. Sorry." He was embarrassed. "There's nothing more boring than listening to an old man ramble on about things that don't matter to anyone but him."

She knew better than to argue; he would think it condescending. She eyed him.

"What?"

"I'm trying to picture you at sixteen."

He chuckled. "I was short and skinny and had a cowlick that axle grease and a brick couldn't hold down."

Their entrées arrived. Lucy made a show of eating her first bite, licking her lips and closing her eyes in rapt appreciation.

"Well done," Jessie said.

"I want you to remember this when it comes time to answer the other nineteen questions I have coming."

Seven

Lucy

After lunch Lucy drove Jessie to the meeting, insisting, despite his protests, that they enter the law offices through the back entrance. She wanted Jessie at an advantage when he met his daughters, even if it was only making them come to him in this final step of the process. She settled him in the small conference room at the head of the table facing the door, then brought him coffee laced with a splash of his favorite bourbon. He took a sip and shot her a questioning look. She smiled and held up crossed fingers.

"Stop worrying." He put the coffee aside. "Even if the only reason they've come is to tell me that they hope I burn in hell, it's a whole lot more interesting than sitting and waiting for hell to come to me."

"Sitting and waiting is your choice. I told you I could find things for you to do."

"You've got enough on your hands as it is." He gave her one of his slow smiles and a wink. "Now, if you were serious about volunteering to go with me on these excursions, I might rethink the offer."

The remark left her momentarily speechless. He was flirting

with her. Why now? Why not five years ago? Ten? Twenty? "Be careful, Jessie. I just might take you up on the offer."

In response to her outrageous remark he chuckled and then sighed. "We could have been something special, Lucy."

"So why weren't we?" she challenged.

"I would have missed knowing you." He held her in direct eye contact, not shying away from the words or their meaning. "You're the best friend I ever had, and I didn't want to chance losing you."

She nodded, acknowledging her agreement. If she stayed to answer she would turn the afternoon into something it wasn't supposed to be. Today belonged to Jessie and his daughters. "I'll be right back."

She went down the hall to the glass-paneled waiting room, pausing behind a ficus and at an angle where she knew the women inside were unlikely to notice her.

There were only three, each feigning interest in a magazine while surreptitiously casting sidelong glances at the other two. Lucy could only imagine the thoughts that must be going through their minds. Looking at each other, they were seeing bits and pieces of themselves, trying to figure out how and why they knew each other, just as sure they'd never met.

The features they had in common weren't startling or unusual— dark hair, lean builds, and square jaws. What set them apart was the sharp intelligence that shone from their eyes and the way they consumed the space around them, filling it with purses and discarded magazines to create a protective barrier.

Lucy glanced at her watch and then at the entrance. She could call the limo service to see if the missing daughter was on her way but decided to give her another minute or two. Even if she was a no-show, three out of four wasn't bad. More than she'd expected.

Christina was there, obvious in her youth and the bronze skin tone she'd inherited from her mother. She appeared nervous one second and excited the next, smoothing her skirt, glancing at the clock, tucking her long, startlingly black hair behind her ears and then pulling it forward to lie over her shoulder, exposing a flash of brilliant pink. In between she turned the pages of *Sacramento Magazine*, studying it as if it were written in a foreign language she had to translate.

Like Christina, Elizabeth's age gave her away. At forty-eight she'd developed the same upward-slanting lines at the corners of her eyes that gave Jessie's face its compelling character. She looked the most like her father—something Lucy had a feeling Elizabeth would not appreciate hearing. Unlike her sisters, who'd worn skirts and heels to the meeting, Elizabeth had come in jeans and a denim jacket. Whether the informal attire was a subtle sign of disrespect or an attempt to downplay the importance of the meeting, she'd negated both by wearing a pair of three-hundred-dollar Cole Haan loafers.

The third woman wasn't just pretty—with a good haircut and makeup a lot of women fell into that category—she was the kind of woman who made all but the most egocentric men feel inadequate and other women feel intimidated. Hers was the kind of beauty that was an asset only when it was capitalized on—in the movies or on the runway. In ordinary life, under ordinary circumstances, turning heads every time you entered a room was a burden, one that brought little understanding or sympathy from women or men.

The door in front of the receptionist's desk opened, drawing Lucy's attention. In seconds her position would be exposed. A quick assessment of the new arrival told Lucy that this was the executive daughter from San Francisco, which meant the beauty in the waiting room was the singer's daughter, the one who'd been adopted.

Lucy strode toward the woman dressed in an Armani suit, one that she'd tried on during an annual seasonal shopping trip to

San Francisco and rejected as too expensive. Her hand extended, she gave Rachel a welcoming smile.

"So glad you could make it, Ms. Nolan."

Rachel shifted the narrow strap of her Marc Jacobs purse higher on her shoulder before shaking Lucy's hand. "You're . . . ?"

"Lucy Hargreaves," she supplied. "Your father's attorney."

"Is he here?"

"He's waiting for you in the conference room." She hesitated in adding the rest but realized it was pointless to delay any longer. "Your sisters have already arrived."

"I don't have any—" The indifferent mask slipped. "I suppose I should have expected something like this." She drew in a deep breath. "You said sisters—plural. How many are there?"

"Your father has four daughters."

"That he knows of, I presume."

The hostility was disappointing, but not unexpected. "If you'll follow me I'll introduce you to your sisters first, and then I'll take you all in to see your father."

"We're all to see him at the same time?"

"If you'd prefer a private meeting, I can arrange that for you."

"Never mind. I just want to get this over with."

Eight

Elizabeth

Two women came into the waiting room, drawing Elizabeth's attention. She put her finger on the paragraph she'd been reading in *Architectural Digest,* about using color to make a small room appear larger, and looked up. Both women appeared stamped from the same mold, a type that was everything Elizabeth wasn't—career-oriented, self-assured, independent. Women who could wear linen and not look as if they'd slept in it.

Abandoning the article, she closed the magazine and put it aside. Her hands felt clammy, her mouth dry. For the first time she was sorry she'd refused Sam's offer to come with her. She'd wanted to do this on her own—Jessie could have met Sam at her wedding but had chosen not to. It was the last time she'd asked her father for anything.

The older of the two women introduced herself. "Good afternoon. I'm Lucy Hargreaves, your father's attorney." She indicated the woman beside her. "And this is Rachel Nolan, your sister."

Convinced she hadn't heard correctly, Elizabeth stared at Lucy and then Rachel. She glanced at the other two women. They were looking at Rachel also, seemingly as confused as Elizabeth.

"I'm sorry," Elizabeth said. "Were you talking to me?"

"You're Elizabeth Walker? Jessie Reed's daughter?"

"Yes." She heard a quick intake of breath from the two women seated opposite her and turned to look at them. Of course. Whatever made her think Jessie hadn't had more children?

"Wait a minute," the young one said. Her gaze swept the room. "Are you telling me these women are my *sisters*?"

"Half-sisters," Elizabeth supplied.

She turned to Elizabeth. "You can't be my sister. You . . . you look old enough to be my mother."

"What does that tell you about your father?" Elizabeth snapped.

"He's your father, too," the girl said coolly.

"You must be Christina," Lucy said stepping in to referee and redirect the conversation. "How was your trip from Tucson?"

"Great," Christina said. "Terrific. Tap-danced the whole way along that yellow brick road in the sky. Damn near wore out my shiny red shoes. I'm not sure I would have made the sacrifice if I'd known I was being called to a gathering of the clan."

"I *know* I wouldn't have come." The third woman uncrossed long, elegant legs and came forward in her seat. "I don't know what made Jessie Reed think I'd be interested in meeting his dysfunctional family, but he couldn't have been more wrong. I'm only here today to tell him to stay the hell out of my life."

"And you must be Ginger," Lucy said.

Elizabeth had to give the attorney credit. She took the salvos without flinching. But then, unlike them, she'd had time to prepare.

Elizabeth surreptitiously studied her "sisters," seeking something that connected her to them. She saw nothing, felt nothing other than a knot of anger in her stomach. The woman the attorney called Ginger was plainly used to having things her way, her startling beauty a coin spent with mercenary abandon.

Christina was a smart-mouthed kid who must have come

thinking she was going to slide down a rainbow and land in a pot of gold. It probably wasn't discovering her father's lack of moral fiber that had Christina upset, but the idea of sharing what she'd believed was hers alone. Typical for someone her age and generation. Elizabeth flinched at the depth of meanness in her bitter assessment. Whatever Christina might be, she hadn't asked for this meeting any more than the rest of them.

The third woman, Rachel, exuded confidence, as comfortable wearing a designer suit as Elizabeth was with dirt under her fingernails. This type of woman was as alien to Elizabeth's world as debutante balls.

The questions Elizabeth had come to ask were answered. She'd discovered the reason Jessie had abandoned her and her mother. He hadn't had time for them, for *her*. New women, new daughters had taken her place in his life. If she'd gained nothing else by coming there, she finally understood that much.

She tucked her purse under her arm and stood. "I don't need this. Please tell my father that I only came here today to tell him that when he chose to live without knowing me, he chose to die that way, too."

Lucy nodded. "I understand why you're upset. But you need to know that I'm not here to act as intermediary. Whatever you want said to your father, you're going to have to say yourself."

"What point is he trying to make by having us all here at the same time?" Rachel interjected, her cool demeanor slipping.

"I don't know," Lucy admitted. "You'll have to ask him. I'm sure your father is prepared to answer all of your questions."

"He's not my father," Ginger said emphatically. "My father is in Denver. Jessie Reed was a sperm donor. He means nothing to me."

Rachel shot Ginger a questioning look. "If you feel that way, what are you doing here?"

"I received—" Ginger turned on Rachel. "I don't have to explain myself to you."

Rachel studied Ginger for several seconds. "What are you—about thirty-six?"

Ginger flinched. "What has my age got to do with anything?"

Rachel laughed. "I'm thirty-six, too. Now what does *that* tell you about our father?"

Christina looked from one to the other, reaching behind her neck and pulling her long, black hair forward, twisting a strand around her finger in a nervous gesture. "This just gets better and better."

Elizabeth was overcome with memories of herself at twelve asking, begging God to find her father and send him home. He was the only one who could make her mother stop crying, the only one who could make her care there was no food in the house because she never went shopping, the only one who could convince her that going to the cemetery every day wouldn't bring Elizabeth's brother back. Now, knowing where Jessie was and what he'd been doing was like tossing kindling on a fire that had been smoldering for over thirty years. With her illusions destroyed, the thought of seeing him again actually made her physically ill.

"Okay, so what kind of man *is* my father?" Christina's youthful bravado slipped. Disappointment hung heavy in her voice.

Before anyone could answer, Lucy stepped forward. "You can answer that question for yourself. Your father is waiting in the conference room. If you'll follow me, I'll take you to see him."

Elizabeth held back when the others moved to follow the attorney. She'd come thinking she had the upper hand, believing her father couldn't hurt her anymore. God, she could be such an idiot.

Sam was right. She shouldn't have come. The speech she'd prepared wasn't going to set her free. Nothing would. The mark Jessie Reed had left on her was indelible.

Elizabeth left the waiting room. But instead of following the others, she headed for the etched glass doors opposite the receptionist's desk.

Lucy caught up with her at the elevator. "Please don't go."

In the time it had taken Elizabeth to walk away, a profound weariness had settled over her, dampening her anger and allowing her to answer without rancor. "There isn't anything for me in there."

"How do you know?"

"Because I don't care anymore."

"You wouldn't be here if you didn't care." The elevator doors swung open. Lucy put her hand on Elizabeth's arm. "Please, see him just this once. For your sake, if not for his."

Elizabeth shook her head. "I'm sorry . . . I'm not going to put myself through that."

"There isn't time for you to change your mind later," Lucy said gently. "He really is dying. This could be your last chance to see him."

Elizabeth put her hand out to keep the door from closing. "Has he told you how many times I begged to see him after he left my mother and me?" Lucy didn't answer. "I didn't think so."

Elizabeth stepped into the elevator and pressed the button for the first floor. Lucy didn't try to stop her again.

Nine

Jessie

Jessie rose from the leather chair Lucy had had moved in from her office and went to the window. He stood there for a full minute before he touched the wall for balance. The need for a cane would come next, but not for a month or two, not until pain became stronger than pride.

Outside the window, Capitol Mall was quiet, even for a Saturday. No smartly dressed women walking with determined strides as they shouldered the responsibility of keeping the State's business in order. No men with cell phones pressed to their ears so caught up in conversation they missed the pleasure of watching the women who passed them.

The capitol stood to his left, its green copper dome rising above a sea of verdant trees as old and stately as the building. Jessie had spent enough hours in the capital lobbying for one cause or another to know the governor and several legislators in the back-slapping, meet-and-greet way someone came to know people who moved in the social and business circles created by money and influence. But for the most part, if politics didn't directly involve him or one of his companies, he stayed away.

He glanced at the walnut door behind him, soundproof by its sheer size, anxious to get started. If his daughters were anything like him, he was in for a rough ride. Expecting heavy doses of fireworks and hostility to be an integral part of their righteous indignation, it was the reason he'd decided to gather everyone on a Saturday, when they would have the office to themselves. He wanted them to vent. Hell, he was looking forward to it.

The waiting wore on him. He glanced at the door before he dug in his coat pocket and withdrew four dog-eared photographs. His hands shook as he fanned pictures already embedded in his mind's eye—Elizabeth in the fifth grade, Rachel at nine, her hair in pigtails, freckles dotting her nose, Ginger at four, leaning back in a swing, her legs stretched out in front, a grin that stole his heart, Christina at three, her eyes dark and questioning.

Jessie slipped the photographs back into his pocket. It didn't matter what any of them looked like now. They could be tall or short, fat or thin, could look like him or their mothers—or neither of them—and it wouldn't make any difference. The only thing that mattered was finding a way to make them understand he hadn't stayed away because he didn't care. Too late he'd come to realize how important it was for them to know this. The regret had become its own cancer.

He went to the sideboard to get a glass of water before returning to his chair. He'd give Lucy five more minutes to put on the show her way, then he would take things into his own hands. The door opened before he'd settled into a comfortable position. Lucy moved to the side and mouthed that she would be right back.

Jessie stood to greet the three women who came into the room single file and on guard. He smiled and tried not to stare or show disappointment that there were only three. Elizabeth had rejected him again. Even in his death she could not reach back and find a glimmer of the love they'd once shared.

Overcome with emotion and momentarily speechless, Jessie

motioned to the chairs gathered around the table. He waited until his daughters were seated before he joined them. Careless in the excitement of the moment, he sat down too hard and sent a searing pain shooting through his hip, a brutal reminder.

"I tried to imagine what you would look like as grown women, but I see now I didn't do any of you justice." He offered a smile. No one responded. "You're nothing like I'd pictured." His hand shaking, he started to reach for the photographs in his pocket but changed his mind. It was too soon.

"You're wondering why I asked you here." It was everything he could do to keep from staring at Christina as memories of her as a little girl caught him in the same compelling web he'd experienced watching her onstage in Tucson. So close now he could reach out and touch her, he could see that she was not the slightly altered version of her mother he'd believed. Instead, when she tilted her head and nervously touched the river of black and pink hair that flowed over her shoulder, he saw his sister, Rose.

"I want to try to explain something to you, and to apologize. I know it's not enough, nothing could be enough after all this time, but I thought it might help you to know that I only left each of you because I thought it was the right thing to do." This wasn't what he'd planned to say. "It doesn't make sense now, but at the time I believed I was doing the right thing. There were so-called experts who thought so, too." He was trying to defend something that was indefensible. "They've changed their minds since then, of course," he went on, digging the hole deeper. "For all the good it does any of us now." Now he was rambling.

While Christina appeared wary at his stilted speech, the other two, Ginger and Rachel, looked at him with equal amounts of hostility and negative curiosity. Jessie had hoped for a connection, the kind he'd read in books and laughed at in movies, the kind where strangers latched on to each other because it just seemed right. But beyond an intriguing familiarity in Ginger's eyes and a propensity toward freckles that Rachel had inherited from her mother, his daughters remained the strangers they were in reality.

"But then maybe you're not here because I asked you to come," Jessie added, giving them an opening. "Could be you're here for reasons of your own."

Again, no one responded. The air thickened with anticipation. Finally, taking charge, Rachel came forward in her chair, her hands splayed against the edge of the antique pine table, a gold Gucci watch exposed beneath an exquisitely tailored sleeve. Her voice was deceptively calm when she said, "I don't know about the others, but curiosity brought me. I wanted to see what kind of man you are."

"Go on," Jessie prompted, admiring the way she was ready to take him on.

"Frankly, I'm disappointed. I'm not sure what I expected, but it wasn't this. You look so. . . ." She shrugged. "I don't know any other way to put it—you look *ordinary*. I can't imagine what my mother saw in you. What *any* woman would see in you."

Jessie smiled at her show of spirit. "Ordinary is a good way to put it. It's how I've always thought of myself, too, Rachel. But you shouldn't take that to mean you come from common stock. The Reeds and Boehms have produced long lines of extraordinary women. My mother—"

She stopped him. "What about the men? Are they extraordinary, too? Or are the women exceptional because they have to be when the men abandon them and their children? How many wives did your father have? Do I have half-uncles and -aunts scattered everywhere, or was infidelity your specialty?"

She'd gone too far. "I've been with a lot of women, but I've never been unfaithful to any of them."

"Oh?" Rachel pointed to Ginger. "Then how do you explain her?"

Jessie's eyes narrowed. There was something going on with Rachel that had nothing to do with him or her sisters. "Her name is Ginger," he said. "Her mother and I were friends."

"Friends? That's supposed to make it all right that you were screwing around on my mother? That's your idea of fidelity?"

He had never explained himself to anyone, and it was hard to do so now, no matter how much Rachel deserved an answer. "What makes it all right is that your mother had moved out weeks before I was with Barbara. When she left, she made it clear she wasn't coming back."

"Because of *Barbara*, I assume."

"Not even close."

"Then why did she leave?"

"That's something you'll have to ask her."

"So let me get this straight," Ginger interrupted. "You never loved the woman who gave birth to me. You were just 'friends.' I was an unfortunate accident, the consequence of some night out on the town? Were you drunk? Or did you just figure, what the hell, haven't had sex in a while, might as well stick it to a friend."

A flash of rage gripped Jessie. For an instant he was young and strong again, ready to do battle to protect the memory of the woman who had given herself to him and in doing so, saved his life. But with whom should he fight? Barbara's daughter? The child she'd agonized over, the fetus she'd refused to abort? What sense did that make?

Did Ginger have a right to an explanation that superseded his right to privacy? He met her gaze, matching her outrage. "Barbara took the bullets out of the gun I was going to use to kill myself the night you were conceived. She stayed with me until I understood that dying wasn't the answer."

The statement was like a hand that touched Rachel's shoulder and pushed her back in her seat. Anger turned to confusion. "You were going to kill yourself because my mother left you?"

Anna's leaving had been the one bright spot in his life that fall, but that wasn't what Rachel wanted or needed to hear. "Let's just say it wasn't one of my better years."

He turned back to Ginger. "I would have known you anywhere. You're the mirror image of your mother."

She gave him an icy look. "My mother and I don't look anything alike. But then," she added pointedly, "I don't look like my father either. My real father, that is. He has red hair and blue eyes."

Jessie smiled. "I didn't ask you here to try to insinuate myself into your life, Ginger. We both know nothing I do or say can change the way you feel about Delores and Jerome."

"So why did you want to see me?"

"I wanted you to hear about the woman who gave birth to you from someone who knew her." Such an easy lie because it was wrapped in truth, a truth he hadn't realized until that very moment. And so much easier to say than his own plea for forgiveness.

"What possible difference could it make now?" Ginger asked.

"None, I suppose. It's just something I feel I owe her. And it's something you have a right to know."

"Wait a minute." Rachel held up her hand, the Gucci watch flashing in the sunlight coming through the window. "Are you saying you gave—" Rachel looked at Ginger. "I'm sorry, I forgot your name."

"Ginger," Jessie supplied.

"That you and Ginger's mother gave her up for adoption?" She shook her head in wonderment. "This just keeps getting better and better. Well, now we know why you brought *her* here. You want to apologize for screwing up her life so you can die with a clear conscience. But why me?"

Ginger turned on her. "What makes you think my life is screwed up?"

"Are you saying it isn't?"

"If it is, it's no more screwed up than yours."

Rachel bristled. "My life is fine. As a matter of fact, it's never been better."

Ginger purposely studied Rachel. "What happened to your wedding ring? Whatever it was, it couldn't have happened very long ago. There's still a mark on your finger. Was it your idea? A case of like father like daughter?"

Rachel exposed herself in her fury. "You don't know the first thing about—"

Christina's eyes widened at the bruising exchange. She'd perched on the edge of her chair, giving no clear clue whether she was fascinated by the people around her or ready to flee from them.

Jessie sat back and folded his hands in his lap. He'd anticipated fireworks, not the Fourth of July, and certainly not directed at each other instead of him. God, he had missed so much with these women. How had he let himself become such a coward? The justifications he'd used seemed so insignificant in hindsight that they no longer offered so much as an emotional handhold.

"If what Ginger says is true, I'm sorry, Rachel," Jessie offered. "I hope you can work things out—if that's what you want."

"What I want is none of your business." She turned on Ginger. "Or yours either." She reached for her purse. "I was an idiot to have come here."

Ginger put her hand on Rachel's arm. "I'm sorry. I was out of line."

Rachel hesitated and then yielded. Several seconds passed in an electrically charged silence. "You had no idea you were adopted?"

"Not until I got the letter to come here."

"Wow," Christina said, speaking up for the first time. "That must have been a killer."

Jessie looked at his youngest daughter. In the twenty-three years since Carmen had convinced him that his irregular appearances in Christina's life were hurting, not helping her, child psychologists had made his calculated disappearance from her life an emotional crime. There was no way now that he could make her understand or believe that he'd abandoned her out of love.

"And you, Christina? What did you come here to find out? What questions do you have for me?" The pain in his hip shot to his side, settling under his ribs and burrowing in. This was something new. And frightening in its force. Yesterday he wouldn't have cared. Today, cruelly, time had become important again.

Christina hesitated, frowned, started to speak, and then stopped. Finally, in a rush, she said, "I thought you were dead. My mother *told* me you were dead. Why would you let her do that?"

"I was sixty-two years old, and in the middle of an ugly lawsuit that I eventually lost that bankrupted me again. When your mother moved back to Mexico I couldn't have bribed or blackmailed a judge into giving me custody. Then she married Enrique, and he wanted to adopt you."

"He didn't, you know. He just made me take his name. My mother decided it would be better not to muddy my U.S. citizenship." Christina stared at him, blinking to keep from crying. "I loved you. How could you turn your back on me?"

Christina pulled her sweater cuffs over her hands and wiped her eyes. When she'd finished, she tucked her hands under her legs and from somewhere found a dazzling smile. Like a sleight of hand in a magic show, the vulnerable child disappeared. In her place sat a composed, reserved woman. "So, Dad, just how many kids *do* you have?"

It took a second for Jessie to follow Christina through the abrupt transition. "You have three sisters." He cleared his throat. "You had a brother. Frank. He was killed in the war before the three of you were born."

It was time to show them the pictures. He dug them out of his pocket and put them on his lap.

"Which war?" Christina asked.

Was it that she was so young or that he was so old? "Vietnam," he said simply.

Rachel came forward, zeroing in on Jessie. "Can we cut this pseudo reunion garbage and get to the reason you asked us here?" She made a point of looking at her elegant watch. "I'm due at a soccer game in a couple of hours."

An incredibly effective put-down. Jessie was impressed. With a minimum of words, Rachel had dismissed the possibility that meeting her father and sisters for the first time held any real meaning. "It's nothing complicated," he said, suddenly incapable of telling them the real reason, of revealing his guilt, of asking for the forgiveness he so desperately needed. "I wanted to see you. And I wanted you to meet each other. I'm sorry Elizabeth didn't come. Maybe next time."

Ginger was the first to react. "You can't be serious. Why would any of us want to put ourselves through this again?"

"Curiosity," Jessie offered hopefully.

Rachel reached for her purse. "Count me out. I have as much family trouble as I can handle right now. And as for seeing you— I lived thirty-six years without the privilege. Nothing you've said or done today has made me think I missed anything."

It was Christina's turn. "You're wrong," she said softly. "You missed a lot. We all did." She looked at Jessie, her heart on her sleeve, a catch in her voice. "I wish I could understand why you did what you did. Maybe it would make a difference. Maybe I'd be able to forgive you."

She looked from Ginger to Rachel. "I won't be back either. It's not that I don't care that you're my sisters, just that I don't think you care that I'm yours." The corner of her mouth lifted in a half-smile. She settled her gaze on Rachel. "You say you already have enough family trouble. Well, I get enough of feeling like an outsider at home. I sure don't need any more from the likes of you two."

An overwhelming fatigue gripped Jessie. He knew it was his last chance to say something to alter the ugly outcome of their meeting, but the words wouldn't come. He looked down at the bent and tattered photographs and understood that it was too late. He slipped them back inside his pocket and silently watched his daughters file out of the room, waiting for a backward glance from Christina that never came.

Ten

Lucy

Lucy stepped into the elevator and hit the button for the sixth floor. She'd followed Elizabeth to the parking garage, trying to talk her into changing her mind about seeing Jessie. Not surprisingly, Elizabeth had proved as stubborn as her father. Nothing Lucy could say, none of the appeals she'd made, had penetrated Elizabeth's resolve.

Lucy wished she could convince herself that a couple of days would make a difference, that with a little time Elizabeth might have a change of heart and agree to another meeting, but there hadn't been a hint that it was a possibility. Now the best she could hope for was that Jessie had had more success with the three who had stayed.

That hope died when the elevator doors swung open. Rachel didn't wait for Lucy to exit, sliding past her as if she couldn't get away fast enough. Ginger and Christina followed. Stepping out of the elevator, Lucy turned to look at them. None met her gaze.

"Thank you for coming," Lucy said. "I know seeing you meant a lot to your father." The door slid closed. She faced the wood-paneled doors, rooted to the moment.

After several seconds, the receptionist asked, "Are you all right, Ms. Hargreaves?"

Lucy had a smile in place when she turned to answer. "I'm fine, Margaret. This meeting was the only thing I had scheduled for today, so if you'd like to take off now, I can lock up when I leave."

"Are you sure? I don't mind waiting."

"Thank you, but I'm sure." Lucy unbuttoned her jacket as she walked down the hall. Despite being hand-tailored, the suit just didn't fit right. Every time she wore it she swore she would never wear it again. Then, when she took it off, the little girl who had never owned anything that hadn't come from a Sears catalog would rebel at getting rid of a perfectly good piece of clothing just because she didn't like it. Invariably, the suit wound up in the closet instead of a bag for Goodwill.

Jessie liked to tease her about her frugalness, saying that if he'd hooked up with her in the beginning he would have saved himself three bankruptcies. When she countered that without him she would still be handling cases that belonged in small claims court, he impatiently dismissed her ride on his coattail as serendipity. Jessie had spotted her ability where others only saw her gender.

In fifteen years her firm had grown from an office in a strip mall to eight senior partners, twenty-five associates, and turn-away business. Financially, the firm would survive the loss of Jessie as a client. Privately, Lucy's world would spin a little slower. Worst of all, her days would lose that spark of expectation that she would pick up the phone and hear Jessie's voice challenging her with yet another complex partnership idea that she was convinced held more problems than potential.

She stopped outside the conference room, removed her glasses, and pressed the tips of her fingers to the bridge of her nose. She needed new glasses—but stopping to think about it now was a delaying tactic. She didn't want to face Jessie, didn't want to hear him try to convince her the meeting had gone better than it had, and most of all, she didn't want to see the loss of anticipation that had animated him that past month.

Wishing she were anywhere but there, Lucy opened the door and went inside. Jessie sat with his back to her, turned toward the window. "Well, how did it go?" she asked.

"I hate to admit this, Lucy, but you may have been right."

She moved to join him. "You knew the first time would be hard. We'll give them a couple of—" She caught her breath when she saw him. Beads of sweat dotted his forehead. His eyes radiated pain. "What is it?" When he didn't answer, she dropped to her knees to study him closer. "What's going on?"

"I'm okay. Just give me a minute. It takes a while for the medicine—" He gasped and bit his lip as another wave of pain struck, this one nearly doubling him over.

"I'm calling an ambulance."

"No—don't do that. They'll take me to the hospital and—" He gasped again and folded his arms across his chest. This time he did double over. "Damn, damn, damn," he moaned. "Why today? Why now?"

Lucy ran for the phone and dialed 911. She fought to remain patient as the dispatcher asked what seemed an interminable number of questions. Finally, it occurred to her that the doors had to be unlocked for the paramedics. She hung up and ran down the hall, saw Margaret about to leave, shouted quick instructions, and returned to Jessie.

"They're on their way," she said.

"I'm not going to the hospital."

"You need help, Jessie."

"Call the doctor. He'll know what to do."

"It's Saturday. You're going to have to take whoever's covering for him, and they're going to want to see you in the hospital."

"And the hospital is going to insist on admitting me. If I let that happen, they're going to make me walk the fires of hell to get out. I'm not going through that again, Lucy."

"Give me your doctor's number. I'll call him right now." She waited as he struggled past the pain to reach inside his jacket. In all the years they had known each other, by mutual, unspoken consent, their physical contact had been limited to a handshake and then only in the beginning. There had been no hugs, no comforting hand on a shoulder, not even a casual touch to brush lint from a lapel. To do so would have opened a door to a place they knew they could not enter. Now, her heart breaking with the knowledge that it no longer mattered, Lucy gently reached inside Jessie's jacket and removed his wallet.

Eleven

Jessie

"Feeling better?" The doctor stood at the foot of the bed and read the lab results attached to a metal clipboard. Sporting a week-old attempt at a mustache and dressed in a T-shirt and jeans, he looked more like an undergraduate than a partner in the most respected oncology practice in the city.

"Good enough to get out of here." Jessie didn't just hate hospitals, he feared them. His idea of hell was a place with industrial colors and shiny floors and beds that crinkled when he moved. What could be worse punishment or more humiliation than ringing for help and having a disembodied voice come through a speaker on the wall and demand that he shout his need to go to the bathroom?

"I'm going to have you spend the night."

"Sorry, doc, but that's not going to happen."

"I've substantially increased your medication, and you need to be monitored until we see how you handle it."

"I'm dying, doc." Jessie sat up and shifted his legs over the side of the bed. "What can be worse than that?"

"The way it happens," the doctor answered bluntly.

Lucy moved from the head of the bed to stand beside Jessie. The green-and-orange-striped privacy curtain caught on her shoulder and slid along the overhead bar, making a sibilant, metallic sound. "He has a nurse at home who can watch for side effects," she lied.

The doctor looked from her to Jessie. "I thought Dr. Morrison told me that you'd fired your nurse."

Without missing a beat, Lucy answered for him. "I hired another one. Between the two of us and Mr. Reed's housekeeper he will have whatever care you feel he needs in order for him to be released today. I'm assuming you'll send written instructions?"

The doctor didn't stand a chance. When inspired, Lucy could talk a leprechaun out of his pot of gold.

The doctor widened his stance and crossed his arms over his chest, hugging the clipboard. "You reached another stage today, likely the final one. If you have things that you've waited to do, I'd do them now."

The irony that this was the day he'd chosen to start something, not end it, was not lost on Jessie. "Thank you for telling me."

The doctor nodded. "If you're sure this is what you want, I'll get the paperwork started to get you out of here. I'm going to send some new prescriptions home with you. If these don't work and you're still having pain, Dr. Morrison will probably order a morphine pump."

Jessie knew better than to ask, but couldn't help himself. "How long?"

The doctor didn't answer right away. Finally, reluctantly, he said, "I don't like to make those kinds of predictions. They tend to become self-fulfilling."

"Well, the hell of it is that I started something I probably shouldn't have," Jessie said. "Without another two or three months to set things right. . . ." Frustration sat on his chest like a weary elephant. "Let's just say I've got some work to do. What I need from you is a time frame."

"I can order another MRI. It would tell us how far the cancer has spread."

"And what would that do?"

"Confirm what we already know. You haven't been in remission these past months, you've been dying the way you lived. But sheer will and stubbornness can only take you so far against cancer." He wiped his hand over his face. "You'll be lucky if you can push this out another three or four weeks."

Jessie nodded. "I appreciate your candor." He glanced at Lucy, saw a tear slip down her cheek, and immediately wished he'd looked anywhere else. He gave her a wry smile. "Seems there's something to be said for just stepping in front of a bus and having it done with."

Twelve

Elizabeth

With each mile, Elizabeth lost a brick in her wall of self-control. She would never make it all the way to Fresno like this. Coffee. Something strong and black, or better yet, sickeningly sweet like a caramel macchiato with extra caramel and whipped cream—venti. A distraction. No matter how on edge she was, she would never break down in front of a Starbucks full of strangers.

She took the first Lodi exit and drove along the frontage road. By the time she found an empty parking lot in front of a Mexican restaurant her hands were shaking so badly she had trouble hanging on to the steering wheel. She tried to put her reaction off to fury—she couldn't remember ever feeling as angry as she had when she discovered that the three women sitting with her in that lawyer's office were her sisters—but that was too easy.

Here, alone, without anyone to question what she was feeling or why, without anyone to witness her pain, she could be honest. But it was hard. If she admitted how she felt she couldn't hide behind the lies anymore.

After all this time, how could Jessie Reed still have the power to hurt her? She was almost fifty, and somewhere in her mind she was still his little girl, abandoned thirty-five years ago and abandoned all over again today.

What had she done that was so wrong? What sin had she committed that he couldn't forgive? She'd studied pictures of herself at thirteen. Was she too skinny, her hair too straight, her teeth too big? Would he have stayed if she'd been smarter? If she'd been a better athlete? If she'd been a boy?

All these years she'd harbored a secret fantasy that he'd been kidnapped or imprisoned or lost on a desert island. She'd created a hundred reasons he'd never come to see her or called or answered her letters. The one time he'd tried, years too late, she'd almost been as angry that he'd destroyed her fantasy that he couldn't come to her as she had that he'd stayed away so long.

And now she knew the truth. He'd replaced her.

A pain filled her chest that made each breath a conscious effort. A sob rose in her throat. She put her hand over her mouth, afraid of the sound that might come out.

Sam came out of the house as Elizabeth pulled into the driveway. He opened her door and gave her a quick kiss. "You're home early," he said. "I take it the meeting didn't go well?"

"I don't want to talk about it." She couldn't. Not yet. Maybe never.

He put his arm around her shoulders. "Come on, Lizzy. It will do you good."

She stepped away from him. "Since when do you know what's good for me?"

"Whoa—where did that come from?"

"What if I hadn't come home tonight? What would you have done?" God, what was wrong with her? Why was she trying to pick a fight with Sam? Even knowing what she was doing, she couldn't stop. "Would you have bothered calling me or looking for me?"

He considered her question. "Probably not. I would have figured you were having a good time and that you'd be home when you were ready."

"What if I were in a wreck?"

"The highway patrol would call." He frowned. "What's going on, Lizzy?"

"I hate it when you call me Lizzy."

"I've always called you Lizzy."

"And I've always hated it. It's condescending."

He threw his hands wide in frustration. "All right. From now on it's Elizabeth. Now would you please tell me what in the hell is going on here?"

She moved to step past him. "Nothing's going on."

He blocked her way. "I don't believe you."

She couldn't tell him. She didn't want him to know how easily her father had replaced her, how unimportant she'd been to him when he'd been everything to her. She was ashamed, too ashamed to let Sam see how hurt she was. And in her shame she lashed out at the one person she knew would forgive her anything. "If I wanted to talk to you about this, I would."

"All right—have it your way."

"Thank you." In a modifying tone, she added, "What time are we supposed to meet Jim and Karen for dinner?"

"When you didn't call, I canceled."

She'd been counting on the distraction. "Why don't I see if they can still make it?"

He gave her a sheepish look. "I made other plans."

"What plans?"

"Steve asked a bunch of guys over to watch the fight on pay-per-view. I told him I'd be there if you were going to be late."

"You could have called me."

"I didn't want to interrupt."

"What time are you leaving?"

"Six—but I could make it later. The fight doesn't start until eight."

"No—go."

"What will you do?"

She had no idea, but he needed an answer before he could enjoy his night out. "I'm tired. I'll probably take a bath and catch up on email."

"There's a message from Eric." Sam led the way inside, waiting when Elizabeth stopped to put her purse in the closet. "Sounds as if he's getting serious about that girl he told us about at Christmas."

She wrote short personal notes to the kids two or three times a week and a longer update to all three on Mondays. She heard from Eric in fits and starts, and Michael only when he had a joke to pass on or when she called them after coming up with a plausible excuse. To their credit, the boys rarely cut her short and actually seemed to enjoy catching up. "What makes you think so?"

"They're going to Mexico together over Memorial Day."

"I wonder how Michael feels about that." Elizabeth went into the kitchen and took a bottle of chardonnay out of the refrigerator.

"None for me," Sam said. "I should be leaving soon. What did you mean about Michael? Why would he care?"

"Last I heard he and Eric were going hiking in Montana the end of May."

Sam chuckled. "Then it's serious, all right." He reached for Elizabeth and pulled her to him. "So, how do you feel about being a mother-in-law?"

Sam was the most forgiving person she'd ever known. He simply didn't know how to hold on to anger or to hold a grudge when he suffered the brunt of her frustration. "Eric's too young to get married."

"He's older than you were."

"It's different now."

"Which is exactly what our parents said." Sam planted a kiss in the middle of her forehead. "The good thing is that it's their problem, not ours. All we have to do is show up for the wedding."

"And pick up the pieces when it falls apart."

"Lighten up, Elizabeth. It's just a trip to Mexico. Knowing Eric, it's more likely a case of testosterone overload than undying love." He kissed her again, this time on the lips waiting for a response before he let her go. "You know where I'll be."

"Wait—" She couldn't let him leave. Not this way. "I'm sorry." She put her hand to her mouth to hide her trembling lip. "I had no right to—"

"Fire away. Anytime. I can take it." He came back and wrapped his arms around her. "Besides," he said gently, "if not me, then who?"

She put her cheek on his shoulder. "I'm going to owe you big time for this one."

"Hmmm, I like the sound of that. Are we talking German chocolate cake big time, or peanut butter cookies?" He gave her a salacious grin. "Or something even better?"

No matter how blue she felt, he could find a way to make her smile. She ached for a way to tell him how much his love meant to her, but there weren't words that hadn't become clichés, and he deserved more.

"Thank you." She tilted her head back to look at him. "I promise I'll handle this better from now on."

He kissed her forehead, her nose, and then her lips. "You're entitled to a couple of off days now and then. God knows you've put up with enough of them from me."

She gave him one more kiss and let him go, her arm at his waist as she walked him to the door. When he was in the car and backing out of the driveway, she went inside and poured her wine. She glanced out the kitchen window and saw the car stopped at the end of the driveway. Sam was waiting to give her one last wave.

She returned his wave and sighed. She was as predictable as

a family dog whose life revolved around the coming and going of everyone else. Her entire married life she'd organized her day around her family. When she left there was no one to see her off because it was her job to be there until they were gone. When she came home, no one was there to greet her because she never volunteered for anything that wouldn't let her get home first.

At what point did predictability become tiresome?

She'd loved being a mother and had never, not for a moment, felt stifled or unfulfilled. She'd never envied women who had careers outside the home, had actually felt a secret smugness at all she experienced that they missed.

How had she failed to realize how empty her life would be when the kids were gone? Why hadn't she done something to prepare herself?

She recorked the wine and started to put it back in the refrigerator, then decided to take it with her into the family room.

The blinds were drawn, which meant Sam had been watching television. She put the glass and bottle on coasters and opened the blinds, stopping to run her finger along several slats, checking for dust.

This was her favorite room, the one she'd designed the rest of the house around and decorated in tans and greens and burgundy. It was large because she'd wanted lots of room for the kids and their friends, and the ceiling had to be tall to accommodate the Christmas tree that never looked as big in the lot as it did when they brought it home. There was a fireplace to hang stockings—putting it in the corner and adding a raised hearth was an afterthought that had doubled the cost and lost them their original mason.

A wall of windows faced the pool that they'd put in four years after the house was built, an addition Elizabeth hadn't agreed to until Stephanie was five and swimming on her own. A doorway led to the kitchen, another to a hall and the downstairs bathroom.

As she watched her children grow she imagined the day the house would be filled with yet another generation. What she hadn't taken into consideration was the possibility her grandchildren would live hundreds, even thousands of miles away. She was too young to live the rest of her life waiting for holidays and vacations that might or might not bring the family together again and too old to change who she was and what she'd become. She wasn't ready for the life she'd known to be over, and there wasn't a damn thing she could do about it.

Seeking an escape from happy memories turned melancholy, Elizabeth took her glass and the bottle of wine outside. She settled into the Adirondack chair Sam had given her for her forty-fifth birthday and drank a toast to all the Saturdays that had gone before when she had not been there alone.

Elizabeth looked up from her book when she heard the garage door open. It was only ten-thirty. She hadn't expected Sam home before midnight and had gone to bed without him. She adjusted the pillow at her back and called, "In here."

He appeared in the doorway. "Not feeling well?"

She closed the book and put it on the nightstand. She'd been on the road over ten hours that day and felt like it had been twenty. "Just tired."

He slid across the bed and put his head in her lap, his hand cupping her thigh. He stayed still as Elizabeth gently ran her fingernails over his shoulders and down his back, then he reached for her hand and turned over to face her. "You ready to talk?"

"About?"

"Your father."

"Is that why you came home early?"

He grinned. "Would you believe me if I said yes?"

"Maybe."

Now he laughed. "No you wouldn't."

"So, why did you come home?"

Serious again, he brought her hand to his lips and pressed a kiss to her palm. "I thought you might need some company."

After twenty-seven years he could still surprise her. She traced his lower lip with her fingertip. "I owe you an apology. I know I've been a bit of a bitch lately, and that you've taken the brunt of it, but things are going to get better. I did some thinking tonight and decided it's time I made some changes."

"In me?"

She was tempted to say yes, to give him a list of things she wanted him to do, just to tease him. But he might think she was still teasing when she finally told him the truth, and she wanted him to know she was serious. "Stop worrying. This doesn't have anything to do with you."

"Before you say anything, if you're thinking you need to change because of me, don't. I love you just the way you are. And I don't care if that does sound like a song title. It's true."

She took a deep breath and let it out slowly, giving herself time to think about what she was going to say. Saying out loud what she had planned made it official. Until then she could change her mind a hundred times without guilt or explanation. "I'm going to go back to school. And I'm going to get a degree in something useful this time. I don't want a job, I want a career."

"Whoa—where did that come from?" Sam rolled over and sat up.

"I think the idea has been floating around in my mind for a long time now. I just didn't recognize it for what it was."

He shook his head like a fighter after a hard blow. "And I thought you were going to tell me something about your father."

"He's part of it—in a way. I told you that if he left me in his will I wasn't going to take his money. Now I am. I figure since he didn't pay for my wedding, he can damn well pay for my education."

"So, he does have money?"

"Yes—or at least that's the way it looks. Of course, whatever is left is going to be split several ways, so it might not be much in the end."

"I don't understand."

Finally, she told him about her day. When she was finished, Sam didn't say anything for several seconds.

"Are you sure you did the right thing by not seeing him?"

"What do you mean by *right*?"

"Don't get defensive. All I'm saying is that this was your chance to tell him all the things you've had bottled up all these years. Once he's gone, so is the opportunity."

"It doesn't matter. He wouldn't care."

"How do you know?"

The pain was too fresh to keep from her voice. "I was one of four, Sam. If I really mattered to him, he would have wanted to see me by myself."

Sam brought her to him in an awkward embrace. She let him hold her until the need to cry had passed. "I'm all right."

"You're not—but you will be. You're the strongest person I know."

She smiled. "Wow, two compliments in one night."

He returned the smile. "Make it three—you look sexy as hell in that nightgown."

She couldn't remember what she was wearing and looked down at her nightshirt, the one with the faded picture of the Grand Canyon that she couldn't bring herself to throw away because it had survived enough washings to be the softest and most comfortable one she owned. She put her hand on his thigh. "You want to fool around a little?"

"Nah—" He came forward again and kissed the hollow at the base of her throat. "I want to fool around *a lot*."

She moved to accommodate him, sliding down from her sitting position and opening the covers.

Their lovemaking was familiar and comfortable. There was little they hadn't tried through the years, keeping what worked and discarding what didn't. By mutual, unspoken consent, they generally saved the more athletic positions and marathon sessions for romantic getaway weekends or times when one of them felt a need for something more.

Sam was the first and only man she'd ever made love with. She'd looked at other men in a curious, speculative way but never with desire. Instead of turning her on, just thinking about another man's hand on her breast made her shudder. It wasn't that she didn't understand when her girlfriends salivated over Johnny Depp or Hugh Jackman or Colin Firth, just not how they incorporated them into their sexual fantasies.

At times Elizabeth had felt so out of step with her mental monogamy that she'd wondered if she was a sexual eccentric. But then Sam's hands would cup her breasts the way they were now and his thumbs would sweep across her nipples, leaving them hard and extended, and she would give herself over to feeling instead of thinking. Soon she would become aware of a familiar warmth stealing through her belly, and then a throbbing would start between her legs. At that moment, even if it were within her power to summon a thought about sexual eccentricities, it was beyond her to care.

Thirteen

Christina

The taxi turned the corner onto Christina's street, the driver swearing as he slammed on his brakes to keep from hitting an oncoming truck navigating through the carelessly parked cars that lined both sides of the narrow road. "Looks like someone's having quite a party," he said.

The throbbing bass of rap music spilled through the open doors and windows of her house. So much for a quiet night and a shoulder to cry on. "Yeah, it looks that way."

Cars were parked three-deep in the driveway, forcing the driver to stop in the middle of the street. He put his arm across the seat and turned to look at her. "Twenty-two fifty."

She handed him a twenty and a five and tried not to let him see that it was all she had in her wallet. A stupid point of pride, something she could have easily pulled off if she weren't so tired, if she just weren't so worn down with being poor. She'd humiliated herself by asking the clerk at the Hyatt for a refund when she'd decided to come home early. Not only had he pointed out that the room had been paid for by credit card, he'd questioned whether the card was hers.

At least the airline let her change her ticket without too much of a hassle, adding the fee to the credit card on file. First-class was full and she'd had to fly coach, a center seat in a row next to the galley kitchen. A nonfunctioning kitchen, her rumbling stomach reminded her.

Flying to Sacramento first-class had been a mistake. Buying generic brands at the grocery store, secondhand clothes at the thrift shop, and gasoline by the dollar instead of the tank, and stealing flowers from her neighbor's yards when she wanted to make the table look pretty, had lost its charm.

She liked the respect she'd been given in first-class, liked having a limo waiting when she arrived in Sacramento, and most of all, she liked having people look at her with a mixture of curiosity and awe because they were convinced the treatment made her someone special.

Opening the door and getting out, she flung her backpack over her shoulder. "Keep the change."

The cloyingly sweet scent of pot swirled around her when she stepped onto the front porch. Instantly furious, she reached for the screen door and flung it open. She'd told Randy a dozen times she didn't want his friends doing drugs at their house. There was a hard-ass cop with the nose of a bloodhound who patrolled the neighborhood on weekends. He loved busting parties and hauling people off, claiming he was doing it for the old folks who'd been there forever and couldn't afford to live anywhere else.

She strode inside where smoke hung over the living room like a layered brown fog. Half-empty, grease-stained pizza boxes littered the tables and floor. Someone had started a pyramid of beer cans between the kitchen and dining room; another six-pack and it would reach the ceiling. Music throbbed from the oversize speakers that Randy had picked up at a garage sale and that doubled as end tables. The few people still sober enough to carry on a conversation shouted at each other to be heard.

Flinging her backpack behind the sofa, Christina went looking for Randy. She found him in the kitchen with Doug, the sound man for *Illegal Alien*. Randy had an open script in one hand and was waving the other, conducting the rhythm of the discussion. Neither looked as if he'd been partying. Instead, they were high on something more intoxicating to them both—the movie.

Unnoticed, Christina leaned against the wall and watched, picking up bits and pieces of the conversation, enough to let her know they were talking about her and her father's money.

The song ended. For that brief time before another began, Randy's words were all that filled the silence. "Now watch the bastard get a second wind."

Doug laughed and lowered his voice. "Maybe you could get Christina to slip him something."

Randy tapped him on the chest. "Don't go there."

Doug shoved Randy's hand away. "Shit, man, I wasn't serious."

"I don't care."

Christina felt a peculiar mix of gratitude and affection for Randy. She started toward him to tell him so but came to an abrupt halt when she heard what came next.

"If she hears that kind of trash talk I'm sunk. As it is, I figure I'm going to have to marry the bitch to get anything out of this."

Doug's jaw dropped. "You're going to marry her? Jesus—there's got to be another way."

The speakers crackled a half-second warning before shooting a staccato bass that rattled the windows and ricocheted off the walls. Randy's reply was lost in the echo, but not the laughter or the high-five that followed.

Love was never as easy or straightforward as Christina wanted it to be. Too often its line was capriciously drawn, the heart pulled one way, the mind another. But not this time. She might, given enough time, be able to forgive a man who abandoned her, but never one who betrayed her.

Christina pulled the plug on the CD player, went to the light switch, and flipped it several times. "Party's over. Get out—and take your shit with you. What I find gets flushed."

"Hey, not so fast." Randy came at her from behind and grabbed her around the waist. To the others he said, "Give us a minute. It's cool."

"Let me go," Christina said.

Instead he pulled her closer, nestling his chin into her neck. "Hey, Doug, take care of things in here. Christina and I need to talk."

She brought her heel down on his foot.

"Fuck—what'd you do that for?"

"I said I want everyone out," she shouted. She turned to Doug. "That means you, too, you son of a bitch." Picking up a purse from the end of the sofa, she flung it toward the door, looked for another, and did the same thing. No one challenged her, no one even looked at her. "And don't come back," she shouted. "I never want to see any of you again."

"Fine by me, bitch," a girl's voice answered.

"Fuck you," a guy said, starting a chorus of fuck you's.

Christina stood in the middle of the room and watched them go. When she turned to look at Randy, he was glaring at her.

"Are you nuts?" he asked, his anger palpable.

"You, too, Randy. Get out."

"You can't throw me out of my own house."

"It's not your house. If you recall, it's my name on the lease and my paycheck paying the rent."

He grabbed her arm and when she tried to pull away, squeezed until she cried out and stopped struggling. "What the fuck is going on with you? You leave all happy and come back a flaming psycho."

Instead of answering, she launched an offensive. "What's with the party, Randy? You said it wouldn't happen again. As a matter of fact, you promised."

He let her go and sat on the sofa arm. "I was celebrating. What's wrong with that?"

"Why were you celebrating? Did something happen that I don't know about?"

He reached for her. She slapped his hands away. "The movie, baby," he said. "What else?"

"The movie or the money?"

"Right now it's pretty much the same thing."

"There isn't any money," she said. "That's what my father wanted to tell me."

Randy's expression went from confusion to disbelief to anger. He started to run his hands through his hair, stopped, and held the sides of his head. After several seconds he walked toward the kitchen, then turned and came back. "He's lying. We'll get a lawyer. We'll sue. He can't cut you off—you're his daughter, his own flesh and blood."

"It won't do any good—*there isn't any money.*"

"Oh yeah? Then how did he pay for that first-class ticket?"

She surprised herself with how quickly she came up with an answer. "He's running up his charge cards. He says it's a return on the twenty-two percent interest they've been collecting from him all these years."

Randy groaned. "That fucker. I was counting on him."

"He's going to feel awful when he finds out what he did to you."

"Don't push me, Christina."

"And I suppose this means you're not going to dedicate the film to him or give him producer credit?"

"I'm tired of your smart-ass mouth." He glared at her. "And I'm tired of you."

"Go ahead, break my heart."

"I'm leaving—but not because you want me to."

She laughed. "Whatever it takes."

She remembered too late that Randy could handle just about

anything—but not someone laughing at him. Out of the corner of her eye she saw him double his fist. He'd never hit her, so her mind stumbled over the warning. Too late she brought her hands up to defend herself. His knuckles connected with her jaw in a head-snapping blow. Shards of pain shot through her cheek, across her eye, and into her scalp. Her world went from blinding white to red to black. She struggled to stay upright, reaching for something to hold on to but finding only air. Her foot caught on the worn sisal rug and she went down.

Randy crouched beside her. "It's over between us, Christina. But not because you say so. I only stayed for the movie." He cupped her jaw and squeezed. She cried out in pain. "Report this or come after me in any way, and I'll make your life hell. I'll tie you up so tight in the Tucson courts that you'll never get to L.A."

She tried to answer, tried to tell him she wasn't scared and that he could go to hell, but her mouth wouldn't work. Pain washed over her in crimson waves. She fought closing her eyes, knowing she needed help and that she was on her own to find it.

Fourteen

Jessie

Jessie turned the micro recorder over in his hand, flipping it between his fingers the way he would a silver dollar. It was May 1, a day the newspapers used to carry a picture of kids dancing around a May pole, the girls with ribbons in their hair, the boys in short pants. Now it was Cinco de Mayo, the fifth of May, that was celebrated. The kids in the picture were Mexican, the girls in brightly colored dresses, the boys wearing sombreros as big as umbrellas.

Had there been a day when editors gathered in the newsroom and decided there was only room for one photograph of dancing children in May, or was it simply a matter of times changing the way lives changed?

Did anyone care?

Jessie leaned back in his chair, closed his eyes, and listened to the wind-driven rain hitting his bedroom window. He'd made his twenty-question bargain with Lucy on a whim, never suspecting how serious she'd been or how far she would go to collect until she arrived with a recorder and a box filled with batteries and tapes. At first he'd claimed fatigue and then disinterest; she'd turned away both excuses, telling him a bargain was as good as a promise, knowing he would never renege on a promise.

He'd finally agreed but balked at her insistence that he begin at the beginning again, retelling the part about leaving home for a second time. As far as he was concerned, once was enough to visit those particular hurts. There wasn't anything to be gained going there again. But then she'd told him she'd been distracted at the first telling and was sure she'd missed some of the details, and besides, she'd eaten dessert not only that day but several times since. Trading the extra time she'd had to put in at the gym for an hour or two with a recorder seemed only fair.

What the hell—there was nothing for him in looking forward, he might as well look back. With a sigh, he closed his eyes and put the recorder next to his cheek.

This second journey into his past was easier than the first. The burden of age and wisdom and hard-won sophistication was shed with careless abandon, like a heavy winter coat at the first sign of spring. It took an hour to retell the beginning, and then, after a break for pills and a cup of coffee, Jessie was back with the recorder and on the road out of Guymon again.

Jessie's Story

Oklahoma looked a lot smaller on the maps I'd studied in the feed store. I'd figured usin' my thumb and travelin' due east to Woodward and then dropping south through Watongo I'd get to the Oklahoma City oil fields in a couple of days. I could last that long easy with the food Ma had given me. Whatever else I might need I could get with the five dollars Pa had shoved in my back pocket last thing before he drove away.

It turned out I wound up walking more than riding.

*It wasn't that folks weren't willing to stop and let me hop
on the back of their truck, it was that none of them were
going much more than a mile or two down the road.
The long haulers I talked to at the gas stations and coffee
shops were headed west to California. To a man they
told me I was headed in the wrong direction. A couple
even invited me to join them, but I told them California
didn't have what I was looking for.*

*A hot, dusty, road-weary week went by, and I still
hadn't seen my first oil well. I'd gone slow on the food,
not eating till my stomach sent out sounds like the Indian
drum Grandma used to call us in from the fields. The
piece of ham I'd saved till last spoiled and stunk up the
suitcase so bad I couldn't stop breathing the smell for
days. I tossed everything but the stuff I'd tucked into a
handkerchief before I torched the house, a shirt and some
underwear—the only things I owned that hadn't been
patched or darned three times over—and rolled them
in a blanket I stole off a clothesline somewhere between
Seiling and Oakwood.*

*I kept what little flesh was covering my bones from
disappearing by stopping at the back doors of farmhouses
and beggin' for a meal. It didn't take long to figure out
the best times were early morning or a little before noon,
when there was something on the stove that could be
scooped or ladled or have a corner broken off of and not
look like much was missing. When I offered to work for
food, as often as not I was given something to make me
feel I'd earned what I was given.*

*I slept in barns when I could and alongside the road
when I couldn't and never once felt sorry for myself or
bellyached I'd been dealt a lousy hand. It didn't take
much lookin' to see someone worse off. Besides, I was*

sixteen and free to come and go as I pleased and full of
the kind of dreams that made graduating from college
seem like coming in second place. I answered to no one,
was responsible for nothing, and was convinced I could
be or do anything I put my mind to.

Not that I didn't stumble a time or two on my glory
road. I learned I wasn't too proud to lick spilled beans off
a dirty rock or eat someone else's leavings at a restaurant.
And my pride didn't get in the way when it came to
asking a pretty girl for a handout. I got so good at
begging it scared me when I stopped to give it more
than a passing thought. I made myself a promise that
when it was over it was done. As soon as I reached the
oil fields and got a job, I'd starve before I took another
dime or bite of food I hadn't earned.

I finally hooked up with a real ride about twenty
miles outside Oklahoma City. I'd put my thumb out for
a truck loaded with pipe, figuring the driver was going
somewhere I wanted to be. He took me to the Sudik
dairy farm, or at least what had been a farm five years
earlier—before the Wild Mary Sudik came roaring out
of the ground and blew the cows and people off the land.

Wild Mary was the biggest thing that had happened
in Oklahoma since the land rush—so big, radio stations
sent reporters to tell the story to folks listening all over
the country. I was eleven, old enough to be caught up in
the excitement of a disaster, smart enough not to let on
that I was secretly hoping it went on a long time. I asked
Pa a hundred questions, most of them starting with why.

I loved hearing the witnesses tell how the well blew
and the escaping gas shot the heavy drill pipes into the
air like pieces of straw. It was everything I could do not
to cheer when several days later the drama increased

*dramatically as the wind shifted and sent gas and oil
over Oklahoma City. For miles around no one dared
light a match to smoke or cook or heat their houses.
Even the neighboring wells were stopped for fear a spark
would set off a fire.*

*The well ran wild for eleven days, roaring so loud the
men working to shut it down wore ear plugs or went
deaf. Oil covered the land and choked the waterways.
Later, I heard somewhere that more than a quarter-
million gallons of the stuff was recovered from creeks and
ponds and yards. I never heard anyone come up with a
reasonable guess at how much was lost.*

*And there I was, standing in the middle of where it
had all happened, gawking up at derricks pulling black
gold out of the ground and making men rich. I stood
on the edge of that man-made forest and let the smell
and feel and sound of it work its way into my mind and
take over my soul. Goose bumps stood up on my arms
like rows of mountains; the hair at the back of my neck
bristled like a brush. Here was my future, my fortune—
and there was no one to tell me different.*

*A month later I had money to stuff in my shoe, but
not enough extra to get me inside a rooming house. I
worked a day or two at a time, doing whatever needed
to be done at one well and then moving on to the next.
There wasn't much call for unskilled labor when men
who'd been working the oil fields all their lives were
standing around with their hands in their pockets.*

*A couple of times a week when I was coming or going
from town to the fields I would run into Clyde Stephens,
the driver who'd given me a ride to the Mary Sudick.
He'd stop and pick me up and ask how things were going.
One day I was jawing about the cold setting in and*

not having a place to stay or money to pay for it when he offered me the best advice I ever got.

"If you want to make money at something, you got to be willing to shoot your dog or skip your mama's funeral if that's what it takes to be first in line. You came to the wrong place, kid. All anyone around here is gonna let you do is pick up the scraps."

"Last I heard my mama was feelin' fine. And I ain't got a dog—but I'll shoot one of yours if you tell me where I oughta be."

"You got to go where the wildcatters are. Pick one of 'em you think looks lucky and desperate and then offer to work for food and a place to sleep till they see you're worth more. Then tell 'em you don't want cash money, but that you'll work for a piece of the well when it comes in. You don't have much to offer so don't go askin' for much right off. Even just a little bit will get you started on where you want to go."

"Where do I find this desperate kind of wildcatter?" Everywhere he'd been the wells were run by big companies.

"Jesus H. Christ, boy, you got to do some of this on your own."

I saw a hole as big as a tire coming up in the road and grabbed hold of the seat and door handle to ride it out. Still, my head hit the top of the cab and cracked my neck. "I don't want to be telling you your business, but it seems your truck might last a little longer if you slowed down once in a while."

"Can't. I got ten more deliveries today. Then I'm leavin' town."

He was telling me something I was too slow to figure out. Finally he tossed me a disgusted look. "Ain't you even gonna ask me where I'm goin'?"

"Didn't figure it was my business."

"I hear there's some interesting things going on down to Yokum County."

"Where's that?"

"East Texas, south of Lubbock, right next to New Mexico."

"That's a long drive—three, four hundred miles at least. Seems to me you could get closer to the front of the line if you had someone to help drive."

Clyde smiled. "Took you long enough."

I had Clyde take me by the creek where I'd set up camp so I could retrieve my belongings I'd hidden in the bushes. We drove straight through and arrived while the celebrating was still going on for a wildcat discovery well they called Ruth E. Bennett.

I couldn't find a desperate wildcatter who didn't laugh at the notion I was worth so much as a barrel of his oil, so I hired on with the Denver Producing and Refining Company. The next morning I told Clyde I'd see him that night. We didn't run into each other again for nearly a month. Winter was setting in hard, and the crew I was on worked sunup to sundown, then fell into beds set up in tents not a hundred yards from the drilling. We had a Chinese man who cooked for us and a Mexican woman who did the wash. Saturday nights a white whore who called herself Marilyn came by. She stayed three hours, no more, then her boyfriend hauled her out of the tent and took her to the next camp. I got in line a couple of times, but worked it so I never got close enough to drop my drawers.

I was three months past my sixteenth birthday and still a virgin, a fact I worked hard to keep from the rest of the crew. They must have figured it out somehow *because that Christmas I got a present that set my head spinning harder than the bottle of whiskey Clyde and me had shared for Thanksgiving. Her name was Wynona. She was Marilyn's friend and there to help out for the holidays. Somewhere between Christmas and New Year I fell in love. Clyde laughed when I told him. He said Wynona was old enough to be my ma. Even if it was true, I didn't care.*

That last night, the one where she told me she was movin' on, I broke down like a baby, begging her not to go, promising things I had no way of delivering, trying to talk her into staying.

"You been good to me, Jessie," she said, my head resting between her full breasts. "I'll remember you—and that's sayin' something." She sat up and perched on the side of the bed.

The tent was small and freezing cold, the only heat coming from a cast-iron stove that leaked as much smoke inside as it drew out. Light came from a lantern hanging off a pole in the corner. I knew that once the sun set what happened inside Wynona's tent was about as private as peeing off the porch, but not even that slowed me down.

Wynona wrapped herself in the Indian blanket at the foot of the bed. "It's time you got a move on, Jessie. George and me is pullin' out early in the morning and headin' for home. My kids ain't seen me in so long I'm thinkin' they forgot what I look like."

The woman I loved was a mother. And married. I grabbed my pants and shoved my legs in them. "What kind of a man is George that he lets other men sleep with his wife? And him standing no more than fifty yards down the road? If I was your husband—"

Wynona laughed. "George ain't my husband. He's just someone I hired to take care of me on the road."

"But you said you had kids."

She looked deeply into my eyes. "How old are you?"

"What difference does that make?"

"You're a sweet boy, Jessie." She handed me my shirt. "But you got a lot of learnin' to do before you're a man."

"You don't need George. I could protect you." My legs should have carried me outside. Instead they buckled and I was sitting on the bed again.

Wynona put her hand under my chin and brought it up until I was looking at her. "Do you know about women who like other women?" she asked gently.

I didn't, but pretended I did.

"I'm one of them. As much as I like you, Jessie, I could never love you. Not the way you want to be loved."

It was funny the way I could feel my heart breaking and at the same time knew I was going to be all right.

Jessie stopped when he saw Rhona at the doorway. She'd been working for him almost as long as he'd been in Sacramento and nothing, not even coming in on him when it must look as if he were having a conversation with his hand, fazed her.

"Sorry about interrupting," she said. "But it's time for your pills."

"You're not interrupting anything," Jessie told her. He pressed the off button and tossed the recorder on the table. "I'm through with this nonsense." No one wanted to hear the ramblings of an old man revisiting his youth. Not really. Lucy was simply taking care of him the only way she knew how, giving him something to do to fill the hours and days, making them seem as if they had purpose.

Rhona handed him the pills and a glass of water. A month ago he could swallow them all at once. Now he took them one at a time and slowly. "My uncle was in the oil business," she said. Jessie finished the water and handed her the glass. "He was a wildcatter, mostly in South America. My father used to talk about all the money he made." She smiled sagely. "My mother told me he spent a whole lot more."

"It comes with the territory."

"Not with you."

"I've only been steady the last twenty years. Before that I was up and down as often as the stock market."

She let out a snort. "Well, I wish you'd let those people on Wall Street know how you finally figured it out."

Now it was Jessie's turn to smile. "There's nothing mysterious about it—you quit while you're ahead."

Fifteen

Rachel

Rachel pulled into the parking lot at the soccer field with the scoreboard showing two minutes into the second half. Mothers and a scattering of fathers were gathered on the sidelines, some pacing, most sitting in folding chairs. She opened the door but couldn't get out of the car.

She'd accepted how hard it would be to face these people—they were the ones who'd watched the affair between Jeff and Sandy develop during practice while she was at work. They'd witnessed the sidelong glances, the intimate smiles, the growing familiarity, but had chosen not to say anything when they saw her at the weekend games. She knew she was being unfair. She knew it was wrong to allow herself to think one of them could have taken Jeff aside and asked him if he knew what he was doing, what he was risking, and stopped the affair before it happened. It was shifting blame when Jeff and only Jeff was responsible. Still, she couldn't get past wondering if it was so wrong to think one of them might have cared enough to step in with a warning.

How did she know they hadn't?

The anger and bravado she'd counted on to get her through this first encounter were buried under a blanket of humiliation. What insane ego trip had gripped her when she'd suggested exchanging the kids at Cassidy's soccer game? What in-your-face-friggin' point was she looking to prove that she hadn't already proven when she moved out and had her lawyer contact Jeff for a formal financial support request?

If she hadn't promised Cassidy she would be there, if she hadn't already missed the last three games because she'd been too humiliated to face the knowing looks of the other parents, she'd leave now. But this was the second to last game of the season, and she'd promised.

She didn't leave. Instead she watched the game leaning against the car feeling a twinge of guilt whenever she saw Cassidy scan the sidelines looking for her. The game ended in a three-three tie. The teams lined up in the center of the field to run past each other, their hands in the air for cursory high-fives. Mothers and fathers gathered chairs and bags and blankets while the coach reviewed the game with their daughters, led them in a final cheer, and handed out snacks.

Cassidy stood apart from the other girls searching the parents on the opposite side of the field. Someone offered her a drink; she shook her head. John danced around her in a five-year-old brother's bid for attention; she ignored him. Jeff came up to Cassidy and put his hand on her shoulder, inadvertently blocking her view; she moved to look around him. At last she spotted Rachel.

Plainly puzzled at finding her mother in the parking lot, she offered a tentative wave. Rachel smiled and returned the wave. Once discovered, she had to do something, to join them, or at least meet them halfway.

She couldn't; her feet simply wouldn't move in that direction. When had she become such a coward?

Jeff turned, saw her, and immediately seemed to understand.

He reached for John with one hand, the athletic bag with the other, and started toward her. Cassidy ran ahead.

Rachel waited, grateful to the point of tears for the small thoughtfulness, a knot of anger in her chest that it was necessary.

"Did you see my goal?" Cassidy called.

"I did. It was amazing. And the assist you gave in the third quarter was downright brilliant." She caught her beautiful, sweaty daughter to her in a fierce hug.

Cassidy leaned her head back and looked up at Rachel. "How long have you been here?"

"Since the beginning of the second half."

She frowned. "Why didn't you watch with Daddy and John?"

A quick lie sat on the end of her tongue, one that would satisfy Cassidy and stop the questioning. Lies and half-truths were becoming commonplace in this new world they inhabited. Would trust be the next victim? "I felt more comfortable in the car."

"Because you and Daddy are getting divorced?"

While it was reasonable to assume this was the direction she and Jeff were headed, neither of them had said so. At least not to each other. "Who told you that?"

"Becky's mom."

"I don't know Becky. Is she a friend of yours?"

"She's the new girl on my team." Cassidy turned and pointed. "That's her next to coach Brady."

Impatient with his father's slow progress, John let go of Jeff's hand and ran to Rachel. She hugged him without letting go of Cassidy and bent to kiss the top of his head. With a quick glance at Jeff, she said, "Does everyone know our private business?"

"No one *knows,* Rachel, they guess."

In a classic case of not realizing what she had until it was gone, Rachel was only beginning to realize that by losing Jeff, she'd also lost her best friend. She had no one to talk to about what was happening to them, no one to give her helpful clichés that promised a better life at the end of this hellish journey. In the middle of the night when the loneliness was overwhelming, she could imagine a day when she would get past the affair, but would she ever forgive him for destroying their friendship?

Parents were headed their way. "Did you bring their clothes?" she asked Jeff.

"The suitcases are in the car." He gave her a pointed look. "Do you want me to get them now?"

The way he asked made her recognize just how big a mistake she'd made suggesting they meet where they would be on exhibit. For the past month, while they'd tried to work out what would be best for the kids, she'd stayed at the house on weekends and Jeff had gone to a motel.

Finally, in the middle of a sleepless night, she'd decided it made more sense for Jeff to stay at the house and for her to get an apartment. He was the primary caregiver and needed to be there to take the kids to school and pick them up and to take care of all the day-to-day moments that made up their lives.

This was the first time the kids would be staying at her new apartment. She'd been so caught up in trying to make the adjustment run smoothly that she'd missed the obvious.

"Why don't I drop their clothes by later?" Jeff suggested.

His kindness, so typical, so *Jeff*, infuriated her. She wanted him to act as small and deceitful now as he had when he'd been in the middle of the affair, not remind her why she'd loved him. "I made plans."

"Then I'll follow you now."

"All right." Her stubbornness touched on stupidity. Rachel opened the back door to the Lexus. John got in first and crawled across the seat. Cassidy followed, leaving the door open halfway.

"Cassidy has a birthday party tomorrow at three. I can pick her up at your place and take her if that would be easier."

Rachel nodded, fighting the urge to tell him that nothing was easy for her anymore. She'd been in her apartment a week and still hadn't gone grocery shopping—one of the "plans" she had scheduled for that weekend along with a trip to the cleaners and half a dozen other errands Jeff used to take care of for her. "What about John?"

"He can come with me when I come for Cassidy or you can bring him by the house later." When she didn't answer right away, he added, "Or I can meet you somewhere."

She didn't know what she wanted. "I'll let you know tomorrow."

"Call me on the cell. I'll be out all morning."

It was everything she could do to keep from asking where he would be. She moved to open the front door. "Are you sure it won't be inconvenient for you to take Cassidy to the party?"

"I'll be back by then."

"If you're sure." She mentally cringed. Cellophane was less transparent.

"I'm going to be at the lumber yard. I figured it was time I fixed the back porch railing."

Jeff had threatened to tear the entire railing off and start all over again so often it had become a running joke between them. "Why now?"

He looked away, took a deep breath, and shoved his hands in the back pockets of his jeans. "I've been working on getting the house ready to sell."

Of course. They couldn't afford the house and an apartment long term. Still, hearing the words was like adding another mile to the distance between them. Soon everything they knew, everything they had been would be gone. The life she had loved and taken for granted would be a questionable memory. Tears filled her eyes, yet another thing she'd lost control over. "I hate you for doing this to us."

He automatically started to reach for her, then at the last second drew back. In a voice only she could hear he asked, "What can I do? How can I make it right between us again?"

"You can't."

"I won't accept that."

Foolishly, her heart did a skipping dance of hope. Her mind refused to follow. Out of the corner of her eye she saw one of the parents headed their way. She got in the car and opened the window. "Don't bother meeting me. I'll pick up whatever the kids need for tonight at the store."

He nodded and bent to wave to Cassidy and John. "I'll see you tomorrow then."

Rachel backed out and started to drive away. Almost as an afterthought, she glanced into the rearview mirror and saw Jeff watching them. The anguished look on his face stole her breath. For an instant, unwillingly, she was drawn into his pain.

The apartment was like a new toy to Cassidy and John, one to be explored, played with, and tossed aside after a couple of hours. The novelty had worn off by bedtime, and they were ready to go home.

Up for the third time to go to the bathroom, John stood at the doorway to the living room and stared at Rachel. "When is Daddy coming to get us?" he asked softly.

Rachel put her laptop aside and fought a flash of frustration bordering on anger. The feeling was gone as quickly as it had come. John and Cassidy were suffering as much as she and Jeff, if not more. "Tomorrow," she said gently. "Now go back to bed."

"I don't like that bed. It's too hard." The Spiderman pajamas he'd chosen at the store were so big they would be worn out before he could grow into them.

"I can make it softer, but not tonight. We have to wait until the stores open in the morning."

His lip quivered. Another minute and he would be crying. "Do you want to try my bed?"

He considered the blatant bribery, then bobbed his head in a slow nod.

Rachel crossed the room and took John's small warm hand in her own, leading him down the short hallway. Her bedroom looked even less inviting than his, the only furniture a queen-size bed with no spread. The clothes that couldn't be put on hangers were in boxes lining one wall, and there was only one light, a lamp that sat on the floor beside the bed.

John stopped at the doorway and stared at the sad-looking room. The only way he was going to stay without argument was if she stayed with him. She sat on the edge of the bed and patted a spot beside her. John climbed onto her lap instead.

"I'm not very happy, Mommy."

She put her arms around him and hugged as hard as she dared, knowing any harder would scare him. "I'm not very happy either, John."

"I don't want you to live here. I want you to come home with me and Cassidy and Daddy."

"I can't."

"Why?"

"Because sometimes mommies and daddies stop loving each other, and when that happens they can't live together anymore."

"Daddy loves you. He told me so. He told Cassidy, too." He sat up to look at her. "See? You don't have to stay here. You can come home."

Damn you, Jeff. By telling John he loved her, in their son's eyes, the separation became her fault. He would undoubtedly grow up believing she'd broken his father's heart. When he was old enough to be told what really happened, it would be too late.

What was it with her and men? She wasn't good enough for her real father to stick around when she was a child, she'd been everything from a nuisance to a temptation to a half-dozen stepfathers, she'd married a man who'd betrayed her, and she had a son who preferred his father over her.

What was it that she lacked that men looked for in a woman?

She'd not only loved Jeff, even more important, she'd trusted him in a way she'd never trusted any man. Implicitly. Without question. He'd had her from the moment he climbed onto the lab stool next to hers in chemistry class their junior year and told her he'd had to bribe his friend to let him sit there. She'd believed him. More importantly, she'd believed *in* him.

"Mommy?"

She opened the covers for John, then settled in beside him. "What?"

"Do you love Daddy?"

She knew where he was going and how it was bound to end. "John, is it okay if we don't talk about this now?"

"How come?"

"I'm tired."

He didn't say anything for a long time. Then, softly, "Will you still be tired in the morning?"

Under other circumstances she would have cheered his tenacity. He was fighting for something he wanted in the only way he knew how. She pressed her cheek against the silkiness of his freshly shampooed hair. "Would you like to hear a story?"

"What kind of story?"

"About a little boy and his big sister and their mommy and daddy and how they started a new life that seemed really scary at first but turned out okay."

"I don't think so. I'm kinda tired, too."

Rachel kissed him again and brought him closer. "Maybe in the morning then."

Sixteen

Lucy

Impatient with the delays that had kept her in the office that afternoon, Lucy looked up from the phone and waved off her assistant, Patty, when she appeared in the doorway. Patty stood her ground. Lucy glared at her. Patty didn't flinch.

Lucy cut the caller short by promising a return phone call the next morning. "Well—what is it?" she asked Patty.

"There's a Ginger Reynolds on line three."

Lucy came forward in her chair. "Well, I'll be damned."

"I told her you would call her back, but she said she didn't mind waiting. I thought you might want to make an exception for her."

"You're right. Thanks." Lucy picked up the phone again and switched to line three. "This is Lucy Hargreaves. What can I do for you, Ms. Reynolds?"

"I want to see Jessie Reed. Can you arrange it?"

There was no mistaking the thread of hostility in Ginger's voice. "Would you mind telling me what this concerns?"

"Yes, I would."

"There's something you need to understand about my relationship with your father, Ms. Reynolds. I'm his attorney—but more than that, I'm his friend. As much as I know he would love to see you, I'm not going to let him be harassed by an angry woman who can't seem to understand that giving a child up for adoption can be an act of love. He doesn't have much time, and I want whatever is left to be as peaceful as possible."

"He doesn't strike me as someone who's led a peaceful life. I find it hard to believe he cares all that much about dying peacefully. And he really doesn't seem the kind of man who wants a woman running interference for him."

The words brought her up short. Wasn't this what Jessie had been telling her all along? "All right. When would you like me to arrange this meeting?" Before Ginger could answer, Lucy added, "The sooner the better."

"Tomorrow?"

"Morning is best. He's stronger then."

"I'll be at your office at nine."

"It would be better if you met him at home." She gave Ginger the address and directions.

"Will you be there?" Ginger asked.

She wanted to be, but couldn't do that to Jessie. Ginger was right. He'd spent his entire life on the edge and never asked to be protected. He sure as hell wouldn't want it now. "Unless there are legal questions you want answered, I see no reason to be there."

"I just thought—never mind. It isn't important."

Lucy was about to end the conversation when something stopped her. "I know this has been hard on you. After you left I tried to imagine what it would be like to live thirty-six years believing one thing and then be told it was wrong. I couldn't. Not really. It's not possible for anyone who hasn't gone through what you're going through to understand what you're feeling."

"You're good," Ginger said. "But that doesn't surprise me. Jessie strikes me as the kind of man who only hires the best."

"I wasn't trying to work you. My comment was simply an observation. As I told you, Jessie is my friend as well as my client. I care about him, and in extension, his family."

"You can save it for the others. I already have all the friends I need or want."

The oddly defensive reply puzzled Lucy. Ginger was acting like the last kid picked for a softball game, pretending she didn't care. Was it possible that a woman who naturally possessed the looks and figure that made other women run to their plastic surgeons was lonely? The possibility was too much of a cliché for Lucy to swallow.

"I'll call your father and let him know to expect you. If there's a problem with the time, I'll let you know."

"Thank you."

Seventeen

Ginger

Warm, heavy air swirled around Ginger as she opened her car door and stepped outside. Nine o'clock and according to the temperature readout in the car, two degrees shy of eighty. It was going to be a tar-oozing-through-the-asphalt kind of day, and she'd stupidly put on heels and SPANX for her meeting with Jessie. She wanted to look her best, wanted him to know that she'd gotten along fine without him. Most of all she wanted him sorry he had missed knowing her. By looking as much like Barbara as she could pull off, she hoped to make him just a little sorry he'd given up his only link to the woman he'd lost all those years ago.

Her only other trip to Sacramento had been for the "family" get-together at Lucy Hargreaves's office. She had no idea what to expect from a city whose skyline was developing with the speed and abandon of carelessly planted flower bulbs.

Jessie lived in an area east of downtown filled with stately homes on tree-lined streets. The residential community didn't so much scream money as whisper it with a genteel accent. Whether the mostly two-story houses were brick or stucco or wood, there were no lawns that needed mowing, no weeds to pull, no peeling paint or crooked shutters. Windows sparkled in the dappled sunlight and elaborate summer wreaths hung on front doors. Sidewalks were swept, driveways clear, yards free of children's toys. People who lived here had help maintaining these houses. Lots of help. Expensive help.

Marc dreamed of living like this but was two or three promotions shy of what it would take to make the move. She'd be content with a three-bedroom, two-bath in the suburbs as long as it was with him. And soon. The wait was an anchor on everything from her mood to her ability to have children. The biological clock she heard ticking every month was starting to sound like Big Ben. She'd foolishly assumed her mother's late pregnancy was evidence she could pull it off, too. Now, no matter how hard she tried to convince herself nothing had changed, she knew it was a lie. Her life had turned into a game of checkers with her pieces on the red squares, her opponent's on the black. No matter how well she played, winning wasn't possible.

She didn't want to be here, had fought coming, but the need to know more about her mother grew stronger every day, as did the realization that time and opportunity to ask Jessie about her was running out. She'd told no one she was coming, not even Marc. Her mother would say she understood, but she wouldn't, not really. It would hurt her, feel like a betrayal when it was nothing more than curiosity.

Ginger's need to know Barbara had gone from a pride-filled spurning of the woman who'd rejected her to a fantasy-filled belief that Barbara had grieved over her decision the rest of her short life. Jessie was her one chance, her last chance, to learn the truth.

Ginger adjusted her jacket, smoothed her skirt, and headed for the front door. A middle-aged woman, dressed in slacks and a polo shirt, her hair in a ponytail, answered immediately, as if she'd been standing on the other side of the door waiting.

"I'm Ginger Reynolds. I have an appointment with Mr. Reed."

"He's expecting you." She stepped aside for Ginger to enter. "I'll take you to him."

Ginger's heels clicked noisily on the foyer's travertine floor, disturbing the quiet like an inept cat burglar. At the beginning of a short hallway the travertine gave way to dense wool carpeting. The woman stopped outside an open door and rapped lightly on the frame. "Ms. Reynolds is here."

She glanced at Ginger, an unmistakable warning in the look. Plainly Jessie engendered a loyalty in all of his employees that went beyond their paychecks. "If you need anything, I'll be in the kitchen. My name is Rhona."

"Thank you."

Ginger entered the room in time to see the effort it took Jessie to stand to greet her. She resented the wave of compassion that swept over her. She didn't want to feel sorry for Jessie Reed. She didn't want to feel anything for him. "Please, don't get up."

"As long as I can, I will." He motioned for her to join him, pointing to a high-back chair covered in green and black striped silk. He lowered himself into a matching chair and openly studied her. "Forgive me if I stare. Seeing you last week brought back memories I hadn't indulged in years. I'd forgotten how beautiful your mother was. . . ."

She returned his stare, seeking something, *anything* that connected them, but couldn't see past how old he was, how sunken and wrinkled and gray. "I looked for pictures of her on the Internet. The ones I found were all staged, nothing candid."

"Could you see yourself in them?"

"No." She had, but only superficially, and only after comparing them to what she had looked like in her twenties.

"You will one day—when you get past your anger."

"Don't assume you know me because you knew her. I'm nothing like her."

"How do you know?" he asked with a half-smile.

He might be old and dying, but he wasn't slow. "I believe in nurture over nature."

He chuckled. "I guess it's a good thing I didn't mention how you seem to have inherited the infamous streak of Reed stubbornness."

"What makes you so sure you're my biological father? You couldn't test for things like that back then." It wasn't something she'd planned to say and was immediately ashamed that she'd done so in an attempt to hurt him.

"What possible reason would I have for claiming you as my daughter if I didn't know it to be true?"

"She could have lied to you. Women have been known to do that."

"Not Barbara."

"I've listened to her songs. She sang a lot about being free to love when and where and who you wanted. It seems reasonable to assume she practiced what she preached."

"You can accept Barbara as your mother, but not me as your father? Is that it? You would prefer a faceless, nameless man you would never have to acknowledge?"

She felt cornered. "I don't . . . know."

"Why did you come here today?"

"I want to know if there are any family medical problems that I could pass on to my children."

"That's it?"

"Yes."

"No other reason?"

"I want to know about Barbara," she admitted. "What she was like. What the stories written about her don't tell."

Jessie closed his eyes for so long, Ginger couldn't determine if he was in deep thought or had gone to sleep. When he opened them again he looked at her, ready for whatever she had to throw his way. "All I know medically is that she didn't have any problems carrying you or having you. For anything else you're going to have to ask your grandmother or one of Barbara's sisters. I don't know that I would recommend doing that, though."

"Why not?"

Jessie chuckled. "They're a tight-ass bunch who'll have you slit your wrist to prove your blood runs blue. They loved Barbara, but she swore there was a collective sigh of relief when she moved out west and they didn't have to explain her to their friends anymore."

"That's a terrible thing to say."

"Even worse to believe."

"You were already an old man back then. I find it hard to believe you were friends. What could you have had in common with someone like her?"

"Believe what you want, Ginger. I'm not going to try to change your mind." Fatigue shadowed the lines on his face, charcoal in the hands of an artistic cancer. "Ask me something that matters," he said with aching tenderness. "Something you'll be glad to know when you stop hating her for what you think she did to you."

He'd found a way past her anger, past her pain and confusion. "I can't think what that would be."

"Then I'll tell you what I remember, what I see when I look back. I knew she was gone before I heard it on the news. I've never told anyone this, it was too personal and didn't matter one way or the other to anyone but me, but she stopped to say good-bye before she took off on that plane. She didn't say anything profound, she hardly said anything at all. She just wanted to let me know she was all right. Now, when I think about her, I see her smiling and remember how she loved raunchy jokes and peppermint candy and whistling.

"Most of all I remember her music and what it meant to her. It was everything, not just a way of life, but life itself. It's hard to understand someone that dedicated and driven. Viewed from a distance, they are the stars we delight in, even envy. Close up, they are the ones who break our hearts."

"Did she ever talk about me?"

"No. But I know she thought about you. Listen to her songs. She was talking to you through them."

"How do you know that? Did she tell you?"

"She didn't have to." Jessie gave her a sad look and shook his head. "Why is it important for you to feel discarded? Barbara wanted you to have the stable home she could never give you. If she'd been your friend you would have admired her decision."

"And how would I have felt about you?"

Jessie stared at her a long time weighing his answer. Finally, with a sigh he said, "Not very good, I'm afraid. I was the last person you needed. Drunks make lousy fathers."

Eighteen

Ginger

Ginger hesitated ringing the doorbell to Rachel's apartment. She still couldn't understand why she'd decided to take I-80 instead of I-680 to get back to San Jose or what impulse had made her take the Orinda exit to stop by to visit her "sister."

Curiosity was the obvious answer, the one Jessie had offered at their first meeting. But it was more than that. Jessie had shown her photographs of his family, but most of them were so faded and cracked, she couldn't recognize him as a young man, let alone see herself reflected in the faces of the people staring back at her.

A month ago she'd paid less attention to family ties than she did her retirement account, taking for granted what she'd known, or thought she'd known, all her life. Now the complex DNA that tied her to complete strangers threaded through every waking thought and even found its way into her dreams.

She had a million questions. Like musical talent. Was it inherited? If so, it had skipped a generation. She couldn't carry a tune in a Prada bag. What about business sense? Obviously Jessie had more than his share. He might have gone bankrupt a couple of times, but he always came back. She couldn't balance her checkbook. Where was the connection?

Was it in her sisters? Did they share mannerisms, stubbornness, gestures? Were those traits inherited or learned?

And where did standing outside someone's door stupidly trying to decide whether to ring the bell fall in the grand genetic scheme of things?

Ginger pressed the bell. Rachel appeared seconds later. At first she looked annoyed, then puzzled. Recognition and curiosity followed in succeeding waves. "Ginger—isn't it?"

Ginger nodded.

"How did you find me?"

"The lawyer, Lucy Hargreaves, gave me your address. Your husband—I assume he's still your husband—gave me this one."

"And you came here because . . . ?"

Ginger considered the question. "Honestly—I don't know."

Rachel seemed as ambivalent. Finally, she said, "You might as well come in while you're figuring it out."

Ginger followed Rachel down a hallway into a living room with a sofa, a coffee table, a lamp, and little else. "I see you're a minimalist. I'm more into the calculated shabby chic myself."

Rachel sat on one end of the sofa and motioned for Ginger to join her. "The proper term is early separation." She offered a polite smile. "I've heard of shabby chic, but not the calculated part."

"My invention. It's where you strive to convince everyone you can afford better when you really can't."

"I spent the first five years of my marriage there. Jeff and I used to cruise the neighborhoods on pickup day to see what we—" Rachel stopped and shook her head. She gave Ginger a glance that was both pain-filled and embarrassed. "I've got to stop doing that."

The action was as revealing as words. Ginger knew with gut-wrenching certainty what had happened between Rachel and her husband. The details—who, why, when—weren't important, only that Rachel had not been the one who'd strayed. She still hadn't learned how to stop loving the creep.

"That's not how I pictured you at all," Ginger said breezily. "I figured one of us had to have benefited from having a father who was a millionaire. I knew it wasn't me, and it obviously wasn't Christina."

"And the other one looked pretty middle-class."

"That would be Elizabeth, the one who bolted when she discovered she had a room full of sisters. Do you suppose she honestly believed she was the only one? She knew Jessie the longest. She had to have some idea what he was like."

She gave Ginger a curious stare. "How do you know that about Elizabeth?"

"I went to see Jessie today."

"I see," Rachel said carefully.

She shouldn't have said anything about Jessie's money. "It's not what you think." Rachel wasn't stupid. "Well, maybe it is, a little," she admitted. "But mostly I wanted to find out about my mother."

"Seems to me that would be pretty easy to do on the Internet."

"I tried that. There's a lot about her music and her public image, but not a lot about her personal life beyond what was in her obituary."

"What about all the books that were written about her after she died?"

"I've ordered a couple, but they haven't arrived yet." Ginger smiled. "You've been looking, too, I take it?"

"A little," Rachel admitted.

"I wouldn't think you'd have the time."

"Yeah, you'd think." Rachel straightened her legs and sat forward. "Look, I don't mean to be rude, but my kids will be here in an hour and I don't have anything in the apartment to feed them."

"You have kids?"

"Two. Cassidy's eight and John's five."

An odd feeling came over Ginger. "I guess that makes me an aunt."

"I guess it does." Rachel seemed as bemused at the idea as Ginger. "I've been so wrapped up in everything else that's been going on, I didn't stop to think that this thing with Jessie involves them, too. What about you? Do you have children?"

"I've never been married, and I'm kind of old-fashioned when it comes to kids and marriage. Came close once, but it didn't work out."

"And there's no one now?"

Ginger had her mouth open to tell Rachel about Marc when it hit her what a huge mistake that would be. There was no way Rachel would understand her reasons for being involved with a married man. "You need to get to the grocery store. I should have called before I came."

"I'm glad you didn't," Rachel said. "I would have found an excuse not to see you."

The statement was too provocative not to ask, "Why?"

"My life is complicated right now."

"Yeah, mine, too." She moved to stand. "Before I go—I know I already told you I was sorry, but I just wanted to say it again. I was a real bitch to you at that meeting. I had no right to put you on the spot the way I did about you being separated."

Rachel smiled. "As I recall, I gave as good as I got. I took out on you what I wanted to take out on Jessie."

Ginger stood and slipped her purse strap onto her shoulder. "He looked a lot worse when I saw him today."

"I'm not surprised. He's dying."

"It was more than that. He was . . . I don't know, I guess it was that he looked sad."

"Sounds like you've forgiven him?"

"I'm still trying to decide whether he needs forgiving—whether either of them do. I can't imagine giving a child away that I'd given birth to, but I've never been in that situation. How do I know what I would do?"

"It's pretty obvious that Jessie wouldn't have been a part of your life even if your mother had kept you. At least with you he had a legitimate excuse for staying away."

"You never spent any time with him?" Ginger asked.

"I never even *saw* him before that meeting. Not once in thirty-six years."

"I think we can safely assume Jessie Reed never came through as a father for any of us."

"There's no way I can tell you how much I hate that man."

"You should tell him how you feel, get it out of your system while you can."

"He would just try to defend himself, and I don't want to hear what he has to say. There's no excuse for what he did to me or to my mother."

"What did he do?" Normally Ginger would never have asked, considering it none of her business. But there was nothing "normal" about Jessie or the situation he'd put them in.

"My mother was seventeen when I was conceived. Jessie was almost fifty. When she told him she was pregnant he said he was too old to have a kid. He changed the locks on the house and told her he would hire as many men as he could to say they'd slept with her if she tried to take him to court for support. Now the son of a bitch wants to claim me because he's dying and has a guilty conscience? I don't think so."

Ginger recoiled at the story. People changed, but she couldn't believe Jessie could have changed that much in thirty years.

Something wasn't right. Rather than argue the point, she decided to switch to a safer subject. "Do you have pictures of your kids?" She smiled. "Of course you do. What I'm really asking is if I could see them."

"I only have a couple of recent ones here. They're in the bedroom. Hang on a minute, I'll get them." Just as she was leaving the room, she stopped and looked back at Ginger. "How do you feel about macaroni and cheese?"

"About the same as I do about liver and onions."

"Is that good or bad?"

"Very, very bad."

Rachel laughed. "How about salad?"

"What woman who wants to stay under a size sixteen hasn't convinced herself she loves salad? Why are you asking?"

"I just thought if you didn't have other plans you could stay for dinner. That way you could see Cassidy and John in person."

Marc was waiting for her, or would be in another hour. He'd been too busy to listen when she'd called earlier to tell him how the meeting had gone. "I can't. I have a conference call—" She saw a quick flash of disappointment cross Rachel's eyes that mirrored her own feelings.

For once she would cancel on Marc. He'd done it to her so often he could hardly be upset. "I'll get out of it. I'd really like to meet my niece and nephew."

Cassidy and John were confused and standoffish at first introduction but came around when Ginger plied them with riddles and knock-knock jokes while Rachel ordered pizza. Jeff wasn't so easy to figure out. She'd been prepared to hate him on sight but saw too much sorrow in the way he looked at Rachel to justify a snap judgment. He was friendly, and obviously curious at meeting a sister Rachel hadn't known she had, but was too conscious of being in a place he wasn't welcome to take the time to socialize.

Later, after pizza and a video and unexpected hugs from her niece and nephew that left Ginger a little breathless with wonder, Cassidy and John were in bed, if not asleep.

"I should be going," Ginger said. It was an offer, made because it seemed the right thing to say at nine-thirty in the evening. She didn't want to leave. She hadn't asked half the questions she'd come there to ask, nor had she found a reason to be glad she'd been raised without knowing she had a sister.

"Do you live far from here?" Rachel asked.

"San Jose." An hour or two from Orinda, depending on traffic.

"Would you like to stay?" Rachel blurted. "Never mind. I know how odd that sounds, but I was just thinking how nice this has been and how long it's been since I've had someone I could talk to—and how much we have to catch up on."

"You mean overnight?"

"All I can offer you here is John's bed."

"Where would John sleep?"

"With me."

"He wouldn't mind?"

"He won't even know he's been moved until he wakes up in the morning."

She shouldn't. She had a dozen errands to run in the morning, including a couple for Marc. "Sure. Why not?"

Rachel smiled. "Great. I'll open that bottle of Merlot I picked up last week." She stood and added, "Is Merlot okay with you?"

"Yeah—it's fine."

"You're wondering why I didn't offer it with the pizza."

"No—not at all." Yes, she was.

"I have a thing about drinking and driving. In college my best friend was killed by a drunk driver. I tried really hard to hate him, but at the trial I wound up feeling sorry for him. His wife died in the accident, too. They'd been at a restaurant celebrating their anniversary. Everything about it was such a waste."

"What happened to him?"

"He went to jail for a couple of years. After he got out, he committed suicide."

Ginger cringed. "Sure you wouldn't rather stick to iced tea?"

"Don't get me wrong, I don't have a problem with drinking. It's when it's combined with driving. And I'd really like someone to try this Merlot with me."

"Okay."

They had a glass, decided it was less than advertised but better than average, and finished the bottle with a bag of microwave popcorn. By eleven-thirty Rachel was sitting on one end of the sofa, yoga fashion, with Ginger at the other end, her shoes kicked off, her feet tucked under her.

"I have to admit this has turned out a lot better than I expected," Ginger said, relaxed to the point of shared confidences, thanks to the wine and an inexplicable, compelling feeling that she'd found a long-lost friend.

"Oh? And what were you expecting?"

"After that first meeting—not much."

"Seeing Jessie was harder than I'd expected. I still don't know how I feel about finding out I'm not an only child."

"I have a brother. Not the brother I thought he was, but it doesn't matter, not really. The funny thing is, I always wanted a sister." She drained her glass. "Be careful what you wish for, huh?"

Rachel let out a humorless laugh. "My mother went through men like race cars go through tires. The only thing that makes Jessie different from the others is that he's the one who got her pregnant. She made damn sure it never happened again."

"I don't understand what he could have had that would make a girl her age sleep with him. When I was seventeen, fifty-year-old men made my skin crawl."

"I asked her about that once. She said she didn't know how old he really was until years later."

"Still—he was *old*. At least to someone her age. Did she ever say what attracted her to him?"

"He was in the movie business, and she was young and dumb and wanted to be a star. She believed him when he said he could make it happen." Rachel set her glass on the polished oak floor and reached for the popcorn. "What about you? Did Jessie tell you anything about your mother today?"

Answering was awkward. When Jessie talked about Barbara his voice was gentle, his memories loving. Whatever their relationship, he would never have used and discarded her the way he had Rachel's mother. "He insists they were only friends, but when he talks about her, it sounds like more than that to me."

"She must have loved him a little, too. At least enough to have his baby."

Ginger couldn't tell whether Rachel believed what she'd said or had said it out of kindness the way you told someone they looked good in a hideous dress. "I'm still trying to figure out why it matters. What possible difference does it make how our parents felt about each other when they were knocking the headboard against the wall?"

"You don't think it will matter to Cassidy and John that Jeff and I loved each other when they were conceived?"

Trapped by her own logic. "I think it's going to matter a lot more how you and Jeff treat each other from now on."

"Maybe someday it will get easier, but right now, at times, it's everything I can do to be civil to him. I think I'm doing okay, and then I see him and I get so angry all I want to do is throw something at him."

"So, I take it the separation was your idea?"

"What would you do if you found out your husband was screwing the mother of one of your daughter's soccer friends?"

"I know what I'd want to do—hire a hit man." She flinched.

Rachel didn't know her well enough to know she wasn't serious. "You know I'm kidding, right?"

Rachel smiled at Ginger's retraction. "Yeah, well, it's not as if I'm the first person this has happened to. I'll get over it."

The flippant answer belied the new-kid-in-school look in Rachel's eyes. "Does he love her?" Ginger asked.

"He says he never loved her. It was just one of those things— one that went on for months."

"Maybe you can work it out," Ginger said carefully. She was about as qualified to offer marital advice as she was to play quarterback for the Forty-Niners. "But then maybe you don't want to."

"I keep thinking about the kids growing up the way I did." She propped her elbow on the back of the sofa and leaned her head into her hand. "And then I see Jeff and think about him with her, and it's like my heart is being ripped out of my chest. It's not just the sex part that bothers me. I wonder what they talked about and whether she made him laugh. Did he buy her things? Did he sneak off to call her when he was with me?"

Ginger was growing more and more uncomfortable with the direction the conversation was headed. "You know you can drive yourself crazy thinking about things like that and not even come close to the way it was between them."

"I can't help it. The harder I try to put it out of my mind, the more it's there." Rachel reached for the empty wine bottle. "I'll be right back." She returned with a fresh one, filled Ginger's glass and then her own, and took a sip. "I don't know if this one is better or my taste buds are numb."

Ginger swirled, smelled, and tasted. "It's better."

Rachel settled in again. "Enough about Jeff. Tell me about the man in your life. I'm assuming there is one."

Marc was the last person she wanted to talk about with Rachel. "We've been going together for almost four years now—"

"Going together or living together?"

"We lived together for a while and then decided it wasn't working, so we each have our own place now." The truth, even if varnished with a wide brush.

"So marriage isn't an option?"

"We haven't ruled it out entirely."

"Are you from here?"

"Kansas. I followed Marc to San Jose when he was promoted about a year ago." She'd given up her own upcoming promotion at the job she'd held for ten years to accept a job with Selex Electronics at half the pay. Half the pay, twice the living expenses, and an unanticipated culture shock she was still struggling to overcome. Not a smart combination.

"It must be love."

"Yeah," Ginger laughed. "Or a sickness."

"Same thing," Rachel said.

"I never wanted some big career, just a hearth and home and two-point-five kids."

"With your looks—"

"Oh, please don't—I've heard that kind of thing all my life. What my looks have gotten me is a lifetime of the wrong men hitting on me and the right ones being afraid to even talk to me. Women automatically assume I'm out to steal their potbellied husbands, and everyone, including kids, assumes I'm stupid."

"So, given the choice, you'd rather be ugly?"

Ginger smiled. "Average would be nice."

Rachel took a sip of wine. "I liked being married." She was quiet for a long time. "I hate living like this."

"How does Jeff feel?"

"He thinks I should move back. At least until we see if we can work things out. But I can't do it."

"Maybe with time. . . ."

"If it were you—if the man you love had an affair—do you think you could find a way to trust him again?"

It wasn't a rhetorical question. The lies Ginger told herself, the reasoning she used to justify her own affair, the promises that sustained her sanity, seemed shallow in the face of Rachel's pain. Was this how Marc's wife felt? Was this the real reason Judy insinuated herself into every moment of Marc's day?

Why was she doing this? Judy was nothing like Rachel. Their circumstances were completely different. And she was nothing like the woman Jeff had had an affair with. She loved Marc. And he loved her.

"I don't know if I could find a way," Ginger said, shaken. "But I know I would look really hard."

Rachel nodded. She offered her glass to Ginger for a toast. "I never would have believed this, but I actually think I might like having a sister after all."

Touched by Rachel's unexpected sentiment, Ginger lightly tapped her glass against Rachel's. "Me, too."

Nineteen

Lucy

"How is he?" Lucy asked, shifting the small overnight bag she'd brought with her to her other hand.

Rhona opened the front door wider to let Lucy enter. "I've never watched anyone die," she said. "But I have a feeling it won't be long now. When he wakes up, it's only for a minute or two and then he's asleep again."

"I tried to get here sooner."

Rhona put her hand on Lucy's arm. "You don't have to explain. He knows how you feel about him. So do I."

The small intimacy almost undid Lucy. She'd been with Jessie every day for the past week, watching, waiting, listening when he could talk, sitting quietly by his side when he drifted off to sleep. "I want to be with him. . . ." She couldn't finish.

Rhona walked down the hall with Lucy. At the door to Jessie's bedroom, she said, "Mr. Reed doesn't know, but Ms. Reynolds was here this morning."

Lucy stopped and looked at Rhona. "Ginger was here?"

"She stayed a couple of hours, but Jessie slept the whole time. He's going to be sorry he missed her."

"Did she say why she came?"

Rhona shook her head. "And I didn't ask."

Lucy glanced at Jessie. "I'll tell him when he wakes up."

"No need," Jessie said. Without opening his eyes, he took a deep, labored breath. "I heard."

"You need something for pain?" Rhona asked.

Still Jessie didn't open his eyes. "No, not yet. I want to talk to Lucy first."

She handed Rhona her bag and moved to the bed, close enough for Jessie to feel her presence. "I'm here."

Finally, with obvious effort, Jessie looked at her. He studied her face for a long time, as if charting every line and angle, and then smiled. "I've been waiting for you," he said softly.

Her heart filled her throat. "Why?" she managed to whisper.

"It's time to say good-bye."

She nodded and reached for his hand, curling her fingers into his palm. "I'm going to miss you."

For long seconds he didn't say anything, his look questioning. He stopped to take several breaths. "I wasn't going to do this. There's no point in it—not really." Almost imperceptibly, his hand tightened around hers. "It's just that I've been thinkin' it so long it seems wrong not to say it at least once while I still can. I love you, Lucy. Always have . . . always will."

In a choked whisper, she said, "I know. I love you, too."

"Can you stay a while?"

A tear stole over her eyelashes and escaped to slip down her cheek. She blinked back its companions. She didn't want his last image of her to be one of her crying. "I'm not going anywhere."

He smiled, winked at her one last time, and closed his eyes. Within seconds he was asleep, his breathing shallow and labored, his hand loose in her grip.

Lucy lost all sense of time as she stood and watched Jessie, knowing his heartbeats were numbered, understanding that he would not yield one of them to ease or comfort. He simply didn't know how to give up; he never had.

The heat of the day gave way to a cooling delta breeze as the sun drifted toward the horizon. Lucy asked Rhona to turn off the air conditioning and open the windows, letting the sheer curtains in the bedroom move and billow with the summer-scented air. With it came the sounds of children playing, lives just beginning. Someone was barbecuing, someone else drove by on a motorcycle. Baby birds frantically chirped to be fed.

Jessie breathed.

Lucy settled deeper into the chair beside the bed and reached for the recorder Jessie had used to make her tapes. She pulled out the one she'd been listening to the day before and put in the one that followed. Settling the earphones over her ears, she abandoned the world Jessie was leaving and followed him to a time when he was still a boy.

Jessie's Story

Doesn't matter how much oil you're pulling out of the ground, it's not worth anything if you can't get it where it's got to go. I learned this my usual ass-backward way when I broke my left arm and the only thing I was good for was driving the truck to Coulter City to pick up supplies four or five times a day. It took a while to figure out how to steer with my knees and shift with my good arm, but I got so good at it I kept right on doing it after the cast came off.

There was always someone in charge of something hitching a ride to the oil fields, and I figured I might as well spend the time learning a thing or two I hadn't known the day before, so I asked a lot of questions.

One of the men, Alden Atkins, was there leasing land from the ranchers to run a pipeline between the fields and the railroad. He told me most of the men he dealt with were glad for the little extra money the deal brought, but once in a while he'd run into one who didn't want anything to do with anyone who had anything to do with oil.

Of course I wanted to know what he did then and wasn't glad for asking when I heard the answer. Where I came from men went to jail for killing a man's cattle or burning his barn. Here it seemed neighbors were willin' to look the other way if someone was standing between them making enough from lease money to keep their ranch or losing it to the bank.

I thought about this a lot when I didn't have anyone with me on my runs. There had to be a better way to get people to do what you wanted than scarin' the hell out of them. I was still thinking about it when I made a night run a week later and picked up a man who'd hit a deer with his car. He was bleeding from where his head had hit the windshield and thinking he was headed to town to get it fixed. But he was walking the wrong way and would have been lying in a ditch with crows sitting on his chest by morning if I hadn't turned him around. When we passed his car a couple of miles down the road, he all of a sudden got it in his head that I'd saved his life and that he owed me for it.

The short of it is that he gave me a piece of information that night that had me working for myself two years later. Six months after that I was living in a house with real wood sides and driving a truck I bought with a fistful of cash.

The man swore me to secrecy when he told about the refinery his company was going to build in New Mexico, closer to Coulter City by fifty miles than the railroad— and in the opposite direction. No one had bothered getting right-of-way leases from the ranchers on the west side of town. There wasn't any need.

The next day on one of my runs into town I stopped at Chapman's, the biggest and best dry goods store in town. In the six months I'd been there, Coulter City had gone from a twenty-foot-wide road scratched through the prairie grass, yucca, and sandsage to a full-blown town. The single service station, lumber yard, and restaurant had grown to twelve grocery stores, twenty dry goods, seventeen lumber yards, thirty-eight cafés, twelve supply houses, and ten drugstores. The people who worked in the oil fields lived in pine-planked houses and canvas tents that emerged from the body of Main Street like a butterfly unfolding its wings.

The clerk at Chapman's helped me spend half my savings on a suit, tie, shirt, new shoes, and what I figured had to be the finest felt fedora ever sold in Texas. My jaw dropped to my knees when the clerk brought me out of the dressing room to look in the mirror. It wasn't a boy looking back, but a man. A stranger.

No one I knew had ever owned clothing so fine as that suit and hat. I stood there for a long time trying to imagine myself walking up to some rancher's door and talking him into doing business with me looking the way I did. What would my pa think if it was him staring at me through the screen door? The shoes were too shiny, the jacket too pressed to convince anyone I wasn't exactly what I was—a greenhorn trying to pass himself off as something he wasn't.

That night I waited till I was sure everyone was asleep before I put on my new clothes and sneaked outside. I tried not to think how hard I'd worked to buy brand

new instead of borrowing someone's Sunday best while I
was out there rolling around in the hard west Texas dirt
workin' to make the new look old. I scuffed the shine off
the shoes kicking rocks but had to close my eyes before I
could take that fine fedora in my hand and fling it into
the air. It caught a gust of wind and landed in a shinnery
oak higher than I could reach without climbing. On the
way down I caught my britches on a branch and tore a
hole that let the sun shine through where it shouldn't. A
woman in town fixed the tear and cleaned the trousers as
best she could, leaving just enough dust for me to brush
away while I was standing on a farmer's porch waiting to
be asked inside.

   I didn't have to do near the talking or persuading
I'd anticipated. Once I explained I wasn't just leasing
their land but offering a percentage of the profit from
every gallon of oil that flowed from the field through
their ranches to the refinery, I had fifteen out of the
sixteen leases within three weeks. I didn't need all that
land, but had to make sure no one else got enough to go
around me. By the time I was done, my share was down
to forty-three percent. The only money I was out I was
wearing on my back.

   The last ranch was the largest and right in the middle of
the others. It was key to keeping the cost of actually laying
the pipe appealing to the investors I would approach next.
The ranch was owned by a man named Wyatt Farnsworth.
I'd been warned that he hated everything about oil, cursing
the derricks as loudly and profanely as the people who built
and lived in the towns that had sprung up around them.
However, it seemed he saved his greatest wrath for the
foreigners who had moved in following the discovery of oil,

and to Wyatt Farnsworth a foreigner was anyone born outside the great state of Texas.

I had two strikes against me before I'd even picked up the bat.

Opening the gate to the Farnsworth ranch that Sunday afternoon wasn't as hard as I'd feared. I'd convinced myself by then that not even Wyatt Farnsworth would shoot someone for trespassing on the Lord's day without at least discovering why he'd come. I didn't expect to make it all the way to the porch without being challenged, so I wasn't sure what to do after I opened the screen, turned the bell on the front door, and waited for someone to answer. As I stood there I tried to decide whether I'd make a better impression holding my fedora or wearing it. I took it off, put it back on, then took it off again. Changing my mind one more time, I had the hat halfway back on when I spotted someone staring at me through the curtains at the side window.

My face caught fire and burned so hot it was like pressing my cheek to the top of a potbelly stove. I said a prayer for the ground to open and swallow me whole, but like most of my prayers, it went unanswered. Instead the door opened and I was greeted by a man trying so hard not to laugh that the veins on his neck stuck out like ropes. Someone, a girl or woman—from the volume and sound of it, likely both—demonstrated less restraint.

My hat wound up pressed to my chest, where I held it like a shield. Wyatt Farnsworth was tall and wide, his head just shy of hitting the top of the door frame, his body as thick as a hay bale. He was nearly bald and had a mustache waxed to form circles at each end. I opened my mouth to introduce myself, but the words stuck in my throat.

"What is it, boy? I haven't got all day."

"Mr. Farnsworth?"

"Who's asking?"

I took a chance and stuck out my hand. "Jessie Reed."

He ignored the gesture. "I've been expecting you."

I'd stressed the need for secrecy with the other farmers, at least until the deal was set. Plainly they'd had other ideas. "You have?"

He crossed his arms over his broad chest. "Figured you had to show up sooner or later. You can't get where you want to go without me and my land."

"I mean no disrespect, Mr. Farnsworth, but you're wrong. It wouldn't be easy, but I can get there." I managed to say it in a calm, clear voice, but I was more knee-knocking scared at that moment than when I was seven years old and my Uncle Jeb convinced me there was a ghost living under my bed. "It would put a whole lot more money in everyone's pocket—including yours—if the pipeline doesn't have to go around you. But as my pa used to say, there's more to life than money. If you don't want what should be your share, that's your choice."

The sentiment brought a derisive snort. "That's the kind of thing a man says after the bank takes everything but his pride."

I took a chance at that. "My pa didn't have a whole lot of that left either when he took off for California." I wasn't looking for pity and I sure as hell didn't want to see it in Farnsworth's eyes, so I looked down at my hat. "That's why I'm here. I don't care how long it takes, I'm going to give my pa back what the bank took from him."

He stared at me long and hard. "I wouldn't have believed there was anything you could say that would get

*you invited inside, but you managed to find something." He
motioned for me to follow then turned and disappeared.*

*I knew I wasn't getting a second invitation, so I
reached for the screen door and stepped inside. There was
a parlor to the left, empty as far as I could see. The room
to the right had a sliding door open barely wide enough
for someone to look through. I figured he couldn't have
gone in there or I would have heard the door close. I
stopped to listen and noticed a painting hanging at the
end of the hall. It was of a young woman sitting astride
a black horse. I moved closer, wiping my sweaty hand
on my trousers, shifting the fedora and wiping the other
hand the same way.*

*I'd never paid much attention to paintings so didn't
know if this was a good one or not. It didn't matter,
good or bad; what was there reached out and grabbed
me—the girl. I'd never seen anyone as beautiful. She
had long black hair and blue eyes the color of a summer
morning sky before the sun baked it dry. Her slim waist
would have fit between my hands, and her breasts would
have filled them.*

*"Better not let Daddy catch you staring at that picture
like that." The warning was spoken in a whisper, the
voice soft, feminine, intoxicating.*

*I turned and saw the girl in the picture looking at
me, a mischievous smile flashing from those amazing
blue eyes. I stared, openly and longer than was polite,
before I found a smile to give in return. I guessed her to
be fifteen, maybe sixteen, close enough to my own age for
me to fall instantly, passionately, irretrievably in love.
If God ever decided my prayers were worth listening to,
this was the woman I would marry one day. She was my
future.*

Her smile faded. I think the way I stared at her must have scared her some, but she didn't look away. She knew, just as I did, that something special, maybe even a little magical, had happened between us.

They weren't the kind of words I could say out loud when I was a month shy of my seventeenth birthday and wondering what I was going to use for money for the next two years while I laid pipe over land leased with promises. Promises I laid awake nights wondering if I could keep.

The tape ended. Lucy slipped the earphones off and glanced at Jessie. She waited to hear the strained pull of air into his lungs, but there was only silence. Sometime, somewhere during her journey into his past, he'd left her.

She reached for his hand. It was still warm. He hadn't been gone long. She stood and brushed the hair from his forehead and kissed him good-bye. "If the fates had been kind, I would have been the girl in the painting," she whispered. "And your daughters would have been mine. I'll take care of them for you, Jessie."

She wasn't aware she was crying until she saw a tear land on his cheek. She squeezed his hand and tenderly kissed him on the lips—for the first and for the last time. "Save a place for me, dear friend."

Twenty

Lucy

Lucy sat up straight and stretched her shoulders. She should go home. It was after midnight and she was exhausted. She'd come to the office to tie up loose ends after the funeral. Now everything was done; there was no reason to stay. But she couldn't leave. Her office was the one place she still felt Jessie's presence, as if he were purposely hanging around, trying to communicate to her that there was something left undone.

There was. The reading of the will. Lucy had hoped to take care of it after the funeral, saving Jessie's daughters another trip to Sacramento. But they hadn't come. Not one of them. There was a moment when she thought she'd spotted Elizabeth at the cemetery, but when she looked again, the woman had disappeared. Elizabeth was the only one Lucy knew for sure was even aware Jessie had died. She'd tried for three days to contact Christina and Ginger and only reached their answering machines. She'd left messages, but had yet to hear from them. Rachel's secretary had told her Rachel wasn't expected back from a business trip to Hong Kong for another week. Lucy asked for a return call that never came.

No one knew about Jessie's daughters, so no one at the funeral looked to the family section and wondered at their absence. No one but Lucy. She had sense enough not to feel hurt. The anger she felt gave way to sorrow as she listened to Jessie's tapes.

They would never know the man their father had been, never understand why he'd done what he had, never forgive him his trespasses. She could make copies of the tapes, but they wouldn't listen. They clung to his abandonment of them like winning lottery tickets.

Lucy left her desk and went to the window. The street below was deserted, the traffic lights flashing from green to yellow to red with no one to heed them. "What should I do, Jessie? Is there a way to get them to listen? Is that why you humored me and made the tapes—because you wanted me to find a way?"

She stood there several minutes waiting, open to inspiration, eager for answers, for a solution. Nothing came. Finally, yielding to fatigue, she locked up and drove home.

The answer came in the middle of the night. There would be hell to pay if what she'd come up with was ever discovered, but she didn't care. Unable to contain her excitement, Lucy got out of bed and went to work drafting an addendum to Jessie's will. When she'd finished, she sat back and smiled.

"It's done, Jessie," she said softly, satisfied. "And damned if I don't think you had a hand in this."

Twenty-one

Christina

Christina handed the cab driver his fare and waved off the seventy cents in change. Five weeks since her last cab ride home from the airport. A lifetime ago.

The small patch of grass that passed for a front yard was all but dead, the flowers she'd planted along the porch, a brittle memory. The wheels on her suitcase bounced and skidded on the debris-laden concrete driveway. Two houses down she heard the Ramirez kids playing in their plastic pool in the backyard. Next to them the Chapman dog barked automatically, without purpose or enthusiasm.

It wasn't even noon yet and one of the signs on the savings and loan buildings they'd passed on the way in from the airport had said it was a hundred and five degrees. It would be a hundred and fifteen by five and likely wouldn't drop below eighty that night. She said a quick, silent prayer that the air conditioning still worked. Someday she was going to live somewhere that didn't need air conditioning—in a house on the side of a hill facing the ocean.

Someday she was going to do a lot of things and have a lot of things that she didn't have now. She hadn't come back to Tucson because she'd wanted to, she'd simply had to get away and there was nowhere else to go. After five weeks of confinement with her mother while her broken jaw healed and the bruising faded, listening to everything that was wrong with her life and why she should move back to Mexico, hell had more appeal. The doctor had tried to talk her into staying another three weeks, at least until her jaw was unwired, but when Christina burst into tears and mumbled something unintelligible about losing her job if she didn't get home, he gave in and let her go. It was one of her finest acting moments.

She stepped on the porch and stuck her hand into her purse to dig for her keys. She was still searching through lotions, fingernail files, a sunglasses case, and the emergency suction bulb her mother had insisted she carry in case she got sick on the plane when she looked past the dusty screen and spotted a note taped to the front door.

Her first thought was that it was a final parting shot from Randy, but she knew from friends that he'd left town a week after the police released him and the note looked relatively new.

Christina opened the screen to get a better look. It was from the landlord—an eviction notice stating the rent hadn't been paid in three months. The seven days she'd been given to pay what was due had passed five days ago. Now she had one day to vacate before an officer of the court came to do it for her.

Panic pressed a cold hand to her shoulder. How could this be? She'd always paid their rent on time. She'd been counting on that goodwill to see her through until she was working again.

And then it hit. *Randy*—the low-life, no-good bastard must have been siphoning the household money for months. No wonder he'd offered to take over paying the bills. How could she have been so goddamned stupid to believe that he was doing it to give her a break? Christina shoved the notice into her purse and unlocked the door.

A wave of stagnant hot air greeted her. The blinds and curtains had been drawn, the only light coming from the open door. She waited for her eyes to adjust to the dark, seeking familiar objects. There weren't any; just mail littering the floor under the slot beside the door. Ten seconds ago she'd wondered what she would do with the furniture, how she could get it moved, where she would store it until she found another place to live. She should have known Randy would take care of that for her, too. Anything worth keeping, anything of any value, was gone—including the bookshelves and the boxes that held everything to do with the movie.

Except the phone. He'd left it in the middle of the room, the message light blinking. Obviously he'd paid the phone bill—she reached for the light switch—and the Tucson Electric Power Company bill. Or they were simply slower cutting her off than her landlord.

Randy had moved quickly, stripping the house, undoubtedly selling what he could, trashing what he couldn't, making sure there was nothing left for her to recover. She considered and rejected the idea of calling the police. Even though the furniture had been hers, it had come from flea markets and garage sales, paid for by working extra shifts at the restaurant while Randy was at their rented studio with Shawn doing the sound dubbing. A petty theft charge wouldn't be worth the effort.

Her gaze settled on the flashing red light on the answering machine. Why leave the phone?

Because he'd left her a message. He wanted the last word and knew she couldn't resist listening. Well, screw him. If he had something he wanted her to hear, he could damn well tell her in person when she tracked him down to get their movie back. He might get away with breaking her jaw and taking her furniture, but no way in hell was she going to let him get away with stealing their movie. Christina picked up the phone and yanked the cord from the wall.

Curiosity more than hope sent her through the rest of the

house. She wasn't surprised to see her file boxes dumped and crushed, the papers littering the floor, her clothes in a pile in the middle of the room, glossy red paint sprayed in an X pattern over the top. Only a pair of jeans, a white shirt, some underwear, and her stuffed bear survived. Which didn't matter. She'd lost so much weight drinking her meals through a straw, none of her old clothes would fit. She'd make do with what her mother bought before putting her on the plane for Tucson. Gathering the clothing along with the papers—everything from school records to payroll stubs to paper clips to receipts from the movie that she'd meticulously cataloged and saved since moving to Arizona—she stuffed it all into her suitcase.

Now all she had to do was figure out who she could ask to put her up for a couple of weeks and how, with her mouth wired closed, she was going to get a job to pay them back.

Christina stared at the foot-high stack of mail, trying to decide whether to take the time to go through it now or stuff it in her suitcase and take it with her. Figuring—hoping—that most of it was junk mail and not worth the effort, she sat down cross-legged and began sorting.

There were two letters from agents she'd queried in L.A., both form rejections, several past due notices from various utilities, and a request for a donation from the University of Arizona Alumni Association. "Someday, when I'm rich," she promised, acknowledging her loyalty and love of the school she'd attended on a whim. Eager to leave home, she'd applied to U of A because that was where her best friend wanted to go. Then the friend was caught in a drug bust six months into their freshman year and sent home. Alone and bored, Christina wandered into an audition for a school play. She was hooked. She changed her business major to theater the next semester and never looked back.

Stuck between an ad for a new grocery store opening in the neighborhood and the telephone bill was a letter from her father's attorney. A chill traveled her spine. Whatever was inside couldn't be good. If Jessie had gone into remission or wanted to see her again or just wanted to know if she was thinking about seeing him again, he would have called.

She glanced at the telephone still sitting in the corner where she'd thrown it. Torn between fear and a need to know, hesitantly, reluctantly, she plugged it in, rewound the tape, and hit the play button. As she'd suspected, the first voice she heard was Randy's. She fast-forwarded through his message and three from the restaurant where she'd worked, the last one telling her she was fired. Calls from several friends, both hers and Randy's, followed. She was almost to the end when she heard a woman's voice she didn't recognize and stopped to listen.

"—peacefully. The funeral is this Saturday. The governor's office requested we wait until he was back from Washington, and I wanted to give you and your sisters enough time to make arrangements to be here. I'm afraid it's going to be a bigger production than your father wanted, but he never had any real sense of how beloved he was in this community." Fatigue rode her words like a dark horseman.

"If you have any questions or need help with your arrangements, I've told my assistant to do whatever she can to aid you. I'm going to be out of the office between now and the funeral, but if you need to talk to me personally, my assistant will tell you how to reach me. Or you can leave a message and I'll get back to you as soon as I can.

"I've reserved the front pew at the church for close friends and family. If I don't hear from you before—" The tape ended and began to rewind.

Christina flashed back to the messages she'd deleted on her cell because she didn't recognize the number.

How could her father be dead? He'd looked tired when she'd seen him, not weeks from dying. She'd only been gone a little over a month.

She'd told her mother she was going to see her father again, as soon as her jaw was unwired and she could put the money together to get back to Sacramento. She'd never seen her mother so angry. Didn't Christina realize what a slap in the face it was to Enrique, the man who had raised her as his own child? What would the rest of the family say if they found out? It would bring up everything Carmen had worked so hard to overcome. She would be gossiped about, embarrassed, shamed all over again. Christina was ungrateful, she was selfish, she had no loyalty to the family that had sacrificed everything for her.

Christina brought her knees to her chin and stared at the sliver of light escaping the drawn blinds. The one person she had once believed loved her without reservation was gone. She had a hundred questions that would never be answered. A thousand.

At least she could tell him good-bye. It was Thursday. That gave her a day and a half to get to Sacramento. She reached for her purse and dug for her wallet. Eighty-six dollars and twenty-three cents. Even a bus ticket would cost more than that. She had a final paycheck coming from Lansky's, enough to get her to Sacramento but not back. She didn't care. There was nothing to come back to. She'd go to L.A. Finally.

She opened the letter.

Dear Ms. Alvarado,

As I'm sure you are aware by now, your father passed away a week and a half ago.

She was too late.

There were several business dealings I had hoped to go over with you and your sisters after the funeral, but since none of you were present, it will have to be done at my office. I have reserved Monday, the fifteenth, at three o'clock in the afternoon for this meeting. It is critical that you keep this appointment. If for any reason you cannot attend, please let me know immediately, and I will attempt to make other arrangements.

Sincerely,
Lucy Hargreaves

None of them had been there? Out of four daughters not one had cared enough to say good-bye?

She grabbed a handful of mail and flung it across the room. How could Jessie come back into her life and not give her more time to know whether to love or hate him, to know whether her memories of him were real and not something she'd imagined? Those fragile memories were the soft, warm, safe corners of her childhood, the place where she'd gone whenever she felt she wasn't pretty enough or smart enough or good enough. Always her father had been there to tell her she was wrong.

And now he was gone, dead to her twice.

She was tired. Too tired to deal with it anymore. She took her bear back out of her suitcase, tucked it under her head, and curled up in the middle of the empty room, her heart as tattered as the sisal rug that dug into her skin.

Twenty-two

Elizabeth

"What did you decide?" Sam swam to where Elizabeth sat on the edge of the pool. "Are you going?"

Elizabeth leaned forward on her hands and looked down to meet his gaze. "No."

"Mind telling me why not?"

"It will look like I'm there for the money."

"Screw what it looks like. This could be your last chance to see your sisters. I think you should take it."

"What makes you think they'll be there—or that I want to see them?"

He shrugged. "Human nature. And they came last time when money wasn't a part of it. Seems to me they'd put in a showing again, if only out of curiosity." He tugged on her foot. "Come on, aren't you even a little bit curious? Don't you want to know if he left you something?"

"Maybe—but it doesn't matter. Even if he did, I wouldn't take it." She'd changed her mind about having him pay her way through school. This, like everything else, she would do without him.

"You're telling me you'd pass up, say, fifty grand just to prove how stubborn you can be?"

She snorted. "Jessie didn't have anywhere near that kind of money."

He pushed off and floated across the pool on his back. "I wouldn't be so sure. How many poor men's funerals do you think the governor attends?"

"I don't know and I don't care." She'd never been to a funeral like her father's. She and Sam had arrived late and stood through the service at a church that easily held seven hundred and was filled to overflowing. The people who spoke talked about a man she didn't recognize, extolling Jessie's compassion and dedication, remarking on his philanthropy and business acumen, calling him the tilt-up warehouse building king of Northern California.

Sam reached the other side of the pool. "What if it were more than fifty thousand? Say it was a hundred."

There was a lot she could do with a hundred thousand dollars. Stephanie could go to graduate school without Sam insisting she get a job to help pay the tuition. And it would take Michael five years to save enough for a down payment on the house he wanted—unless they helped. Eric was desperate to secure financing on the ski shop he wanted to buy in Aspen. With a hundred thousand dollars they could help him with the down payment.

"So, you think I can be bought?" she tossed back.

"We all can, Lizzy—sorry, Elizabeth."

"Would you cut that out? I told you I love it when you call me—" She realized what he'd done the second after she took the bait. "All right, so I change my mind—occasionally. That doesn't mean it's going to happen this time."

He swam back to her, separated her legs, and wrapped them around his waist. "Come closer," he said.

She did. "Now what?"

He gave her a wicked grin. "Well, now that I have you where I want you. . . ."

"Yes?"

"I figure I can talk some sense into you."

She put her hands on his shoulders and tried to push him away. "Is the money really that important to you?"

"I don't give a damn about the money. Do whatever you want with it. Hire a plane and scatter it over the city. I just don't want you to miss seeing your sisters. They're blood, Lizzy. That means something."

"So after we exchange blood types, what do we talk about? I have nothing in common with those women, Sam."

"What if I go with you?"

"You have a meeting with that guy from Chicago on Monday."

"I'll get out of it."

Sam had been trying to set up the meeting for months. "This really means that much to you?"

He grew serious. "Think of all the things you're sorry you didn't do—like seeing your father when you had the chance and telling him how you felt about his abandoning you and your mother. I don't want this added to the list."

"All right," she finally relented. "But you're not canceling your meeting. I'm going alone."

He moved to kiss the inside of her thigh. "Now that we have that out of the way, I think we should move on to other things."

"What did you have in mind?"

He hooked his thumbs on the bottom of her two-piece suit and tugged.

She laughed. "Not here."

"Why not?"

"The neighbors, for one."

"They can't see us."

"They can if they're out in their yard."

He slipped his finger under the fabric and unerringly touched her, stroking with erotic, possessive intent. She caught her breath, making a small, quick sigh with the inhaled air. "You know what it does to me when you make that sound," he murmured.

She laughed. "Everything turns you on."

"Not true."

"Tell me something that doesn't."

"Scampi."

"What if there wasn't any shrimp—just garlic and butter?"

A slow smile lifted the corner of his mouth. "Spread where?"

Again she laughed. "You're incorrigible."

"Admit it—you like having an empty nest as much as I do."

"It has its moments." But only when he was with her. "Did I tell you the catalog for fall classes arrived?"

He pulled himself out of the water to sit beside her. "What did you decide?"

"I have an appointment to talk to a counselor on Wednesday."

He nodded. "I'm going to get a drink. You want one?"

The playful mood had changed. "I'll have a beer."

She heard the sliding glass door open and close again as Sam went inside to the kitchen. Alone, she let down her guard, releasing some of the crippling emotion that she kept concealed like an ugly scar. Tears she managed to control until she was alone took possession.

She used to be stronger, her composure unflappable. Lately, she either felt like crying or actually was crying. She'd tried to put it off to menopause; the tests the doctor ordered came back negative.

She listened for the door, knowing Sam would be back soon. If he found her this way he'd want to know what was wrong. She couldn't tell him. She didn't know. Not really. And Sam couldn't accept that. Sam fixed things. It was the most basic part of who he was and one of the things she loved about him when it didn't frustrate the hell out of her.

She heard him returning and slipped into the pool dipping her face into the water. When he appeared she summoned a seductive smile, reached behind her back, and unhooked the top to her swimming suit.

"What will the neighbors think?" Sam said.

In reply, she did something that surprised her as much as it did him—she winked. "That you're one lucky guy."

Twenty-three

Ginger

"I wish I'd been adopted."

Taken aback by the statement, Ginger chanced a quick look at Rachel before she changed lanes to move onto the Benicia Bridge. Rachel was staring out the side window. "Why would you wish that?"

"Let's just say my mother never would have won a mother of the year award."

"I don't think mine would have either—if she'd kept me. From everything I've read she put her career above everything and everyone."

"Wasn't she married when she died?"

"Engaged. To some record company executive." She slowed for the toll booth. "I think it was more business than love—at least on her part. The articles I read said he was devastated when she died."

Rachel dug four dollars out of her purse and handed them to Ginger. "I thought she was past that 'sleeping your way to the top' stage in her career when she died."

"You'd think. But I saw a picture of the guy, and it wasn't his pecs that attracted her." Ginger paid the toll and merged into traffic. "So, what do you think is in the will?"

"I don't know. I'm assuming Jessie was comfortable. According to his obituary he supported a number of charities."

"I wonder if there was any left over."

Rachel gave her a questioning look. "Things kind of tight?"

"I could really use a new car." Ginger twinged. "Well, that certainly makes me sound mercenary."

"At least you went back to see him again. You never said what happened that last time."

"He was asleep, so we didn't get a chance to talk. Did you go to the funeral?"

Rachel shook her head. "I was in Hong Kong trying to mend fences with a new client."

"I was in Denver. My father's birthday. Ironic, huh? The same day one father celebrated his seventieth birthday, the other was buried. I thought about flying back, but it would have created all kinds of family problems, and I didn't think Jessie was the kind of man who cared who came to his funeral. I should have known he wasn't going to last much longer. He looked pretty bad the last time I saw him."

"I wasn't going to come today," Rachel admitted.

"Why did you?"

She hesitated. "I feel like a hypocrite saying this, but I'm hoping he left me something, too. Jeff and I met with a Realtor yesterday, and we're not getting anywhere near what I'd hoped for the house."

"I thought real estate was creeping up again."

"It is, but we bought high and haven't owned long enough to pay the fees and come out ahead. We're going to be lucky to wind up with enough for a down payment on a place half the size. Jeff thinks he should rent for a while, but there isn't anything worth moving into in the area that isn't almost as much as the mortgage payment. With both of us renting, the taxes would kill us."

"What do the kids think about moving?"

"We haven't told them yet."

"How do you think they'll take it?"

"Not well. Especially Cassidy. There's no way we can afford to stay in the same area, which means she'll have to change schools—the third time in two years she's had to make new friends. Jeff's brother, Logan, said he would come out to help us move, and I'm hoping he'll be able to distract Cassidy while it's going on. He's fantastic with her and John. They adore him."

"Don't you think that as long as you and Jeff are civil to each other, Cassidy and John will adapt to the change? It seems to me that having two homes and, eventually, two sets of parents to love them could be a positive thing." She wasn't just saying it to make Rachel feel better, she really believed it. She would do whatever it took to make a warm and loving home for Marc's children after the divorce.

"Kids don't care if their parents are screwing around or just longing to get back into the dating game. As long as Mom and Dad are sober and not abusive, kids do best in the old fifties sit-com household."

"If you believe that. . . ."

"What?" Rachel prompted.

"Never mind."

"Why haven't I tried harder to work it out with Jeff?"

Ginger didn't say anything. She couldn't.

Rachel turned to look out the side window. "It hurts too much," she admitted, a catch in her voice. "After we talked last time I decided to try—really try—to put it behind me. But no matter what I do, I can't look at him without picturing him making love to her."

"Maybe you just need to give it a little more time." God, she felt like such a hypocrite.

"That's what my mother used to say—time heals everything. It didn't matter what complaint I brought to her, that was her answer. Of course I think she was saying it as much to convince herself as me. Men never stuck around long at our house, and she needed something to get her past the disappointment when they walked out."

"Did you ever get attached to any of your mother's boyfriends?"

Rachel let out a bitter laugh. "For the most part, the men Anna brought home weren't father material. I was grateful for the ones I didn't have to hide from when she left me alone with them."

Rachel's life was so far removed from anything Ginger had experienced that it was like listening to a story told in a foreign language—beyond comprehension. "Where did you live when you were growing up?"

"Everywhere. Anna never stayed anywhere very long. She didn't like paying bills and loved fresh starts, so we were on the road a lot. The first time I went to the same school for an entire year was my freshman year in college."

"That must have been hard." The traffic grew heavier as they neared the Vacaville outlet stores, forcing Ginger to concentrate on the road again.

"It wouldn't have been my first choice." Rachel moved her seat back and crossed her legs. "What about you?"

"Did you ever see *Happy Days*?"

"The television show?"

Ginger nodded. "My parents were the Cunninghams—about as exciting as a white bread and mayonnaise sandwich."

"And you think that was bad?"

Ginger glanced at Rachel to see if she was serious. Rachel looked back with open, simple curiosity. "I did at the time. All of my friends had mothers who were doing something interesting with their lives. Mine was content to stay home and knit socks and sweaters for the church's missionary packages."

"What about your father?"

"He owned a garage. My brother was supposed to go into business with my dad when he graduated college, but Billy's girlfriend wanted to live in New York. It broke my dad's heart. So he retired and sold the garage, and then two months later Billy's wife left him and he moved back home." She smiled. "I've always loved the irony."

"How did Billy react when he found out you were adopted?" Rachel asked.

"He wanted to know if he was adopted, too. I think he was a little disappointed when he found out he wasn't." Her brother was in the midst of a midlife crisis, the kind that demanded new women, new adventures, and expensive new toys. A new family would have been a fresh olive in an old martini.

"What about you? Are you over the shock? I don't know that I would be," Rachel asked.

"I'm okay with it most of the time. At least I'm not angry anymore." She spotted Sacramento's skyline in the distance, concrete and steel fingers protruding through prime agricultural land. They were due at the attorney's office in forty-five minutes. If traffic didn't get any heavier, they would make it with time to spare.

"That's good—isn't it?"

"I don't know. Sometimes I think it would be easier if I had a target for some of this stuff." Ginger pointedly looked at Rachel.

Rachel laughed and held up her hand. "Don't even think it. The disintegration of my marriage is as much as I can handle right now." A stunned expression replaced the smile. "I can't believe I'm actually joking about this."

Ginger repeated Rachel's question. "That's good—isn't it?"

"It scares the hell out of me. It doesn't hurt as much when

I'm mad." She took a clip out of her purse, twisted her shoulder-length hair into a loose knot, and secured it to the top of her head. "That's enough about me and Jeff. Tell me about Marc. How does he feel about everything that's happened to you lately?"

"He thinks I should try to contact my mother's family." A safe enough answer and a perfect segue into something safer yet. "I looked them up after I talked to Jessie about Barbara. Her parents are East Coast and old money and not the kind of people I picture opening their arms to a stranger, even if I showed up with a DNA test proving who I am. According to an article *Rolling Stone* did on Barbara, her mother was furious when she left college to join a band. It didn't matter that she was mainstream rock and sang in as many concert halls as auditoriums. It was way too middle class for them."

"I wonder if she told them about you."

"Not likely. My guess is that she told as few people as possible. I haven't run across anything that even hints she might have had a child."

"How do you suppose she pulled that off?"

"The official version is that she went into seclusion for several months to write the music for *White Lies*."

"I have that CD," Rachel said. "Jeff gave it to me for Christmas a couple of years ago."

"I know a couple of the songs she recorded, but don't own any of her music." Ginger had gone online to buy a couple of CDs, saw her mother's face on the album covers, and changed her mind. She wasn't ready for the intimacy of Barbara's music, realizing she would fixate on the words, searching for hidden meanings, looking for a connection, imagining one that wasn't there.

"What about Jessie? Is he ever mentioned in any of the stuff you found?"

"Not in connection with her. I ran into a couple of old articles about one of his movies, and a lot of fairly recent stuff about his construction and real estate dealings in Sacramento, but nothing that tied him to the music industry."

"What do you suppose he had back then that made two women young enough to be his daughters go to bed with him?"

"Money?" Ginger said, stating the obvious.

"That would have worked for my mother," Rachel said. "I don't think it would have mattered to yours."

"Maybe it was power with her. Or maybe it really happened the way Jessie said it did. They were friends, and she tried to help him when he was depressed, and one thing led to another."

Rachel uncrossed her legs and smoothed her slacks. "Well, whatever it was, it worked. I'm just surprised there are only four of us."

"I was just thinking the same thing."

Ginger saw the off ramp for the Tower Bridge and merged left. She was almost sorry this would be her last trip to Sacramento. She'd begun to like the city Jessie had called home.

Twenty-four

Lucy

Lucy swiveled in her chair, stopped, and tapped her pen on top of Jessie's will, killing time. As anxious as she was to get the meeting with his daughters over with, she needed every advantage to succeed at what she had planned. Initially, she was going for a volatile mix of irritation and surprise that would, with a little luck, provide enough distraction to keep logic from rearing its curious head. It was important to prevent them asking questions that would feed off each other.

A fifteen-minute wait should irritate Jessie's girls, but not anger them. She expected Rachel, with her business background, to react the strongest, Christina the least. Elizabeth was an unknown, but Ginger was easy. For all the seeming physical advantage Ginger's beauty gave her, she lacked the confidence to confront authority.

Unable to sit still any longer, Lucy went to the sideboard and poured a cup of coffee, her fifth that morning. She was actually beginning to understand the adrenaline rush Jessie received from living on the edge. He never went as far as she was about to, at least not that he'd admitted to, but he'd had a whole lifetime to experience something she had never had the nerve to do—until now.

He'd gambled his fortune; she was risking her license to practice law. Not to mention the little matter of criminal prosecution for forgery and perhaps even fraud, depending on the zealousness of the district attorney who took on the case. The firm would suffer a devastating blow, but with her out of the picture, either in prison or disbarred and retired, it would recover in time. It was a hell of a chance she was taking, a criminal act so blatant there was no way she could begin to defend it in court.

Still, even knowing the potential consequences, once her decision was made, she hadn't hesitated or looked back.

She sipped her coffee and stared out her office window at the traffic inching its way along Capital Mall. Finally, she was in a position to give something to Jessie instead of being on the receiving end. It felt good. Almost too good, considering the criminal element. She raised her cup in a salute. *This one is for you, Jessie Patrick Reed.*

Twenty-five

Christina

Christina was late. She'd missed her connection in L.A., the plane sitting on the tarmac for forty-five minutes while the pilot waited for a gate to clear.

Still, she could have made it to the lawyer's office on time if a guy in a wheelchair hadn't crowded in front of her and snagged the last cab in line. Okay, a wheelchair was a bigger handicap than a wired jaw, but rudeness leveled the playing field. Luckily, no one around them understood what she'd shouted at the departing cab.

Arriving fifteen minutes late, she was surprised to see her "sisters" still ensconced in the waiting room. She barely had time to sit before a blond woman in a seventies-style dress that looked designer retro rather than vintage came into the waiting room and told them, "Ms. Hargreaves is ready to see you now. If you'll follow me, please."

Stealing a quick glance at her sisters, Christina judged them as uncomfortable about being there as she was. Even the standoffish one, Elizabeth, had come to this party. Obviously her reasons for not seeing their father hadn't prevented her from attending the reading of his will. Or what Christina assumed was the reading of Jessie's will.

Lucy stood to greet them, nodding to each in turn. She motioned to the four chairs in a semicircle in front of her desk. The "twins," Rachel and Ginger, sat together leaving Christina no choice but to sit on the end next to Elizabeth.

"Is there anything you'd like before we get started?" Lucy asked. "Coffee? A soft drink? Water?"

Silence.

"All right. Do you have any questions you'd like to ask before I begin?"

Silence again.

"Well, why don't I just get started then?" She lifted the top sheet of paper, sky blue and stiff.

Restrained as she was, Christina had to forgo asking if the firm had pink paper for the women clients who'd passed on. Maybe having her mouth wired shut was a good thing.

Lucy peered at them over her glasses. "I can read what's here in its entirety, or summarize the salient points. Your choice."

"Summarize, please," Rachel said. "I have a meeting in the city this afternoon."

"And the rest of you?" Lucy asked.

"Summarizing is fine," Ginger said.

Christina nodded.

"Will we get copies?" Elizabeth asked.

"Yes, of course." Lucy looked at each of them in turn before she put the will aside and leaned forward. "Basically, half of your father's estate is designated to go to the seven charities and organizations he supported while he was alive. The other half is to be evenly divided among the four of you, his only living children." She waited several seconds before continuing. "There are, however, conditions attached to your inheritances."

Several heartbeats later Elizabeth asked suspiciously, "What kind of conditions?"

"I'll go into that in a moment," Lucy told her. "First you need to know what's at stake. The remainder of the estate is slightly over ten million dollars—for each of you."

There was an instant of palpable silence followed by audible gasps from everyone but Christina, who fought to keep from choking.

"What is that after taxes?" Rachel asked.

"The tax has been taken care of," Lucy answered.

Ten million dollars? Christina struggled to get her mind around the figure. For the past eight years her idea of rich was to own a car that had four good tires and an unchipped windshield. Now she could buy a dealership? No way. It just wasn't possible. Try to sell a script with that plot and the writer would be laughed out of L.A.

Ten million dollars—no a little *over* ten million. How much was a little? Ten cents? A thousand dollars? A hundred thousand?

Elizabeth, stepping into her role of eldest daughter, was the first to recover enough to ask, "How did a man like Jessie Reed get that kind of money?"

Christina turned to look at her. Elizabeth's face had turned a pale porcelain. Twin circles of rose-colored blush stood out on her cheeks like cherry lollipops.

"Your father didn't have a dishonest bone in his body," Lucy said with obvious restraint. "If he had, his estate would have been ten times what it is."

"I guess that depends on your viewpoint and how you define honest," Rachel challenged. "There are some of us who saw another side of Jessie Reed."

"Get over it," Christina snapped. "He left me, too. But do you hear me whining about it?" The words came out as crisp as oatmeal and as easy to understand as Latin.

They all turned to look at her, each with the same puzzled expression. Rachel was the one who asked, "What did you say?"

Damn. No way did she want to explain her broken jaw to them. Christina shook her head and crossed her arms, hoping they'd take the hint and leave her alone.

"There is a condition," Lucy said, drawing their attention. "The four of you are required to meet at your father's house once a month for six consecutive months for a minimum of four hours. During this meeting you will listen to the tapes he made the last month of his life. Realizing each of you had questions he would not live to answer, he decided on this form of communication, hoping it would help bring closure to unresolved issues between you."

Ginger started to say something; Lucy held her hand up to stop her. "One last thing. This condition is non-negotiable. If you choose not to participate, you forfeit your portion of the inheritance and it will be equally divided between the charities your father designated. Now, if you have questions I'd be happy to answer them."

Elizabeth stood. "There's no way something like this will hold up in court."

"There is one more provision I haven't mentioned," Lucy said to them all. "Anyone who challenges the will is automatically disinherited. When you do your research, Ms. Walker," she said to Elizabeth, "you'll discover this particular condition has proven binding in wills written in California.

"However, even knowing this, should one of you still decide to challenge the terms of your father's will, I feel obligated to tell you that I will defend his final wishes with absolute conviction, diligence, and vigor. How long all of your inheritances would be tied up during this process depends, of course, on the length of the trial and appeal—should there be one. One last thing I feel you should know. The ten million you would have inherited is certain to suffer appreciably—both in attorney and court costs."

"That sounds like a threat," Rachel said.

"I'm sorry if that's the way it came across. It's certainly not what I intended. I was simply being as thorough as possible in explaining the terms and how they affect each of you. I would be remiss were I to give you the impression your father's wishes could be circumvented without consequence."

"Why?" Ginger asked. "Why would he stay away all of our lives and then blackmail us into doing something like this? It doesn't make sense."

Lucy took a moment to answer. "Above all else, your father was a pragmatist. He anticipated there would be resistance to his simple request."

"Simple?" Elizabeth shot back.

"No, that's not what I meant," Ginger said. "Why would he force us to get together every month? Wouldn't it be easier simply to make copies of the tapes and let us listen to them privately?"

"Like that's going to happen," Christina mumbled behind her hand, doing nothing to hide her animosity toward her sisters. She turned to Elizabeth, the sister she had taken an immediate and lingering dislike to, if for no other reason than she could tell Elizabeth didn't like her. "Your turn, Ms. Personality."

Elizabeth's eyes narrowed in a slow burn. "You know, it's getting clearer and clearer why Jessie left you. I hate to say this, but I think I might have to give him this one."

"Ouch," Christina managed to say, the word dripping sarcasm. She flipped her hair behind her shoulder, making sure as much of the pink showed as possible. She smiled, inadvertently showing the odd way her teeth were held together.

Elizabeth frowned. "What happened to you?"

"My guess would be that someone slugged her," Rachel supplied.

"No way," Ginger said.

Shit.

Twenty-six

Rachel

"It . . . isn't . . . what . . . you . . . think," Christina carefully mouthed, pausing at each word.

But it was. Rachel could see it in her eyes, the same look of embarrassment she'd seen in her mother's eyes when one of her boyfriends left evidence of abuse and someone noticed. God, what was it with women who in their shame protected the men who hit them? If Jeff had ever—no, it wasn't possible. It simply wasn't in Jeff to hit a woman. She'd known men who could and did, and Jeff was nothing like them.

She could push Christina or give her the lie. "Car wreck?" Rachel offered.

Christina nodded and flashed Rachel a look acknowledging the unexpected kindness.

"That's terrible," Ginger said. "Are you okay? Was anyone else hurt?"

Christina waved her off, pointed to her mouth, and shrugged.

Something bothered Rachel about the will, but she couldn't decide whether it was the idea of being under Jessie's control—even if only for six months—or whether it was the will itself. Making tapes and manipulating the four of them into getting together to listen to them didn't fit with the little she knew about Jessie Reed. Or maybe it was not what she knew about him as much as what she imagined. He hadn't cared what they thought when he was alive—why would it matter after he was dead? It didn't make sense.

Whatever the motivation, he'd found the method. Ten million dollars was a hell of an enticement. Especially when seemingly so little was asked in exchange. Twenty-four hours total in the company of three women, one of whom Rachel actually liked, listening to an old man try to justify his reprehensible behavior. She could do that. Hell, she'd lived eighteen years with a woman who hated her, listening to her complain how Rachel had ruined her life. Tuning out Jessie Reed would be nothing compared to tuning out her mother.

"I assume Jessie's house is in Sacramento?" Elizabeth asked.

"Actually it's not very far from here," Ginger said. "It's nice. Not what you'd expect from someone who had this kind of money, but better than I've ever lived in."

The surprised looks coming from Elizabeth and Christina amused Rachel. It was almost as if they were jealous, possessive of someone neither of them had wanted anything to do with an hour ago.

"You've been there?" Elizabeth asked.

"Twice."

"Why?" Christina mouthed.

"Why not?" Ginger said defensively.

Lucy gathered the papers on her desk, drawing attention to herself. "Am I to assume none of you intend to challenge the terms of the will? Or do you need more time to consider?"

"I don't like it, but unless my attorney tells me something different, I'm willing to go along," Rachel said.

Ginger said, "Me, too."

Christina nodded.

They looked at Elizabeth. "It appears I can be bought," she said with obvious reluctance. She glanced at Lucy. "Will you be there?"

"Only for as long as it takes to drop off the tapes and answer any questions you might have. I've arranged for your father's housekeeper, Rhona McDowell, to stay on for the next six months, so she'll be at the house when you're there."

"Don't trust us to actually listen—or to stay the full four hours?" Elizabeth asked.

Lucy nodded, acknowledging Elizabeth's question. "I've asked her to report to me after each meeting to let me know the conditions of your father's will have been met. Depending on the time you choose to meet, lunch or dinner will be provided."

It was everything Rachel could do to keep from laughing out loud at the bizarre normalcy of the minor details. The four of them were being confined for four hours once a month for six months—but not to worry, they wouldn't go hungry.

"Do we pick the days, or do you?" Rachel asked. "If at all possible, I'd like to leave my weekends free."

"Actually, the weekends are best for me," Elizabeth said.

"She has her kids then," Ginger said before Rachel could answer. "I think if at all possible the rest of us should try to work around—"

"Sundays are okay," Rachel said, compromising. "It's only once a month, and Jeff won't mind."

"How does the third Sunday each month sound?" Lucy asked. "Does that work for you, Christina?"

Christina shrugged and seconds later nodded.

"I'll let Rhona know when to expect you, then," Lucy said, pausing to give them time to object. When no one did, she went on. "There are directions to your father's house along with copies of the will in an envelope my assistant has for each of you. Now, do any of you have any more questions?" Again she waited. "No? Then there isn't any reason to keep you any longer."

Twenty-seven

Lucy

Lucy stood and came around the desk. "It's been a pleasure seeing you again. As I said, if I can be of any help, or should you have questions that didn't occur to you today, please don't hesitate to call."

Lucy shepherded them out the door, closed it behind them, and let out a deep sigh of relief to have passed the first hurdle. Rachel would run the will by her attorney—if she found time. Christina and Ginger assumed a will was sacrosanct and wouldn't take the chance of losing everything by challenging the terms. It was Elizabeth whom Lucy hadn't been able to read. She was the wild card, her anger a volatile and unpredictable fuel. If she couldn't be contained, everything Lucy hoped to accomplish would blow up in her face.

This was the hard part—waiting. Something Lucy had never done well. She wasn't a sit-back-and-bide-time kind of attorney, something Jessie had considered her greatest asset and her partners a pain in the ass.

Lucy was back at her desk, her mind focused on working on a solution to the last stumbling block in a merger between the two largest independent grocery chains in Northern California, when she was distracted by a knock on her door so soft it took a second to realize what it was. Puzzled, she went to the door instead of calling out an invitation to come in.

"I . . . can . . . come . . . back . . . later . . . if . . . you're . . . busy," Christina said, pausing on each word to make sure she was understood.

Lucy opened the door wider and waved Christina in, trying not to show her surprise. She was carrying a suitcase she hadn't had earlier. "What can I do for you?"

"I . . . don't . . . know . . . how . . . to . . . ask . . . this." She dipped her head, her long, black hair covering her face. When she looked up again, she met Lucy's gaze and then quickly looked away. "Is . . . there . . . any . . ."

Lucy put her hand on Christina's arm. "You don't have to speak like that. Just say what you have to say, I'm sure I can understand you."

She looked relieved, but still embarrassed. "I'm broke," she said in a rush. "I hate to ask this, but is there any way I could get a small advance on what my father left me?"

Lucy had considered the possibility this could come up and had decided there was no way she could accommodate such a request out of Jessie's account. It was critical to keep things as uncomplicated as possible. "How much do you think you would need?"

"No one is going to hire me to wait tables like this, and the wires don't come off for another two to three weeks. So, whatever it would take to get me to L.A. and enough to eat and pay the rent until I get a paycheck."

"You'll need money to get back and forth to the meetings up here, too," Lucy said, mentally calculating first and last month's rent, food, and incidentals at L.A. prices. "Do you have a car?"

"Not anymore. I sold it to get here."

"You can't get around in L.A. without a car."

"I'll use the buses."

The statement startled Lucy. Christina wasn't just looking for an easier road, she truly was desperate. "Why L.A.?"

"That's where the jobs are."

"What kind of job are you looking for?"

"Something in the production end at a movie studio. It's where I want to end up, and it's time I got started."

"What if I could find you something here?" Lucy didn't have a clue how she'd pull it off, but there had to be someone she knew who had connections.

"How would you do that?"

"There are video production companies in town, some of them first-class." If Christina stayed she would act as an anchor to the others, eventually drawing them to Sacramento to see her because they wanted to, not simply because they were being forced to hear their father's story. "And if you do stay, you could live in your father's house and use his car." Christina would add life to the house, someone who was there to greet the others as they arrived.

"As for Sacramento being a long way from L.A., I'm sure you're aware that several independent film producers have launched careers from here. I'm always reading about them in the newspaper. As a matter of fact, Dixie Reid is a reporter for the paper who does most of the feature stories for new films and happens to be a friend of mine. I could ask her for a recommendation." Before Christina had a chance to comment, Lucy went on. "As for the rest, I'll arrange a small loan against your inheritance to see you through to your first paycheck."

"I guess I could stay until I could afford to move myself."

A wave of guilt washed over Lucy. She was manipulating Christina to remain in town not only because it would create a more home-like base for the sisters to meet, but because it would be more convenient for Lucy to set up those meetings. It was one thing to coerce them into doing things for Jessie, another for herself. "It was only a suggestion. If you'd rather not stay, I'll make sure you have enough money to set yourself up in Los Angeles and to get back here to meet with your sisters."

Christina didn't answer right away. Finally, she said, "Can I stay at Jessie's house a couple of days and think about it?"

"Of course. I'll call Rhona and tell her to expect you."

"I guess all I need now is the address and some directions." She smiled sheepishly, her mouth a jungle gym. "Never mind, I just remembered you said all of that was in the packet your assistant had for us."

Lucy glanced at her watch. "I have a meeting in that direction in a half-hour. I can drop you by. Just give me a minute to get my briefcase and let my assistant know I'm leaving."

Twenty-eight

Christina

Christina was quiet on the way to her father's house. Nothing she had to say was worth the effort to be understood. Lucy didn't want to know that the more Christina thought about Jessie being richer than God the more pissed off she became. She'd been closing in on forgiving him for letting her think he was dead, rationalizing how an old man might think he couldn't properly take care of a kid. Now, knowing he could have hired Mary Poppins for the day-to-day stuff, it was obvious he'd had a choice and the choice he made didn't include her.

"How long did it take my father to make his money? He told me he was broke when he left me."

Lucy gave Christina a quick smile. "The only thing Jessie had when I met him was an ability to get people to believe in him. That's what got him the loan to build his first warehouse."

"Why warehouses?"

"He looked around and saw the need. He could do that better than anyone I've ever known. More important, he wasn't afraid to fail. It made him bold. He took chances when others took a wait-and-see attitude." Lucy stopped at a red light and turned to

Christina. "I have a feeling he passed on more than a little of that trait to you."

"I'm not there yet," Christina admitted. "But I'm working on it."

Minutes later Lucy turned onto a street of two-story houses, large by middle-class standards but not the walls and gates Christina had expected. Lucy pointed to one on her left. "Ronald Reagan lived there when he was governor."

Lucy was taking her on a tour? Puzzled, and not knowing what else to say, Christina simply nodded.

"Jessie wasn't a fan."

Another contradiction. Weren't capitalists supposed to be Republicans? "On personal or political grounds?"

"Pardon?"

Christina shook her head. "Nothing."

Lucy pulled into a driveway. "We're here."

The house wasn't much bigger than the one Christina had grown up in. Where had Jessie spent his money, if not on himself?

A woman came out to greet them. Lucy introduced Christina and explained her communication problem, saving Christina the effort. Rhona responded with surprise and sympathy but not enough to make Christina concerned that it would become the focus of her time there. She could pull off the lie as long as she didn't have to build a fictional world to support it.

Lucy told Rhona she was waiting to schedule the first meeting at the house until Christina's jaw was unwired and that Christina would be using Jessie's car. "Is that it?" Before Rhona could answer, Lucy added, "Oh, no, I just remembered you had something that you wanted to show me."

Rhona put her hand on Lucy's arm. "It can wait."

Christina noted the familiar gesture and wondered about Rhona's role in her father's life. Was housekeeper a euphemism for mistress? Certainly no servant in her mother's household would have been anything but subservient when dealing with a woman of Lucy Hargreaves's position.

Lucy smiled her thanks. "I'll stop by tomorrow morning on my way to work." To Christina she said, "If you need me for anything—you know how to reach me."

Rhona smiled at Christina and held her arm out in a welcoming gesture. "Come in. I'll get you settled, and then I'm off to my book club. I've actually finished the book we're discussing, so I'd really like to make this meeting." She closed the front door. "I hope you don't mind."

Christina shook her head.

"I thought you'd feel more comfortable in the back bedroom." She glanced at Christina. "Unless you'd rather stay in your father's room?"

"The . . . back . . . bedroom . . . is . . . fine."

Rhona led her across the circular foyer and then left down a short hallway. The walls were soft brown and bare. Expecting more of the same, she was taken aback at the bedroom. It was as if it had been decorated with her in mind. Blue and cream toile covered the window and the canopy of the four-poster cherrywood bed. The accent colors were bright yellow and navy blue, used in a profusion of pillows, the bedskirt, and matching chairs.

"Nice," Christina said.

"You're the first to use it. Your father would come in here to read once in a while. He liked the colors."

Blue and yellow were her favorites. How easy it would be to let herself think he'd known that. "Did . . . he . . . tell . . . you . . . about . . . us?"

"I worked for your father for a long time," Rhona answered without elaborating. She went to a door on the opposite side of the bed and opened it, revealing a full bathroom. "If you need anything, please let me know. Also, if you have any food preferences, please leave a note in the kitchen. I'm going shopping tomorrow."

"Blender?" She pointed to her mouth.

"Yes, there's a blender. There're also several protein drinks in the refrigerator. They're pretty awful, but I haven't felt much like cooking since your father died." She smiled. "It will be nice to have someone to do for again."

"You . . . don't . . . have—"

"I know, you can take care of yourself. It's exactly what Jessie would have said. But I'm going to tell you what I told him—taking care of people is my job. I like it, and I'm damn good at it. So you let me do what I do, and I'll let you do what you do, and we'll get along just fine."

Oh, great, someone new to boss her around. Christina knew if she didn't take a stand now it would be impossible to take one later. She started to protest, saw the challenge in Rhona's eyes, and backed down. Besides, what was she going to say? She was standing there with a broken jaw, homeless, penniless, and with little more to wear than the clothes on her back. Yeah, it was pretty obvious that she could take care of herself all right.

Twenty-nine

Rachel

Ginger offered to drive Rachel into the city, but Rachel convinced her that taking BART from the El Cerrito Del Norte station and walking the four blocks to her office would be as fast as fighting the traffic on the Bay Bridge.

She made it to her meeting in plenty of time but was hard-pressed to stay focused on the latest round in the insurance fraud case the company had been pursuing for the past two years. It was one of the quarterly FYI updates that only concerned her division but would eventually involve the entire company and how they did business. She was supposed to find a way to let the information trickle down without alarm or liability. Thankfully, she'd dragged Maria along with her to take notes.

After the meeting, alone for the first time since hearing the details of Jessie's will, Rachel opened her mind to the ramifications and possibilities. *Ten million dollars.* Even at three percent it would earn more than she was making at her job now.

She wouldn't have to work ever again. She could be a stay-at-home mom, learn to cook, even become one of those women who helped out in their children's classrooms. She and Jeff—

But there was no she and Jeff. How could she live with that fact every minute of every day and still make that kind of mistake?

Damn you, Jeff. She thought it so often it had become automatic, losing its impact. Almost.

Everything she did, everything that happened to her, affected him and would for the rest of their lives. Cassidy and John bound them through graduations, weddings, grandchildren—all of life's noted events where they would be expected to be civil, even cordial, to each other, their accomplishments accumulating over the years like ribbons on a battle-weary soldier's chest.

Rachel reached for the phone and dialed Jeff. "I need to see you," she said to his hello.

"Now?"

"Tonight. Can you have Mary watch the kids and meet me at my apartment?" Mary, their next-door neighbor, and Jeff exchanged spur-of-the-moment babysitting on a regular basis.

"What time?"

She glanced at her calendar. There was nothing to keep her past five. "Seven." It would give her time to pick up the apartment a little, maybe even dust. All her life she'd thought of herself as compulsively neat. Living alone she'd discovered she cleaned for the impression it gave others. She was terrified what other revelations were in store down the line.

"I'll be there."

"Thanks." She hung up without saying good-bye, unreasonably annoyed that he hadn't asked why she wanted to see him. She'd never understood his ability simply to go with the moment while she questioned everything.

Her driver dropped her off at her apartment at six-thirty. An accident in the Caldecott Tunnel had tied up traffic for more than an hour, leaving her with the choice of meeting Jeff with a clean body or a clean house. She went inside and walked out of her shoes, bending to pick them up as she moved toward the bedroom. In six months she could hire a live-in housekeeper—hell, with ten million dollars, she could hire someone to do everything.

She should be happy. If not happy, relieved. They no longer had to sell the house and uproot the kids and worry what effect it would have on them. She could buy another house for herself, something close, within walking distance. It would almost be as if. . . .

Rachel sat on the edge of the bed and covered her face with her hands. Within seconds she was sobbing. There was no way she could live down the street from Jeff. It would tear her heart out to see him healing and going on with his life, leaving her behind even in this. She needed distance, a thousand miles might do it, but there was no way she could leave John and Cassidy, not any more than she could expect him to be willing to move away.

The doorbell rang. She wiped her face with her hands and pinched her cheeks to add color the way she'd seen her mother do a hundred times when she wanted to convince someone she hadn't been drinking or crying or sleeping in the middle of the day. Anna Kaplan had been a master of emotional deception, Rachel a captive pupil.

But she'd never been able to fool Jeff. He saw the minute she opened the door that something was wrong.

"You're early," she said, cutting him off before he could question her.

"I finished the meeting with John's new teacher earlier than I expected. You want me to go away and come back later?"

"What happened to his old teacher?"

"She had her baby."

Inexplicably, Rachel was crying again. "I didn't even know she was pregnant." In their division of parental duties, Jeff had taken responsibility for the day-to-day schooling. He told Rachel what he felt she wanted and needed to know and handled the rest without involving her.

As easily and naturally as he had done for the past fourteen years, Jeff put his arms around her. It was a mistake, she knew it right away, but instead of resisting, she moved closer and laid her head against his chest. A hundred thundering heartbeats sounded against her ear before he softly asked, "You going to tell me what's wrong?"

At that she finally moved to step away.

He held on. "It's okay, Rachel. Whatever it is, you can tell me. I'll just listen." He looked down at her and offered an encouraging smile. "No advice. And I promise I won't make more out of it than it is."

She stiffened. "It's not what you think."

After several seconds he shrugged and let go, disappointment a curtain shadowing his eyes. "All right. So what is it?"

"We're rich," she blurted. "Or we will be in six months. We don't have to sell the house."

"You got another promotion?"

"What? No—" Her lips formed a smile, plainly surprising him as much as it did her. "If it all happens the way it's supposed to, I'm going to quit my job. Can you imagine? Me unemployed?"

"As a matter of fact, I can't."

His answer surprised her. "Why?"

"You live for that job."

"No, I don't. I work because I have to. How else would we—"

"Let's not do this, Rachel."

"You're right." They'd careened down that narrow road too many times, their destination predetermined. Rachel went to the sofa and sat on the arm, her legs stretched out in front of her, her arms crossed. "I went to Sacramento today for the reading of my father's will. Turns out he had one last manipulative surprise for his daughters—ten million dollars."

Jeff let out a long, low whistle. "He had that kind of money and he never gave you or your mother a dime?" He was more angry than surprised. "Are you going to take it?"

"Of course I'm going to take it. It's the answer to all our problems. We won't have to sell the house. The kids won't—"

"There is no 'we,' Rachel. The money is yours. Inheritance isn't considered community property."

"I don't care about that. All I care about is getting through this without hurting the kids any more than they have to be hurt. If it takes Jessie's money to do that, then so be it."

"Stop it, Rachel. You know none of that matters. We'll find a way that doesn't involve taking that man's two and a half million."

"It's not two and a half million, Jeff. It's ten million—each. Tax-free." She pinned him with a stare. "Still think I should give it back?"

He didn't flinch or hesitate. "Yes."

The incredible thing was that she believed him. He knew what it would do to her to live under the cloud of compromising her principles to accept money from a man she despised. "I have six months to think about it."

She told him about the tapes and the meetings.

"So, you're supposed to listen to him ramble on, making excuses for what he did, when none of you can call him on any of it?" Jeff said. "He's controlling you from the grave. Why would you let him get away with it?"

The obvious answer, the money, was too easy—the truth, too painful. "Maybe I want to hear what he has to say." The admission humiliated her.

The fire in Jeff's eyes turned to sorrow. "Aw, Rachel, I'm sorry." He knelt down in front of her and took her hands in his. "I should have known."

He was the only one who would, and now he did. They were tied by so much more than history. Jeff knew her like no one ever had or ever would. He'd unmasked the lonely girl she'd kept hidden inside the self-assured woman, shown her love and constancy—and then betrayed her. She would walk away from Jessie Reed's money, she would gladly give it all away, if doing so would give her back what she'd lost with Jeff.

Emotionally exhausted, she leaned forward and touched her cheek to the top of his head. "I miss you," she whispered. The admission came from the depth of her soul, the haunting call of the swan left behind by a hunter's bullet.

Jeff stood and brought her with him. He combed his fingers through her hair, holding her still for a kiss. She didn't fight or try to turn away. Instead, her lips parted and she moaned with a fierce release. Her reasons for holding back no longer mattered. She abandoned all she knew for what she felt. She wanted him. She wanted all they had had, all they had been, even if only for that moment and only in her imagination.

Jeff took her arms and put them around his neck. Her emotional defenses collapsed. She became the aggressor, thrusting her tongue deep into his mouth, bruising her lips in her eagerness. She ground her hips into his, moving hard against the bulge in his jeans.

"Oh, my God, Rachel," Jeff said. "I've dreamed—"

"No—don't say anything," she said. "I don't want to talk about this. I just want to do it." She slipped her hand into his jeans and held him, squeezing and releasing until he let out a cry of pleasure so intense it bordered on pain. "I need you to make me forget, Jeff."

He tried working the buttons on her blouse, gave up and ripped the fabric open. He unhooked the closure at the front of her bra and swept the cups aside, capturing her breasts with a rough urgency, pinching her nipples between his thumb and finger.

"Harder," she demanded. He bent and pulled a nipple into his mouth, sucking, lapping, nipping her with his teeth. She lifted a leg and wrapped it around him, rubbing herself against his erection. In a tangle of arms and legs he removed the rest of her clothes, stopping to kiss and touch and caress until her entire body became an erotic organ that screamed for release.

He picked her up and laid her on the sofa, then stood over her to shed his own clothes. His hands on her knees, he pushed her legs up and open. He tested her readiness with his fingers, massaging her clitoris then thrusting his fingers deep inside. She moaned and moved against him.

"Now," she demanded and reached to pull him down. He took her arms and pinned them to her sides, then did with his mouth what he'd been doing with his hand. She cried out, rocking her hips and arching her back. A sweet tingling ache spread from her clitoris to her stomach and thighs, then contracted to a hard, throbbing urgency deep inside. Her need for release grew, each tongue stroke sweeping her deeper and deeper into a sensual one-way current until she was hit by wave after wave of a climax so intense she tried to curl into herself to contain the ride.

Jeff released her arms and lowered himself, entering her while she was still in the throes of orgasm, thrusting hard and deep and fast. Rachel wrapped her legs around his waist. He reared back and grabbed her buttocks, pulling her closer, rhythmically matching his thrusts.

Rachel had never experienced multiple orgasms. She and Jeff had tried, she'd even tried alone, but it had never happened. She'd finally decided it wasn't possible and gave up. Which was why she didn't recognize what was happening when the sweet ache in her loins at having Jeff inside her changed to something more. She was back in the current, the ride swifter this time, the water deeper.

She looked at Jeff, her eyes wide. He must have guessed what was happening because he smiled and then did something he'd never done before, reached between them to touch her, prolonging the climax longer still. She caught her breath in surprise. Confusion at what had been an automatic reaction turned to anger. She tried to pull back, but it was too late. She'd reached the edge and tumbled over, sent on a sensual ride she resented more than enjoyed. Oblivious to her thoughts, Jeff followed with his own climax, pounding deep until he was spent, then collapsing beside her and pulling her into his arms.

Rachel listened as his panting slowed to deep breaths and then a long sigh. He brushed the hair from her forehead and kissed her. "I love you."

"Don't say that." She turned away from him but didn't get up. She was crying and didn't want him to see.

He put his hand on her shoulder to turn her back, but when she resisted he stopped trying. "What's wrong?"

"You've never done that—never touched me that way."

"What way?"

He knew what he'd done. He only asked because he thought it was expected. "Did she teach you to touch her like that?" Before he could answer she sat up and reached for her blouse. "Was it better for you with her?" God, why was she humiliating herself this way? "Is that why you kept going back—because making love to me wasn't exciting anymore?"

"I give up." Jeff reached for his jeans. "I've told you I'm sorry in every way I know how. I can't give you what you need, Rachel. I can't turn the clock back. There's no way I can make what I did go away." He finished dressing in silence, then headed for the door. "I made a mistake. A huge mistake. It didn't mean I don't love you or that I'm not in love with you." He looked at her for a long time. "I know it's hard for you to believe, but I never stopped loving you, Rachel. If I've really lost you, then that's my punishment. I don't know what else to do. Where we go from here is up to you."

She could have stopped him with a single word but instead watched as the door closed behind him with an indifferent finality.

Thirty

Ginger

Ginger had every intention of going to work after she dropped Rachel off. She'd only taken half a day, intending to spend the afternoon finishing a report on an employee returning from disability leave, due in the morning. But the idea of voluntarily returning to a windowless cubicle in the human resources division of Selex Electronics on this sun-filled day held as much appeal as a pair of four-inch platform shoes. Instead, on impulse, Ginger stopped for a late lunch of crabcakes at Pisces, a restaurant she and Marc had frequented when she first moved to California. They'd stopped going there after running into the credit manager from the Oakland dealership—not because Marc was concerned about someone discovering them together, but because he was looking for an excuse to fire the manager and didn't want anything getting in the way. The crabcakes were even better than she'd remembered, and she left promising herself that she would return soon. Maybe with Rachel on their way home from one of their meetings in Sacramento.

Yeah, she liked that idea and hoped Rachel would, too.

Ten million dollars. She'd had several hours to get used to the idea but simply couldn't wrap her mind around the figure or the possibilities. It was easy to think of things she could do for her mother and father, but she floundered on ideas for herself. She never had to work again. But if she didn't work, how did she fill her days? She could buy a house, almost any house she wanted. But where? It all depended on Marc. She could finally get rid of her seven-year-old Camry—and replace it with what? She didn't like Mercedes, the cars Marc sold, and he'd be hurt if she bought from anyone else.

The thought brought her up short. Where were *her* dreams, *her* goals, *her* ambitions? When had she stopped being an "I" and become a "we"? Her world revolved around Marc. His world included an entire universe.

They weren't new thoughts, just ones that she'd never given free rein. What was the point? She loved him, and that meant accepting the good and the bad that came with loving him.

If only their being together were a matter of money.

Ginger spotted Marc's red Mercedes as soon as she rounded the corner into the parking area behind her condo. Surprise and anticipation fluttered in her chest like butterflies released at weddings. Three years she and Marc had been together, and she still felt this way just knowing she was about to see him. Wasn't that the definition of love?

She glanced at the dashboard clock. Ten minutes after five. He never left work before six. Curious and anxious, she carelessly swung her Camry into the narrow space allotted her, a space made even smaller by her neighbor's monstrous SUV, and had to back out and park again. Infringing on a neighboring parking space was a sure way to start a turf war, something she didn't have the patience to put up with or stubbornness to maintain.

Marc met her at the door flashing his you-are-the-most-important-person-in-the-world smile, the one she suspected came as easy as breathing to him, but that she still found impossible to resist. She was so damn easy. "What are you doing here?"

Instead of answering, he reached for her and took her into his arms, pressing a quick kiss on her forehead followed by a longer, not-for-public-consumption kiss on the lips. "Where have you been? I've been waiting over an hour."

Not exactly accusatory, but close. "There was construction on 580. Traffic was backed up for—"

"What were you doing on 580? I thought I told you it would be shorter to take 680."

It used to amuse her that he automatically assumed she followed his advice, as if by asking a question she subjugated herself to his answer. Lately, she'd begun to find it more annoying than charming. "Rachel went with me. I dropped her off at the BART station in—"

"So, how did it go?" He helped her out of her jacket and laid it over the end of the sofa.

"It was actually a little sad. I wasn't expecting that." Ginger put her purse in the closet and noticed a bottle of champagne sitting in a bucket of ice on the coffee table. "I think Lucy Hargreaves was more than Jessie's lawyer. It was obvious his death affected her pretty deeply. It makes me wonder if—"

"That's not what I meant," Marc said. He paused, waited for her, and when she didn't say anything, prodded gently, "The will, Ginger." When she still didn't say anything, he added, "What was in it?"

Unexpectedly, unreasonably, she resented his asking. "I thought you weren't interested. At least that's what you said when I asked you to go with me." She'd only asked because she knew he'd expected it and was relieved when he'd said he couldn't get away.

"You're right. And since you obviously think it's none of my business, we'll just let it go at that."

Zing, a blow to the midsection, calculated to do the most damage and put her on the defensive. Damn, he was good. "You know that's not what I think. I'm just tired. It's been a rough day."

"Then you should let me take care of you. That's what I'm here for."

That surprised her and instantly lifted her mood. Yeah, he was good, and yeah, she was easy. So what? "Oh, and just what was it you had in mind?" She gave him a smile. A peace offering he readily accepted.

He led her to the sofa, and when she was seated, propped a pillow at her back. He opened the champagne and poured each of them a glass. "Dinner will arrive at six-thirty," he announced, handing her a glass and sitting close beside her. "I had the chef at Luraine's personally prepare all your favorites—Caesar salad, filet mignon with orange Bearnaise sauce, wild rice pilaf with scallions—and fresh whipped cream."

They were menu items, not something out of the ordinary that the chef would have to "personally" prepare, but to say so, to even think it, made her sound petty and ungrateful. "Just whipped cream? Nothing to put it on?"

His slow, answering smile said it all—she was the dessert.

He tucked his head into her neck, nipping her ear, and kissing the sensitive skin at the base of her jaw. "God—you smell incredible. What are you wearing?"

"Too much," she said turning into his kiss.

"Not so fast. You're always complaining there's never enough time for us to talk. Now's your chance."

She licked her lips and then his. "Later."

"But what about the whipped cream? I promise you that you're going to like what I have in mind."

She got up and went into the kitchen, coming back with an aerosol can of low-fat, low-calorie, low-taste whipping cream. "Will this do?"

He grinned. "It'll do just fine."

She held out her hand and led him upstairs, tossing the can on the bed and adjusting the blinds. Slowly, the way he liked her to do, she began undressing. He stopped her when all she had left were her bra and panties. She reached back to unhook her bra.

"Let me do that," he said.

She turned her back to him, the silk parted, and he traced a line of kisses the length of her spine. She sighed and leaned into him when he reached around to cup her breasts, kneading them with gentle insistence. Her nipples grew hard and pressed into his palms.

"You have the most incredible breasts," he whispered against her hair. "They're perfect. You're perfect." He turned her to face him, smiling. "I see other men looking at you, undressing you in their minds, and I want to tell them whatever they're imagining, they don't have a clue." He leaned down to take one nipple into his mouth and then the other, tugging gently, circling with his tongue, and then suddenly pulling hard. She gasped.

He slid his hands down her stomach, caught her panties, and slid them over her hips. When she was naked, he held her at arm's length to gaze at her. "Even like this, no one would ever guess that you're thirty-two."

"Even like this?" she echoed. "What's that supposed to mean?"

"You know exactly what I mean. You could make a fortune as a body double for all those aging movie stars."

"Enjoy it while you can," she teased. "One of these days it's going to head south."

He removed his clothes and hooked them on the bedpost. "When it does, we'll just find someone to prop it back up again."

She would expect Marc to give her gentle jabs if she ever let herself go. Aging wouldn't come without a fight or without regret, but she absolutely would not become a tucked and padded and Botoxed replica of the woman she'd been at twenty. She wanted him to accept her as she aged naturally, the way he accepted the growing bald spot at the back of his head and the beginning of the spare tire riding on top of his belt. Growing old together, sharing the ups and downs, the good and bad, was the best part of loving someone.

Naked, armed with the can of whipped cream and a wicked smile, Marc reached past Ginger and pulled back the bedspread. He brought her onto the bed with him, opening her legs and sitting between her knees. He came forward and kissed her, drawing her tongue into his mouth and then thrusting his tongue into hers. Sitting up again, he shook the can, sending her an erotic, almost malevolent look as he drew a circle of foaming cream that covered her areolas. He then dipped his finger into the center of the cream, brought it to his mouth, took half and transferred the rest to hers. Slowly, deliberately he shared the cream this way until only traces remained on her breasts.

Marc had always been a creative lover, but this was something new, something that left Ginger curious and quivering in anticipation. He drew a line of cream from her breasts to her belly and into the dark triangle between her thighs. He didn't like oral sex, at least he didn't like giving it, saving going down on her for "special occasions" when he wanted her especially sated by their lovemaking. He'd always denied that was the motivation, and she let him. She had her own "special occasion" ways to please him. Wasn't that a part of any good relationship?

What he did next was beyond her imagining. She caught her breath and jerked into a half-sitting position when something cold was inserted into her vagina and she felt the cavity being filled with cream. He discarded the can, put his hand on her shoulder, and pushed her back down, silencing her protests by covering her mouth with his and giving her a long, plundering kiss. He moved between her legs and thrust deep and hard inside of her. The sensation was unbelievable, the cold of the cream, the heat of his body, the hard driving force. Instantly, she was out of control, meeting his thrusts with an insistent, bruising force. It seemed like only seconds and she was aboard the wild horse, fighting to prolong the ride.

Later, fresh from a bath, dressed in oversized robes and sitting on the floor eating their gourmet meal off her everyday dishes, Marc stretched across the coffee table to wipe the corner of her mouth with his napkin. When he leaned back against the sofa he asked the question Ginger had been waiting for him to ask again. "So, are you going to tell me what happened this morning?"

"A half-million." The lie slipped out with stunning ease. It was a first between them, at least on her part. She didn't count the small lies, the ones she told him every day about understanding why they had to wait to be together. They were the thread that held the fabric of their relationship together. This was different.

"That's it?"

She was stunned at how much she resented his disappointment. Half a million dollars was a lot of money. Instead of back-tracking while she still could, she made the lie more complicated. "Divided four ways."

"That can't be right. The investigator I hired said he was worth at least fifty times that."

She tried to wrap her mind around this new piece of information. Her deception no longer seemed so important. "You hired an investigator? Why would you do that?"

"I was afraid something like this would happen. Plainly it's a good thing I did."

"How dare you hire someone without telling me? You had no right. Jessie Reed is my father and my business."

"You used to say Jerome Reynolds was your father."

"That was a low blow."

He tossed his napkin on the coffee table. "You know, I gave up a lot to be here with you tonight. If you think I'm going to stick around and let you attack me just because I didn't tell you everything I was doing to look out for you, you're crazy. That's the kind of shit I get from Judy. I'll be damned if I'm going to take it from you, too."

She knew what he was doing, how he was manipulating her by comparing her to Judy, but after three years the pattern was as set as her reaction. If she didn't find a way to pacify him, if he left with the argument unresolved between them, she wouldn't hear from him for days.

She stared at Marc trying to decide what to do and was bemused when she realized she didn't have the energy or desire to make the effort to keep him there. She wasn't going to fall apart or curl up in loneliness if he left. She'd had too much practice getting through such evenings.

Besides, she had someone to talk to if she needed to talk, someone to see if she needed company. Someone who was just as screwed up when it came to men as Ginger was—the sister she actually liked, Rachel.

"Well?" Marc prodded.

"Well what?"

"Are you going to apologize?"

"Absolutely not." Even that surprised her. "If anyone deserves an apology, it's me."

He got up and stood over her. "I should have gone to the opera with Judy."

She glared at him. "Be my guest. I'm sure if you hurry, you can still make it." Later, when she was alone and waiting for the phone to ring even knowing it wouldn't, she would regret saying what she had. But right now it felt too damn good to let what might or might not happen bother her.

Thirty-one

Elizabeth

"I really have to go, Stephanie." Elizabeth cradled the phone against her shoulder as she closed the dishwasher with her hip and made one last swipe of the counter. "I'm going to be late if I don't get out of here right now."

"Where are you going?"

"I told you, I'm meeting friends." She still hadn't told anyone but Sam about her father and sisters. At times she wondered if it was a mistake excluding the kids in something this big, wondered if they would feel left out or angry when the time finally came to tell them. But she wasn't ready to answer the questions that were sure to come, mostly because she was still asking questions herself.

"They'll wait. This is important, Mom. You have to talk to Dad for me. You know if I ask him for the money he's going to tell me to get a job. This is my last summer of freedom."

"What about graduate school?"

"God, must you always be so literal?"

"I have some money set aside." She was taking the easy way out even knowing it was a mistake. And it was wrong. It was like eating a piece of pie on a diet. The five- or ten-minute sugar high was never worth the agony of knowing there was no way to exercise enough the next day to burn off the calories. "It's not as much as you want, but it's the best I can do. Just don't tell your father." She wanted to be the one to tell him.

"I love you, Mom. You're the best."

"Yeah, yeah—I've heard it before." She believed it, too. She just wished it was said more often and under other circumstances.

"I mean it. I knew you'd come through for me."

"How?"

Stephanie laughed. "You always do."

"This has to last you. I don't—"

"I have to go now. Sharon's waiting. Love you." She hung up before Elizabeth could say anything more.

Elizabeth struggled to sort through her feelings. Was it so bad to be taken for granted? Wasn't that what parents were for—to be there when their children needed them? And weren't children entitled to unqualified emotional and financial support as long as their parents were able to give it?

The argument didn't work. At least not completely. Elizabeth would send Stephanie the money she'd been saving to buy something for Sam that didn't come out of the checkbook or show up on the credit card. But she was only going to send half—not nearly as much as Stephanie wanted. If it wasn't enough, Stephanie could damn well work to earn the rest, or ask her father.

Elizabeth didn't need the extra time she'd allowed to find Jessie's house, which meant she arrived a half-hour early. There were no other cars, not even one that could have been Lucy's, someone she had expected to be there early. She could either drive around to kill time, find a coffee shop and stoke up on caffeine, or go inside to wait and look around her father's house—if she could manage it without getting caught.

She decided to go inside.

Christina answered the door dressed in flip-flops, cutoff jeans, and a tank top. A tattoo of a lizard appeared perched on her shoulder as if it were a pet impregnated into her skin. "Well, Elizabeth, how nice to see you again." She opened the door wider, making room for Elizabeth to enter. "You're early, you know."

"How did you get here?"

"What? No nice to see you, too? How have you been? What's new with you?"

Elizabeth stepped into the marble tiled foyer. "Sorry. I was just surprised when you opened the door. I didn't see your car outside."

"It's in the garage. At least that's where the car I'm using is. I'm living here now." Responding to Elizabeth's stunned expression, she added with a coy smile, "Daddy always did love me best, you know."

Elizabeth blinked and then laughed at the pure insanity of the statement. "I guess I should be jealous."

"Oh, please do," Christina smiled in return. "I have an almost pathological need to feel superior. I feed on jealousy." She pointed to a room off the main hallway and breezily added, "You can wait in there if you want. I have some stuff to finish in the kitchen."

Elizabeth glanced into the living room and decided to follow Christina. The room was something she imagined a decorator with an unlimited budget and illusions of grandeur would put together, more model house than home, the fabrics rich silks and brocades, the wooden surfaces shiny and labor-intensive. A television would be as out of place there as a toddler. The only thing that gave it any warmth at all was a fireplace, and even that was surrounded by a carved marble mantle.

The kitchen was at the back of the house, the nook overlooking the backyard. It was in keeping with the architecture of the house, made to look original but filled with state-of-the-art appliances and granite countertops. Christina was at the island sink chopping celery. "Pretty spectacular, huh?" she said.

"The living room reminds me of the houses the robber barons built along the Hudson River in New York—meant to impress." Elizabeth sat on one of the bar stools at the island. She and Christina would never be friends, but circumstances dictated she at least make an effort to be civil to her younger sister. "I see your jaw is unwired. How are you feeling?"

"Great. I'm even working." She scooped the celery into a bowl. "Gotta pay the rent, you know."

"To stay here?" Elizabeth said, putting the clues together.

"What, did you think that I'd move in and—"

"I'm just surprised that Lucy would charge you to live in your own father's house."

"She didn't. It was my idea. I pay my own way or I don't go." She picked up a bunch of red grapes, plucked them off the stem, cut each in half, and added them to the bowl. "Well, shit. After that I guess I have to admit that I'm not paying to use the car. But I am thinking about buying it. It's a nineteen-sixty-five Mustang. Unbelievably cool." She laughed. "And I thought I was through with old cars."

A memory hit Elizabeth as bright and intrusive as the shaft of sunlight coming through the window behind Christina. She saw her father pulling into the driveway of their home in Bakersfield, honking the horn on a shiny new car, calling her and Frank outside. Her mother came to the door but refused to go outside or let them out either. Frank grabbed Elizabeth's hand and ran for the side door, urging her to hurry as he dragged her around to the front, shoving her in the backseat and then climbing in to sit next to their father.

"Sweet," he said, running his hand over the dash. "Is it mine?" You could tell by the way he asked he didn't believe it. He was nine months shy of his license. There was no way a brand-new car was going to be dropped in his lap.

"As soon as you can pay for the insurance," Jessie said.

Frank let out a whoop and turned to look at her. "Did you hear that, Lizzy? We got us a set of wheels."

It wasn't the car, it was the *we* that etched the day forever in her mind. She was the tagalong little sister, ten years old to his fifteen, and he'd thought to include her. No one had ever given her a better gift, no one ever did.

The car started moving, backing out of the driveway. Elizabeth knew there would be hell to pay later with her mother if she went with them, but she didn't care. No way was she going to miss this moment.

She told herself to close her eyes, not to look at her mother as they pulled away, but a thought drew her. If she smiled and waved and let her mother see how happy they were she would understand and it would be all right. Instead, she saw her mother crying. The glitter of the moment turned to sand.

"What color is your Mustang?" Elizabeth asked.

"Dark green—with black upholstery and no air conditioning." She tossed a grape in her mouth. "Just what you want to be driving around in when it's a hundred degrees outside."

"My brother had a car like that."

"Oh, yeah? That's right. I remember Lucy saying something about Jessie having a son. Did he die a long time ago?"

"Two years after he got the car."

"Bummer."

"Yeah—*bummer*."

"Don't go turning hostile on me. It's just an expression."

One her own kids used all the time. "I'm sensitive about Frank," she admitted.

Rhona came into the kitchen from a side door that led to the garage. She put a paper grocery bag on the counter and extended her hand. "You must be Elizabeth. I'm Rhona McDowell, your father's housekeeper. Can't tell you how pleased I am to meet you. I've seen your picture, of course, but you couldn't have been more than ten or eleven when it was taken."

"Jessie had a picture of me?" God, now they were going to think she actually cared.

"Would you like to see it?" Rhona asked.

"No." That only made it worse. "Maybe later."

"He had a lot of pictures of us," Christina said. "Surprised me, too."

Elizabeth changed the subject. "You said you had a new job. What do you do?"

"I work at River City Studio." She came around the counter to sit on the stool beside Elizabeth. "Where in less than two weeks I have made myself indispensable. No one who's worked there has ever managed empty the trash on a regular basis or given better unsolicited editing advice. I answer phones with a sickening cheerfulness and convince clients they really can wait an extra day for their videos because the quality will be better than anything they can get without going to L.A. and paying twice as much."

"How did you get a job like that?" It was the kind of question someone asked to keep a conversation going, but Elizabeth genuinely wanted to know.

"Lucy knew someone who knew someone. What about you? What do you do?"

"I'm a home— I used to be a homemaker. I'm starting college this fall semester."

"Why?"

"You mean why would I want to go back to school at my age?" It took effort, but she managed to suppress the testiness.

"Well—yeah."

Rhona laughed. "Out of the mouths of babes."

"I'm not *that* old," Elizabeth protested.

"So what are you studying?"

"I don't know yet," she reluctantly admitted. "I'm going to get the basics out of the way and then decide. Right now I'm leaning toward a degree in library science."

"Oh, that makes a lot of sense. Get a degree in a field that's disappearing."

"Are you always this mouthy?" Elizabeth asked.

"Yep. It's one of my more charming personality traits." She handed Elizabeth a grape. "Don't worry. You'll get used to it."

"There will always be libraries," Elizabeth said defensively. "Maybe not as we know them now, but—"

"Where have you been the last ten years? What used to be a sacred cow is now one of the first things to go in a budget crunch. A kid with a laptop hooked up to the Internet has access to more research material than any library on earth."

She was being lectured by someone young enough to be her daughter, and it infuriated her. "You don't know what you're talking about," she shot back for lack of a more clever retort.

"I've been doing voice-overs for political ad campaigns for the past six years. It's kind of a hobby of mine to see how many of the politicians keep their promises once they're elected and discover there isn't money to fund dying, antiquated institutions." She pinned Elizabeth with a stare. "How many politicians' careers do you follow?"

"Libraries are not dying, antiquated institutions."

"Maybe not university libraries—" The doorbell rang. "I'll get it."

With that the conversation ended, saving Elizabeth from strangling Christina. She glanced at Rhona.

"Times and ideas change," Rhona said. "People, too. Christina's a smart one. She has a lot of anger bottled up inside, but give her some time. She'll come around."

"Honestly? I couldn't care less whether she does or not. Once this is over I doubt that any of us will ever see her again."

"With all due respect, I believe you're wrong."

Was ten million dollars really worth putting herself through this for six months?

To her shame, she didn't even hesitate with the answer. It was. Plainly she wasn't the pillar of moral certitude she'd believed herself to be.

Thirty-two

Elizabeth

The first tape ended just as Jessie was meeting Elizabeth's mother, a woman, a girl, Elizabeth didn't recognize. She'd only known her mother as an angry, bitter old woman who spouted venom whenever she talked about Jessie Reed. What had gone wrong? Why had Jessie abandoned a woman he'd fallen in love with at first sight, a woman he believed to be the most beautiful woman in the world? And where was the rancor in his voice now at the way the marriage ended?

"There's a second tape," Rachel said, looking inside the envelope. By tacit approval Rachel had become the organizer of their disparate group, the one Lucy had instinctively given the tapes and instructions to. Seemingly, as the oldest, the job should have been given to Elizabeth, but she preferred the spectator role. Something she had no doubt that Lucy had detected. Elizabeth was as wary as she was impressed with her father's attorney. She didn't know what prompted the wariness, only that she was convinced Lucy Hargreaves was more deeply involved in her father's life and in his estate than she wanted any of them to know.

"Does anyone need a break before I put it in?" Rachel asked.

"I do." Ginger grinned apologetically. She was sitting on the floor, cross-legged, her back propped against the damask-covered sofa. "Too much tea."

"Down the hall and to the left," Christina said.

Elizabeth had taken the chair by the fireplace, straight-backed and incredibly uncomfortable. She looked longingly at the second chair of a pair of upholstered Bergères opposite the sofa, but to move would put her next to Christina. With an inward sigh, she got up and moved.

"You lasted longer than I thought you would," Christina said.

"That chair is a relic from the Inquisition. Another ten minutes and I would have been on my knees confessing."

"Oh my God, you *do* have a sense of humor," Christina exclaimed.

"What is it with you two?" Rachel asked.

Christina reached for the tea pitcher. "Oh, you know how it is with sisters. But then maybe you don't. You and Ginger seem to be hitting it off okay. What's with that?"

Rachel appeared unfazed by Christina's aggressive posturing. "You want me to explain why I like Ginger?"

"Sure. Maybe it will make me like her a little, too. Just don't tell me it's because she's beautiful and sweet and wants to work for world peace."

"Aren't you afraid of the fall from such a high horse?" Rachel asked.

"Not at all. I'm an excellent rider."

Rachel kicked off her shoes and tucked her legs under her, settling deeper into her corner of the sofa. "She is beautiful, but so what? I can't see that it's gotten her anything the rest of us don't have—except hostility for winning the genetic gene pool. She's open and honest and isn't carrying the shitload of emotional baggage the rest of us are. Which, in my book, makes her an ideal companion."

"You forgot about the happy homemaker over here," Christina said. "She comes across as pretty solid."

"Are you?" Rachel asked Elizabeth.

"Keep me out of this."

"Come on," Christina prodded. "Tell us something about yourself. I promise we won't bite. Well, I won't."

Ginger appeared in the doorway. "Me either."

They were all looking at her expectantly. Elizabeth wasn't about to open a vein for them, but she'd give them something, if only to show she wasn't the isolationist Christina portrayed. "If I've seemed distracted, it's because I did something this morning that I wish I hadn't and it's been bothering me since."

"So tell," Christina said.

Elizabeth hesitated. "It's my daughter's last summer at college—or could be if she decides not to go to graduate school— and she decided to spend it with friends in New York." She left out the *rather than coming home* part, fearing it would sound needy. Besides, it was missing the point. "Her father told her that if she ran out of money she wasn't to come to us for more. She did of course—this morning. It was either send her some money I had set aside and tell her not to tell her father or wind up in the middle of a huge fight with the two of them going at each other and me getting it from both sides. I'm mad at Sam for not understanding how important this summer is to Stephanie, and I'm mad at Stephanie for putting me in this position."

"I would have done the same thing," Ginger said.

"Me, too," Rachel added. "It's just not worth all the crap you'd have to take in the middle. So what's a couple hundred dollars if it buys a little peace?"

"Jesus, I don't believe this. What's wrong with you people?"

Christina asked. To Elizabeth she said, "Stephanie knew exactly how to work you, and you let her get away with it. I'll bet the first thing she did when she got off the phone was high-five her friends."

"She's not like that," Elizabeth said, seething at the criticism.

"Oh, *please*. I know the routine. I've seen it pulled a hundred times. Hell, if I could have gotten away with it, I would have been one of the people making one of those phone calls home."

"So what do you think Elizabeth should have done?" Rachel asked, challenging her.

"Told her no and meant it. And she should have started a long time ago. I'm the last one to give my mother credit for anything, but that's one thing she got right."

Elizabeth begrudgingly agreed with her. Christina spoke to a fear that had been developing in Elizabeth for a long time. When did love become indulgence? At what point did the pleasure she derived from doing for her children become destructive to their ability to do for themselves? "It's too late now," Elizabeth said.

Christina reached for a cookie. "Have you told her about Jessie's money?"

Elizabeth shook her head. At least *that* she'd gotten right, and without Sam having to reason her through it.

"Good luck when you do," Christina said.

"I hated college," Rachel said, putting a new twist on the conversation. "I couldn't wait to get out. I don't know if I would have made it through if Jeff hadn't been there to push me."

"I was just the opposite," Ginger countered. "Loved every minute of every class." She waved off the plate of cookies Christina now offered to everyone. "I could have made it through in five years, but I managed to stretch it to six, much to my father's annoyance." She thought about what she'd said. "My *other* father. The one who paid the bills."

"I couldn't wait to get there and couldn't wait to get out," Christina said.

"Wanted to get started on your career?" Elizabeth asked. There it was. She'd sunk to Christina's level. So much for taking the high road.

"Oh, good one, Betty," Christina fired back.

"*Now* what?" Ginger said.

"She knows I'm working at a bottom-feeding job while I'm waiting for Daddy's ship to dock."

"I didn't mean that the way it sounded," Elizabeth said. Well, not exactly. At least not that she wanted to admit to.

Ginger looked from Christina to Elizabeth and then back again. "What kind of job are you looking for?"

"I'm a filmmaker," she said.

Elizabeth felt an abrupt, surprising softening toward Christina at the defensive, vulnerable admission. It wasn't like her to step on other people's dreams, even people she didn't like. "Too bad Ginger's mother isn't still around. From what I've read, it isn't what you know but who you know in the movie business."

"Ten million dollars is all the introduction I'm going to need."

"We probably should get back to the tape," Rachel said. "Elizabeth has a long drive home."

"You know, you could stay here next time if you didn't want to make the trip in one day." Christina seemed as surprised at the blurted invitation as Elizabeth. "It's still Jessie's house, at least it still belongs to the estate. He was your father as much as he was mine, and I'm sure Rhona wouldn't mind."

To dismiss the invitation out of hand would diminish the effort it had taken to make it. "Thanks. I'll think about it."

Rachel put the tape in and hit play.

Jessie's Story

I left the Farnsworth ranch with the lease in my pocket and stars in my eyes. I was in love. It wasn't what I'd felt for Wynona, but something that was pure and complete and let me know love was more than sex, it was a house and kids and coming home every night to sit by the fire and talk about the things that had happened that day.

With marriage in mind and the leases locked up, I started working on the pipe companies, offering them the same deal I had the ranchers and first dibs on the money when the oil started flowing. I couldn't get workers to give up paying jobs for a lick and a promise, but a number of them were willing to give me nights and Sundays.

I rolled along thinking I was the biggest bull in the barnyard when what I was up to got back to some powerful people who didn't care for the idea that a hayseed like me had bested them. They tried talking the ranchers into canceling their leases, but west Texas produced men with stubborn streaks wider than the Rio Grande. What they were slow to give they refused to take back.

With the ranchers holding firm, they came after my workers, beating a couple of them senseless just to show they could, and that they could get away with it. The threats worked on about half of the men, but the rest, the really tough ones, got together and decided they would give up their paying jobs to sign on as part owners the way the ranchers had. They moved into the field, living together for safety, working every hour they weren't eating or sleeping. The pipe went down twice as fast as it had before. We were a month ahead of where I figured we'd be come September—halfway to the New Mexico border, where the new refinery was even further along—when the pipe shipments stopped.

I tried begging and bribing, but whoever got there before me knew the magic words and there was nothing I could say that mattered. I was watching the last of the pipe being laid and feeling as close to giving up as I'd ever been before or since when I looked up and saw a streak of dust coming at me across the horizon. In the thirty minutes it took Wyatt Farnsworth to reach me I'd imagined myself doing battle with the half-dozen thugs I was sure were on their way to fit me for a pine box.

The first thing Wyatt did when he eased himself out of the truck was check his mustache to make sure the curl hadn't come undone in the heat and wind. He ambled over to where I was standing, touching the brim of his dust-laden Stetson and nodding his head in greeting. "Hear you been havin' some trouble getting across my land. Cattle don't much care for you boys hanging round."

"Can't lay pipe I don't have."

"Yeah, heard about that, too." He reached into his back pocket and handed me an envelope.

"What's this?"

"Another five percent of the business added to what I have coming if you take it. Think it over and let me know." With that, he turned and headed back the way he'd come, leaving me holding a blank check and the directions to a pipe manufacturing plant in Mexico.

Another five percent left me less than twenty. But twenty of something was a hell of a lot better than twenty-five of nothing. And there was an upside that I'm sure Farnsworth hadn't figured when he'd made his offer. With him as the second biggest shareholder, I found it necessary and convenient to ride out his way for a little jawing whenever I felt the need to cast eyes on his daughter.

Either he wasn't as smart as I'd given him credit for or I was better at hiding my feelings than I thought, because *it took him almost six months to warn me off Denise. Turned out she wasn't the fifteen or sixteen I'd guessed but thirteen. That should have dumped water on the fire I had going for her, but I was too far gone for anything like that to get in the way. Her being thirteen gave me time to get the business going without worrying she'd get tired of waiting or that someone else would come along.*

It took another year before the first shipment of oil left the fields of west Texas in the Reed and Company Pipeline and landed at the refinery in New Mexico, and another year and a half after that before I had enough money put aside to go out to California to find my folks and keep my promise.

It wasn't a big secret that I planned to ask Denise to marry me when I got back. I'd been heading that direction for almost three years and had become such a regular at the farmhouse that Denise's mother moved another chair into the dining room and left it there.

When it came time to leave, Wyatt drove me to the train station up in Lubbock, surprising both me and Denise when he let her come along to tell me good-bye. With twenty minutes before my train left, figuring it wasn't near enough time to get into any real trouble, Wyatt left us alone to find himself a box of Cuban cigars.

I decided then was the time to give Denise the locket I'd bought for her birthday. She cried when I put it on. I puffed up more than I had a right, thinking it meant more than it did. I caught people looking at us as they passed, the women with curiosity, the men with envy. She must have seen it, too, because she did something she'd never done before. Right there in front of all those strangers she held on to the front of my jacket, came up

*on her toes, and kissed me. It wasn't full on the lips—
she'd closed her eyes and missed hitting me square by
half my mouth. But it didn't matter. I was seeing stars
and my heart was pounding so hard I thought it was
going to break one of my ribs.*

"How was that?" she asked.

*"Fine," I mumbled, not knowing if I should kiss her
back right there or haul her someplace more private and
do it right.*

"Just fine?"

"It was wonderful, Denise. The best."

She smiled. "Want me to do it again?"

"More than anything."

She looked around. "Right here? Right now?"

*I took her arm and led her to a doorway where I
figured Wyatt wouldn't see us. "I dream about kissing
you all the time."*

*"You do?" She asked in such a way that I knew it
excited her to have that kind of power. "Want me to do
it again now?"*

*I didn't wait for her. I put everything I was feeling
into the kiss I gave her, hitting her square on the mouth.
I didn't realize until I let her go what a huge mistake I'd
made. I'd scared her. Her eyes opened wide, the white
showing all the way around the blue. She started crying,
this time for real.*

It was a lesson I never forgot.

Thirty-three

Rachel

Rachel slid the frozen lasagna into the oven. She was making an actual sit-down meal for the kids tonight, one that included green beans, fruit salad, and John's favorite—garlic bread covered in Parmesan cheese. For fun she'd picked up a CD of an Italian opera she'd found in the discount bin at the store where she'd gone to buy candles.

This was going to work. It was time to make the kids realize that being with her on the weekends wasn't a temporary thing but the way it was going to be from now on. And the three of them weren't just going to make the best of it, they were going to thrive.

She'd been moving toward this decision for the past two weeks, ever since listening to the first two tapes. Hearing Jessie talk about his life, how he'd pulled as much energy from his defeats as his victories, made her realize she'd been spending her days with Cassidy and John as if there were a bank where she could withdraw more. This time with them was too valuable to spend casually.

The doorbell rang. They were early. She smiled in anticipation.

Not for an instant did she doubt that she would open the door to find Cassidy and John standing there. No one else, well, no one except Ginger, had visited her apartment.

But it was Jeff, and he was alone, a bouquet of daisies in one hand, a drugstore box of chocolates in the other. He'd lost weight since their separation and looked as cut and fit as he had in his twenties. His hair was a week or two past needing a trim and long in back the way she liked it. Dressed in jeans and a white polo shirt that hugged his chest and arms as if it had been tailored, he looked disarmingly sexy. She leaned against the door frame and crossed her arms. "Where are the kids?"

"Home. With a babysitter."

"Why?"

"We've tried picking up the pieces and going on, and it's not working. I figured it was time we tried starting over." He handed her the flowers. "This was all I could afford the first time I took you out. They're still my favorite."

"Then why do you always buy me orchids?" He sent her flowers for everything, once just to celebrate Tuesday, a day of the week he insisted was normally neglected. She'd come to expect his little surprises and then, sadly, to take them for granted.

He shrugged. "Our lives changed. I thought you weren't a daisy kind of girl anymore. My mistake, not yours."

He'd been withdrawn since the night they made love, dropping the kids off and picking them up with a minimum of communication, letting her believe he'd finally given up on them. She'd gained an odd kind of strength in his aloofness and was afraid of being pulled back again. "I remember that night," she said softly. She took the flowers from his outstretched hand and held them to her chest. "You sold your autographed copy of the Doors' *Waiting for the Sun* album to get the money to take me out."

"The best investment I ever made." He held out the candy and grinned. "Sorry—I couldn't remember what kind I bought back then. I just remember it was cheap, and this was the cheapest I could find."

"It was chocolate-covered cherries. Pretty provocative for a first date. My roommates thought it was hysterical."

"You never told me."

"I didn't want to hurt your feelings."

The statement hung between them like a broken promise. "Can I come in?" When she hesitated he added, "While you get ready."

"For what?"

"Our date."

She glanced at her silk shell and linen slacks. "What's wrong with what I'm wearing?" She hadn't meant it to sound like an acceptance, but did nothing to correct the impression.

"You're overdressed. This is a jeans and T-shirt kind of date."

She could still say no, could still save herself from getting back on the roller coaster. "I don't know if this is a good idea, Jeff. We're getting along better than we have in months the way things are. The kids are—"

"This isn't about the kids. It's about you and me. I don't want to look back ten years from now and wonder if we should have tried harder. I want to know we did everything we could before we gave up."

"And what about what I want?"

He took a deep breath. "You can't have what you really want, Rachel. I can't make what I did go away. Nothing can. Whether it's with or without me, for your own sanity, you've got to find a way to get past it."

"I can't. I've tried."

"That's bullshit. You're the strongest woman I know. Look at what you went through growing up. Look who you had as a role model for a mother and then look at the incredible mother you became. Look at where you are at work, the promotions you've earned, the money you make. How many women coming from your background could have pulled off any of that?"

She smiled despite herself. "You get so passionate when you're in your cheerleading mode."

"Well? Are we on for tonight?"

Why was she fighting something she wanted? "Give me a couple of minutes." She started to leave, then turned back. "You might as well come in—and make yourself useful. I put a lasagna in the oven that will need something done with it."

He moved past her, lightly tossing the candy on the table by the front door. She caught a whiff of something that tweaked a memory but that she couldn't identify. "What is that you're wearing?"

"Old Spice."

She laughed. "I didn't know they made that anymore. You really did go all out."

"Wait till you see where I'm taking you for dinner."

The neon light over the converted boxcar said TINY'S ELEGANT URGER AR. When Rachel hesitated going in, Jeff assured her he'd eaten there twice in the past couple of weeks and had survived unscathed both times. After surreptitiously checking out the food on the tables they passed on their way to the counter, Rachel gamely ordered a cheeseburger, fries, and a root beer milk shake. To her embarrassment, she finished it all.

"You realize what this indulgence in gluttony means, don't you?" She tilted her glass to gather the last drops of milk shake. "I'm going to be eating salads for a week."

"Ah, but was it worth it?"

"Ask me next Wednesday."

Jeff reached across the table to wipe a trace of salt from the corner of her mouth. "Hey," she protested. "I was saving that."

He caught her hand in his and twined their fingers together. "When did we get caught up in believing money mattered more than time?"

"Somewhere between not having any and thinking we were immune to its effects?" Because she liked having her hand in his, liked pretending it belonged there, she untangled her fingers from his and put her hand on her lap, out of his reach. "I don't know. It just kind of happened."

He pretended not to notice her withdrawal. "Ready?"

"Date's over?" She didn't care that she was giving him mixed signals. She wasn't ready to go home.

"Not yet."

They drove with the windows down, the remnants of the ninety-degree day rushing into the car with sensuous summer abandon. It was an evening of untucked shirts and unbuttoned collars, of deep, contented sighs and hair lifted languidly off the neck.

Jeff wandered through the Oakland hills, finally stopping at a wide spot in the road with a turnout that looked across the bay to San Francisco. The sun was still a half-hour from setting, the sky an explosion of pink and orange, the lights on the Bay Bridge and in the city dim promises of the spectacular land-bound milky way they would become in an hour.

"It seems I never stop to just look at anything anymore," Rachel said, transfixed by the beauty of something she saw every day but failed to notice.

"Me either," Jeff admitted. "If the kids don't point it out, I don't see it."

She unbuckled her seat belt and turned to face him determined to be more than a passive participant in the evening. "So, tell me what's been happening with you lately."

"Not much. I was offered a job last week," he said, making it sound casual. "One of the firms I've been doing consulting work for had something open up that they thought would be a perfect fit. They're being pretty persistent. I assume it's because they've gotten it in their heads I'm holding out for them to sweeten the deal more than they already have."

The news stunned her. It wasn't even within shouting distance of anything she'd expected. "If it's something you want, I'm sure we could work things out." She didn't mean it. She counted on him being there for Cassidy and John. *They* counted on him.

"The job is in Michigan, Rachel."

"Oh." Her mind raced with the ramifications of his taking a job half a continent away. She had no right to ask him to refuse. Their agreement was that he would stay home with the kids until they were in school, use his consulting work to maintain his contacts, and then rejoin the workforce. He was already a year behind schedule. "What are you going to do?"

"I'm not going to take it."

Her heart started beating again. "Are you sure it's what you really want to do?"

"You know what I want, Rachel. There isn't a job anywhere at any money that would change that."

For an instant there was an opening to the world she used to know, a place where she had loved Jeff with irreproachable trust. She was filled with an ache to stay there. "I don't know what to say."

"You don't have to say anything. I only told you because I have a feeling they might contact you. I wanted you to be prepared."

"You know that half of the money I'm getting from Jessie is yours."

"What brought that up?"

"It's just that in case you think we need the money."

"We've never *needed* money, Rachel, we wanted it."

"It doesn't matter. Now we have it. Or we will in five months."

"I know we've had this discussion before, but it's worth saying again—*you don't have to take it.*"

"Face it, Jeff. As much as you want to believe I could walk away from ten million dollars, I can't. It sounds noble as hell in theory, but there's no way I want to spend the rest of my life looking back wondering if I made a mistake. What if something happened to one of the kids and we couldn't get the help they needed because I made this grand gesture?"

"I guess he knew what he was doing."

"If you're saying Jessie knew his daughters could be bought, then you're right. We all showed up at Jessie's house, even Elizabeth."

"Why 'even' Elizabeth?"

"She was the one who walked out of the first meeting at the lawyer's office when she discovered she had sisters." Rachel had told Jeff some of the details at one of Cassidy's soccer games, using it as an excuse to fill an awkward silence. Tonight she told him because she wanted to. "Elizabeth and Christina aren't like me and Ginger. They seem conflicted about their feelings for Jessie—kind of a love/hate thing. But then they're the ones who actually knew him. Ginger's already forgiven him. Why wouldn't she? She didn't know he existed until a couple of months ago, and he never did her any real harm."

"And you?"

"All these years I've had a picture in my mind of who he is and he's not anything like I expected. At least not on the tape."

"He's putting on a show. Of course he's going to make himself sound good."

"But that's just it, he's not. At least not yet." She leaned her head against the seat. "He talks about the most remarkable things in this completely off-hand, self-effacing way. I actually think I might have liked him if I didn't know who he was and what he did to my mother."

"Has he talked about her?"

"Not yet. At the rate he's going it will probably be another couple of months before he gets to me and Ginger."

"Do you think he'll tell the truth?"

"His version of it." And it scared her because she was afraid she would believe him. He was going to take away the fantasy that with him her mother had been different, that she hadn't used him the way she'd used all the other men in her life. Growing up, Rachel's hatred for her unknown father had been a crutch, an excuse for what her mother became. He was the target for her hurt and humiliation and disappointment, an enemy who allowed her to love and protect her flawed mother with the fierce tenacity of a neglected child.

"The kids like Ginger," Jeff said.

"I do, too."

"And the other two—Elizabeth and Christina?"

"They haven't met them."

"I meant you. How do you feel about them?"

"I don't know. Christina's smart and funny, but she's got a lot of baggage. Some guy—I'm assuming it was her boyfriend—broke her jaw a couple of months ago. She wanted us to think it happened some other way, but I could tell it was personal."

"Is she still with him?"

"I don't think so. At least there isn't anyone living with her at Jessie's house. I'm hoping eventually she'll get comfortable enough with the rest of us to tell us what really happened. I think we could help her."

"I'll be damned," Jeff said softly. "Did you hear what you just said?"

She went back over it in her mind. "It's not what you think."

"They're family, Rachel."

"So is my mother's brother, but you don't see me claiming him."

"What about Ginger?"

"She's different. We have a lot in common, and we look at things alike." She gave Jeff an acknowledging smile. "Okay, so I'll add her to the list."

He glanced at his watch. "Time to go. I promised the sitter I'd be back in time for her to meet her boyfriend." He put his seat belt on and started the car. "You want to pick up the kids tonight or have me bring them over in the morning?"

She'd been worried she was going to have to be the one to end the evening and to insist that things went no further. Now that it had happened, she was disappointed, not ready to end what had been the best hours between them since the separation.

They were halfway home when Rachel asked, "Have you heard from her?"

Jeff let out a heavy sigh. "Why would you do that? We managed to capture a little of our old life tonight, Rachel. Why try to destroy it?"

"Have you?"

"How many times do I have to tell you it was over a long time ago before you believe me?" His voice rose in frustration. "I'll give you the phone bills. You can see for yourself—nothing to Texas." He sent her an angry glare. "Is that what you want?"

"No, of course not." She said it knowing if she were still living at home she would look because she'd find it impossible not to. "I'm sorry about ruining tonight."

"I don't want you to be sorry." The words were darts thrown with piercing emphasis. "I want you to think about how ready you are to listen to your father and forgive him, and I want you to give me a little of that consideration, too." A minute passed and then another before he slammed a hand against the steering wheel. "Do you honestly believe that when I'm not with you I'm out there looking for another soccer mom to fuck?"

"Don't yell at me." Jeff rarely raised his voice, and never to her or the kids.

"Well, do you?"

"She had to mean something to you. It's the kind of man you are. You wouldn't fuck someone you didn't care about. And you don't stop caring just because you got caught."

"If I wanted her, if I believed for a minute that being with her would bring me one-tenth the happiness I had with you, a tenth the love I still have for you, all I would have to do is pick up the phone and she'd be here. She doesn't love her husband, she hasn't for a long time. She went back to him for the sake of the kids.

"Think about it, Rachel. With the ten million you're going to be getting, we could set up split custody—the summer with me, the rest of the year with you. I could move to Michigan and not have this back-and-forth weekend crap to contend with. But I'm not. I'm staying here. I'm doing everything I can to make it as easy on you and Cassidy and John as possible. *What more can I do?*"

She looked down at her hands, at the harvest moon cresting the Oakland hills, at the lights in houses they passed, anywhere but at Jeff. "Give me time," she said softly.

"I told you I'd give you as much time as it takes. The rest of my life if necessary."

Jeff crested the hill and dropped down into the back side of Orinda, headed for her apartment. Ten minutes later he pulled into her parking area and turned the key on the Range Rover. He put his arm out the window and stared straight ahead, the tension brittle between them. "You want to come by for the kids, or do you want me to drop them off?"

"I'll get them. Is nine okay?"

"Fine. Cassidy has a game at ten. John has to be at Jason's by two-thirty. His mom is taking them to the movie and pizza. I told her I'd pick him up around seven."

"I can do that."

"You don't know where they live."

"So, tell me."

"It's just easier if—"

"Stop it, Jeff." Less harshly she added, "You're entitled to a night off. Take it."

He stared at her. "And do what?"

"Whatever you like."

"Right. I'll do that." He reached for the key. "I have to get back."

She didn't want the evening to end this way. "Walk me to the door?"

"You're kidding."

"Isn't that what you do on a first date?"

He came around the car to open her door, waiting with his hands in his back pockets while she retrieved her keys. When the door was open he said, "I'll see you in the morning."

"Not so fast."

"Now what? Why all the mixed signals, Rachel?"

"I'm trying, Jeff. It's hard." Standing on the step in front of him she was near his height, so it didn't take anything but leaning forward to come within kissing distance. She gave him a chaste kiss, her lips together, her body inches from touching his. "Thank you. I had a wonderful time."

"You're welcome."

"Are you going to call me? I'm free this Wednesday. Or next weekend would be okay, too."

He frowned. "Are you serious?"

"As I recall, the kiss was better on our second date." Tears welled but didn't spill.

Now he smiled tenderly. "I don't suppose there's any way we could skip the second one and go straight to the third? As I recall, the kissing was even better then."

She caught her breath in a sob. "I do love you, Jeff."

"I know." He brought her into his arms and held her for a long time. "We'll find a way back," he told her. "I promise I won't stop trying until we do."

Thirty-four

Elizabeth

"I'm pregnant."

The words struck Elizabeth like a giant wave hitting a sand castle built too close to the shoreline. Her hands gripped the steering wheel, hanging on tight to something she could control. White-knuckled, she looked for a place to pull over but was trapped in the left lane in rush hour traffic.

She struggled to make sense out of something she desperately didn't want to believe. "Are you sure?"

"Of course I'm sure," Stephanie wailed. "Why else would I be here now?"

Elizabeth recoiled. "Look, I understand why you're upset, but that doesn't mean—"

"*Upset?*" Stephanie brought her foot up and propped it on the seat, wrapping her arms around her leg. "My life is over. Upset doesn't begin to describe what I'm feeling."

The only warning Stephanie had given that she was coming home was an email she'd sent that morning giving her flight time and asking to be picked up at the airport. Elizabeth's attempts to call had gone straight to voice mail.

"How far along are you?" Elizabeth asked, reeling. How was she going to tell Sam? He'd be devastated.

"What difference does that make?"

"If you wanted rational questions, you shouldn't have waited until now to tell me."

"I wouldn't have had to tell you anything if you'd sent the money I asked for."

"I did send you money."

"Not enough." She propped her elbow on the door and stared at the passing cars.

Elizabeth had plainly failed as an intuitive mother, had been tried and found guilty in absentia. Somehow, in Stephanie's mind, Elizabeth should have known that her daughter was in trouble, that this request for money wasn't like the hundred others that had preceded it.

"You could have told me." The traffic was still too congested to merge, the cars in the right lane either ignoring her signal or oblivious to it.

"I couldn't. I was too embarrassed," she admitted.

Elizabeth looked at her daughter. Stephanie's chin trembled, tears spilled onto her cheeks. She was a little girl again, her heart broken, her mother expected to make the pain go away as she always had.

Frustrated beyond reason, Elizabeth swung into the turn lane and gunned the engine, shooting across the oncoming traffic and barely missing the rear bumper of a green Honda. She hit the curb and scraped the undercarriage on the concrete, then pulled into the nearest parking place and slammed on the brakes.

They sat in strained silence until Stephanie let out a low moan. "Everything is ruined. All of my plans. . . . My friends are going to graduate and go on without me. It's not fair. I've worked so hard."

Elizabeth waited.

"I tried to get an abortion, but I couldn't go through with it." She dug through her purse for a tissue. "It's murder, Mom."

"Where did that come from?" As far as Elizabeth knew, Stephanie had always believed in a woman's right to choose.

"Sharon's mother showed me some pictures of what my baby would look like when they took her from me. She said abortion was the one sin God couldn't forgive and that I would burn in hell forever if I went through with it."

Elizabeth was speechless with anger. What right did Sharon's mother have to impose her dogmatic beliefs on Stephanie? She'd taken advantage of Stephanie when she was at her most vulnerable. "Why did you tell Sharon's mother and not me?"

"I didn't tell her. Sharon did."

Elizabeth was torn between wanting to shake Stephanie and hug her. She waited until the hug won out and reached for her. Stephanie sobbed and laid her head on her mother's shoulder. The tears turned messy with sniffs between the sobs. Elizabeth dug into the glovebox and handed Stephanie a napkin. "What about the father?" Elizabeth hadn't even known Stephanie was seeing anyone.

Stephanie didn't answer right away. She took time to wipe her eyes and blow her nose. Finally, the delaying tactics becoming obvious, she said, "What about him?"

"Have you told him?"

"No."

"Why not?"

Stephanie shifted, avoiding eye contact. Finally, softly, she said, "It was a party. I was high. It happened. I don't even like him, and I'm pretty sure he doesn't like me." Her chin started trembling again. "Not exactly a foundation to build a relationship on or take care of a kid."

"Oh, Stephanie. . . ." Crushing disappointment filled Elizabeth's chest. She brought her daughter into her arms again. "Have you seen a doctor?"

"No."

"Then how can you be sure you're really pregnant?"

"Five pregnancy tests are a pretty good indication."

"Then that's the first thing we have to do."

"Not Doctor Cummins. I can't face her."

"You're pregnant, Stephanie." Were those words really coming out of her mouth? "You're going to be seeing a doctor for months. Don't you want it to be someone you know?"

"Do I have to tell her? About the baby's father, I mean."

"She might ask you if there's any reason for an amnio." At Stephanie's puzzled look, she added, "If there's a genetic problem on his side of the family."

"What do I tell her?"

"We'll talk about that later." They would come up with something, a way to put reason to an incredibly foolish mistake. "Right now we need to get you home and settled in."

"What are you going to tell Dad?"

"The truth." He was the one person she would not lie to about this, not even for Stephanie.

"You can't. He'll never understand. He'll hate me."

No, he wouldn't understand. But he wouldn't hate her. He would be upset and disappointed and feel the need for a dozen after-the-fact lectures. It would take him a day or two, but he would come around and deal with it in the same steady way he dealt with everything. "What did you have in mind to tell him?"

More tears. More sobbing.

Elizabeth mentally pulled back and stared at her daughter, the sage warning to be careful what you wished for echoing like a shout in a cave. Stephanie was home for the summer, and Elizabeth would give anything to have her back in New York calling to say what a wonderful time she was having. She leaned over to press a kiss to Stephanie's cheek. "You'll get through this. We'll find a way. I promise."

The words were the security blanket her daughter had come home to have wrapped around her. Snuggled into their comfort, Stephanie wiped her eyes and ran her hands through her thick, glistening auburn hair, righting her world. "I'm tired. Can we go home now?"

Elizabeth skipped the planned stop by the grocery store, settling on frozen corn instead of fresh, ice cream instead of strawberry shortcake, making do with what she had. She could stretch a meal for unexpected company, turning a single steak into Stroganoff for a crowd or salmon for two into fish tacos for half a dozen. She could dig through the bargain bin at a fabric store and come up with a prize-winning Halloween costume. She was Sam's partner, his emotional support, his companion. She was a fierce, protective, loving mother who would give her life for her children without a second thought.

Knowing this, believing this, how could she be so upset with her youngest child, her beautiful daughter, for bringing her heartbreaking problem home and dumping it on her doorstep?

"Are you going to keep the baby?" Sam asked.

Elizabeth didn't miss a step clearing the table, even though she felt as if someone had come up behind her and hit her in the knees.

"How can I?" Stephanie said. "What would I do with a kid? I still have school to finish, and then I have to find a job." She gave her father a hopeful look, seeking approval and confirmation of the wisdom of what she was saying. "And it's not like I wanted to get pregnant."

Elizabeth busied herself at the sink. She didn't want Sam or Stephanie to see how disturbed she was at the thought of a stranger taking her first grandchild, the baby she had dreamed would one day come into their lives to fill her heart and give her purpose again.

"Well, you have some time to think about it," he said.

"I thought you would be mad."

He took her hand in his. "What good would that do?"

"Are you disappointed in me?"

Stop pushing, Elizabeth wanted to shout. *Give him a day or two to get used to the idea before you start asking for absolution.* But Sam surprised her.

"What would be the point? It's done, Stephanie." He passed a hand wearily over his face. "If there was a lesson to be learned from all this I would hope you learned it. If not, nothing I say is going to make any difference."

"I'm sorry." She was crying again.

"I know. And it isn't fair. It took two of you to create this child, and only one will pay the consequences."

"I just wish I could make it go away."

"You can," he said flatly.

"An abortion? Is that what you think I should do?"

Elizabeth looked at their reflections in the kitchen window. Stephanie was staring at Sam, her look almost hopeful.

"I can't make that decision for you. I just want you to know that, whatever you decide, I—your mother and I—will support you."

"You don't believe it's murder?"

"No."

"A lot of people do."

"And a lot of those same people believe in the death penalty. You can't listen to the fanatics on either side, Stephanie. You've got to go with what's in your own heart."

"Could you do it?"

"You want something from me I can't give you. It isn't my body or my decision—it can't be."

Elizabeth had never loved him more than she did at that moment. Maybe someday Stephanie would realize the gift her father had given her, but now was too soon. Now it was enough to know she was home.

"I told Sharon I would call her when I got here," Stephanie said, bringing an end to the conversation. "I'll be in my room."

"Wait—" Elizabeth said. "I know there's no way to keep this from your grandmother forever, but I'd rather—"

"I know what you're going to say, Mom. And don't worry, I don't want her to know about it either. I'll check caller ID before I answer the phone, and if it's her I'll let the machine pick up."

"What about Michael and Eric?" Sam asked.

"Do they have to know?" Stephanie said.

"Yes," Elizabeth answered. "But we don't have to tell them right away. We've got time."

Stephanie nodded, fresh tears shimmering in her eyes. "I'm so sorry."

"We'll deal with it," Sam said. "Now go make your phone call."

When she was gone, Sam brought his glass to the sink. "Don't you have class tonight?"

"I decided not to go."

"Why not?"

"It's her first night home."

"And she's in her room on the phone. She could be there all night."

"I couldn't concentrate anyway." Tears she'd been holding back since Stephanie shared her news gripped her throat like a vise. "I can't go off to school every day, living the life she had to give up."

"What are you saying?"

"I'm going to withdraw." Before he could protest, she added, "Just this semester."

He rinsed the glass and put it in the dishwasher. "She's twenty-one, Lizzy—two years older than you were when we were married. You'd had Michael by the time you were her age. You've got to stop babying her and let her grow up."

"Things are different now. Kids don't grow up as fast as we did."

"And whose fault is that?"

"You make it sound like it's a bad thing."

"Since when is arrested development a good thing?"

Now she was crying. She put her arms around him and burrowed her head into his neck. "I don't want to fight with you. Not tonight."

He pulled her closer. "Promise me you'll think about this some more before you drop out."

"I will." It was an easy promise. She would think about what she was doing right up to the moment she did it. Stephanie needed her. Tough love would have to wait.

Thirty-five

Ginger

Ginger held John's hand while they waited in line to buy cotton candy. Rachel and Cassidy were next in line to ride the roller coaster, something John was too small to get on and Ginger too cowardly. "So, what do you think, pink or blue?" she asked John.

"Blue."

"What about Cassidy?"

"She likes blue, too."

"You're absolutely sure your mom lets you eat this stuff? I don't want to get in trouble with her."

"She buys it for us all the time."

Ginger laughed. "Yeah, I'll just bet she does." She paid for the spun sugar and looked around for a bathroom. As she remembered, wet paper towels were a necessity with cotton candy.

They found an empty bench under a tree to wait for Rachel and Cassidy. "Are you really my aunt?" John asked.

"Yep, I really am."

"How come I never saw you when I was a little kid?"

"I didn't know I was your aunt when you were a little kid." She ruffled his hair, smiling when he tilted his head to get away from her. She loved being around him and Cassidy, loved talking to them, listening to them, hearing them call her Aunt Ginger. If she wasn't careful she was going to turn into one of those obnoxious relatives who pinch chubby little cheeks. "If I had known, I would have come to see you all the time."

"Uncle Logan sends us presents."

She had a feeling she was being set up. "What kind of presents?"

"He got me a fire engine for my birthday."

"A real one?"

John laughed. "No, silly, a ride around one. It has a bell and goes really fast downhill. But my dad won't let me go downhill anymore 'cause I almost got hit by a car. It was an accident. I didn't turn fast enough and went out in the street." The story was important enough to pause eating for the telling.

Ginger took a tuft of candy off his nose and popped it in her mouth. It was as sweet and gritty as she remembered. She pulled a small cloud off the bottom of his wand, bit into it, and let it melt in her mouth the way she had as a child. "Where does your Uncle Logan live?"

"Washington." Bite. "We went there to see him one time." Lick. "He took us to his firehouse." Wipe hand on pants.

"I'll bet that was fun."

"I didn't like it when he turned on the siren. It hurt my ears."

If anyone would have told her a year ago that she would eagerly give up a day at a spa to spend it in an amusement park with an eight- and a five-year-old, she would have said they were nuts. That the trip was her idea was even more unbelievable. The tickets were sent as a thank-you for the lateral transfer she arranged for a woman who wanted to be in Houston to be near her dying mother. Normally Ginger would have passed the tickets on to someone who had kids. This time the first thing she did was call Rachel.

"Is your Uncle Logan your daddy's brother?"

He frowned. "Huh uh, he's my Uncle Logan."

She considered explaining the connection but decided to leave it for another time. She heard a series of clicks that indicated the roller coaster was on its way up the first big climb. "There they go. Can you see your mom and Cassidy?"

He turned to look. "I don't see them. Yes I do," he squealed. "There they are."

Ginger wasn't looking. A tall man in a yellow shirt and tan shorts had caught her eye. He had his back turned to her, his arm around a woman who had her arm around his waist. There was something strikingly familiar about the man—his build, the way he stood, the way he wore his sunglasses propped on top of his head, the careful comb-over to cover a growing bald spot on the back of his head. The woman tilted her head to look up at him. He bent to give her a kiss, exposing his profile. Ginger's stomach did a slow roll.

It couldn't be. She had to be mistaken. Marc was in Kansas City at a meeting of district managers and wasn't due home until Wednesday. He'd tried to get out of the meeting. They'd had plans for the weekend, important plans. They were going to the wine country. Ginger had made dinner reservations at Mustards months ago. It was someone who looked like him. A double. Supposedly everyone had one.

Two kids, a boy and a girl, came up to talk to him. The girl tugged on his back pocket. He turned. Oh, God—it was him. He wasn't in Kansas City. He'd lied to her.

He'd lied so he could be with them.

Despite the ninety-five-degree heat, goose bumps covered her arms. She couldn't let him see her. Not now. Not like this. Not when he was with Judy—with his children.

But she couldn't get up to leave. She felt weighted, anchored to the bench, the sight of Marc with his family was so painful it stole her breath. Still, she couldn't look away. They seemed so happy, the perfect unit, his daughter laughing and hanging on to his hand, his son waving them toward the roller coaster line. Judy looked up at him and smiled.

The cotton candy Ginger had eaten rose on a swell of bile. She was going to be sick. She put her hand over her mouth and swallowed hard. Once. Twice.

John pointed and shouted, "See, there they are."

Ginger was sure Marc would turn at the noise, but as usual he was caught up in his own world and oblivious to everything and everyone else.

"Here they come," John announced. "Let's go." He jumped up and started toward the line.

She ran after him, grabbing his hand and steering him in the opposite direction. "They get off this way."

Rachel and Cassidy were disheveled and grinning as they relived the ride on the way down the ramp. Rachel's smile disappeared when she got a good look at Ginger. "What's wrong?"

"I don't know," she lied. She had to get out of there. *Now.* "John and I were sitting over there waiting for you. I felt fine one minute and like this the next." She chanced a quick glance behind her. She panicked when she couldn't see Marc. "I'm sorry. I have to leave."

"We'll all go."

"No—please don't." Thankfully they'd met there, each bringing their own car. "That would make me feel even worse."

"Are you sure you can make it home by yourself?"

"Positive. It's not that far." She handed Cassidy the second cotton candy. "Have fun. I'll call you later."

Ginger threw up in a privet hedge near the park exit and again on a freeway off ramp. Her hands were shaking so violently by the time she arrived home that she had trouble fitting the key in the lock on her front door. She held on long enough to call Ra-

chel and leave a message on her machine telling her she'd made
it home and was going to bed. She promised to call back later.
Finally she crawled into bed and curled into a fetal position. The
first tears spilled silently onto her pillow. The sobs that came later
rose from a dark, lonely place filled with indescribable pain.

She had never felt so desolate, so alone—so embarrassed. Not
even when Marc first told her he was going back to Judy had she
experienced this kind of pain. But then his reason had been so
noble, so kind, so loving. He was doing it for the children. She
understood. She loved him even more because of it.

She'd felt no shame in loving him, in being the other woman.
She was his refuge from a controlling, manipulating, evil woman,
a woman who made his life hell when he was with her.

How could he show a woman like that the affection she'd witnessed between them? How could the children respond to the
two of them as a couple if there was the constant tension Marc described? How could every day be the misery he'd described when
he was the one who reached down to take Judy's hand?

Now shame overwhelmed her. She was not the love of Marc's
life. She was the other woman, the one he used for the kinky sex
he couldn't get at home. She was safe, disease-free, and cheap.
Bottom line, what did that make her?

What had she been thinking when she gave up friends and
family to follow Marc to California? Why had she hung on for so
long? Most humiliating of all, where had she found the blinders
that kept her from seeing herself for what she really was?

She was still in bed six hours later when the phone rang. It was
Rachel checking up on her. She was sure of it. She rolled over,
cleared her throat, picked up the receiver, and chirped what she
hoped was an acceptable "Hello."

"I was beginning to think you weren't there and I was going to
have to tell your answering machine how much I miss you," Marc
said. "Where'd I catch you?"

"Where are you?" she asked, her voice monotone.

"At the hotel. I would have called sooner, but I missed my connection in Denver and just got settled in my room."

He was making this easy. She should be grateful, but all she could think about was how many times he'd lied to her in the past and how readily she'd believed him and how much those lies hurt now. Why had she never questioned him when he'd insisted she only call him on his cell, never on the hotel phone?

"How was the flight?"

"I got stuck next to an old couple who'd been visiting their grandkids. They insisted on showing me a hundred pictures they'd taken on their visit." He laughed. "That might be an exaggeration. But only a small one."

Did he spend time making up these kinds of stories or did they just come naturally? The details were always intimate, utterly believable. "And the ride in from the airport?"

"Other than the cab driver not speaking a word of English, it was okay. Why do you ask?"

"No reason. I guess I just miss Kansas City. How does it look?"

He laughed. "The same. It's always the same. I don't understand what you love about this place."

"I miss my friends. It gets lonely out here."

"I keep telling you to get out more. What did you do today?"

He only asked to prove his point. "I went out with Rachel."

"Good for you."

"And her kids."

"Oh?"

"Remember me telling you about the woman who sent me the tickets for Great America?"

A long pause followed. "Now that you mention it."

"We used them today."

A longer pause this time. "Did you have a good time?"

"For a while."

He let out a deep sigh. "I can explain."

"I know. You always have an explanation—for everything."

"But not on the phone. Give me an hour."

"Take two. After all, you could miss your connection again."

"Okay, I deserved that. Just promise me you're not going to do anything stupid."

"Like?"

"Talk yourself into anything."

"Like?"

"I'll be there as soon as I can."

She put the phone back on the base, got out of bed, and went to the closet to examine her luggage, trying to decide which piece she should use to pack his things. None of them. It was a matched set her mother and father had given her for her birthday. Paper bags would have to do.

It didn't take as long as she'd anticipated to strip her condo of everything belonging to Marc. A razor, aftershave, underwear, his favorite wine, cigars and the humidor she'd bought him for his birthday. She considered throwing in the gifts he'd given her over the past three years but decided they'd be put to better use at a battered women's shelter.

Or Goodwill.

Or the Dumpster downstairs.

She put the bags by the front door and sat on the sofa to wait. Like always. She was good at waiting for Marc. Too good. If she had a dollar for every hour she'd spent this way, she could donate it to the local PBS and receive every premium they'd offered at their last beg-a-thon.

Why was she waiting for him anyway? They were really finished this time, and there wasn't anything he could say that would make her change her mind. Her heart lightened at the conviction. It wasn't the absolution she would have liked for what they had done to his wife and his children, but it was a start.

She grabbed her purse and keys and moved the bags to the small porch outside her front door. Marc would think she was still inside and be slow to accept her not answering his summons. She liked imagining him knocking on the door, waiting, expecting, impatient, and finally giving up believing her strong enough to wait him out.

Without a destination in mind, she headed north. She'd gone twenty miles before she realized she'd subconsciously headed for Rachel's, the one place she knew without question she would find what she desperately needed—a friend.

Oddly, and completely unexpectedly, she had a flash of longing for her other two sisters, too. Elizabeth was wise in a wounded way, her battle scars a shield for the vulnerable little girl she still sheltered inside. Christina was young and bold and brash and lived her life poised for a fight, passionately looking for proof she was worthy of being loved, poignantly expecting to be disappointed.

Despite the baggage they all carried there was a strength of character that shone through. Ginger felt a wondrous and deep sense of pride knowing she was connected to them.

Thirty-six

Christina

Christina looked at Ginger across the walnut dining table. Ginger fascinated her. Four out of the four times they'd been together she'd looked as if she was about to step onto a runway—makeup, hair, clothes, skin, everything perfect. "Have you ever had a bad hair day?"

Ginger looked up from her shrimp and avocado salad. "No. Never. Well, maybe when I was on the track team in high school, but I try not to dwell on things that upset me." She reached up and flipped her hair over her shoulder. "I wake up looking exactly like this every morning. Don't you?"

Christina self-consciously ran her hand through her recently cut and colored hair. Lucy had recommended a hairdresser who'd done miracles with what remained of the coal black and pink mess she'd lived with for the past six months. "Okay, I admit that may have sounded a little sarcastic, but it wasn't intended. I was just curious how someone like you always looks so put together."

Ginger took a second to wipe the corners of her mouth. "Someone like me?"

"You know—beautiful." Hell, all she'd been trying to do was liven up the luncheon conversation. She'd decided that as long as she was forced to spend time with these women she might as well learn something about them. "Haven't you ever wondered how some people seem to have it all and others look like they were beaten by an ugly stick? Or maybe you don't notice things like that."

"We're both freaks of nature."

She said it so easily, it was obvious she had given it thought— lots of it. "So, is it hard being that different from the rest of us?"

Ginger smiled, exposing impossibly white, perfectly aligned teeth. "Are you baiting me?"

"Leave her alone," Rachel said in tandem. "She's had a rough week."

"So have I," Elizabeth said softly. "I found out I'm going to be a grandmother."

They all looked at her. "That's bad news?" Rachel asked.

"I don't know why I said that," Elizabeth answered. "Of course it isn't bad news."

"Then why do you look as if you caught your best friend in bed with your husband?" Christina asked.

Rachel flinched, Ginger shot Christina an angry look, Elizabeth looked as if she was about to cry. "Sorry—bad analogy," Christina said. To Rachel she said, "I didn't mean anything by—"

"It's all right. I think we're starting to get the picture, Christina," Rachel said. "You spend a lot of time with your foot in your mouth."

"Boy, do I. Even when it was wired shut."

"Are you ever going to tell us about that," Elizabeth asked.

Christina hesitated, looking from one woman to the next. Innately she understood that she could trust them not to judge her the way her mother had. "My boyfriend broke my jaw."

Ginger gasped. "What a low-life bastard."

"I hope he's in jail," Elizabeth said.

Rachel didn't say anything. But then, Christina hadn't expected her to. She'd figured it out a long time ago. "I don't know where he is. He stole everything, including the movie I'd financed and we'd worked on together for two years, and bailed while I was in Mexico recuperating."

"What are you going to do?" Rachel asked.

"I don't know."

"You have to do something," Ginger said, outraged. "You can't let him get away with assault and battery—and, and robbery, or theft, or whatever you call it when someone steals something like that."

"He already has gotten away with it. He had a half-dozen witnesses swear he was with them the night he hit me. There wasn't anything the police could do."

"What about him stealing your movie?" Elizabeth asked. "You have to be able to do something about that."

"I've been watching to see if he's submitted it to any of the film festivals, but if he's changed the title and submitted under a different name, there's no way I would recognize it without being there or at least seeing a synopsis."

"Can you prove it's your movie?" Rachel asked.

"Yes—at least I think I can. He'll have the same people lined up to lie about my involvement in the production, but it won't work this time. When he stripped the house he stupidly left behind all the receipts showing that I was the primary investor. I'm going to talk to Lucy to find out what she thinks I should do."

"I agree with Ginger," Elizabeth said, animated with anger. "You can't let him get away with it."

Christina sat back in her chair bemused and more than a little surprised and pleased by their fierce concern. "If I were a sheriff

I'd want the three of you on my posse." Ready to change the subject, she looked at Elizabeth. "You never did say whether congratulations were in order about being a grandma."

Elizabeth chased a shrimp around her plate with her fork. "My daughter is twenty-one, she's never worked a day in her life, she's dropped out of school because she's too embarrassed to go through the pregnancy in front of her friends, she decided against an abortion because someone showed her some pictures, she can't decide what to do with the baby when it's born, and she's annoyed because she's going to miss the rest of the summer in the Hamptons. Oh, and to top it all off, she doesn't want to tell the father because she doesn't like him and she says the feeling is mutual." She folded her napkin and put it beside her plate. "I'm not even fifty and I feel like there are three generations instead of one separating me from my daughter. When—no, *how*—did women start treating sex like a box of tissue—use it, toss it, forget about it? Is that the equality everyone fought for? I'm not saying you should wait for the honeymoon, but shouldn't you at least feel something for your partner? You don't have to love him, but shouldn't you at least like him?"

"So . . . I guess we can assume you haven't been spending a lot of time setting up the nursery," Christina said.

"Sorry. I had no right to dump my problems on all of you, but this is something that's been eating at me since Stephanie dropped her little bomb." Elizabeth tried to smile but couldn't pull it off. Instead, she started crying. After several stunned seconds passed in silence, Ginger went to her and gave her a go-ahead-just-let-it-all-out hug.

"Well, hell." Rachel tossed her napkin on the table. "Elizabeth's daughter screwed up Elizabeth's life, Christina's boyfriend screwed up hers, Ginger dumped the man she thought she was going to marry, and I can't decide what to do with my philandering husband. There's no way Jessie can top any of this."

Jessie's Story

It took me almost a month and over a thousand miles on the old Studebaker I bought when I got to California to discover it wasn't going to be the piece of cake to find my family that I thought it would be. They weren't any of the places Ma had told me to look when they left for California, and no one at any of the camps remembered them. I finally ran across a cousin in Salinas, and he told me, last he'd heard, they were living in a Farm Security Administration camp near Bakersfield.

I passed a ragged city of tar-paper shacks a half-dozen times looking for their camp before I stopped and asked about them. Never once did it cross my mind that she and Pa would have come to this, not with four able-bodied people in the family to work the fields and put money aside. Yet, there she was, living on the generosity of people who had nothing to give.

I'd let myself believe they were getting on all right because it was what I wanted to believe. Pa had always found a way to get by, even in the worst of times. I was busy living an adventure, the hero of my own dime novel, never for a minute thinking the people I'd promised to help could be dying and discarded like so much roadkill.

Ma told me my brother went first, in a senseless fight. No one knew what started it, Bobby Ray using his fists, the other guy a knife. Grandma caught a cold the second winter that took her in the spring. My sister just up and disappeared one day, leaving for the fields in the back of a truck with a dozen others in the morning, missing when it came back that night. Ma never saw her again. She said she believed losing his girl that way was what finally did Pa in. She couldn't get him to eat after that, *even when out of desperation she traded her wedding ring for a side of fatback and cooked up his favorite beans and cornbread. He left her long before he stopped breathing. When it came time, burying what was left was just a formality.*

I tried to get her to come back to Texas with me, thinking she'd want out of California any way she could. But she said she'd never liked Texas much and didn't feel right leaving Pa behind. I think it was more the hope my sister would turn up one day that kept her there.

I bought her a house with a bus stop close by and as much new furniture as I could before she told me that it was more than she wanted to take care of and she was sending the next delivery back to the store. I'd come with money enough to buy a farm, money I believed would make me a man in my father's eyes. I was determined not to take any back with me, so I bought a good-sized piece of land outside Bakersfield, thinking eventually Ma might want to settle on something where the neighbors couldn't see in her windows.

I had a long time to live with the guilt of knowing I could have come sooner if I'd been willing to come with less. Ego never carried a heavier price tag.

When I got back to Texas I proposed and Denise accepted. We were going to be married that next summer, but then Pearl Harbor came along, and a year or so later I wound up a paratrooper in Europe instead. We jumped on D Day, fought in France for a month, and came back to England. I had a letter waiting for me from Ma's neighbor saying that she'd died peacefully in her sleep and asking what I wanted done with the house.

About all I remember of the next two months is

*drinking or being hungover. I sobered up in Holland
and, with the exception of a couple of memorable lapses,
stayed that way until the fighting was over.*

*The war changed me. Growing up changed Denise.
If us getting married hadn't been something her family
thought of as certain as the sun coming up every morning,
and if I hadn't owed what I did to Wyatt for taking care
of the pipeline business while I was gone those three years,
I don't know that we would have gone through with it.*

*The wedding pulled ranchers and oil men from all
over the panhandle and west Texas. The party was big
and wild and still in full swing when we left on our
honeymoon two days later.*

*We came home not knowing each other any better
than when we left. We moved into a house just outside
town that was too small to keep Denise busy past ten in
the morning. She was bored, and I was gone too much
looking for ways to put excitement and growth into a
business that had become static. The life we settled into
bred discontent instead of the babies Denise wanted to
give her purpose.*

*We were two years into the marriage before Denise
got pregnant. She was sick most of the nine months and
laid up the rest, but I'd never seen her happier. It was a
good time for us. I was home more, and we were talking
like we hadn't talked since we were kids, making plans
and looking forward like we believed again that we were
meant to be together.*

*We had a boy. I didn't get to see either of them for
more than five hours after they took Denise into delivery.
I'd paced a gully in the linoleum floor before someone
finally came to get me.*

A nurse with a starched white hat appeared in the doorway. "Mr. Reed, you can come in now."

I followed her down a hallway and into a green-and-white room. Denise sat propped up in the bed, a white bundle in her arms. She wore a pink nightgown and a blue bow in her hair, her cheeks had twin circles of rouge, her lips a slash of red. She looked like she'd been ridden hard and put away wet and someone had come along to try to hide the evidence.

"Are you okay?" I asked.

She gave me one of the smiles she saved for special times, the kind that turned her eyes into pools I wanted to swim in the rest of my life. "Come see your son."

My son. I couldn't imagine sweeter words. I went to the bed and kissed Denise, believing I said what needed to be said in that kiss, that she would understand how I was thanking her for what she'd gone through and how proud I was. I should have used words. I should have seen the light leave her eyes when I picked up the baby and walked to the window to show him the world instead of settling in next to her. I named him Frank, after my grandfather, foolishly assuming it was a man's prerogative to name his son. If it had been a girl, I figured Denise would have picked the name. It was the way it had been done in my family for generations. Had I known it would start the wedge between Denise and our son that lasted and grew over a lifetime, I would have let her name him after her father the way she'd secretly planned.

I had something pushing me even harder now to make the business grow—I had a son who one day would be a part of everything I built. Oil was what I knew, so when I heard about new fields opening in Colorado, I went there *to see for myself. What I didn't stop to realize was that it wasn't the finding, it was the transporting where I could hold my own. I went in a sheep ready for shearing and came out as naked as one of those Greek statues. In the end I had enough left to get us to California and settled on the land I'd bought for Ma.*

I've always believed real luck comes from the blisters you get working. But then there's dumb luck. That's the only way I can think to describe what happened while I was looking to sell the land to get enough money to buy into a couple of blacksmith shops—oil was discovered half a mile down the road. As quick as that, I was a recognized player in the California oil business.

Denise wanted another baby, but no matter how we kept to schedules and the crazy doings that Denise's mother and grandmother said were never-fail ways to get pregnant, it didn't happen again. We started thinking the only way we'd ever get another one was to adopt. Turned out those were the magic words. A month after we started looking into it seriously, Denise was pregnant. She was as sick as she'd been the first time, so I took Frank to work with me, thinking I was doing her a favor. Most days we'd leave before sunup and not come home again until after dark. It was an exciting time in the fields with new wells coming in every week. I wasn't needed there to oversee it, but staying home was like setting up a high-stakes poker game and telling a gambler he had to sit out.

Denise might have forgiven me for not being around all those months if I'd made it to the hospital when Elizabeth was born. I knew she was ready. I'd cut my days down to a couple of hours in the fields in the morning and a quick trip to the office in the afternoon. But that day we had a gusher come in that we couldn't get a cap on, and I didn't get home until almost midnight. Elizabeth had arrived at four o'clock.

I left Frank at a neighbor's and rushed to the hospital. I used to wonder if it might have helped her feelings for me if I'd taken time to wash up a little or pick some flowers from the yard instead of coming as I was, my clothes covered in crude, smelling like I'd been living in a barn, bare-handed. But lookin' back, I can see our troubles ran deeper even then.

"It's a girl." This time there was no smile. "She's mine, and she's the last. I'm not going through this again."

"I'm sorry I wasn't here. There was—"

"Don't. I don't want to hear it. I know all I need to know."

I nodded. "The baby's okay?"

"Her name's Elizabeth."

"Elizabeth . . ." I let it roll around my mind. "I like it. Did you pick a middle name?"

I wasn't sure what I was seeing at first. The light was low, and Denise had looked down at her hands folded across her belly. But then I heard a quick intake of breath and knew I was right. She was crying. I came closer. I put my hand out to touch her and pulled back at the stark contrast between the black coating my nails and knuckles and the white of her skin. "It seems I'm always telling you I'm sorry about something," I said. "I know you're tired of hearing it, but I don't know what else to say."

"Her middle name is Mary."

My mother's name. I thought for a minute that I was through breathing. My chest felt so heavy, I simply couldn't make it move. That was when Denise looked up

*and saw that there were tears in my eyes. She frowned
when I said, "Thank you." I didn't understand why
until I remembered that she'd never heard me call
my mother by name. It was an accident, one I'm sure
Denise would have rectified had I told her. I let it be.
She'd find out one day when I told my baby girl about
the woman whose name she carried.*

Thirty-seven

Christina

Christina shuffled her feet on the concrete floor, rolling her chair closer to the editing monitors at the studio. "I'd go with the second shot," she said. "The lighting is better on the mustard."

Greg ran the tape backward to get another look. "Yeah, but I think the catsup looks better in three."

"It's a dancing hot dog, for Christ's sake," Dexter Landry said from the doorway. "And it's already over budget."

"And it's never going to make it off cable," Greg said in a singsong voice without looking up.

"And we're not being paid to be artists," Christina added, mimicking Greg's voice. "The client just wants to get the job done as cheaply as possible."

"Okay, you've heard it before. That—"

"Doesn't make it any less true," Christina finished for him.

"All right, so I need to get some new lines." Dexter waved a piece of paper at Christina. "I have something I think you might be interested in."

She rolled her chair toward him and held out her hand. He

pulled back and made a motion for her to follow him into the other room. "I'll be right back," she told Greg.

"No rush."

"Yeah, there is a rush," Dexter said. "I want that hot dog dancing out of here by this afternoon."

As owner of River City Studio, Dexter was caught between the business and artistic ends of film production. Coming from two years of supporting and working on *Illegal Alien*, Christina understood the financial and creative pulls Dexter operated under. He wasn't a hack. She'd seen the work he produced when given a reasonable budget, and it had blown her away. He just couldn't afford to give in to his artistic side as an editor when it involved raw footage brought in by a part-time videographer that would be shown strictly on cable.

Christina followed Dexter into his office. He surprised her when he closed the door behind them. Dexter's office door was always open. "What's up?" she asked.

He handed her the paper. "I think we found your movie."

Her heart did a tap dance against her ribs. She'd been looking for *Illegal Alien* for months, reading the synopsis of every film in every festival she could find in the United States, Canada, and Mexico. Randy could change the title but not the content. She'd considered contacting friends in Tucson to help but decided it was too risky. Everyone she knew had been friends to them both and would have divided loyalties. Dexter and her sisters were the only ones she'd told about looking for her movie, and Dexter only after he'd found her doing a search on the Internet. What she had in mind had to be done clean and fast. Randy couldn't know she was looking for him.

She looked at the paper, reading the description of the film Dexter had circled halfway down the page—*Fast Food at the Border*: a poignant portrait of a twenty-four-hour period in the life of an illegal alien. She glanced at the header—Willow Creek Film Festival in Grants Pass, Oregon. And then the dates—the winners would be announced and their films screened October 15. That gave her time, but not much.

"Is that it?" Dexter prompted.

"It sure looks like it."

"What now?"

"I make an appointment with my father's attorney. I want everything tied up in a nice legal bundle before I go after him."

"Can you do that in a month?"

"I don't know. But I can sure as hell try."

Christina followed Lucy's assistant, passing the office where she'd last seen her father. An unanticipated lump filled her throat as she was hit with the memory and the growing awareness of the missed opportunity to know him again. She vacillated between sorrow and anger, blaming him, blaming herself, looking for answers in the tapes, and heritage in her sisters—although she would never tell them that. Let them believe she saw nothing she had in common with them. That way, in four months when they turned their backs on her and went on with their own lives, they would think it was what she wanted, too.

The assistant tapped lightly on Lucy's door. "Ms. Alvarado is here."

Lucy stood and came around her desk. As always, she was dressed in a suit and heels and she made Christina feel unkempt and out of place, not as blatantly or completely as Ginger, but enough to make her check to see if her shirt was still tucked into her jeans and her hair was still secured in the clip she'd used that morning.

"How nice to see you again," Lucy said, extending her hand. Christina figured it was a standard greeting, but Lucy managed to make it sound sincere. "I appreciate you fitting me into your schedule."

Lucy led her to a chair. "You said it was important."

"I need help with a legal problem, and I didn't know who else to ask."

Lucy sat down and smiled. "Well, it's not the best reference I've received, but it will do."

"My dad trusted you."

"What's going on, Christina?"

She told Lucy about Randy and the film and how she was determined to get back what was hers. "I found him today—at least I found the film. He's entered it in one of the smaller festivals in Oregon. Unless he's done something stupid with it since he stole it, it's going to win. I want to be there when he shows up to get the prize."

"Does he have to be there?"

"No, but he will. Randy lives for the attention. He belongs in front of the camera, not behind it."

"And you say you have documentation that you financed the film as well as worked on it?"

Christina reached inside her bag and handed Lucy the sheaf of papers she'd rescued from the apartment. "I was the original narrator, but I'm sure he replaced me."

Lucy spent several minutes going through the papers. "These handwritten notes on the script—did you make them?"

"Yes."

She held up a receipt for a camera rental. "Whose credit card was used to pay for this?"

"Mine."

"Was he a signee on the card?"

"No."

"And all these other charges? Were they made with your card, too?"

"Randy didn't own a credit card. He quit his job a couple of months after we got together to work on the film full-time. I was our only source of income."

"Did you have a contract outlining ownership of the film?"

"Nothing written."

"But you discussed it?"

"From the beginning we agreed we were equal partners."

Lucy gathered the papers and set them aside. "All right—why have you come to me?"

"I want my film back."

"You want your half," Lucy corrected.

"I can't stand the thought of that son of a bitch getting away with stealing my movie, too."

"Too? I think you'd better tell me what else is going on here."

Christina hated telling her. In a sentence she would go from someone seemingly in charge to a victim. "It isn't important."

"Let me be the judge of that."

Still she hesitated. How could she admit to being someone she'd once looked at with contempt—a woman who would knowingly let herself become involved with a user. Only she hadn't known. She'd let her passion for a project she believed in blind her to the reality of the man she'd been convinced loved her. "My jaw wasn't broken in an accident."

Lucy's face reflected her thoughts from questioning to understanding as she absorbed the information. "I see. . . ."

"He had witnesses who swore that I was fine when he left the party with them. They swore he was with them the rest of the night. I couldn't prove them wrong."

"Sounds as if he's the type who's used to winning." A slow, mercenary smile formed. "Well, not anymore." She looked at Christina. "But first—are you sure you want to do this? Have you thought what it's going to mean to see him again?"

Christina knew she'd made the right choice coming there by

the personal concern she saw reflected in Lucy's eyes. "He stole the person I thought I was, and there was nothing I could do about it. I'm not going to let him steal my movie."

"That's all I need to hear."

"What are you going to do?"

"First, we'll get a temporary restraining order. That will keep him from taking any action that has anything to do with the movie."

"He won't be able to enter any more contests?"

"He won't be able to do *anything* until the hearing. I'm assuming the majority of the filming and the verbal contract took place in Arizona?"

Christina nodded.

"Then we'll have to file for a preliminary injunction there. I have a friend who's an attorney in Phoenix. I'll have him take care of the paperwork." She picked up a pen and made several notes on the tablet in front of her. "When is the award ceremony?"

"October 15."

"Do you want me to arrange to have him served before or after the ceremony?"

"I want to do it myself."

"Bad idea. I understand—to you it's personal. But moments like that are never what we imagine and certainly not worth the danger you'd be putting yourself in."

"You can't talk me out of this." She wanted to see the look on his face when she confronted him and he understood she hadn't just survived, she'd won. She wanted revenge, and not just because he'd broken her jaw but because by doing so he'd denied her the chance to see her father again.

"If you're dead set on doing this, at least take someone with you."

"I don't know anyone who—" She could see Lucy wasn't going to back off. It was easier to go along. "I just thought of someone."

"Mind if I ask who?"

Christina hadn't expected that. She'd already said she didn't trust any of her friends in Tucson. Lucy knew how long she'd worked at the studio and would never believe Christina would ask someone there. "Elizabeth."

Lucy's surprise was almost comical. "Your sister?"

"Do you have a problem with that?"

"Are you serious?"

"Why not? Isn't that the whole purpose behind the tapes—to throw us together until we either kill each other or become friends?"

"What makes you think Jessie—"

"Come on. Those tapes weren't meant to make us feel all warm and fuzzy about our disappearing father. If my dad gave a shit what the four of us thought about him he would have done something about it a long time before he was on the way out."

"I'm sorry, I can't respond to that. It wasn't something Jessie and I discussed."

"But he told you to take care of his girls for him, I'll bet."

"That one I'll give you. Which is why I'm concerned about you taking a fifty-year-old woman to Oregon with you to act as your bodyguard."

"She's forty-eight."

Lucy stared at her, unbending.

"What happened in Tucson was an aberration. It was the first time Randy hit me—or even threatened to hit me. I'm not crazy. If I thought there was any chance he'd try it again I wouldn't go near him." She had to give something if she wanted Lucy's cooperation. "But I can understand why you'd be concerned, and I'm willing to take Elizabeth with me as a witness on the off chance he thinks that since he got away with it once he might as well try again."

"Having Elizabeth as a witness might put him in jail, but it's not going to keep you out of the hospital."

"You're just going to have to trust me on this. Randy won't do anything that could fuck up his future in the business the way something like this would."

"Have you asked Elizabeth?"

"Not yet," she reluctantly admitted.

"I'd appreciate a call after you do—just to let me know everything is in place."

"Sure." Trapped. Now she really was going to have to ask. God, what if she said yes? Christina shuddered at the thought. "Is that it?"

"I think I have all I need to get started. If not, I'll call."

"Thanks."

"You're welcome." She stood to walk Christina to the door. "This is going to be fun."

Christina smiled, feeling better than she had in months. On a whim, one she didn't understand or stop to analyze, she asked, "Did you love my father?"

Lucy answered without hesitation, "Yes."

"Me, too," Christina told her.

Thirty-eight

Elizabeth

"Daddy said you were going back to school." Stephanie adjusted the cushion on her lounge chair, then put a protective hand over her still flat stomach. "But that you quit because of me."

Elizabeth shook water out of the net she'd been using to skim leaves from the pool. "I wasn't going *back* to school. I never started."

"You never went to college at all? I thought you dropped out after a couple of years."

She was always amazed how little Stephanie knew about her. Did she never talk about herself or did Stephanie tune her out when she did? "It didn't seem important at the time."

"Why go now? What's the point?"

How did you make someone Stephanie's age understand what it was like to be facing fifty and discovering your life had no meaning or purpose? "I thought it would be fun."

"It isn't. It's hard work. The pressure is unbelievable, especially during finals. All you ever think about is tests and grades." Stephanie put her head back and closed her eyes against the sun. "At least that's the way it is when it really matters."

"Are," Elizabeth corrected.

"What?"

"All you think about *are* tests and grades."

"Whatever." She put her hand to her forehead to shield her eyes from the sun. "Is there any more of that tea you made out of that herb stuff?"

"There should be a whole pitcher in the refrigerator."

"Would you mind getting me a glass?"

That did it. Elizabeth had been pushed too far. "Of course not," she said sweetly. "I want you to enjoy your last day of sitting around and doing nothing. Tomorrow you're going to start looking for a job and you're going to keep looking until you get one."

Stephanie laughed. "Good one, Mom."

"I'm not kidding."

"Who's going to hire me? I'm pregnant—remember?" The last dripped sarcasm.

"And you think that's going to make a difference?"

"Why would anyone want to hire someone who's only going to work for them a couple of months?"

"I'm not talking about a career position. There are a lot of un-skilled jobs that—"

Stephanie sat up and swung her legs over the side of the lounge. "All of this because I asked for a glass of tea? Jesus, I'll get it my-self."

"You might as well pick up the newspaper while you're at it."

"Why?"

"To look through the help-wanted ads."

Stephanie glared at her. "Why are you doing this?"

"Because you have some grown-up decisions to make. It's time you started growing up so you can make them."

"I should have had the abortion and taken my chances in hell. It couldn't be any worse than being here with you."

The statement was so over the top that Elizabeth couldn't come up with an answer. Sadly, it made her even more aware of how far Stephanie had to go. "I'm going to give you the benefit of the doubt and assume raging hormones prompted that last statement, but I would suggest you do everything you can to make sure it doesn't happen again. I'm not going to be your target every time you feel like lashing out at someone."

That brought a sob, followed by tears. It was the second time that day. "Why are you being so mean to me? What did I do that was so wrong?"

Where to begin? First was getting high and having unprotected sex with a boy she didn't even like—for what Elizabeth had concluded wasn't the first time. Then there was dropping out of school. Rounding out the short list was Stephanie allowing a woman with her own agenda to steal her emotional right to choose. "You're a year from graduating and you've never held a job. You need some experience in the real world."

"No one I know has ever worked—except doing stuff at school. You're just doing this because you think it will teach me a lesson." She swiped her hands across her cheeks, clearing the tear tracks. "Well, what kind of fucking lesson do you think I'm going to get working with a bunch of losers making minimum wage? I came home because I thought you loved me and cared what happened to me." Stephanie headed for the house. "Obviously I was wrong. I should have stayed with Sharon." She slammed the sliding glass door so hard, it bounced open again.

Weary of the non-ending emotional turmoil, Elizabeth sat on the lounge Stephanie had vacated and buried her face in her hands, closing out the real world and sinking into a sheltered moment of solitude.

Sam came out of the bathroom with a towel wrapped around his waist and shaving cream on his chin. "Why isn't Stephanie going with us?"

"She's mad at me." They'd decided at breakfast to go to Fernando's for dinner—Stephanie's favorite Mexican restaurant. It was a tradition of sorts, started when Stephanie went east to go to school and discovered what passed for Mexican food on the East Coast.

He grinned. "Then we can go where we want. How about that new Italian restaurant Harold was telling us about?"

Elizabeth pulled a sleeveless cotton dress out of the closet. "I don't care where we go, I just want to get out of the house for a couple of hours."

"That bad, huh?"

"Worse."

Sam went back in the bathroom to finish shaving. Elizabeth stepped into her flats and followed, squeezing past him and picking up the hairbrush. "What were we thinking when we decided this bathroom was big enough for two?"

"That we'd never be in it at the same time." He rinsed the washcloth and wiped the cream off his face, then reached for her, drawing her into his arms. "I'm sorry you're getting the brunt of this. Why don't I see if I can get Stephanie to come to work with me tomorrow? I'll find something around the office for her to do. She needs to get out of the house."

"She needs to get a job."

He pulled back in surprise. "Wait a minute, isn't that my line?"

"I'm worried about her, Sam, and for more than the obvious reasons. We've babied her too long." He gave her one of his looks. "All right, *I've* babied her too long. I didn't want her to grow up. And now she has to and she's not ready. It's as if she thinks she's going to have the baby and then go on as if nothing happened."

"Wait a minute. When I talked to her last night she said she didn't know what she wanted to do, and now she's decided to give the baby up for adoption?"

"No—at least not that I know of. Every time I ask she tells

me she doesn't want to think about it, that she has lots of time to make up her mind."

"Are you sure she isn't waiting for you to make the decision for her?"

"That's not going to happen. It wouldn't matter what I told her, five minutes later it would be wrong."

"I'm glad you realize that."

She leaned her head against his shoulder. "I don't know what I'll do if she decides on adoption. It would kill me to know we had a grandchild growing up without us."

"I was thinking about that on the way home tonight, remembering what it was like when the kids were little and how much fun we had with them. This would be twice as much fun because we could send him home when he got cranky."

"What would you say if she asked us to take care of the baby until she finished school and got on her feet?"

Sam let out a pent-up sigh, let her go, and went into the bedroom to get dressed. "I've been waiting for that."

Elizabeth followed him. "It would only be a couple of years."

"And then you'd turn the kid over to a woman who didn't have a clue how to be a mother? Right in the middle of the terrible twos?"

"She would have to finish school here so she could help raise him, and so they could get to know each other."

"And you think she would agree to that? She doesn't want to be a mother, Lizzy. She has all the maternal instincts of a sea horse—drop 'em, take off, and let the father raise them. Only in her case that's not possible."

"It's done, Sam. Like it or not, there's never going to be a boy showing up on the doorstep to lay claim to his child."

He tossed his shirt on the bed. "How could she do that? How could she not have more respect for herself? I get sick to my stomach just thinking about it. She was being used, Lizzy, and she let it happen."

She'd been Daddy's little girl, the light of his life, the twinkle in his eye, the father who questioned her dates and stayed up until she was home, convinced she would be a virgin until her wedding night because it was what he wanted to believe. "We don't know all the circumstances."

"Please tell me you're not defending her," he said.

"There isn't anything to defend." Stephanie and Sam had locked horns so many times since she'd come home, Elizabeth had finally gotten him to back off by telling him the stress on Stephanie wasn't good for the baby. It wasn't that Stephanie didn't need to hear what he said, it was that she wasn't listening. He had to find a different way to get through to her. They both did. "All I'm saying is that we have to find a way to get past how it happened so we can focus on what needs to be done now."

He picked up his knit shirt and pulled it over his head, then tucked it into his pants. "We need to get away for a couple of days. What about next weekend?"

"I have to go to Sacramento on Sunday."

"That's another thing. When are you going to tell Stephanie about your sisters?"

"I don't know yet."

The phone rang. Stephanie picked up in the other room. Seconds later she shouted from the hallway, "Mom, it's for you."

Elizabeth grabbed the phone on the nightstand. "Hello?"

"It's Christina."

Elizabeth looked at Sam, shrugged, and frowned. "Oh, hi."

"I have a favor to ask. A pretty big one. It's okay to say no. Actually, I've already come up with a couple of reasons why you should say no. Feel free to use one of them if you can't think of one of your own."

"I'm pretty good at thinking up my own excuses when I don't want to do something."

"Good. That makes it easier to ask. I should tell you it's not going to hurt my feelings or anything if you do say no. I don't even know why I'm asking you—not really. It's not like we're friends or anything."

"What is it, Christina? The suspense is killing me."

"I have to go to Oregon for a couple of days next month, and Lucy doesn't think I should go alone. I just thought if you weren't doing anything that you might want to go along. I can't pay your way now, but I can pay you back. If you haven't seen it, Grants Pass is beautiful in October. Or so I hear."

Elizabeth could only imagine how much pride it had cost Christina to ask. She had to be desperate. "Okay."

"What?"

"I said, okay."

"You're sure?" Christina asked, plainly surprised at the answer.

"Sam was just telling me that I should get away for a couple of days." Of course he'd meant with him. "And I've always wanted to see Grants Pass in October. You can fill me in on the details on Sunday."

"Okay." She started to hang up. "Uh, thanks."

"No problem." She handed the phone to Sam to return to its base.

"What was that all about?"

"I'm going to Oregon with Christina for a couple of days next month."

"Isn't she the one you don't like?"

"You mean the one I said I'd rather eat snails than be around? I don't know if she's mellowed or I have, but she's not as bad as she used to be."

"Why Oregon?"

"She didn't say, but I have a feeling it has something to do with the old boyfriend."

"The one who broke her jaw? I'm not sure I like you getting

involved with something that involves him. As a matter of fact, I know I don't."

"If it makes you feel any better, I'll take the pepper spray Michael got me for Christmas." She smiled. "If I can find it."

"Any man who uses a woman as a punching bag isn't going to be put off by a can of pepper spray."

"I'll get one for Christina, too. Not even Jackie Chan could get through two women armed with pepper spray."

"Stop joking, Lizzy. This is serious."

She put her arms around his neck. "I know it is. And I promise I'll be careful."

"I want to know exactly where you'll be and everything you're going to do before you leave or I'm not going to let you go."

Her hands on her hips, she glared at him. "*Let* me go?"

"Okay, poor choice of words. How's this—before I let you go alone?"

"Better, but it still needs some work."

He brought her back into his arms and kissed her. "Hmm, you smell good. Sure you want to go out?"

"I don't know. . . . What did you have in mind?"

"Get rid of that dress and I'll show you."

"Now?"

"Why not now?"

"Did you forget about Stephanie?"

He groaned. "How long do you think this is going to last?"

Elizabeth kissed the tip of his nose. Sam didn't expect an answer, but she gave one anyway. "Six months? A year? It all depends on what she decides to do with the baby."

"So, I guess that means we won't be making love on the rug in front of the fireplace anytime soon?"

He was joking, but she was serious when she asked, "When did we start thinking of the house as ours instead of theirs, too?"

He considered her question. "For me it was a couple of Christmases ago when everyone left and we were taking down the tree. I was repairing that ornament we'd picked up on our honeymoon, and I started thinking about all the places we'd talked about seeing and the things we'd talked about doing when the kids were grown. I miss what we had when the kids were little, but I don't want it back. It's our time now."

Stephanie knocked on the door. "I'm hungry. There's nothing to eat."

"Seems I've been forgiven," Elizabeth whispered. She went to the door and opened it. "There's soup and tuna in the cupboard."

"Yuk."

"Peanut butter?"

"Double yuk."

Sam sat on the bed to tie his shoes. "You're still welcome to come with us. But we're leaving in five minutes."

"Where are you going?"

He pinned her with a stare. "A new Italian restaurant near the mall. Take it or leave it."

"Give me a second to comb my hair."

Elizabeth reached out to pat his rear end as he passed. "I love it when you act tough."

"Then you're going to be ecstatic when you get ready to leave for Oregon."

She put her hand over her chest. "Be still my heart."

"I'm going to remind you of this."

She hit the light switch. "I have no doubt."

Thirty-nine

Ginger

Ginger finished her stretching exercises and went to the living room window to look outside before leaving for the track. Seven-thirty at night and heat waves still undulated throughout the city. She tried to remember if it had been this hot a September ago, but to her weather was like the new crop of sitcoms promised for the fall lineup—easily forgotten. She'd had it with the sunshine that had baked the hills surrounding San Jose a crusty brown and turned the air a smog-laden gray. Even knowing their potential destructive power, she missed the dark menacing rain clouds that rolled across the plains of Colorado and Kansas.

In California it didn't rain in the summer. Couldn't. Too many crops would be ruined. She imagined an army of elves stationed offshore that beat the rain clouds into fog before they could reach land. Four more months and she could go home. All she had to do was figure out where home was. Her mother was pushing for Denver, on the good days reminding Ginger how much she loved to ski, on the bad ones finding reasons to mention how old she and Ginger's dad were getting. Ginger recognized the gentle coercion for what it was and rarely commented. Love traveled a convoluted path in the Reynolds household.

Not up to hearing pseudo-sympathy or, worse yet, jubilation, Ginger still hadn't told her mother about Marc. She needed distance and a little objectivity before she could answer the questions that would follow the announcement. Besides, she'd given Delores enough turmoil that summer with exposed secrets and unimagined wealth.

The phone rang. Ginger knew before she picked up that it was her mother. It seemed all Ginger had to do was think about talking to her mother lately and she called.

"Hi, Mom."

"How did you know it was me?"

"I was channeling you."

"What?"

Ginger laughed. "Nothing. What's up?"

"Are you busy? You're not in the middle of dinner, are you?"

"Just getting ready to go running."

"Did you know running is hard on your knees? Bicycling is supposed to be better."

"You've been reading again."

"I read all the time. It wouldn't hurt you to pick up a magazine now and then."

"I know this isn't why you called."

"I've been thinking about Jessie and what was on those tapes. Maybe I've been too hard on him."

Ginger sat down on the sofa and put her feet on the coffee table, settling in for the duration of the call. "In what way?"

"Men were different back then. They weren't expected to know anything about raising kids, and most women wouldn't put up with having them try. Nowadays you think nothing of seeing a man in a grocery store pushing a cart with a child in it. Back then everyone would have stopped and stared. It could be that Jessie didn't give you up because he didn't care, but because he didn't know how to take care of you."

It was as close to a speech as Ginger had ever heard her mother make. "What brought this on?"

"I don't know. I guess it's that I don't feel as threatened as I did six months ago." Delores paused, but it was obvious she had more to say. "I know it sounds corny, but a heart has room to love a lot of people. What I'm trying to say is, it's all right with me and your father if you love Jessie, too."

She thought she did, at least a little, but it was nothing like the love she had for the man and woman who had raised her. "You're always surprising me."

"That's nice to hear. I'd hate to be old and predictable."

"You're never predictable."

Delores laughed. "Just old, huh? I'll have you know your father signed us up for six weeks of ballroom dancing."

"Dad did that?"

"Just yesterday. He was at his investing seminar and saw a notice on the bulletin board."

"Investing seminar?" she repeated, fearing what was coming. Every dime her parents had managed to put away had been spent on college tuition for her and her brother Billy. They didn't have any money to invest. "Is Dad studying to become my financial adviser?" she joked halfheartedly.

"He just wants to make sure you don't get taken."

"Tell him to study hard. I'm going to need all the advice he can give me." It wouldn't be her investments he would have to keep an eye on, but his own. She knew it wouldn't be easy to get them to take any of the money, which was why she was waiting until she actually had it before she said anything. But like it or not, her parents were only months away from becoming millionaires.

Delores laughed. "He's going to like hearing that."

"Maybe this will convince him he needs a computer." Ginger

got up and went to the window to look outside again, checking the progress of the sun. She liked to time her run to get back before it was completely dark and she had to walk home looking over her shoulder. She started to turn away when a movement caught her eye. It was a car coming into the complex. A Mercedes. Red. She didn't have to see the personalized plate to know who was behind the wheel.

"Mom, I'm sorry, but if I don't get out of here I won't get back from the track before dark."

"Just think about what I said about Jessie."

"I will. I love you, Mom."

"I love you, too, sweetheart."

Ginger hung up, tossed the phone on the sofa, and stood to the side of the window so Marc wouldn't see her. He got out of the car and reached into the backseat, withdrawing an enormous bouquet of white roses.

He'd come to the condo twice since the night she broke up with him, called her at home daily, and sent flowers to her office six times. So far she'd avoided talking to him, hoping he would simply give up. Plainly he had more stamina than she did.

She met him at the door. "What are you doing here?"

"Just give me five minutes. I promise you won't be sorry."

The condo manager waved from the mailbox stanchion. Ginger smiled. She either let Marc in or became fodder for gossip. "All right. But just five minutes."

He came in and tried to hand her the roses. She refused to take them. "They're your favorite," he said.

"Not anymore."

"Kind of petty, don't you think?"

"Get on with it, Marc. You don't have much time."

"I've left Judy."

Shit. It was the last thing she wanted. "Why?"

"You made me realize what a fool I've been. No matter how

hard I tried, there was no way I could make everyone happy. I finally saw that I had to make a choice, and the choice I made was you."

"You forgot one thing. I didn't choose you."

"But now that I'm free—"

"It doesn't matter."

"How can you say that? You love me. I love you."

Did she love him? Was what she'd felt really love, the same kind of love that had seen her parents through forty-five years of marriage? Or was Marc an addiction fed by her fear of growing old alone? "Whatever I felt for you, it's over."

"Is it the money?"

At first she didn't understand. And then it all made sense. He was trading Judy and his children for her inheritance. Somehow he'd discovered how much money Jessie had left her.

"Because if it is," he added, "I'm willing to sign a prenup. I know Jessie Reed left you a lot more money than you admitted. He had to. I don't understand why you lied to me, but I know you must have had what you thought was a good reason. We can work this out, Ginger."

She stared at him, speechless. If there had been one small corner of her heart where she still harbored love for him, one part of her mind where she wondered if she'd made a mistake, one corner of pride that wanted to convince her she really wasn't the world's most poorly paid prostitute, it was gone. "Go back to your wife."

"I can't. I told her about us. I wanted to show that I was ready to commit, and it was the only way I knew to convince you. I had no right to ask you to wait as long as you have. I'm ashamed to admit that I thought you'd always be here for me, that it didn't matter how long it took me to come to my senses." Again he tried to hand her the roses. "Give me a chance and I'll spend the rest of my life making it up to you."

She folded her arms across her chest. She couldn't stop thinking about Rachel and Jeff and how Rachel must have felt when she found out about Jeff's affair. "Don't you care that you broke Judy's heart? What could she possibly have done to deserve what you've done to her—what I've done to her?"

"You know that as well as I do. She's a leech. She's sucked me dry for years with her neediness. I can't take it anymore. Not even for the kids. If it weren't for you, I would have left a long time ago."

"Wait a minute." In her mind's eye she saw him with his arm around Judy, smiling, kissing her. "Are you admitting you went back to Judy because you knew you could have me on the side?"

"You're twisting my words."

"Then straighten them out."

"I went back because of the kids. You knew that. You even agreed they had to come first."

"What happened?"

"I don't understand."

"Why aren't they first anymore?"

"I lost you."

"So now I'm first?"

"You always were." He took her hand. "It took this to make me see it. I can't face a future without you."

She pulled free. "You're full of shit."

In a flash of anger he tore the green tissue from around the roses and reached inside, digging through the stems until he found a small, velvet box. He held it out to her. "I wanted this to be special—the whole nine yards. I was even going to get down on my knees to give this to you. I have a reservation at LaHarve's—and you know how hard it is to get that, especially on short notice. The best champagne. *Whipping cream.*"

She stared at the box, knowing what was inside, thinking of all the times she'd dreamed of this moment. She was tempted to look, to see what he believed it would take to impress her. A carat? Two? Three would border on ostentatious but wasn't out of the question. She could tell him she would take it but only as a gift, not an engagement ring. Then she could donate it to the SPCA auction.

She pushed his hand away. "I'm not interested."

"You don't even want to see it?"

"Nope."

He either didn't believe her or thought she would fold once she caught sight of the ring. He opened the box and shoved it at her. "It's the largest stone available on the West Coast."

It looked like a faceted golf ball. "My God, I can't believe you actually thought I would wear something like that. Go home, Marc."

"I am home." He took the ring out of the box and held it up for her to get a better look.

"You're making this too easy." She bent to retrieve the flowers, then handed them to him. With his hands full, she took his arm and shoved him out the door. Super-heated air surrounded them, a cloying embrace that quickly turned suffocating. "Good-bye, Marc."

"I'll give you a couple of days to think about it."

"I'm not going to change my mind."

He stopped on the first step and turned to look at her. "You still love me, Ginger. I can feel it."

"If I do, I'll get over it."

"No, you won't."

"Give it up, Marc. It's not going to happen. Take the ring back to where you bought it and see if they'll—"

He tossed the roses onto the sidewalk, grabbed her, and kissed her, grinding his mouth hard against hers, his tongue demanding what she refused to give. "Remember that when you're all alone in bed tonight."

She wiped her mouth with the back of her hand. "I'm good at being alone. I've had a lot of practice."

It was his last card. The game was over. Still, he couldn't simply walk away. "You know my number."

She'd put on a good show, let him see exactly what she wanted him to see, done everything she could to convince him she didn't care anymore. And he'd believed her because he'd measured her feelings with the ruler he used for his own. He would only look back with regret when he thought about her money. She would be easy to forget—and to replace.

Abandoning the idea of running that night, Ginger went inside and poured herself a large snifter of Grand Marnier, then put on a Bonnie Tyler CD and skipped to the song "Holding Out for a Hero."

Never again would she settle for anything less.

Forty

Elizabeth

Rachel raised her glass of iced tea. "Here's to the third installment of Jessie's Girls."

"What did you call it?" Christina asked, looking up from some papers Lucy had dropped off with the usual envelope of tapes.

"Jessie's Girls."

"I like it," said Ginger, raising her glass in return.

Elizabeth didn't—not only wasn't she a "girl," she didn't like being claimed by Jessie even if he was gone. But she went along. She touched her glass to the others and tried to catch a glimpse of what Christina was reading. Christina caught her.

"It's a preliminary injunction," she announced.

"You found your movie," Ginger squealed. "Congratulations."

"Tell," Rachel said. "We want details."

"I knew he would enter it in a festival. An unknown needs the buzz that comes from winning festivals to get a distributor interested. He probably figured Grants Pass was safe because it's small."

"If you can prove the film is half yours," Rachel said, "what difference does it make whether you catch him now or later?"

"The more successful a film becomes the more people show up claiming they were cheated out of a part of it. If I let Randy make all the decisions about which festivals to enter and who to sign distribution deals with, that gives him priority and makes it look as if he has a bigger claim. Besides, I might not like the deals he wants to make."

"And the injunction will keep him from doing that?" Rachel asked.

"Which is why I want to serve him as soon as I can find him."

"You're not thinking about doing it yourself?" Ginger said.

"She's not," Elizabeth said. "I'm going with her." Ginger and Rachel whipped around to look at her.

"No way," Ginger said.

Christina made a long-suffering face. "Lucy wouldn't take me as a client unless I promised I wouldn't go alone."

"And you picked *Elizabeth*?" Rachel said, incredulous. "Sorry, Elizabeth, no offense, but you don't look the martial arts type. If it were me, I'd be looking into hiring a couple of those washboard-ab guys at the gym."

"I'm not an idiot," Christina said. "When I serve him it's going to be in a public place with plenty of witnesses."

"And I'm taking a can of pepper spray just in case," Elizabeth added.

"You're what?" Christina said.

"It was the only way I could talk Sam into letting me go."

Rachel tipped her glass to them. "So, when is the big day?"

"October fifteenth."

"Aren't we supposed to meet on the seventeenth?"

Christina stood to clear the table. "We'll be back in plenty of time."

"Anyone else have any news?" Ginger asked. "I'm thinking about moving back to Kansas City when this thing with Jessie is over. Or maybe Denver."

"Why Denver?" Christina asked.

"It's where I grew up."

"I've lived in California all my life," Elizabeth said. "I can't imagine being anywhere else. I love it here."

"You've been here forty-eight years?" Christina said.

"Forty-nine actually. I had a birthday last month."

"Happy birthday," Ginger said. "We'll remember next year and do something special." They all stared at her as if she'd planted a flag in the middle of the table and laid claim to it and the surrounding chairs. "What?"

Christina was the first to say something. "You're not even going to be here—and you're assuming we're still speaking to each other a year from now."

"Why wouldn't we?"

"Why *would* we?" she shot back.

Ginger put a perfectly manicured hand to her throat and looked at Elizabeth and Rachel. "Do you feel that way, too?" When neither answered, Ginger pushed her chair back and stood. "Guess I went off on one of my Pollyanna trips again. Maybe we should get to the tapes so we can get out of here."

She'd been rejected and her feelings were hurt—the last thing Elizabeth expected from someone like Ginger. "I think it would be nice if we stayed in touch," Elizabeth gave her.

"Me, too," Rachel added. "I just didn't think any of the rest of you felt that way."

"Don't look at me," Christina said.

She's not as tough as she pretends. The realization came to Elizabeth the same way she innately understood Christina's need to hold everyone at arm's length. Rachel and Ginger were insulated from the kind of abandonment she and Christina felt. Jessie had never known them. They hadn't been tested and found lacking. Elizabeth only had to look at Christina to see what she would have been without Sam.

"Sorry," Elizabeth said to Christina, "but if we want to send you birthday and Christmas presents and drop by for unexpected visits at your Beverly Hills mansion, we're going to. And there's not a damn thing you can do about it."

"You go, girl," Ginger said raising her hand for a high-five.

Christina smiled in spite of herself. "Try, and I'll have you arrested."

"Like that's going to happen," Ginger shot back. "I can see the headlines now. Big Hollywood producer has sisters arrested for attempting to visit."

"*Prominent* Hollywood producer," Christina corrected.

Rachel added her plate to those Christina had gathered. "I hate to be pushy about this, but could we get to the tapes now? I'd like to be back before five."

"She has a date," Ginger said. Rachel sent her a silencing look. Ginger ignored her. "With Jeff. It's the third one. Isn't that great? And I get to watch the kids."

"I've tried to imagine what I would do if I found out Sam had cheated on me," Elizabeth said. "It seems obvious in the abstract. I hope you can work it out, if that's what you want."

"Six months ago I was convinced it wasn't possible. Now I'm not so sure."

Rhona came in from the kitchen. "Leave that. I'll take care of the dishes."

"Lunch was incredible," Elizabeth told her.

"I normally don't like salmon," Rachel said, "but that was amazing."

"Your father liked simple things prepared in interesting ways," Rhona said.

"If you're ever looking for a job," Rachel said, "let—"

"I'm going to buy a flower shop as soon as you don't need me anymore. Jessie knew it was a dream of mine, and he left me the means to make it come true."

Elizabeth was incredulous. "You've stayed here all this time because of us?"

"No, ma'am," she said gently. "I stayed here for your father." She shooed them out of the kitchen. "Go listen to him some more. You need to hear why he was so beloved by all of us who knew him."

Jessie's Story

Denise tied Lizzy to her apron string with a knot I was never allowed to mess with. As far as she was concerned, she'd given me a son. Frank was mine, Lizzy was hers. She fed me and Frank in the morning and saw us off. The rest of the day was hers and Lizzy's. Most days I dropped him off at school, did what needed doing at the office, and picked him up in the afternoon. He spent the rest of the day with me doing his homework at a desk I had set up behind mine or bouncing around in the truck when I had things to do or people to see.

Then when Lizzy was four Denise hit a telephone pole with the Oldsmobile I'd given her for her birthday and wound up in the hospital for two months. Lizzy had been asleep in the backseat and came through without a scratch, but she had a real hard time adjusting to being with me every day. She wouldn't say, but I think she was afraid of me. Then one evening her loneliness overcame her fear and she crawled into my lap, staying there until bedtime. Just like that, we were friends.

It didn't take long to learn she had a stubborn streak longer and wider than the Central Valley we lived in. Her stubbornness was a pain in the butt when it came to getting her in a dress she didn't want to wear and a blessing when Denise came home and wanted to take up where they'd left off. Lizzy wouldn't have it. She'd made her way to the outside of the bubble her mother had put her in, and she liked what she saw. Denise never forgave me. As soon as she was well enough to travel, she left for Texas and took Lizzy with her. They stayed the summer and half the fall.

I found out later that while she was back there she ran into the boy she'd been seeing while I was off fighting the war. I don't know that it was anything more than friends getting together, but she was different when she came back.

Me and Frank met them at the train station. He was about to turn ten and had taken off growing while they were gone. Instead of fitting under my arm, he was shoulder high and anxious to show off. Denise was so caught up in making sure her luggage made it off the train, she never noticed how he'd changed. I think it was the last real chance he gave her. After that she could have gone to every one of his basketball games or gone out of her way to understand and accommodate his passion for fishing and it wouldn't have made any difference.

I was sure Lizzy would come home with the bricks put back in the wall Denise had built between us. But she came running at me, never doubting my arms would be open wide, knowing without being told that I'd missed her as much as she'd missed me.

It might have worked out with Denise and me if I hadn't bought that land down in Anaheim back when the money from the wells started coming in. I still believed in land over banks for my money, and I'd heard a rumor that Walt Disney was thinking about building an amusement park. I looked at places I thought it could go, places I could get to first. Just like dumb luck, sometimes you're the windshield, sometimes you're the bug. This time I was driving the car, not outside flying around.

I walked away from the deal with too much money to keep locked up or put into land. Or at least that's what I told myself. Maybe if I'd stopped to think about what I was doing I might have realized where it could lead me, but I doubt it. I was years away from being that self-aware. Some men work to have money and some see money as the barometer of their success. For me it was a game where playing and winning were more important than the prize. I didn't so much care what the final numbers were when I sold the land, only that the amount was proof I'd guessed right.

I was looking for the next game when I met Joe and Charles McKinney. They were movie producers with talent and connections but no backing. There's an expression in the wine industry—the way to make a small fortune is to start with a big one. It's the same in the movie business. I was starstruck and having too much fun to care about the bottom line. Like a gambler convinced that all it would take to get back in the game was one more hand, I watched movie after movie struggle to move into the black, believing the next one would be the runaway hit and make back everything I'd lost and then some. A good part of my life has been spent wondering how I could be so right about some things and so wrong about others.

Denise disliked Bakersfield, but she hated Los Angeles and refused to join me there. I spent more and more time away, and when I was home it seemed she was either yelling at me over something that didn't matter any more than who was running for Congress, or not speaking at all. Finally Denise gave me an ultimatum—stay home or stay away. I came home every weekend for the next year—until Denise told me she'd found someone else and wanted a divorce.

I looked at her and tried to remember a time when she'd looked back at me with love instead of hatred. "Is it because you think I've been unfaithful?"

"I don't think, Jessie. I know."

"You're wrong." I knew she hadn't believed me when I told her I came home alone from the parties I went to in L.A., and maybe it would have made a difference if I'd cared enough to try harder to convince her. Instead I let her suffer in her belief because she did it with such enthusiasm.

"I have pictures of you with that singer."

"She's a friend. And she's half my age."

"It doesn't matter. I don't care anymore. I found someone who makes me happy. After putting up with you all these years, I deserve some happiness."

"What about Frank and Lizzy?"

For the first time she seemed unsure of herself. "What about them?"

"Frank's old enough now that he could live with me. And Lizzy could—"

"The lawyer told me you would try something like this."

"You talked to a lawyer?"

"He said there's no way a judge would give you custody."

"How long have you been planning to leave me?"

"Since I came back from Texas," she admitted.

"Why did you come back at all?"

"My father made me."

What could I say after that? I took Frank and Lizzy to dinner, then dropped them back at the house and headed to Los Angeles.

Against the advice of the lawyer I hired, I gave Denise the oil rights and most of the cash I had in my personal accounts. In exchange she agreed to let me see Frank and Lizzy one weekend a month and three weeks in the summer—no holidays or birthdays.

Frank was sixteen, old enough to bridge the twenty-eight days between visits with phone calls. Lizzy was twelve and carrying a burden her brother didn't have— her mother. Denise fought with Frank and filled Lizzy's head with real and perceived injustices, all involving me. I saw that I was losing her, more with every visit, but didn't know how to keep it from happening without filling her head with my own form of poison. I decided I'd rather lose her than do that.

I needed something to distract me, something to keep me from hating Denise for doing what she was doing. I was ready for anything when Joe and Charlie stumbled across a project floundering for lack of financing—bestselling book, compelling script, Academy Award–winning director, A-list stars already signed on. If ever there was a movie guaranteed to do big box office, this was it.

It wasn't our normal kind of project. For the most part we were B-list producers with a couple of pictures the critics loved that were financial failures. We were ready for something big.

I'm convinced we would have made it—if our lead star had left the premier party and gone home instead of to a park where he was arrested for exposing himself to a twelve-year-old boy.

Forty-one

Elizabeth

"Are you busy?" Stephanie asked.

Elizabeth put the sweater she'd just finished folding into the suitcase. "Not too busy to talk. What's up?"

Stephanie came into the room, kicked off her shoes, crawled onto the bed, and propped herself against the headboard. "I got my first paycheck today. It was so pathetic, I thought it was wrong. The accountant went over it with me. Talk about embarrassing."

"You've only been working a couple of weeks." Sam had arranged an office gopher job with one of his suppliers. It was perfect for Stephanie, temporary and unskilled.

"I can't believe people actually live on this kind of money. I went to the mall to look at maternity clothes and couldn't afford *anything* I wanted."

"Did you try one of the chains?"

"You mean like Nordstrom?"

"Like Target or Sears."

She looked horrified. "I wouldn't even know where to look in a store like that."

"Perhaps it's time you learned."

"Why?"

"Options, Stephanie. You should give yourself as many as you can."

She grabbed a pillow and hugged it. "How long are you going to be gone?"

"Three days." Elizabeth had checked the weather report for Grants Pass in October and decided to take things she could layer. It was hard fitting everything into a small suitcase, but she knew Christina would pack light and she didn't want to come across looking like one of those women who empty the closet every time they go somewhere.

"I talked to Sharon today."

That was never good news. Sharon triggered emotions Stephanie couldn't handle, and the repercussion could last for days. "How is she?"

"Fine. Dating a guy she met in a chat room."

"That's scary."

"He wants her to go skiing with him in Colorado in November, so she won't be coming out here after all."

"That's too bad," Elizabeth said, working hard to hide her excitement. Thanksgiving would be the first time in almost a year that the whole family would be together. Having Sharon a part of the mix, especially with Michael and Eric there seeing the physical evidence of Stephanie's pregnancy, had all the ingredients for one of those god-awful family holiday movies.

"Nice try, but I know you didn't want her here."

Stephanie was crying; it happened a lot lately. Elizabeth wasn't sure how much was hormonal and how much was depression. "Maybe she can come out at semester break after Christmas." Stephanie would be eight months along by then, big and uncomfortable and unlikely to want to do the things that Sharon considered necessary parts of life, like checking out the local singles scene.

"She won't. And I don't care." She rolled to the side, snatched a tissue from the box on the nightstand, and blew her nose. "I told her I felt the baby kick. She said it sounded gross."

Slowly, as her body changed and she became more and more aware of the child she carried, Stephanie was developing a protective instinct that made Elizabeth happy and sad at the same time. "If she acknowledges what you're going through she has to accept it could happen to her."

"I wish it would."

"No, you don't."

She grabbed another tissue and wiped fresh tears. "I don't belong anymore. No matter what I do, it won't be the same. I'm different."

Elizabeth moved the suitcase to the floor and sat with Stephanie. "If I could, I would make this all go away and let you go back to being the girl you were. But I can't. From the moment you got pregnant that girl was left behind. Whatever choice you made, the consequences became something you had to live with forever. There were no easy answers, Stephanie. There never are."

"You think I should have had the abortion," Stephanie said flatly.

They were back there again. Stephanie simply couldn't let it go. "Just because I believe in a woman's right to choose doesn't mean I believe it's the right choice."

"What would you have done?"

"It doesn't matter."

"I want to know."

"I'm not going to tell you. Whatever you do has to be your choice. All you need from me or your father is to know that we will support you whatever you decide is right for you and your baby."

"Why do you always say *your* baby instead of *the* baby?"

"You can't distance yourself from what's happening with words. Next week when you find out if you're carrying a boy or girl, then the baby will become he or she." After months of insisting she didn't want to know, Stephanie had changed her mind.

Stephanie turned sad, haunted eyes to her mother. "Why are you doing this to me? Why are you making it so hard?"

Elizabeth put her arms around her daughter, her baby, the child she loved beyond reason. "Because it is. I don't want you to live your life wondering if you made the right decision. When you're my age I want you to be able to look back without question." She purposely didn't say anything about what Stephanie would tell the child who grew up and came looking for her, how she would explain that her life was too complicated to include a child. Women had fought for the right to have choices, but they still hadn't found one that didn't leave scars.

"I don't want to be a mother. Maybe someday, but not now. I'm not ready. Is it so wrong for me to want to give it away?"

Yes, she ached to tell her. This baby wasn't just Stephanie's child, it was Elizabeth's grandchild. How could she be there for the delivery and hold a baby with Stephanie's eyes or nose or chin and know she would never see her again? Did Ginger's mother regret giving her away? Did she look into the eyes of the children she saw on concert tours and wonder if one of them was hers?

Elizabeth lovingly tucked a strand of hair behind Stephanie's ear. "No, it's not wrong."

"God, how could I have been so stupid?"

"It's done. Stop beating yourself up."

Stephanie leaned her head into Elizabeth's shoulder. "If I do decide to give it away, I hope it gets a mother like you."

Elizabeth closed her eyes against the tears burning to be shed, her heart breaking that she could not give Stephanie what she needed.

*** *

Elizabeth was in bed reading when Sam came home from the Fresno State University football game. She slipped a bookmark in to save her page and put the book aside. "Who won?"

"We did. A blowout."

"Where's Stephanie?"

"Lu called. They went to a movie."

"Did you remind her not to drink if they went out afterwards?"

"Give her some credit, Lizzy. She knows what she's not supposed to do."

"If that were true, she wouldn't be in the shape she's in."

She was tired and not in the mood for moral pontificating. "Just what do you think your sons were doing on all those spring breaks they attended in college? How do you know we don't have a whole raft of grandchildren out there who look like Michael and Eric? Nothing's changed, it's still all the girl's fault, she's the slut, and she's the one who has to take care of the *problem* if something happens. I'm sick of it. Stephanie didn't get pregnant by herself. But where's the boy? He's still in school working on his degree, going out on weekends and having sex without a condom because they cramp his style."

"Bad day?"

He knew her so well. "I just have this gut feeling that Stephanie is going to ask us to adopt her baby."

"I've been waiting for this."

"Me, too," she admitted.

He sat on the corner of the bed. "What did she say?"

"That she wanted her baby to have a mother like me."

"And what did you say?"

"Nothing."

"What are you going to say if she just comes out and asks?"

"Don't you think we should talk about it before I say anything?"

Sam shifted position to sit with his back to the headboard. "Are you asking me how I feel about it?"

She was, but she already knew his answer. Sam didn't have it in him to refuse her anything. He was fifty-two. By the time the baby was through college, he would be seventy-four. "It isn't fair," she said. "Not to us or to the baby. I know there are women in their fifties having babies, but every time I hear about it I cringe. We were damn good parents the first time around, but we're not those people anymore. We don't think or act the same, and we've seen too many news broadcasts and been through too many presidents to look at the world in the same optimistic way.

"And we don't eat pizza. How can you have a kid in any kind of sport nowadays and not eat pizza? Every end-of-the-season game, every award ceremony takes place in a pizza parlor."

"Now there's a winning argument."

"I'm serious in my ass-backward way."

"I know you are." He reached for her hand.

"She's never going to understand. She's going to think we don't want the baby because it would get in the way of me going to school and you retiring."

"It would."

"But that's not the point."

"Why not? When did our lives become secondary to hers? This is her baby, Lizzy, not ours."

"But it's our *grandchild*." Damn, she was crying again. "I keep asking myself what we would do if Michael or Eric had a family and something happened to them. I know what we would do, Sam. We would take their children and raise them and do whatever it took to make their lives the best they could be. Why is this any different?"

"Because if something happened to Michael or Eric, the choice to walk away from their children wouldn't be theirs. I grant you it won't be easy for Stephanie if she decides to keep her baby, but we'll be there to help her as long as she needs help. I know things are different now, but when you had Michael you were even younger than she is."

"I had a husband who loved me."

"She has parents who love her." Sam put his arm around Elizabeth and drew her into his side. "How do you think this kid would feel being raised by us and seeing his real mother meet someone and get married—I sure as hell hope that's the way it happens next time—and have children that she keeps?"

"The same way I felt when I saw my sisters for the first time."

Sam handed her a tissue. "Multiply that by three-hundred-and-sixty-five days a year every year for the rest of your life."

"There's a perverse kind of comfort in the fact that Jessie didn't keep any of us."

"Equal opportunity abandonment." He pressed a kiss to the top of her head. "Speaking of which, you didn't say much after your last meeting."

"I'm still thinking about it. Jessie's version of his marriage to my mother doesn't sound anything like hers—especially the part about her being the one who wanted to end it. It's not as if he tries to make himself sound blameless. It's more that he seems to think what happened was his fault because he went through with the marriage in the first place and then hung on as long as he did."

"It surprises you that your mother 'remembers' things differently?"

"Why would she lie?"

"I've never understood why your mother does a lot of the things she does. Maybe you should ask her."

"I will—but not yet. I'm starting to remember things on my own, and I don't want her version getting in the way."

"What kind of things?"

It hurt to say it aloud. "How happy I was when I was with Jessie. I thought I'd made up all those early memories when it was just my dad and me and Frank. Now I know they're real. They happened when my mother was in the hospital.

"So many things are coming back." She burrowed deeper into Sam's side, pressing her face into the soft cotton of his shirt, breathing in faint traces of deodorant and aftershave. "Just the other day I was at the grocery store and this image came to me of Jessie starting my orange. He'd take a bite out of the peel and run his thumb under the circle until it was separated enough that I could finish it myself.

"Then on the way home last month I started thinking about the time I was sitting in the back of the truck watching him and Frank throw a football. I saw a huge spider on the truck window. I was convinced it was about to attack me and let out a scream that scared the birds out of the cherry tree. Frank threw the football where I was pointing. It ricocheted off the truck and sailed through the kitchen window where my mother was putting the finishing touches on the cake she'd baked for her Bakersfield Beautification Committee meeting. Daddy laughed so hard he was wiping tears. Frank and I knew better. We took off for the neighbors'."

"How long did you stay?"

"I don't remember that part."

"You were that afraid of your mother?"

"Everyone was." She frowned. "Our friends didn't respect my mother, they feared her. She was never overt when she went after someone, she was intractable."

"What else do you remember about Jessie?"

A flood of warmth washed over her. "So many things now that I let myself," she said softly. "Like how small my hand felt in his." She sat up to look at Sam. "How could I remember things like that and forget how much I loved him?"

Forty-two

Elizabeth

Christina pulled the Mustang to a stop in front of a log-cabin-looking lodge. "How did you find this place?"

"On the Internet," Elizabeth said. "Clark Gable used to stay here. I thought it was fitting."

"And you used that as a recommendation?"

"Give me a little credit." Elizabeth had expected Christina to be edgy, not bitchy. So far she'd had more fun on Eric's fifth-grade outing to a sewer plant.

"Looks a little pricy."

"Actually, it wasn't bad."

"How much do I owe you?"

"Six-hundred-and-eighty dollars."

"For one night?"

"I got separate rooms."

"I don't care if they've got Gable propped up in the bed, there's no way I'm going—"

"You're rich, what do you care?"

"I'm not rich yet."

Elizabeth smiled slyly. "And it didn't cost that much either. Loosen up, would you?"

"You bitch." It was said with a return smile and an odd affection.

"Stop worrying. This thing is going to go down like a fireman on a greased pole."

Christina glanced at Elizabeth before she opened the car door. "You're showing your age."

"Bitch," Elizabeth mumbled.

"I heard that."

"You were meant to."

They checked in, cleaned up, and met in the lobby. Christina arrived first. Elizabeth found her talking to the desk clerk. She gave Elizabeth a toothy smile. "You'll never believe this. Joey here"—she nodded toward the clerk—"has a film in the festival. He says a lot of the film people who came in early have been meeting at the Wandering Moose Bar and Grill. What do you think? Doesn't it sound like fun to go there and listen in?"

"Yeah . . . I guess." They weren't supposed to see Randy until the next night, after the awards. She took Christina's arm and steered her away from the counter. "What if we run into Randy?"

"Then we serve him the papers a day early."

"I thought you wanted to—" What difference did it make when Christina confronted him? "Never mind. Just give me a second. I forgot something in the room." Elizabeth couldn't fit the pepper spray in her purse without taking everything else out, so she'd left it in her suitcase.

The Wandering Moose was big and dark and noisy, although not even half full. Christina looked around. "I don't see Randy. Let's take that table over there so we can watch the door."

Now she was having fun—which made it even harder for Elizabeth to appear blasé. She told herself this was as close as she

314 ❖ *Georgia Bockoven*

would ever get to being in a detective novel, her all-time favorite kind of book, and she was going to make the most of it, even if only in her imagination.

A tall bleached-blond girl with thighs that looked liposuctioned and breasts that looked like the depository of the fat came up to them. "What can I getcha?"

"Coffee," Elizabeth said.

"Decaf?"

What was it with this under-thirty crowd? Elizabeth wasn't even fifty and felt like she'd been labeled. "No, regular. Black and strong."

"Whoa," Christina said. "Impressive." She looked at the cocktail waitress. "I'll have the same."

"So, what are we looking for—tall, short, skinny, fat?" Elizabeth asked when the waiter had gone.

"Tall, dark, shoulder-length brown hair, blue eyes, an athlete's build."

"Careful, you're sounding wistful."

"He'll show up with a girl. She'll be beautiful. If she's not," Christina added, "she'll have money."

"Hindsight?"

"What?"

"I'm assuming you wouldn't have stayed with him if you'd figured this out earlier." The waitress brought their coffee. Elizabeth put a ten on her tray and told her to keep the change. When Christina shot her a questioning look, she said, "I thought she could use it. Her roots are starting to show."

Christina burst out laughing. "You go, girl."

Elizabeth settled deeper into the corner of the booth. Fresno had bars like this—rough-and-tumble, located on the seedier side of town, guys coming and going wearing Levi or leather vests, the women in tight clothes and big hair. Fresno, Bakersfield, and all the surrounding small towns in between were pockets of country—

music, attitude, and style. The region had as little in common with its liberal neighbors in Los Angeles and San Francisco as George Bush and Al Gore. When she finally talked Sam into taking her to a bar like this at home she was a little disappointed at how ordinary it was—a little like a roadside diner only with less light and more junk sitting around.

Someone young and good-looking appeared in the doorway. She touched Christina's hand to get her attention. "Is that him?"

Christina's eyes narrowed against the light pouring in behind him. "Nope."

"Close?"

"Not even." She studied his companion. "But I know the guy with him." She scooted out of the booth. "Excuse me, I'll be right back."

"You want me to come with you?"

"For crying out—" Christina paused to rethink what she was about to say. "No, it's okay. He's an old friend from school."

The waitress appeared. "You ready for a refill?"

"Sure," Elizabeth told her. She watched Christina approach the guy, saw him pull back in surprise, grin, and give her a quick hug. They talked for several minutes, his facial expression going from surprised to serious to commiserating. After several more minutes they hugged, Christina gave a little wave, and she returned to the booth.

"Let's get out of here," she said, reaching for her purse.

"Why?"

"Randy pulled out this morning."

"Why?"

"He found out the film didn't place."

Elizabeth couldn't tell whether Christina was more disappointed that she'd missed Randy or that her film had been rejected. "I thought they weren't going to announce the winners until—"

"He knew one of the women on the panel."

"Well, shit."

"My thoughts exactly."

"Now what?"

The waitress came by holding the coffeepot, giving them a questioning look. Changing her mind about leaving, Christina sat down again. "Screw the coffee. I'll have a beer."

Bailey's over ice, Elizabeth's usual bar drink, seemed embarrassingly quaint. "I'll have a Cosmo," she said, having no idea what it was, only that her kids talked about them.

The first sip of the innocent-looking drink took Elizabeth's breath away. The second went down easier. To keep from drinking on an empty stomach, she started shelling and eating the peanuts the waitress had brought with their drinks.

"How long were you and Randy together?" she asked, looking for something to distract Christina from her disappointment.

"Two years. I was still in school when we met." She ran her finger down the icy glass in a zigzag pattern. "We started dating and discovered we were both fired up about doing an independent film. I wanted it to be something with social conscience. He didn't care, so we settled on *Illegal Alien.*"

Elizabeth caught the attention of the waitress and motioned to her empty glass.

"Thirsty?" Christina asked pointedly.

"Yeah, a little." More than that, she needed something to do with her hands, something to hang on to. "Have you noticed that guy at the bar keeps looking at us?" she said, changing the subject.

"That's what guys in bars do," Christina said. "He probably thinks we're here looking to hook up with someone."

"You mean he's flirting with us?"

"Oh, please," Christina groaned. "When was the last time you had a night out with the girls?"

"I go out with 'the girls' all the time." To afternoon teas and movies and shopping, never anything like this. "None of them are like you, of course."

"Meaning?"

What *did* she mean by that? "All of my friends are pretty much like me."

"Oh—you mean boring."

"Why do you do that?" Elizabeth shot back, disappointed. Every time she thought they were past the sniping, Christina hit her with a zinger.

Instead of snapping back the way she usually did, Christina took her time and glanced around, looking at everyone except Elizabeth. "I don't know," she finally admitted.

"Does your mother talk to you that way?"

"My mother? Where did that come from?"

"I see my mother in myself sometimes. It kills me when it happens, but there it is. I figure you had to have gotten your defensiveness from somewhere—or someone."

"My grandmother once told me that my mother and I didn't get along because we were too much alike. I thought it was the meanest thing anyone had ever said to me."

"Are you? Alike, I mean."

"If she's had any influence over me it's my determination to be nothing like her. Every decision she makes is based on how it's going to look to others. My whole life everything revolved around what will Grandpa think, or Enrique, or the neighbors. When I came home with the broken jaw, she had a whole story worked out about how I fell off the stage during rehearsals. I didn't have any choice but to go along with a lie that just kept growing."

Elizabeth wasn't going to say anything, then thought what the hell and stuck her neck out. "Was it her idea to let me and Ginger and Rachel think that was the way it happened, too?"

Christina glared at her. "And your point is?"

"Maybe she was just trying to protect you."

"She was ashamed of me."

"How can you be so sure?" Elizabeth asked gently.

"She's always been ashamed of me."

The waitress came by to check on their drinks. Elizabeth nodded that they would take another round, even though Christina wasn't half through her first beer. "Why do you think that?"

"I'm not going there with you. It's none of your business."

"Give it a rest, Christina. What possible harm could it do to open up a little? You think there's some big reward waiting for you at the end of your life because you kept everything inside?"

"You're not going to let this go, are you?"

"Nope."

"All right—I'm lighter-skinned than anyone else in my family." When Elizabeth didn't respond, she added, "That makes it obvious I don't belong. It's like flashing a great big neon sign that Enrique wasn't my mother's first husband."

"And that's a bad thing?"

"In a Catholic society? Are you kidding?"

Their drinks arrived. "So why didn't she just give you to Jessie?"

"Probably because he didn't want me either."

The pain in Christina's voice stopped Elizabeth cold. "Fuck."

Christina laughed. "Well put."

Elizabeth finished her drink and motioned for another. "I'm surprised you turned out as well as you did."

"Thanks—I think."

"Oh, I mean it in the best way."

Ten minutes later, when Elizabeth had finished her third drink and started on her fourth, Christina stared at her and asked carefully, "Do you always drink like this?"

It was one of those have-you-stopped-beating-your-wife questions that Elizabeth wasn't sure how to answer. "No. Never. But don't worry, I'm fine." She grinned. "My kids drink these all the time. How strong can they be? Besides, they're really good and I'm really thirsty."

"Personally, I think they taste like lighter fluid."

Elizabeth laughed, a little too long and a lot too hard, a sure sign she was relaxing. Plainly she hadn't realized how tense she'd been over the prospect of confronting Randy. She was actually having a good time just sitting and talking to Christina. "I'm beginning to think I might like you after all."

Christina groaned and rolled her eyes. "You're a sloppy drunk, aren't you? Maybe we should order something to eat."

"Not for me. These peanuts are plenty. And I'm not even close to being drunk." Only the peanuts were gone. When she held up the empty bowl the waitress assumed she was asking for another drink, too, and brought both.

"Last one," she told Christina. "Soon as I'm finished, we'll find someplace to eat." But first she had to go to the bathroom. "I'll be right back. If one of Randy's friends should happen to come in while I'm gone, don't do anything. Wait for me."

"And what am I supposed to do if they see me?"

If it wasn't sarcasm Elizabeth detected in Christina's voice, it was something close to it. "Cover your face."

Christina shook her head. "Oh great. I've got a drunk for a bodyguard."

"I'm not drunk," Elizabeth insisted. And she wasn't, or at least she didn't feel like she was. Until she stood up. Then it was as if the room had tilted one way and she'd gone the other. Her hands and feet felt numb, her lips nonexistent. When had that happened?

She'd never experienced anything like this. With concentrated, towering effort, she grabbed hold of the part of her mind that still functioned with some lucidity and directed her feet to transport her to the bathroom.

Her hand on the back of the seat for support, she stood very,

very still, plotting her course across the room. She could do this. One step at a time, threading her way around the tables. No. She'd never make it that way. Too many obstacles. Around the room then, booth by booth. That way she could hang on to the backs of seats and no one would notice. It was dark in the bar. People held on to things in the dark. Normal. Natural.

She started. She could do this. She had to do this. Christina couldn't know. She'd never hear the end of it.

She made it, only weaving once or twice, covering the seemingly odd steps by stopping to study butchered, dusty heads of deer and elk and moose hanging on the walls along the way.

Once safely inside the bathroom, she stumbled to the sink and looked at herself in the mirror. "*Ohmygod*," she murmured to the stranger looking back. "Ohmygod, ohmygod, ohmygod."

"Do something," the stranger demanded. "Christina can't know."

She soaked paper towels in cold water and plastered them to her face, then slapped her cheeks and wrists. It didn't help. *Ohmygod*. She wasn't getting better, she was actually getting worse. Now the room was spinning. How could that happen? She closed her eyes. Bad idea. More water, more slapping, still drunk.

She had to get back before Christina came looking for her. She took one last look in the mirror. Her hair was wet and looked scary. She opened her purse to dig for her comb and remembered she'd taken everything out to accommodate the pepper spray. The hell with her hair.

Christina wasn't at the table. She was at the bar, talking to a guy with dark, shoulder-length hair—a guy with a cute girl at his side.

Christina had an envelope in her hand. *The restraining order.* What the . . . and then it hit her. The friend had lied. Randy hadn't left. Christina tried to give him the envelope. Suspicious, he looked down at her outstretched hand. He must have realized what she was trying to do because he jerked back and threw his hands up in the air. His face contorted in anger, he said something to Christina and began backing toward the door. She went after him, slapping the envelope against his chest. He grabbed her wrist and twisted her arm behind her back. She aimed a kick, missed, and tried again, the second time connecting with his shin.

A blinding protective instinct hit Elizabeth with the force of a mother defending her child. "Let go of her, you son of a bitch," she roared. She dug into her purse for the pepper spray as she flung herself across the room. Out of the corner of her eye, she saw the man who'd been flirting with them earlier leap up from his bar stool.

Randy had a friend and he was coming after her. She had to get to Christina.

Elizabeth brought the pepper spray up and pointed it at the friend's face. Somehow the instructions Sam had made her memorize cut through the Cosmo fog and she managed to get off a shot. But not in the direction she'd intended. A woman beside her screamed and fell. Elizabeth ignored the woman writhing on the floor and tried to get off another shot, but nothing happened. She did the only thing she could think to do next—hit him with the can. Hard. He swore, brought his hand up to touch the wound, and glared at her.

"What the fuck?" he moaned.

Blood poured down the side of his face. The sober corner of Elizabeth's mind reassured her it wasn't serious. Any mother of sons knew even small head wounds bleed a lot.

Without warning, something hit the backs of her knees and she dropped to the floor in a heap. The man looked down at her, dripping blood on her blouse, a mixture of concern, anger, and something she couldn't identify on his face. "Get away from me," she shouted. Or at least she thought she shouted.

She still had the pepper spray in her hand and brought it up, pointed it at him, and this time managed to get off a shot in the right direction.

He howled and grabbed her arm. "Jesus, lady—you're crazy."

"Elizabeth?" Christina pushed the man out of the way. "What happened? Are you all right? What's going on?"

"That man"—Elizabeth pointed to the man desperately wiping his eyes and spreading blood all over his face—"that man—" Again the sober part of her mind spoke up, this time sending a warning. She was going to be sick. She tried to get up but only made it to her knees. Disgusting sounds came from her, followed by disgusted sounds from everyone around her. Oh, God—she would never ever eat peanuts again. And she would never drink again. Not ever. Not even at her children's weddings.

With Christina's help, she managed to stand, but when she tried to walk it felt like her legs had flesh but no bones. Christina clamped her hands around Elizabeth's arm to keep her from falling. "Did he hurt you?" Elizabeth asked, determined to fulfill the role she'd come to play.

She saw Christina's lips moving but couldn't hear the answer. The room started spinning, then turned into a shrinking circle that grew smaller and smaller. She blinked. The circle disappeared. It was the last thing she remembered.

Later, when she woke up in a hospital room and opened her eyes, it felt like knives of light were being shot into her pupils. She immediately closed them again. She had an Academy Award–winning headache, a runaway contender in a field that included sinus and migraines.

"It's about time," Christina said.

"What am I doing here?" she asked, moving her lips and jaw as little as possible.

"Waiting for lab results to see if someone slipped something into your drink before the police officially arrest you for assault and battery," she said casually. "The officer said something about charging you with drunk and disorderly conduct and disturbing the peace, but I think they're going to drop those and concentrate on the charge that carries the longest jail term, assault and battery."

"I'm going to be sick."

"Impossible. There can't be anything left."

"I'm serious." Elizabeth sat up, her hand over her mouth. Christina handed her a kidney-shaped plastic container. Elizabeth gagged, her stomach heaved, nothing came up.

"I told you, you're empty," Christina said.

"Ohmygod," Elizabeth groaned. The evening was coming back to her in horrifying snatches. "Please tell me I didn't do what I think I did."

Christina dragged the chair she'd been sitting in over to the bed. "You don't know the half of it. The man you assaulted? Sam hired him. He's a private detective."

It took several seconds to absorb this latest bit of news. "A private detective?" she repeated, incredulous. "Why?"

"To protect us. He was on our tail the whole way."

And then it hit her. "Sam knows what happened?"

"Every detail."

Elizabeth groaned again. "I need to be sick." Christina reached for the plastic container. "Not that kind of sick, the kind that will keep me in Oregon until he misses me more than he's mad at me."

"I think the cops might take care of that for you."

"Am I really going to be charged with all those things?" People went to prison for assault. She tried to picture herself behind bars, confined in a cell with a toilet attached to the wall, sleeping on a hard narrow bed, Sam taking time off work to visit, her children humiliated.

"Don't you dare cry," Christina threatened. "I've been through enough histrionics in the past couple of hours to last a lifetime. By the way, nice shot with the pepper spray. That was Randy's girlfriend."

"I was aiming for the detective."

"I figured as much. But not to worry, you got him, too."

The scream and string of profanity that followed the misdirected shot came back to her in horrifying detail. "Is she all right?"

"They brought her in and cleaned her up, and according to Randy, she's back to her good old double-D-cup self." Christina propped her feet on the railing under the bed. "I thought Randy had better taste in women. How could he go from me to her?"

"Did you at least get him served?" Elizabeth was looking for a bright spot in the fiasco.

"Yeah, but I changed my mind. Seeing him made me realize I want my freedom more than I want my movie. I have a hundred movies ahead of me—fighting for this one isn't worth being connected to him again."

"So after all of this you just gave it to him?"

"Pretty much."

A nurse appeared in the doorway. "Good. You're awake. I'll let the officer know."

"I need a lawyer," Elizabeth said when the nurse was gone. "Do you suppose Lucy knows anyone up here?" She thought about trying to explain to Lucy what she'd done and groaned. "This is so embarrassing."

Christina responded with a half-ass grin. "I guess you've suffered enough. I might as well tell you, the detective isn't pressing charges. Neither is the bar—not after I told them you'd pay for the damages."

"What damages?"

"Some broken glasses, a couple of broken chairs. You created a panic when you let loose with that spray."

"What about Randy's girlfriend?"

"She's taken care of, too."

"And the detective?"

"I think Sam must have offered him something, because he was really happy when he left. He said we weren't to worry about anything, that it was all taken care of."

"How did you get Randy to—" But then she knew. Her heart sunk. "That's the real reason you gave him the movie."

"That's why he *thinks* I gave him the movie. I told you the real reason."

"So he gets away with both the movie and breaking your jaw? It's not fair."

"We'll cross paths again someday. I can wait."

A uniformed police officer came to the door. "How are you feeling?" he asked Elizabeth.

"Like an idiot."

He chuckled. "Can't say I blame you."

"I'm really sorry about the mess I caused."

"Looks like everyone's willing to forgive you. But I'd leave the pepper spray home next time."

"Does that mean she's free to go?" Christina asked.

"As long as you don't travel outside the area." At her stunned expression he grinned. "Just kidding. You can leave whenever you want."

"A cop with a sense of humor," Christina said.

Being careful not to move her head too quickly, Elizabeth sat up. "That lets him out of an airport job."

"Cute."

"Do you know what shape my clothes are in?"

"I brought clean." She went to the closet and retrieved Elizabeth's suitcase.

Elizabeth looked at her. "I owe you an apology. A big one."

"No, you don't. You were only trying to help."

"You needed that kind of help like a drowning man needs an anchor."

"You were willing to risk life and limb to protect me. Besides, turns out you're a pretty cheap drunk. What more could a girl ask for in a sister?" Christina smiled and added a wink.

The action jolted Elizabeth. "Dad used to do that."

"Do what?"

"Wink when he smiled."

"I don't do that," Christina said. "Do I?"

"You just did."

"Show me."

Elizabeth did, then saw by Christina's stunned expression that the wink held memories for her, too. "I wonder if we'll ever be able to truly forgive him."

"I just want to understand," Christina said softly.

Forty-three

Rachel

"It's my birthday," Rachel announced.

"Today?" Ginger took the P Street off ramp, dropping them off the elevated freeway onto Sacramento surface streets. "You should have said something. I know Lucy would have let us change the meeting date."

"I don't celebrate my birthday." Rachel didn't understand why she was telling Ginger. She never talked about her birthday, not even to Jeff. "I never have."

"Never? Not even when you were a kid?"

"When you're a kid, you need a mother who remembers. Mine never did. I don't think the day I was born was one of her better days."

"I can't imagine what it must have been like growing up the way you did."

"Did you ever move and have to change schools?"

"Once."

"Do you remember how lost you felt?"

"Like it was yesterday. It was Mrs. Springer's fifth-grade class.

I was terrified that everyone would make fun of me and that I'd never make friends."

"I was that new kid in class twenty-three times. I almost didn't take my last promotion because it meant Cassidy would have to change schools, but then Jeff convinced me she was young enough that it wouldn't bother her."

"This is leading up to something, isn't it?"

Rachel laughed. "You know it's spooky the way we connect sometimes, almost as if we really were sisters."

"Aren't we?"

"Sisters with history. If biology mattered, I would have felt a connection with my mother."

"Does she know about Jessie and the money?"

"My mother's dead," Rachel said.

Ginger gasped. "When?"

"I was a senior in high school—prom night." The theme was "Romance Under the Stars," and Rachel had been excused from class the entire day to help with the decorations. "We were living in an old two-story house that had a beautiful curving staircase." They'd been there almost nine months, longer than they'd ever stayed anywhere. Rachel had promised her mother she would move out the day she graduated and give Anna her long-desired freedom—if she would let her finish high school in Portland.

What came next she said in a flat, expressionless voice. "I was at the prom when she tied a rope around her neck and stepped over the railing. I came home, kissed my date good-night at the door, and went inside to find her hanging there."

"Jesus. What a rotten thing to do to you. You must have been devastated."

"She didn't leave a letter, so I don't know why she picked that night. Years later my therapist tried to convince me it had nothing to do with me being at the prom, that Anna chose the time she did because she knew she wouldn't be disturbed. He said most suicides manage to convince themselves they are doing a favor for those they leave behind. And, in a way, he may have been right. I thought we were broke and that I'd have to work my way through college. When I went through her things, I found statements that totaled over a hundred thousand dollars scattered over half a dozen bank accounts. I always figured the money must have come from one of the married men she'd been with who'd bought her off. Now I'm pretty sure it was Jessie."

"If Jessie gave Anna that money, it was because of you. Why would he do that and never try to see you? It doesn't make sense."

"I don't know. I was furious when I got the letter from Lucy saying Jessie wanted to see me. I didn't want to have anything to do with him. Now I'm furious because he died so soon. There are a hundred things I wish I could ask him."

"Maybe some of the answers are on the tapes." They were less than half a block from Jessie's house. Ginger pulled over and stopped. "You were about to say something before we got distracted."

Rachel smiled. "Jeff and I are going away for a couple of days."

"But that's good news—isn't it?"

Now Rachel laughed. "You thought it was something bad just because I led up to it with my mother's suicide?"

"Well . . . yes."

"We're going up the coast to a bed-and-breakfast in Gualala. If it works out, I'm going to move back in."

Ginger stretched across the seat to give her a hug. "That's the best news yet. Have you told Cassidy and John?"

"We don't want to get their hopes up."

"Can I watch the kids?"

Ginger's enthusiasm was like a beautifully wrapped present. "You don't even know which weekend."

"I don't care. Besides, it's not as if I've got anything else to do."

"There's someone out there for you. Someone special."

Ginger waved her off. "I've decided to learn to live single and love it." She glanced in the rearview mirror, but instead of heading for Jessie's, made a U-turn.

"Where are you going?"

"We passed a bakery a couple of blocks back. I'm going to get you a birthday cake—whether you want one or not."

"I really wish you wouldn't."

Ginger affectionately patted Rachel's knee. "Better come up with another wish because you're not getting that one."

The cake was chocolate with blue roses and tasted awful. "I guess it's the thought that counts." Christina put her plate on the coffee table and picked up her coffee.

"I should have chosen the carrot cake," Ginger said.

"I have a great recipe for carrot cake," Elizabeth contributed.

"Now why doesn't that surprise me?" Christina tucked her legs under her and settled deeper into the sofa.

Elizabeth ignored her. "Whose birthday is next?"

Christina and Ginger looked at each other. "I'm August," Christina said.

"February," Ginger said. "But we won't be meeting anymore by then."

A strained silence followed that wasn't broken until Elizabeth said hesitantly, "There's nothing to keep us from getting together for birthdays. It would only be four times a year. Or we could combine them and meet twice a year."

Christina's immediate reaction was to reject the possibility. She was anxious to put the past year behind her. She had places to go, people to meet, a life to get on with. But she was curious to hear what "the twins" had to say before she jumped in with her opinion.

"I think it's a great idea," Ginger said. "If I do move, it will give me a reason to come back."

No surprise there. Ginger had pep rally leader written all over her. Christina waited for Rachel.

"Count me in," Rachel said.

Three pairs of eyes focused on Christina. "I suppose I could make it if I didn't have anything else to do."

"She's not as hard-nosed as she sounds," Elizabeth assured the other two.

"Hear that, Christina? Elizabeth's got your number. So do I, by the way," Rachel said.

"Me, too," Ginger added. "So you might as well forget trying to impress us with how tough you are."

"You don't know the first thing about me. None of you. If you think—" What was she doing? And why? "Okay, I'll give you that sometimes I come off a little strong, and I don't always mean things the way they sound. But that doesn't mean I'm looking to fill my shopping cart with sisters."

"She'll come around," Elizabeth said confidently.

Christina sent her a hostile look. She grabbed the envelope of tapes, dumped them on the table, and put the tape marked number one in the player, then hit the play button. "I should have let them put you in jail."

"Hold on," Ginger said, hitting the stop button. "What's this about jail?"

"Later," Elizabeth answered for her.

Ginger clapped her hands. "My God, you're actually blushing. This has got to be good."

This time Elizabeth hit the play button. Jessie's deep voice and soft Oklahoma drawl brought them up short and reminded them why they were there.

"Later," Elizabeth repeated.

Jessie's Story

We managed to keep our star out of jail on the exposure charge—everyone in L.A. has a script to sell, including, in this case, the boy's father. All parties agreed it was an unfortunate misunderstanding, but the press wasn't buying it. We were front-page news for two days—until Jayne Mansfield's limousine hit a truck. Her story came with better photographs, which moved us to an inside page. A day later we were old news and out of the papers entirely.

We talked ourselves into believing we'd squeaked through and that good reviews would overcome bad publicity and build momentum. We just had to hang on and ride it out. For my part, I was doing everything I could to put a good face on something that made me sick to my stomach. There were big parties every weekend and smaller ones in the middle of the week. I went to them all.

At one of them I met a young woman, Anna Kaplan. She was pretty in the Hollywood way, flashy clothes, too much makeup, eyes filled with promise. She said her date had taken off without her and she needed a ride home. We were in the car when she admitted she didn't actually have a home and would I mind putting her up for the night. She stayed six months. When she left she was pregnant, something I didn't find out about until ten years later when a photograph of a nine-year-old girl in pigtails and a letter asking for money arrived from her lawyer. Anna was in New Orleans at the time. I flew there and arranged to meet her in a hotel coffee shop.

She spotted me right away but took her time crossing the room, giving me opportunity to notice she was still as

*soft and round as Monroe in her prime. She bent to kiss
my cheek before she slid into the chair next to mine.*

"You haven't changed," *she said in a new, thick southern
accent.*

"Neither have you," *I said because I knew it was what
she wanted to hear.*

"Did you bring the money?"

"That's it? No, how have you been, what are you
doing?"

"You've been fine, and you're doing better than I
thought you'd ever do again or I wouldn't have left you.
I read all about your strawberry business in the* Wall
Street Journal *and your Mexican wife and baby in some
business magazine at the doctor's office." She crossed her
legs and leaned in close. "Let's not pretend this means
anything to either of us. I was young and dumb, you
were old and horny—we made a kid."*

"You were never dumb."

She gave me a slow smile. "Please tell me you're not
thinkin' 'bout making this hard on little old me. Wait,
make that young me."

"What's that supposed to mean?"

She reached in her purse and took out her birth certificate.
"Check the date, Jessie. Do the math."

*I did, twice, just to be sure I hadn't made a mistake.
There was no way around it—I'd had sex with a sixteen-
year-old.*

"Now, I realize you can afford some pretty good
lawyers, but it won't matter. How long do you think you
can keep that strawberry business of yours going if you
have to operate it from prison?"

*She was bluffing. She'd researched everything else,
she had to know there was a statute of limitations on*

334 ✤ Georgia Bockoven

statutory rape. I looked at her, trying to decide if she was conniving or desperate and decided it was probably some of both. "I want to see Rachel."

She handed me a photograph. I wanted to look, but needed to make a point, so gave it back without even glancing at it. "The real thing."

"Are you questioning the blood tests?"

"I want to see that she's all right."

She was instantly furious. "What? You think I don't take good care of her?"

"She's my daughter. I want—"

"I knew you would try something like this." She stood and glared at me. "My friend warned me about you. She said you'd pretend to be nice and that you'd try to sweet-talk me into trusting you. And then if I let you see Rachel you'd take her and run away and I'd never see her again. Well, you're not getting her. You can keep your fuckin' money." She was screaming now. "I don't need it."

I went to her lawyer's office and told him what had happened. He said Anna was a little high-strung at times and that she had occasional spells where she heard voices and believed there were people out to get her, but that she came around eventually. He wouldn't give me her address, so I looked for her on my own. I found where she and Rachel had been staying, but by then they'd packed up and were gone.

I hung around talking to her friends and the teachers at Rachel's school. The stories they told were different, but with a common theme. Anna ran because there was someone chasing her. She was good at running, better at hiding.

I went home and mailed the check to the lawyer's

office. It was cashed a couple of months later at a bank in Tulsa, Oklahoma. I never saw or heard from Anna again.

Years later I was talking to a friend about his schizophrenic brother and realized that Anna likely suffered from the same thing. By then Rachel was a grown woman, and there was nothing I could do to help. I'm ashamed to admit I was relieved that I hadn't found out about Anna earlier. I had nothing to recommend me as a father, and Rachel had no reason to trust me.

The first tape ended.

Forty-four

Rachel

"Did you know? Ginger asked.

Feeling like a feather in a tornado, Rachel frowned and tried to focus on the question. "No—I never even guessed. You lose perspective when you live with something like that every day."

"Do you think he's right?" Christina asked.

"I don't know." Could she have been so blinded by her own desperate struggle to survive that she missed seeing that her mother was sick? It explained so much—the mood swings, the paranoia, the deep depressions. Most of all, it explained the long talks Anna had with "Donald" alone in her room. Rachel had always assumed Donald was her mother's euphemism for God. A lot of people talked to God. No one thought they were crazy.

Rachel looked at each woman in turn. "I lived with her for seventeen years. How could I have missed something this important?"

"Not seeing the forest for the trees?" Ginger suggested gently. "Jessie didn't figure it out until years later. Why would you? Personally, I wouldn't know a schizophrenic from a manic depressive from a multiple personality disorder."

"Neither would I," Elizabeth added.

Rachel couldn't sit still any longer. She had to move, to pace, to hit something, to scream. She jumped up and headed toward the hall and the bathroom. "Don't start the second tape. I'll be back in a minute."

She started past Jessie's study, stopped, and looked inside. She'd spent her entire life hating Jessie Reed for sins he hadn't committed, her hatred forming the foundation of her beliefs, the cellophane through which she viewed the world. Now, everything she'd known to be true was a lie, even her mother's tortured existence. Anna Kaplan had died insane and alone at thirty-four, two years younger than Rachel was now. Had the demon who inhabited Anna's mind guided her to the stairs or, exhausted from the battle, had she made the decision on her own?

If she believed Jessie, she had to forgive her mother all the moves in the middle of the night, the men, the missed birthdays, the broken promises. And she had to forgive Jessie for not coming to rescue her, and God for not answering her prayers.

How could it be that after all these years of hurt and anger there was no one to blame for the lost child who had cried herself to sleep at night?

Jessie's Story

It was in October when I got a telegram from Denise saying Frank had joined the Army, completed his basic training, and that if I wanted to see him before he shipped out, I'd better get home. At first I thought it was some kind of sick joke. He was only seventeen, due to graduate high school early that coming January and start college the next fall. He'd been accepted to Stanford— something I busted buttons telling everyone who would listen. No one in my family had finished high school, and my son was going to college. And not just any college, Stanford. There was no way he'd joined the Army. And if he had, if he'd forged a birth certificate, they were damn well going to let him out.

I'd been in Mexico almost half a year drumming up investment money for a movie that was going to shut down production if I couldn't come up with another half-million dollars by the end of the year. I'd tried calling Frank and Elizabeth when I was in Mexico City but either couldn't get through or wound up talking to Denise, who always promised to have one or the other of the kids call me, but neither ever did. I should have tried harder or wondered more that I never got an answer to any of my letters, but figured we'd make up for lost time when I got home. I've lived the rest of my life with dreams where I go back and change things, where I come home to find out the things I needed to know. They bring me a strange peace that's all wrapped up in a ribbon of sadness for what might have been.

I made it to Bakersfield in two days. It was hot, and the wind was blowing the sand and dirt so hard even the birds were walking. Denise met me at the door and talked to me through the screen. She asked how I was. I answered with, "How the hell did this happen?" I shouldn't have shouted. It stiffened her spine and set the tone for what would follow.

"Don't you dare yell at me."

"Goddamn it, Denise, I don't have time for this. Where is Frank?"

"He's gone. You missed him." I swear she was about to smile but thought better of it at the last second. "I told you that you didn't have much time."

"What do you mean, gone?" I didn't want to find out later that he was at a friend's house.

"Shipped out."

The words were her bullets, my soul the target. Even though I knew the answer, there was no way around asking, "Where?"

"Vietnam."

Men came home from war. I had. But a lot of men didn't. Some died from stupid mistakes, some died from being in the wrong place at the wrong time, some just died. "He's seventeen. They wouldn't have let him in without someone signing for him."

"It was what he wanted. I saw no reason to stop him."

I hit my fist on the wood surrounding the screen, splintering it. Denise jumped, the smug look gone. "If something happens to him it's on your shoulders."

"My shoulders?" she screamed. "You're the reason he went. He thought he could get your attention. He wanted you to be proud of him." She added the last with a sneer.

"I've always been proud of him."

"How was he supposed to know that? You haven't seen him—or Elizabeth—in over five months, and it was three months before that. They had no idea where you were. You didn't call, you didn't write. What was he supposed to think?"

I didn't try to defend myself against accusations she knew as well as I did weren't true. I had no defense for what was true. I'd let myself get caught up in trying to save my business, believing Frank and Lizzy would understand and that I could make it up to them that summer. Some people are slow learners, others it takes *getting hit up-side the head with a two-by-four. Nothing had ever hit me harder.* "Where's Lizzy?"

"She's not here."

"I want to see her."

"She doesn't want to see you."

"Since when?"

"Since Frank left. She blames you."

"Then I need to talk to her."

"You can't."

It was everything I could do to stop myself pulling what was left of the screen door off its hinges. "Why not?"

"She's in Texas with my mother and father."

She might as well have told me that Lizzy was sitting on the moon. "Why isn't she in school?"

"She is in school—in Texas." *She put her hand up to the screen and showed me a diamond ring.* "I got married, and Mama offered to let Elizabeth stay with her a couple of months while me and Harry settled in."

"When is she coming back?"

"We're going there for Christmas. She'll come home with us then."

"I'm not waiting that long to see her."

"You know how my father feels about you. The minute you step foot on his land he'll have you thrown in jail—or he might just shoot you. And don't even think about calling. They won't let you talk to her."

The threat would have had teeth twenty years before, but I'd made enough men in Yokum County rich that I figured I had some pull. What I needed was to know where I stood in California if I went to Texas and brought Lizzy home with me.

I never found out. I got a phone call from Denise telling me Frank was dead the same day I had an appointment to see the attorney about bringing Lizzy home. Frank hadn't been off the plane two full days and he was gone. He didn't die in the jungle in one of the battles that made the evening news. He was in a mess tent when a Vietnamese girl that Frank's lieutenant said couldn't have been more than sixteen years old set off a grenade. It killed her and Frank and sent seven others home for good.

I got on my knees that night and prayed like I had never prayed. I'd accepted what I'd been taught in Bible School as a kid that it was God's will and His mysterious ways that had taken Ma and Pa and my brother and sister and grandmother the way they had gone, but I was having trouble with Frank. I was doing some hard bargaining with God, my soul for ten seconds with Frank, just long enough to tell him I was sorry and that I loved him and that no man had ever been prouder of his son.

The sun was peeking over the Los Angeles mountains when I gave up on God and made the same offer to the devil. He didn't answer either. I'd offered my soul and had no takers. I'd saved a movie and lost a son. Perhaps I didn't have a soul.

The second tape ended.

Forty-five

Elizabeth

"It's a lie," Elizabeth said, shaken. "That's not the way it happened. Frank didn't want to join the Army, my mother made him." The memories fought for the surface like bubbles from a diver's mask. "They got into a terrible fight about Daddy. I remember Frank said he was sick to death of living with my mother and that he was going to call Daddy to see if he could go to Mexico with him. He was so mad he was yelling. We were in big trouble when we raised our voices to my mother, but he didn't care. He kept on until he got it all out.

"It went downhill after that. Frank said he hated her and that the day he turned eighteen he was moving in with Daddy no matter how she felt about it. She went crazy and took a pan off the stove and hit him. He knocked a chair over when he fell. The way it sounded and the way he reacted, I thought she'd broken his arm for sure, but she didn't stop to check. I'd never seen her so mad. She stood over him and screamed that if he wanted to get away from her so badly, she was going to help him. She made him get up and change his shirt, and then she took him away in the car. When they came back Frank told me he was in the Army and leaving for basic training at Fort Ord the next day.

"He promised to write, but I never got any letters. I guess he never wrote to Daddy—" She paused and thought about what she'd called Jessie. "I guess he never wrote to Jessie. One of his friends told me later that he came to see me before he left for Vietnam, but I was in Texas. He didn't say whether Frank spent any time at home."

"Did he get along with your stepfather?" Rachel asked.

"There was no stepfather. At least none that I know of. I don't know why she told Jessie she was married."

"She had to know he would find out," Christina said, incredulous.

Rachel took the clip from her hair and tossed it on the table, shaking her hair free and running her hands through the sides. She toed off her loafers and pulled her legs up to sit yoga fashion. "If there was no stepfather, then why did your mother send you to Texas?"

The question threw Elizabeth. She remembered the time on the ranch vividly, her mornings filled with school, afternoons riding horses with her grandfather or baking bread with her grandmother. Her nights were filled with shadows on her bedroom ceiling, images she manipulated into moving pictures of happier times. She'd asked why she was there and when she was going home, but no one ever answered. "I never understood why I was sent there."

Christina got up and left the room without saying anything. She was back less than a minute later, a small, velvet-covered box cradled in her hand. "I think this belongs to you."

Elizabeth hesitated, afraid of what she would find. "It's all right," Christina said, intuitively understanding.

Elizabeth took the box and opened it. Inside was a medal— the ribbon worn to the point of fraying, the features on the face stamped on the heart-shaped metal almost indistinguishable. "It's Frank's Purple Heart," she said in a hushed whisper.

With reverence afforded holy objects, Elizabeth removed the medal. An image she hadn't been able to summon clearly for years came to her—Frank turning to wave at her as he boarded the Greyhound bus for Fort Ord. "Don't forget me," he'd said. They were the last words he'd spoken to her.

She held the medal in her palm and looked at it through mist-filled eyes. She could feel the love and regret and yearning that had poured from Jessie with every thumb stroke across the metal heart. He must have carried it constantly, a reminder of what he'd lost.

Frank would forever be her older brother, locked in her memory as someone she'd looked up to, wise and caring. As she stared at all that was left of him, for a blinding moment she saw him as he really had been—a boy, never to become a man. He was seventeen years old when he died, four years younger than Stephanie was now. He was scared when he got on the bus. She wasn't old enough to understand why. Looking back, she was heartbroken as she remembered the fear and loneliness in his eyes. She mentally wrapped the child he'd been in the arms of the mother she had become. Pain filled her anew as she thought about how he had never known the joy of finding the girl of his dreams, the feel of his child's hand cradled in his, or the adoration of his nephews and niece.

"Where did you get this?" she asked Christina.

"In Jessie's study on a bookshelf by itself."

"Did you find anything else?"

"I haven't looked through his personal belongings. I didn't think I should without the rest of you."

"Do you have a photograph of Frank?" Ginger asked.

"Not with me—" As strange as it was to contemplate, Frank was their brother, too. "I'll bring it next time." She smiled.

"He looked like Jessie. Maybe that was why my mother didn't like him."

Rachel held out her hand. "May I?"

Elizabeth handed her the medal.

"How sad," she said softly. "You can almost feel Jessie's pain."

"How did your mother treat you?" Ginger asked.

"After Frank died she almost suffocated me with attention. I couldn't go anywhere without her."

"What about Jessie?"

"I never saw him again."

"Never?" Christina asked.

"Not one time. My mother wouldn't let me come home for the funeral, she said it was more important for me to finish my school year in Texas and that she would visit me there. When we came back to California and I asked about seeing my father, she told me he'd become a drunk and didn't want anything to do with her or me."

"Did you try contacting him?" Rachel pushed.

"The telephone number I had was disconnected. I wrote letters, but he never answered."

"And gave them to your mother to mail?" Rachel pushed again.

An ugly truth, almost forty years gestating, began its birth process. "Are you saying you think she didn't send them? Why would she do that?"

"I'm not saying anything. It just strikes me as odd that Jessie would drop out of the life of someone he loved as much as he obviously loved you and never make any attempt to get back in. He may have become a drunk, but it couldn't have lasted long. We know he met Christina's mother, and we know he started a strawberry business and then lost it. We also know he started whatever it was that he did here in Sacramento that made him so rich. There has to be more to the story."

"Like?" The memory of the attempts Jessie had made to see her made Elizabeth feel as if a lead jacket had been slipped over her shoulders.

Instead of answering, Rachel asked, "Is your mother still alive?"

"Yes."

"I think she's the one you need to talk to."

There were some things Denise Reed wouldn't discuss, and Jessie Reed was one of them. If knowing the truth would make a difference, whatever battle she had to fight with her mother to gain that truth would be worth the effort. But maybe not. Nothing could bring Frank back. And nothing could give her the years she'd missed with her father.

Forty-six

Elizabeth

On her way to her mother's house, Elizabeth drove by the home she'd lived in as a child. The new owners had removed the porch and extended the living room, torn off the clapboard, and replaced it with stucco and brick. The only thing they hadn't changed or updated was the sprawling oak on the front lawn. Frank used to perch there in the summer, stretched out on a thick branch high enough to be hidden from the people passing below whose gazes never rose above the horizon. Once in a while he would let her join him, but she never lasted long—sitting still was hard enough, not talking was impossible.

Her mother had lived in the rambling two-story house until five years ago, when failing eyesight and an inner ear problem made climbing stairs a hazard. Now she lived in a bright, two-bedroom, cookie-cutter house in a senior citizens' complex on the opposite side of Bakersfield. The complex boasted a golf course, shopping center, and clubhouse with enough scheduled activities and classes to satisfy the most discriminating senior—a guaranteed social life, according to the sales brochure. No more sitting around the house waiting for a call from the children and grandchildren. Now, when the call finally came, odds were they wouldn't find anyone home.

Elizabeth pulled into the driveway of the pseudo-Spanish stucco house, painted the prescribed brown on tan, surrounded with community-dictated landscaping and fencing. She rang the doorbell, and within seconds heard her mother shuffling across the terra cotta tile to answer.

"You're late."

Elizabeth kissed her cheek and handed her the potted orange chrysanthemum she'd picked up at the grocery store. The plant was wrapped in orange cellophane with a big black bow, a ghost and witch peeking out of the ribbon. "Happy Halloween."

Denise looked at the plant with suspicion. "We don't decorate for Halloween in Rancho Villa. No sense to it with no kids around. I'm surprised you didn't figure that out for yourself."

"It's a plant, Mom, not a pumpkin. You can take the decorations off if they bother you."

"Don't get snippy. I was just letting you know in case one of the kids was thinking about doing something special for me." She went into the living room and put the mum on an end table. "This way I'll be able to see it when I'm working in the kitchen."

Elizabeth followed, dropping her purse on the rocker opposite the fireplace. As much as Elizabeth missed the old house, she had to admit that moving had been good for her mother. Not only had she traded in her polyester wardrobe and learned how to use a computer, she'd started traveling. The plaid crop pants and matching short-sleeve top she had on today weren't flattering, but they were more stylish than anything she'd owned for the past twenty years. And finally, after a lifetime of wearing her stick-straight hair in a bun at the back of her head, she'd had it cut and permed. The soft curls that framed her angular face made her look years younger and half as fearsome.

Elizabeth gave her mother points for trying, something new to their relationship and welcome. "The house looks nice. I like the sofa. When did you buy it?"

"I didn't. I saw it sitting in Betty's driveway last week and went over to ask what it was doing there. Her kids said they were getting ready to haul it to the dump." She grinned. "I told them they could haul it over here and take mine to the dump instead."

"Betty's redecorating?"

"She died. Two weeks ago. Went to bed and never got up. Coffee?"

"Uh, sure." The quality of her mother's coffee was dependent on whether it was the first or second time she'd used the grounds. Ten o'clock in the morning usually meant recycled. "Do you have any cream?"

"I made it fresh. You don't have to doctor it." She handed Elizabeth a mug and refilled her own. "You might as well have a seat and get started on why you came. No sense dragging this out."

Elizabeth settled into the sofa. "I want to talk to you about my father."

"I figured this was coming." Denise moved Elizabeth's purse and took the rocker. "I already told you that I don't want anything to do with the money he left you. Whatever it was, it's yours. I'm doing fine without it."

"It's not about the money." Elizabeth stopped to take a deep breath. With her anger modified by curiosity, confronting her mother wasn't as easy as she'd expected. "I didn't tell you before, because I didn't want to upset you, but Jessie left tapes. I've been listening to them for the past couple of months with my sisters."

Denise started rocking slowly, pushing herself back with her toes. "So now they're your sisters," she snorted. Seconds later it was, "What kind of tapes?"

"About his life. He talked about how he left his family in Oklahoma and went to Texas to work in the oil fields. And he talked a lot about how you met."

"That's it?"

Elizabeth shook her head. "He told how the two of you came to California and what it was like when Frank and I were born."

Her mother rocked faster.

"And what happened when Frank died."

Denise reached for her coffee, took a sip, and then paused to stare at Elizabeth over the rim of the cup. "Do you believe him?"

How could her mother not realize that she damned herself simply by asking the question? "Why would you think his version was different from yours?"

Trapped. Denise's gaze darted around the room as if the answer were hidden there. "You know as well as I do that Jessie always put his own spin on things."

"This wasn't something he'd put a spin on, it was just plain wrong. You lied to him about why Frank joined the Army."

Long seconds passed before Denise lifted her gaze from her lap and looked at Elizabeth. There were tears in her eyes. "I had to. I was afraid of what Jessie would do to me if he ever discovered the truth. You never saw that side of your father. He kept it hidden from you and Frank."

"Are you saying you were physically afraid of him? That he hit you?" She'd overheard a hundred fights between them, but she'd never seen her father raise a hand to her mother or to anyone else. The only spankings she and Frank had ever received were from their mother. She'd seen her father angry, especially the night Frank sneaked out to meet his girlfriend and caught the barn on fire, but even then Jessie had been in control of himself.

"You don't know what Frank meant to your father." Denise clasped her hands and started rocking again. "The two of them were boards cut from the same tree. Every time I looked at Frank I saw Jessie." She rocked harder. "After your father left us it was everything I could do to look at Frank sitting across the table from me every night."

Elizabeth couldn't believe what she'd just heard. "You hated Frank because he looked like Daddy?"

"He didn't just look like him," Denise insisted. "He acted like him. He even thought the same things in the same way. No matter what it was, Frank took Jessie's side over mine. There was no pleasing him, no way for me—" She stopped and stared at Elizabeth. "You were there. You know how it was. You must remember how Frank defied me at every turn."

"He thought you hated him."

"He hated me—just like Jessie. Do you know how hard it is to love someone who feels that way about you? But it didn't stop me from trying. God knows I tried. He was my son. I wasn't going to give up on him. Not after seeing what happened to you when your father gave up on us, how it broke your heart."

"Jessie said you were the one who asked for the divorce."

Denise jerked as if ducking something Elizabeth had thrown. Her mouth opened and immediately snapped shut again.

"He said that you told him you'd found someone else." Elizabeth had tried, but couldn't remember another man in her mother's life. If she'd dated, she'd done it in secret.

"I was desperate," Denise stuttered. "I thought if I told Jessie someone was interested in me he would come around more. I did it for you. You were a little girl then. You needed a father."

"Is that why you told him you were married when he came to see Frank?"

"By then all I wanted was to hurt him, to show him I'd moved on." Her chin quivered. "He didn't care. All he cared about was seeing you kids. I meant nothing to him."

"It had to occur to you that he would find out eventually."

"I didn't think about that." Tears flowed freely, unheeded. "I had this stupid ring that I'd picked up at the five-and-dime, and I showed it to him. All I wanted was for him to pay attention to me. You don't understand how it was between us. You can't. And I'm sure it wasn't something Jessie talked about on those tapes of his. It tore me up inside that he didn't need me as much as I needed him. I'd been in love with him since I was thirteen. I didn't know how to stop loving him."

A profound sadness hovered over Elizabeth like a cloud. "Why did you send me to Grandma's?" she asked, already knowing the answer.

"You would have told Jessie about the fight between me and Frank, that I was the one who took him to the recruiter. I was going to keep you there until Frank came home."

"A whole year?"

Denise held her hand out in a pleading gesture. "I knew Frank would never tell Jessie what happened. Even while he hated me he protected me. But I couldn't trust you not to tell. I was afraid. You didn't see your father when he came to the house looking for Frank."

The pieces were coming together like letters in a crossword puzzle. "You never sent my letters to Daddy." It wasn't a question, it was a statement.

"I couldn't."

"And you never called him about coming to my wedding." The cloud enveloped her.

"You would have said something. He would have found out. I couldn't let that happen."

"He tried to see me, didn't he?" The emptiness, the anger, the hurt she'd carried like precious cargo throughout her life slipped from her shoulders, replaced with a profound sorrow. "How did you stop him?"

"Why are we talking about this? What difference does it make now?" Denise left the rocking chair and crossed to the patio door, staring outside at the postage stamp–sized backyard, her back to Elizabeth. "Jessie's dead. In a couple of years, I will be, too. It will all be over. Why can't you leave it alone?"

"How can you even ask that?"

"Because it doesn't matter."

"It matters to *me*. It sure as hell mattered fifteen years ago when I refused to see him and then eight months ago when I walked away from my last chance to see him. Do you have any idea what you stole from me?"

"I told him that you blamed him for Frank's death and that you refused to see him." Denise's shoulders slumped and she crossed her arms over her chest as if trying to pull into herself. "None of it mattered. He still wanted to see you. I . . . I convinced him otherwise."

"How?"

"I answered his letters and signed your name."

An impotent rage filled Elizabeth, usurping the corners of her heart and mind where love and understanding had resided. "What kind of monster are you? How could you hear me crying in my room at night, how could you watch me sitting on the porch waiting for the postman, how could you wipe my tears on my wedding day when I realized he wasn't coming, how could you—"

"*Don't you dare talk to me like that*," Denise shouted. "I was the one who stayed home and took care of you when Jessie was off in the oil fields or at those parties in Hollywood. I was there when you were sick. I made your breakfast every morning, took you to school, and tucked you in bed every night. I always put you first. *Always*. I loved you the best way I knew how."

Elizabeth couldn't give what her mother needed. Her own pain was too consuming, too new to have found boundaries, still bottomless, still expanding.

"I think about Frank every day." Denise put her hands over her face. Her breath caught in a sob. "Every day I ask for forgiveness. When will it end? When will the day come that I've been punished enough? I loved him, too, you know."

Elizabeth reached for her purse. "I'm going home."

"Go ahead. Do what your father did. Walk out on me. It's what Frank did, too. I may have taken him to the recruiter, but he didn't have to sign those papers. He could have told them that he didn't want to go, that joining the Army was my idea." She followed Elizabeth to the door. "I'm not the only one to blame. His dying was just as much his fault as it was mine."

"My God, Mother. Did you hear what you just said?"

Denise grabbed Elizabeth's arm. "I didn't mean it the way it sounded. You're forcing me to say these things. I'm afraid of losing you, too. I'm eighty years old, Elizabeth. I don't have much time left."

"You want me to feel sorry for you because you're old?" The injustice choked her with rage. "You've had thirty-six years that Frank missed."

"I didn't send him to Vietnam," she shot back. "The Army did."

"Is that how you've lived with what you did?" Elizabeth wanted to leave and never come back, but she knew that wasn't possible. Eventually she would forgive Denise for this, the way she had forgiven all the other seemingly unforgivable things her mother had done over the years. She needed time. And she needed distance. "Don't call me—I'll call you."

"I'm your mother."

"I'm a mother, too," Elizabeth shot back. "But I never—*not for one moment*—believed that gave me the right to play God with the lives of my children."

Forty-seven

Rachel

Rachel put her hands on the balcony railing at the Whale Watch Inn, closed her eyes, and listened to the waves hitting the shore thirty feet below. The air was still, a calm between tides, a time when the earthy smell of the pine and cedar forests surrounding the inn mixed with the ocean's salt spray and created an intoxicating fragrance. A gull called in the distance. Rachel opened her eyes and saw a lone pelican skimming the water, headed north for the day's foraging.

She'd lived on mountains and in the desert, in cities, and once, when her mother hired on as a cook, on a ranch three hours from the nearest town. Only the ocean imbued her with a sense of home. She was at peace here, the waves settling her mind and soul the way an infant calmed listening to the sound of its mother's heartbeat.

Jeff came up behind her, swept her hair aside, and kissed the nape of her neck. "What time do you want to leave?"

"Never."

"Sounds good to me."

She turned and slipped her arms around his waist. Tilting her head back, she looked into his eyes. "I love you."

Jeff took her hand and put it on his chest. "Did you feel it?"

"What?"

"My heart is skipping beats." This time he kissed her on the lips, his mouth open, his tongue gently touching hers. "I'd given up ever hearing that from you again."

"From now on I'm going to tell you so often that you'll get bored hearing it."

He cupped her face with his hands and stared deeply into her eyes. "That can't happen. I will never forget how empty my life was without you."

"I can't wait to tell the kids."

He smiled. "I don't want to disappoint you, but I'm pretty sure they've figured it out already. I heard Cassidy tell Ginger that we were going away this weekend to decide what to do with all the furniture from your apartment."

"What did Ginger say?"

"That we could have a garage sale."

"Does everyone know?"

He gave her a disappointed look, wildly exaggerated. "So, what you're saying is that I should take back the WELCOME HOME banners?"

Rachel laughed. "Pretty sure of yourself, were you?"

"Determined. There was no way I was going to let this weekend end any other way."

She turned to face the ocean again, snuggling her back into Jeff's chest. "I'm almost afraid to say this." She made a fist and knocked on the wooden railing in an uncharacteristically superstitious gesture. "But I've never been happier than I am at this moment."

"Not even on the day we were married?"

"Our wedding was a naive kind of happiness that just happened. This one we had to earn."

"And when the kids were born?"

"I thought my heart would burst." She crossed her arms and laid them on his where they circled her waist. "Today is cumulative—like all of those happy times rolled into one." She laughed. "I can't believe how corny I sound."

Jeff tucked his chin into her neck and whispered against her hair. "You want to hear corny—listen to this. If there was anything good that came from what I put us through, it's realizing that I have loved and been loved beyond what I expected or dreamed, and far beyond what I deserved. If I died today I would die complete."

The hair at the base of Rachel's neck stood on end. She turned to look at Jeff. "Why would you say something like that? The dying part, I mean?"

He kissed her, long and with infinite tenderness. "It was just an expression. Nothing is going to happen to me, Rachel. I won't let it. You'll just have to trust me on this one. I'm going to be around for a long, long time."

She couldn't shake the uneasiness. "I don't think I could go on without you. I know I couldn't."

"Yes, you could. And you would—for the kids." He put his arm around her and guided her back inside. "It was just my stupid way of telling you how much I love you. I didn't mean anything by it, and I sure as hell didn't have a premonition. Now stop worrying."

She put her arms around him. She was consumed with a need for physical contact. Whether it was making love or just holding hands, she needed and responded to his touch the way a flower responds to sunlight. "What would you say if I told you I've been thinking about quitting my job?"

She'd plainly surprised him. "Why would you do that? You love that job."

"Not as much as I love you and the kids." This was the first time since her promotion that Rachel had taken a day off so she and Jeff could be together. She'd anticipated a twinge or two, at least some worrying about the meeting that was taking place without her, but neither had happened. Now she was sorry she hadn't taken Monday off, too. "And besides, it's your turn. We made a deal that once the kids were in school you could concentrate on your career."

"You wouldn't last a month. I mean this in the kindest way, Rachel, but you're not cut out to be a full-time soccer mom."

She grinned. "You think?"

"I know."

"Yeah, me, too. But in less than two months we're going to have ten million dollars that's going to need managing." She hesitated telling him the rest. The idea was still forming, and the intent needed scrutiny. Her motivations were reactionary, a result of Jessie's unscientific diagnosis of her mother's illness. Curious, afraid it could be genetic and inherited, for the past two weeks she'd been researching schizophrenia. While her mother wasn't a textbook case, she'd had enough symptoms that with a little education, someone, somewhere, should have picked up on her illness.

"I've been thinking about setting up a charitable trust," she ventured.

"I think it sounds like a great idea. And I think you should call it the Anna Kaplan Foundation."

"I didn't say anything about—" She smiled, realizing that not only was he in step with her, he was walking ahead, leading the way. "I need to think about it some more. I feel like I'm a coin that's been tossed in the air and I'm still spinning. After all the years of hating my mother, I've done such a complete about-face that I'm suspicious of my feelings."

"You never hated her, Rachel. You told yourself you did because it hurt too much to admit you loved someone you believed didn't love you back. After all, how could she love you and let you be the one who found her? Now you understand. You know about the demons that drove her and that what she did had nothing to do with how much she loved you."

Rachel's heart swelled with a love she had denied almost her entire life. Her eyes filled with tears. "I wish I could have helped her . . . I wish I had known."

"And look who you have to thank that you finally found out."

"Jessie Reed—my father."

"Was that a note of pride I heard in your voice?" he teased.

"Maybe."

"I told you that you came from good stock."

She smiled, finally believing him after all the years he'd insisted she had no reason to be ashamed of her background. "Get ready," she warned. "I'm going to tell you again."

"Go ahead—hit me with it."

"I love you."

Jeff swept her into his arms and swung her around. "I must have done something incredible in a past life to deserve you in this one."

She gave him a seductive smile. "How much time do we have?"

"The rest of our lives."

She laughed. "Before checkout."

"My God, woman, you're insatiable." He took her to the bed, stopping to give her a kiss that was both tender and urgent. "Which makes me the luckiest man in the world."

They stopped for saltwater taffy at a roadside stand in Gualala and for dinner at Sanducci's, a restaurant that overlooked the ocean and encouraged lingering with slow, meticulous service. For the first time in months Rachel indulged in dessert, crème brûlée. Jeff had a rich chocolate cake topped with vanilla gelato and covered with a caramel sauce. Rachel ate all of her crème brûlée and half of Jeff's chocolate cake.

Inside the Land Rover and on the coast highway again, Rachel adjusted her seat belt, pushing it lower, off her overly full stomach. She rolled down the window, letting the unseasonably warm air fill the car, leaned her head against the headrest, and groaned. "Why did you let me eat the rest of your cake?"

"*Let* you?"

She looked at him and grinned sheepishly. "I thought you were finished."

"With the fork still in my hand?"

"Next time I'm going to skip the meal and head straight for dessert." Turning her head to the side and snuggling against the soft leather, she looked at the sky, a glorious palate of pinks and oranges dripping from the vivid autumn sunset. The road was nearly deserted, with lights just beginning to show on the hillsides in the distance.

Jeff reached for her hand and gave it a squeeze. "I've been thinking. . . ."

"Yes?" she prompted.

"It's not anything I'm stuck on, just something I've been mulling over since you said you wanted to quit your job."

"And?" she prompted again.

"I don't know—maybe I should think about it some more before I say anything."

"You're doing this on purpose."

He gave her hand a second squeeze. "What do you think about having another baby?"

She would have been less surprised if he'd asked her to live on the space station. They'd agreed that two was a good number when she'd insisted it had to be more than one. She knew what it was to grow up an only child. When they'd had a girl and then a boy, it seemed a logical place to stop. "I don't know," she admitted.

"No pressure. I was just remembering what it was like to have a baby around and how perfect the two we have are." He leaned over to give her a quick kiss.

Rachel moved to meet him and saw something out of the corner of her eye. A cow—standing in the middle of the road. She screamed, but it was too late. Jeff must have seen the cow at the same time because he jerked the steering wheel and veered to the right before Rachel's scream cleared her throat. The Land Rover's right wheel caught the soft shoulder and pulled the SUV forward, jerking it toward the cliff.

The SUV hesitated at the cliff's edge, giving Rachel a second to see everything—the terrified cow, the dry grass, the jagged rock, the ocean. But it was Jeff's image that fixed in her mind, his look of horror and fateful understanding, the desperate search for escape, the frantic silent message he sent to her in a glance, telling her that he loved her.

The SUV tilted slowly and gently slid over the edge. For an achingly long second it seemed they would ease down the cliff, escaping the jagged rocks and wind-twisted shrubs. But then they picked up speed. A tire caught and the SUV whipped to the side, slamming nose-first into a boulder. Airbags exploded, filling the cab, crushing Rachel against the seat. As fast as they'd opened they deflated. Now she was flung against the door, the seat, the dashboard, Jeff.

She screamed, or at least she thought she did. It could have been the sound of the car scraping the rocks as it rolled and turned and bounced on its descent to the small sandy cove at the bottom of the cliff.

After what seemed an eternity and yet only a blink, it was over. They had landed right side up, the only sound a hissing and creaking from the engine and the roaring thunder of waves hitting the rocks beside the cove.

"Are you okay?" Jeff asked in a choked whisper.

Her head hurt. She put her hand to her temple and felt a slick, sticky wetness. She was bleeding. A lot. "I think so."

"I'm sorry." He reached for his seat belt. "I should have—" He gasped in pain.

"What is it?" she demanded. "What's wrong?"

"Jesus—my leg. It hurts." He leaned forward and reached down with his right hand. "I can't move it."

Rachel fumbled for her seat belt, struggling with the release. Twisting in the seat made it hard to breathe. She felt like knives were being shoved between her ribs. Finally the release caught and the buckle came apart. "Let me see."

"You can't. It's pinned between the door and the seat."

"Are you sure?" She tried to picture his leg in that position and couldn't. There wasn't room and his leg couldn't twist that way. He had to be mistaken.

"It's there. I can feel it."

"Can you open the door?"

"No, it's jammed into the rock. And my arm's caught under the seat." He put his head back and closed his eyes, his face contorted in pain. "The phone . . . ?"

Jeff kept his cell phone in a cubby hole by the radio. "It must have fallen out."

"Get yours. Call 911."

His voice faded; she could barely hear him over the sounds of the waves. Frantic, she pushed the deflated airbags aside and searched the cab. "It isn't here."

"Try again."

She shoved her hand between the jumbled luggage and bags of silly souvenirs they'd bought for the kids. "It's not here. It must have fallen out."

He reached for her hand. "Are you okay?"

"Yes."

"Are you sure?"

"Yes," she insisted. *He couldn't see the blood.*

"Then you have to go . . . get help."

The sun was gone. The horizon was a fading crimson. Soon, within minutes, there would be no light and no moon to show the way back up the hill. "I'm not leaving you."

"We won't make it if you don't."

"I can't." The thought of leaving him alone terrified her. "Someone will find us. They'll see the skid marks." She reached for the switch to turn on the headlights. "They'll see our lights."

"The tide, Rachel."

At first she didn't understand. And then, her heart in her throat, his fear became hers. He was trapped. If they waited, if the tide was coming in, this cove, like half of the coves on the coast, would disappear. Jeff would drown.

She pressed her face into his hand. "Promise me you'll be okay." The words were ripped from her soul. "Jeff?" She touched his face. "*Jeff?* Goddamn it, Jeff—don't you dare die on me."

He squeezed her hand. Blood trickled from his ear and nose. "Go. . . ."

He was going to die. She knew it the same way she knew she'd never been destined for true happiness. She was tainted, one of life's misfits, not deserving, unworthy. There was a dark corner of her mind that reminded her of these things, a voice that warned her and kept her from being surprised when something bad happened. She was the dog raised alone on a chain in a backyard with a clear view of the dog next door, the one that had never known a boot in the ribs or a night in the rain.

"All right. I'm going." She reached for the handle; the door was jammed. She climbed through the window and dropped to the sand. She caught her breath as pain shot through her body. Everything hurt, her head, her lungs, her knees, even her breast where the seat belt had lain across her chest.

Rolling to her side, she put her hand down and pushed into a sitting position. Seconds later water washed over her fingers. A new, terrifying reality gripped her. The water was only a few feet from the car. Was Jeff right? Was the tide coming in—or was it going out? Frantic, she tried to remember what the ocean had looked like that morning, at lunch, at dinner. Nothing.

She rose to her feet and took a final look inside the car. A hundred things came to mind to tell Jeff, how lonely she'd been before he came into her life, how happy he'd made her, how much she loved him. She reached inside to touch his hand. "I love you," she said softly. Determined that he should hear her, she shouted, "I love you."

Tears mixed with the blood smearing her cheeks and neck as she dropped his hand and stepped away from the car. Steadying herself on the crumpled rear fender, she stopped to study the hill, seeking the easiest climb while looking for her purse or the car phone and finding neither. A rock wall blocked her to the right; on the left was a cliff so sheer the top extended out over the bottom. The only way up was the way they'd come down, a steep slope covered with rocks, dry grass, and twisted shrubs.

The slick soles of her Prada loafers slipped on the tall grass. She took them off and tucked them in her waistband. If she had to walk when she reached the road, she'd make better time in shoes. She searched for hand- and footholds, grasping the tough grass, praying it would stay rooted while she hung on and swung from one toehold to the next. Fingernails tore as she clung to rocks; the skin on her arms and legs shredded on the rough bark of shrubs.

Inch by inch, she made her way up what had taken only seconds to descend. She talked to God, saying the same prayer over and over again, begging Him to give her and Jeff more time, begging Jeff not to leave her. By the time she reached the road her hands were raw, the stumps of her fingernails bleeding, her feet numb. She reached for her shoes, but they were gone. It didn't matter. Nothing mattered but getting help.

The highway was deserted. How could that be? This was the only coast road, the path to every ocean tourist destination north of San Francisco. On summer weekends, the traffic was bumper to bumper. She stood next to the tracks the SUV's tires had dug into the soft soil, a trail that led over the cliff, and waited, ready to do whatever was necessary to get the first car that came by to stop. None came.

She followed the tracks back to the edge of the cliff, wanting, needing contact with Jeff even at a distance. Confused by what she saw, she wiped her eyes and blinked. Something was different. The sand was gone . . . there was water under the car. *The tide was coming in.*

Sick with fear and frantic with the need to do something, she stumbled into the middle of the narrow, twisting two-lane highway and headed toward the only lights she could see—miles away, on the side of a hill.

Forty-eight

Rachel

Rachel sat on the edge of her bed at Santa Rosa Memorial Hospital and stared out the window at a city still asleep. She was alone in the two-bed room, the only sound the voices of the nurses exchanging patient information and gossip as they made their rounds and the low drone of a television coming from another room, tuned into a late-night infomercial.

She was freezing. The thin hospital gown hung open in the back, and she couldn't reach around to close it. She listened for footsteps, her heart dancing in fear and anticipation when she convinced herself they were headed her way.

The ambulance that brought her to the hospital arrived an hour and a half after the helicopter that brought Jeff. They'd taken him into surgery immediately, and now, five hours later, she still hadn't heard anything other than that he was "doing fine" from a nurse she'd begged to call the operating room and ask.

Rachel didn't believe her. Jeff wasn't fine. He couldn't be. She'd seen him after the local fire department pulled him up the hill in a wire basket, stood at his side while the highway patrol closed the road to let the Search helicopter land. She'd looked into the faces of his rescuers—the policemen, the firefighters, the ambulance attendants, the medical people on the helicopter—seeking something, anything to give her hope. There was nothing, not even a flickering smile.

A moment's inattention, a kiss, and a goddamned cow. Jeff's life couldn't be over because of a cow. It wasn't possible. They'd been on the coast road a half-dozen times since moving to California. She remembered seeing warning signs about free-range cattle and remembered going over the cattle guards, but not once had she actually seen a cow—until last night.

Rachel took a tissue from the nightstand and blew her nose. She was crying again. She'd acquired an inexhaustible supply of tears and had no control over when they began or ended. Her stomach was a hard knot of fear that radiated into her chest, squeezed her throat, and made her feel as if she were choking. She tried but couldn't swallow the pain medication the nurse had given her, so she'd been given a shot instead.

New footsteps. Not the soft swish of nurses' shoes but a hard click, moving fast. Rachel looked at the window, her gaze fixed on the door's reflection. Instead of the hoped-for doctor in scrubs, a woman appeared.

"Rachel?"

Ginger. Rachel tried to stand but was too stiff to get up. "What are you doing here? Where are the kids?"

"Christina has them. I didn't think you'd want them at the hospital yet."

"Christina? How did she—"

"I called her. She drove up to take care of them so I could be here with you." Ginger came around the bed and stopped dead, as if she'd run into a Plexiglas wall. "My God," she gasped. "You look like sh— . . . like you were in a really bad accident."

"I'm not as bad as I look." She had to be better than the horror she saw on Ginger's face.

"What happened to your head?"

Rachel gingerly touched the bandage covering the four-inch-long cut on the side of her head. The nurse had apologized when he cut her hair, saying he would only take as much as necessary. Still, she had a bald spot that would be impossible to hide. "I'm not sure. I think I might have hit a rock. I had my window open."

"You're going to have a couple of black eyes, too."

"The worst is the cracked ribs. Three of them. They hurt all the time. Especially when I try to lie down."

"That's it? You go over a cliff and end up with three cracked ribs and a cut?" Ginger moved in to get a closer look. "What's that on your arm?"

Rachel frowned and held up her arm. The scratches looked like someone had come at her with coarse sandpaper. "I must have scraped them when I was climbing out." She looked at her legs. They were worse than her arms.

"Have they told you anything about Jeff yet?"

Rachel shook her head, wincing at the movement. "Nothing beyond he's doing fine."

"All this time and no one has told you anything? You must be going out of your mind."

Rachel's jaw quivered as she struggled unsuccessfully against a new wave of tears. "I keep asking, and they're nice enough about it, but no one does anything. It's like they're all just patting me on the head."

"Do you want me to see what I can do?"

"I don't know. I'm so scared," Rachel whispered, as if it were a dangerous secret. "At least this way I still have hope."

"How long has it been?"

Rachel glanced at the wall clock mounted next to the television. "Almost six hours."

"I finally managed to get through to Jeff's brother. He was at the firehouse. He said as soon as he could get someone to cover for him he'd be down. I don't know if he's flying or driving."

Rachel had called Ginger from the ambulance. She'd asked her to call Logan and let him decide whether to try to reach his parents, who were on a South Pacific cruise celebrating their fiftieth wedding anniversary.

"He's really good with the kids," Rachel told her. "He can take over for you and Christina when he gets here."

"Like that's going to happen. He's going to have to wrestle the kids away from Christina." Ginger smiled. "As for me, I'm due a vacation. Hell, I just may quit. It's not like I love this job and I have enough savings left to last me another six months at least."

Rachel didn't know what else to say, so she simply said, "Thank you."

"For what?"

"Everything. For being my friend—for being my sister."

"Being your friend is easy. The sister thing was Jessie's doing."

Rachel saw a reflected movement in the window—a man dressed in green. She should have known she wouldn't hear the cushioned footsteps that brought the surgeon to her room.

"Mrs. Nolan?"

Ginger jumped at the male voice. "She's here." She moved to the end of the bed. "Come in—please." Ginger held out her hand. "I'm Ginger Reynolds, Mrs. Nolan's sister."

He shook Ginger's hand. "Joseph Kenton."

Rachel slowly stood, holding on to the mattress with one hand, the windowsill with the other. "How is he?"

"He's still in recovery, but you should be able to see him in about an hour. We were able to save enough of the leg to—"

"What does that mean—save enough of the leg?"

He swore softly as he swept the green surgical cap off his head and crumpled it in his fist. "No one told you?"

"No—no one has told me anything."

"The femoral artery was crushed in the accident, cutting blood flow to the lower leg. Without blood, there is no oxygen and the tissues become ischemic and acidosis develops. When that happens, there isn't anything we can do except remove the limb."

"You cut off his leg?" she repeated, sure she couldn't be hearing him correctly. People didn't have legs cut off anymore, they had them reattached. There were newspaper stories about it all the time. Jeff still had his. Why couldn't it be saved?

"Progressive acidosis of a large area of the body can cause shock and death," he said. And then, with a sigh, he added, "Even though his arm was more damaged, the blood supply was never diminished and we were able to save it."

Ginger moved closer to Rachel in a protective gesture. "Otherwise he's okay?" she asked.

"His spleen ruptured and had to be removed. He has five broken ribs, which will heal on their own. The broken pelvis will take a couple of weeks, the bones in his arm considerably longer. Those we had to plate and pin and will have to go back in to remove." He paused, plainly exhausted. "With your husband's body compromised from his other injuries and the majority of the cells in his leg already dead or dying, there wasn't any other option. Frankly, Mrs. Nolan, he's lucky he got here when he did."

"How much of his leg did you have to take?" Rachel asked.

"Mid-thigh. I went high enough to assure good tissue coverage for the stump. He won't have any trouble being fitted for his prosthesis."

"If I could have gotten help sooner would it have made a difference?" Rachel asked.

He shook his head. "From where the accident happened, even if the fire department had been on the opposite side of the road, the helicopter couldn't have gotten him here in time." He stuffed his cap into his back pocket, crossed his arms, and leaned a shoulder into the wall. "I know how difficult this is, but it isn't all bad news. Barring complications, your husband is going to make a full recovery. He'll need a couple of months of physical therapy and time to heal before he can be fitted for his prosthesis, but he's young and in good shape, and there really isn't anything to keep him from doing whatever he wants to do."

"Does he know?"

"Not yet. We'll tell him as soon as he's fully awake." He straightened and prepared to leave. "You're going to have questions when you've had time to absorb this. If they're something the staff can't answer or if you'd rather talk to me personally, you can reach me at my office. Leave a message and a phone number and I'll get back to you as soon as I can."

Rachel held out her hand. "Thank you, Dr. Kenton."

He took her hand between his. They were enormous, and warm. "You're welcome."

When he was gone and Ginger had eased Rachel back into bed, she looked up from adjusting the blanket and asked, "Are you worried how Jeff will take it?"

"Of course. How would you react if you woke up and found your leg gone?"

Ginger considered the question. "After what the two of you went through, I think I'd be thrilled we were both still alive."

She knew Ginger was right, but was logic enough compared to the reality of a missing leg? It wasn't as if Jeff had been offered a choice, his leg or his life. If so, the aftermath would have been easier to accept because he'd been in on the decision. "If the accident had to happen, I'm glad it happened on the way home instead of the way there. Now at least Jeff can't question my reasons for moving home."

"So you did it?"

Rachel stared at her. In one of those compelling moments of lunacy that sometimes accompany tragedy, she answered, "More than once."

Ginger frowned, plainly confused. Seconds later she burst out laughing. "Shame on you."

Infected with the same insane laughter, Rachel's mind credited the small joke with high humor. A torrent of emotion slipped the dam she'd built to get her through all that had happened after the wreck. Almost immediately the laughter changed to sobs. She held her sides at the pain both created. "I'm sorry. That was stupid."

Ginger handed Rachel a tissue and then crawled into bed beside her, bracing her back against the headboard and crossing her legs at her ankles. She took Rachel's hand and locked fingers.

"I'm going to get all sloppy and sentimental for a minute," Rachel said. "I get a knot in my stomach when I think how easily I could have missed knowing you. I wanted a sister from the time I was old enough to know what they were. And now I have you and Elizabeth and Christina, and my life doesn't just seem more complete, it feels as if I'm connected to something wonderful that's forever."

"I used to dream about having a sister, too," Ginger admitted. "Someone I could talk to who would keep my secrets and tell me hers, someone who would laugh and cry with me, someone—"

"—who would let me borrow her beautiful clothes," Rachel finished for her.

"My closet is your closet," Ginger said. She laughed. "I can say that because I know there's nothing in there you would want."

"I don't know—that cropped sweater you had on last week was pretty cute."

"It's yours—spaghetti stain and all."

Rachel appreciated Ginger's efforts to distract her, but it wasn't working. She couldn't stop thinking about Jeff and how he was going to deal with losing his leg. "I have to be with Jeff," she said. "Would you help me get there?"

Ginger swung her legs over the edge of the bed. "I'll get a wheelchair."

Rachel sat next to Jeff's bed, resting her head lightly on the pillow they'd used to support his arm. He'd been awake once long enough to see that she was there and to ask if she was all right and immediately fell asleep again. The nurse told her he could sleep for hours and tried to get her to go back to her room, but she'd refused. She wanted her face to be the first one Jeff saw when he woke up again.

"How long have you been here?" he asked hoarsely, startling her out of her insulated world of "if onlys" and "might have beens."

With effort she got up and leaned over the bed to give him a kiss, biting back a groan at the pain in her side. It was time for another shot. "Since they brought you to the room."

"You look terrible."

She had to struggle to hear his throaty whisper. "It's just surface stuff."

"Are you sure?"

"Absolutely."

"Why are you crying?"

"They're happy tears." She swiped her hand over her cheeks. "We made it, Jeff."

"I know about the leg, Rachel." He brought up his good hand, the one with all the tubes and IVs attached, to touch her chin. "They told me in the recovery room."

"It doesn't matter."

"I know," he said softly. "It's just going to take some getting used to."

"I was so scared."

"You saved my life."

A sob caught in her throat. "I wish I could have saved your leg, too."

"I saw this dumb show a while back about a two-legged dog. He didn't give a damn how weird he looked running around with half his legs. I remember wondering if it took someone special to love an animal that looked like that."

The pain spread from her ribs to her heart. She turned his hand over and pressed her cheek into his palm. "It's not how you look that makes me love you, it's who you are."

His fingers caressed her forehead. "When the water started coming in the car and I thought I wasn't going to make it, I looked for something I could write on to tell you how much you mean to me. I couldn't find anything, but it didn't matter because I realized there weren't any words. What I feel for you is so much a part of me that you're like the air I breathe. I wanted you to feel what I feel. . . . To know how my heart beats faster just knowing you're going to walk into a room."

The monitor beside the bed let out a pinging noise. Jeff smiled. "See?"

She returned his smile, a quiet knowledge laying a comforting hand on her shoulder. They were going to be okay.

Forty-nine

Ginger

Ginger got out of the car at Rachel's house and took a minute to stretch stiff aching muscles. She was long past the second wind that had seen her through the hours at the hospital with Rachel. Christina met her at the door. "You look awful."

"You should see Rachel. I don't think there's a place on her body that isn't black and blue or on its way."

"How was she doing when you left?"

"Physically, the broken ribs seem to be the worst. Her left breast is purple where the seat belt came across and it's swollen twice the size of the right one. Mentally, I think she's still in shock, more numb than traumatized."

"Any change in Jeff?"

She'd called with the results of the surgery while Rachel was with Jeff in intensive care. "The same. They're talking about moving him in a week or two if there aren't any complications."

"Why?"

"So he'll be closer to home."

A tall blond man came up behind Christina. "This is Logan, Jeff's brother," Christina said. "Logan—Ginger."

They shook hands. "I came to get some things for Rachel," Ginger said.

"I can take them back for you," Logan said. "I was just about to leave for the hospital."

"I didn't know you were here or I would have called with the list," she said. To Christina she said, "Where are the kids?"

"Upstairs."

"What did you tell them?"

"I didn't, Logan did."

"Well?" she questioned.

"I told them the truth."

"How did they take it?"

"They asked a few questions, then wanted to know when they could go to the hospital. I told them they probably couldn't right away but that I'd ask."

"The doctor said Rachel could be released as soon as tomorrow, so I thought I'd look for a hotel near the hospital. Not that she's going to stay there, but at least it will give her a place to get cleaned up."

"I can do that, too," Logan said. "You can stay here and get some sleep."

"I'd rather be at the hospital. I want to be there if Rachel needs me."

The doorbell rang. Ginger answered. It was Elizabeth, suitcase in hand. "What are you doing here?" she asked.

"Same thing you are. She's my sister, too, you know."

Ginger introduced Elizabeth to Logan before giving her an update.

"How high did they remove his leg?" Elizabeth asked.

"Mid-thigh."

Elizabeth winced. "Too bad he couldn't have kept the knee, but he'll do fine. They have some incredible prostheses now."

"How do you know about artificial legs?" Christina asked.

"You live forty-nine years, you pick things up along the way." She gave Christina an unexpected, spontaneous hug.

"Wait a minute," Logan injected. "What's this about Rachel being your sister? She doesn't have any sisters. She's an only child."

"I'll tell you about it on the way," Ginger said. And then, feeling oddly on the outside, blurted out, "Don't I get a hug, too?"

"What the hell," Logan said. Before Christina or Elizabeth could move, he put his arms around Ginger.

Ginger was speechless. So, in addition to being tall and handsome and caring, he had a sense of humor. She liked the way the family was expanding.

As soon as Logan let Ginger go, Elizabeth took his place. "I certainly never thought I'd see this day."

Christina opened her arms. "I believe that sound you hear in the background is hell freezing over."

"Why don't you give me the rest of the directions before you fall asleep?" Logan said.

They were still forty-five minutes from Santa Rosa. "I'm fine."

"No, you're not. Your head has been bobbing for the last ten miles."

"I'll sleep when we get there."

"Then talk to me. Tell me about this sister thing."

She did, telling him everything except about the money, leaving that to Rachel.

"I wonder why she never said anything," he said.

"I think we were all a little shell-shocked in the beginning. And why talk about something that's going to be out of your life in six months?"

"That's not the way it looked to me."

"Things change."

"Sounds like your father got around."

A powerful defensive streak stiffened her spine. "Be careful," she warned. "We're all a little sensitive where Jessie is concerned."

"I thought you said you didn't know he existed until a couple of months ago."

She looked at the car beside them, at the woman driving, at the child strapped in the car seat. "It was my loss," she said softly.

Minutes passed. "I'm sorry," Logan said. "I was out of line."

So, he had a sense of humor, asked directions, and apologized when he was wrong. "You're a firefighter?"

"Going on twenty years."

"That must mean you like what you do?"

"Most of the time."

"Meaning?"

"Not every call ends the way you want it to."

"Firefighters got Jeff out of the car and carried him up the hill."

"That's what we're trained to do."

" 'Just doin' my job, ma'am.' "

"Yep."

Firefighters and modesty supposedly went hand in hand, but throw in someone who looked like Logan—tall and muscular with perfect teeth, gorgeous eyes, and a drop-dead smile—and she wasn't buying it. "Are you for real?"

Logan laughed. "As real and as ordinary as this car."

"What's wrong with my car?"

"Nothing. It's just not what you'd call a classic."

Oh, God, she liked him. This was not a good thing. "Wife?"

"Are you asking if I have one or if I want one?"

"If you have one."

"Did once, don't anymore." He shifted lanes. "What about you?"

"Kids?"

"Nope. What about you?" he repeated.

"Neither—wife or kids."

He glanced at her. "So, why all the questions?"

She shrugged. "Just figured it was time I got to know the relatives."

"You're quick. I like that."

"You're bossy," she said.

"And?"

"I'm not crazy about that."

He grinned. "Hits too close to home?"

"Don't take this the wrong way, but you don't seem very worried about your brother."

"I'm not—at least not now. Jeff's a survivor. He has some tough times ahead, but he'll come through okay. Rachel's the one who needs help. It's going to fall to her to hold everything together while Jeff recovers. And she's the one stuck with the nightmares. It's my understanding Jeff was unconscious for most of what happened."

"We'll be there for her."

He pinned her with a look. "Will you? Really? For the long haul?"

"Yes," she said with absolute conviction. "We really will. All three of us."

Fifty

Christina

Christina stopped to look at the drawings decorating the refrigerator. John's was the outline of his hand made into a turkey, the head his thumb, the fingers the tail feathers. Cassidy had made a Pilgrim couple, the woman with flaming red hair and dangling earrings, the man sporting a buzz cut and headband. She was crazy about her niece and nephew but not so enamored she was blinded to the truth—neither was a budding Rembrandt.

She reached inside for the cream, poured it into the small ceramic pitcher shaped like a cow, and put it on the tray with mugs of coffee. She'd spent so much time in Rachel's kitchen the past three weeks that she was almost as familiar with it as she was the one at home.

Only it wasn't her home. It was Jessie's. It just felt like home. But soon, probably the first of the year, Lucy would put the house on the market and it would be someone else's home. And she'd be in L.A. looking for a new place to live, starting a new life.

Elizabeth came into the kitchen. "Need some help?"

She picked up the tray. "I got it."

"Wait a second. I want to talk to you."

Christina put the tray down again. "What's up?"

"What are we going to do about Thanksgiving? Jeff should be home by then, and there's no way Rachel can take care of him and fix a dinner, too."

She should have known this was coming. Elizabeth was half Martha Stewart and half organizational freak—a lethal combination for those related to her who just didn't give a damn about holiday traditions. Christina's last four Thanksgivings had been unmitigated disasters—the best of which was the one she'd spent at a friend's house where everyone celebrated by getting stoned. The turkey hadn't made it into the oven until eight o'clock that night, its only stuffing the plastic bag of giblets, plastic included. "There has to be a restaurant around here that does catering."

Elizabeth looked horrified.

"God, you're so predictable. Okay, what did you have in mind?"

"We could do the cooking."

"We?" Christina questioned.

"The three of us."

"Like that's going to happen. You're assuming a lot if you think I can cook."

"Doesn't matter."

"Okay, so we throw some Stove Top stuffing in a pan and open a can of gravy. What are you going to do with Sam and Stephanie and the boys?"

"Would it be so bad if I brought them?"

"All of them?"

"Yes."

"And me and Rachel. That's seven. With Rachel's four that's nine. Then there's Logan—"

"He said he won't be here. He has to go back to work next week, but he'll be here for Christmas."

Christina was fighting a battle she didn't want to win. "Sure. What the hell. Why should I care?"

"Be careful," Elizabeth said sarcastically. "You might give someone the wrong impression with all that enthusiasm."

"Well, what did you expect me to say? It's not like I know how to do any of this stuff."

"I'll teach you."

Christina picked up the tray again. "I'm thrilled." She pushed open the swinging door between the kitchen and family room with her hip. "Hey, guess what," she said to Rachel and Ginger. "Elizabeth has decided we should all have Thanksgiving here."

A stunned silence followed. Rachel was the first to say something. "Would you do that?"

"*Should* we is more like it," Ginger said. "Jeff will be home by then. You don't need a houseful of people when——"

"Oh, but I do," Rachel protested. The bruises around her eyes had faded to a yellow-green that she'd stopped trying to hide with makeup. "Jeff can't wait to get some normalcy in our lives again. And the kids would love it."

"What about you, Ginger?" Elizabeth asked. "Are you going to Denver for Thanksgiving?"

"I'm going home for Christmas this year. I never do both."

Elizabeth beamed. "Then it's a done deal. I'll pick up what we'll need before I leave today. Does anyone have any family recipes, any traditions they want to include?"

Christina groaned.

"Oh, shut up," Ginger said without malice. "We're on to you, you know. If Elizabeth hadn't thought of this, you would have found a way to suggest it yourself."

"Not likely. My domesticity begins and ends with cleaning moldy takeout from the back shelves of the refrigerator. And remember, I was raised in Mexico. Mexicans don't celebrate Thanksgiving."

"I hate canned sweet potatoes," Ginger said.

"I love mince pie," Rachel added.

They all looked at her as if she were some kind of alien creature. Christina made a face. "You're kidding, right?"

"Well, I like fruitcake," Elizabeth confessed.

"Okay," Ginger said, "if we're admitting dirty little holiday secrets, I like giblet gravy."

"*Euww*," the others said in unison.

Rachel laughed. "Sounds as if we'd better stick to the basics."

Elizabeth nodded. She could handle basic; she could handle elaborate. The meal itself didn't matter, the company did. They had one more meeting after today, in December, to listen to Jessie's final tape. After that, geography would create barriers between them when Christina moved to Los Angeles, Ginger to Kansas City, and Rachel . . . she didn't know about Rachel other than how hard the road ahead was for both her and Jeff. They would likely stay through Jeff's recovery. After that, it made sense to leave California, if only to escape bad memories.

"Basic it is," Elizabeth said, already planning special touches. If this was their only Thanksgiving together, it would be one none of them would ever forget.

They settled into the chairs and sofa in Rachel's family room that overlooked a tree-filled canyon and were warmed by a fire in the stone fireplace. Their mugs of coffee creamed and sugared, a plate of cookies nearby, Christina opened the manila envelope she'd picked up at Lucy's office. "I told Lucy I'd write a summation to prove we actually listened to today's tapes, but she said it wasn't necessary." She reached for the portable tape player she'd brought with her.

"By the way, she sends her best," she said to Rachel. "And she wanted me to tell you that if there's anything she can do, just let her know."

Elizabeth leaned back in the Queen Anne–style recliner and sipped her coffee. Over the past four months, as she listened to Jessie's voice on the tapes, she'd gone from resentful to curious to melancholy. She'd forgiven her mother because not forgiving her was burdensome. More important, she allowed herself to feel love for her father again.

"Ready?" Christina asked.

Elizabeth started to nod, then impulsively said, "Let's go outside." She looked at the others. "I love fall."

"Me, too," Christina said.

"It's my favorite season, too," Rachel and Ginger said simultaneously.

Minutes later they settled in again, this time in weathered Adirondack chairs. Surrounded by a landscape of gold, crimson, yellow, and orange, they listened to a now-familiar voice that transported them to another time and place.

Jessie's Story

I'd never cared much for whiskey, not even the aged and mellowed kind. It always seemed a little like punishment the way it burns all the way from the back of the tongue to the stomach and then hangs around to burn some more. It became my drink of choice after Frank died, the first thing I reached for in the morning and the last thing I had in my hand when I fell down at night. I'm ashamed to say I was drunk at Frank's funeral and to this day can't remember anything past the church being filled to overflowing and the snap and slap and crack of rifles being raised and lowered for a twenty-one-gun salute.

I didn't go to the house afterward, although I told everyone I would. I couldn't take one more person telling me what a good kid Frank had been and what a shame it was the way he died. Never had a chance. What a waste. So young. Life just beginning. How proud I must be. I remember I wanted to kill the son of a bitch who said that bit about being proud.

I didn't know Barbara was at the funeral until she slipped into my car at the cemetery and took the keys. She drove me home, not minding or thinking less of me that I cried most of the way.

I made a couple of attempts at finding a reason to get up in the morning, at caring that bills had come due and gone unpaid so long that cars were disappearing out of my garage and furniture out of the house. Most everything I owned had been repossessed except the house itself and a closet full of clothes. When I tried to write a check for a case of whiskey and it was refused it scared the hell out of me. How was I going to face life sober? I needed the numbness the whiskey provided, the punishment of feeling it burning a hole in my stomach.

I had a gun—everyone in L.A. did back then, or at least everyone I knew. The more I thought about using it, the more appeal it had. It wasn't a perfect solution, but it was damn close. Oblivion didn't seem so bad compared to where I'd been living. As soon as the whiskey was gone I'd use the gun and my pain would be over. I didn't hold any hope of seeing Frank. I'd called on God, offered Him my soul, but there wasn't anyone on the other end of the line.

Barbara must have sensed something because she showed up that night after her concert. I tried, but I couldn't get rid of her. She just sat and watched me drink and held my hand when I'd let her. Finally she got me talking, and I spilled like rice out of a gunny sack with a split seam. She flat refused to believe it was my fault Frank had joined the Army. Her reasoning didn't change my mind, but it let me know that not everyone saw what I'd done in the same light.

The whiskey was gone, and I still had enough pride not to ask her to get more. She stayed with me for three days, holding me, talking to me, loving me. I'd never had a better friend. I'd never had anyone do more or ask less in return. It damn near tore my heart out three months later when she told me she was pregnant. She was riding a wave, a song away from her dream of a number-one record, and in the music business second chances were as rare as real overnight successes.

I offered to find someone to take care of it, but she wouldn't listen. She was determined to have her baby and just as determined that the baby would be raised far away from show business. She was smart enough to know the break in my slow dance with whiskey was just that. I was still a couple of years away from leaving that partner in the dance hall.

I always wondered if Barbara didn't have some kind of premonition that she wasn't going to be around long enough to raise a child. She was the only one I ever knew who could squeeze seventy seconds out of a minute and still worry she didn't have enough time.

She got her hit record the next year and saved me a seat at every concert after that. I had enough sense to step back and let her go when her star shot into the heavens. She would call me on the baby's birthday from wherever she was in the world, and we would talk about everything except her little girl. Three years before she died I hired someone to find Ginger. All I wanted was to know she was being loved and cared for the way she deserved. The detective thought I'd want proof, so he brought back some photographs of Ginger on a swing, grinning ear to ear like her life was nothing but sunshine and rainbows. I thought about it a long time before I gave one of the pictures to Barbara. She cried and tried to convince me they were happy tears, but I've always wondered if such a thing is possible.

Barbara kept the picture. It was in the plane debris and among the personal things she'd left me in her will. When the box arrived I was in Mexico, trying to work out export problems with the government for a strawberry crop that was rotting in the fields. By the time I arrived home the following week Carmen had looked at everything and put the clues together to make an educated guess at my relationship with Barbara. She refused to believe the affair was over before I'd married her and used it as a reason to leave me and take Christina home with her to Mexico City.

I was in my fifties when we met, Carmen barely into her twenties. She was the niece of my partner and from a powerful, wealthy family in Mexico City. And she was pregnant. Despite the threat of being disowned by distraught parents, she refused to name the father. I offered her a place to stay, she thought I'd proposed, and as easily as that I was married again. The marriage was doomed before it began.

We could have and should have had it annulled when Carmen lost the baby a month later. But by then we were living in San Diego, and she wasn't ready to go home. The taste of freedom she'd experienced away from her family was as intoxicating as cheap tequila and produced the same kind of headache years later when being with me in San Diego lost its charm.

I was an old man in her friends' eyes, an embarrassment.

We had nothing in common except a child we both adored.

"Come with me to Mexico City," Carmen offered unenthusiastically.

"My business is here."

"You don't have to sell the strawberries here, you can sell them somewhere else."

"The business is based on bringing them into the States." It was an old argument. "That's how we make our money."

"What money?" she shot back. "There hasn't been any money around here for months. I tried to use my credit card last week, and the clerk told me I couldn't, that the bill hadn't been paid." She stood in the middle of our small kitchen and folded her arms across her chest, glaring at me. "Do you have any idea how humiliating that was for me?"

"Things will turn around. They always do."

"I don't care. I don't want to be here anymore. I want to go home. I want to be with my family. And they want me back with them."

This was the first I'd heard of it. "You've talked to your mother and father about this?"

"Yes," she admitted. "They miss me and they want to be near their granddaughter."

Christina was sitting at the table, book and crayons spread out in front of her, intently coloring Mickey Mouse's ears a bright green. "I'm not going to lose her," I said.

"You won't. You can see her whenever you want."

"Be reasonable, Carmen. Mexico City is hundreds of miles from here."

She opened a cupboard, took out a pan, and slammed

the door. *"You don't see her now. You and Mario are always off doing some business thing."*

"You know the problems we've had lately."

"No, I don't know. You never tell me anything." She held up her hand to stop my reply. *"I don't want to know. Not now. It's too late."* Her expression softened. *"It's always something with you, Jessie. I'm tired of living like this. I'm not going to do it anymore."*

I didn't know what to say, so I didn't say anything.

She put a hand on my arm. "I know you never loved me. And you know I never loved you. You were being kind when you asked me to marry you, and I was so grateful I thought it would be enough. But it's not. I want more. I'm still young. I have a lifetime ahead of me. I don't want to spend it in a loveless marriage."

Again, there was nothing I could say. She and Christina left the following week. The strawberry business folded that summer. Mario and I salvaged enough for him to start another business and for me to get back and forth to see Christina while I looked around for something else to do. I'd never learned to read Spanish and yet didn't bother hiring a lawyer to look through the divorce papers when they arrived, foolishly trusting Carmen and not knowing I was dealing with her father. It never occurred to me that I was relinquishing parental rights to Christina when I signed.

To be fair, neither did Carmen. Domination was the toll extracted by her father for being allowed into the family circle again. She'd paid without realizing the consequences. When my visits were cut off I used what money I had left to hire my own lawyer, but it was useless. Carmen sneaked Christina out of the house to see me when she could, but our time together was strained and awkward and never long enough.

One day a man came with them to the park, Enrique Alvarado. Carmen said he was a friend, but I could see he was much more. She adored him, as did Christina. He was in his midthirties, well spoken, and wore his custom-made suit as if it were an entitlement. In comparison, in my shorts and flowered shirt, I looked like an aging surfer who'd had too many mai tais and too many years in the sun.

Carmen took my arm. "Can we talk? Alone? There are some things I need to tell you." Before, she'd spoken English with only a trace of an accent, never teaching Christina a word of Spanish. Now, suddenly, English seemed like a second language to her.

I knew I wasn't going to like what was coming. "Now?"

"Enrique will watch Christina."

I followed her to a bench while Christina stayed behind and Enrique watched her climb the slide. Hearing Christina's laughter and excited calls to Enrique, I was consumed with jealousy. The torment became almost unbearable as Carmen laid out the reasons she wanted me to stop seeing my daughter.

"You can see how Enrique is with her, and how she feels about him," she said. "We're going to be married next month."

"Congratulations."

"She already calls him Papa," she added gently, not responding to my sarcasm.

I watched Christina a long time without saying anything. She was the one bright spot in a life without direction or reason. For the past year my existence had centered on the efforts it took to see her.

But what was I to her? I knew she loved me. I could see it in her eyes when she first caught sight of me waiting beside the palm tree at the park. Was it enough? Was dividing her love and loyalty between me and Enrique too high a price to ask a four-year-old child to pay?

"Give me some time with her," I finally said.

"You can have the rest of the day. I'll meet you back here at five."

I don't like zoos, even the best seem like animal prisons, but I didn't know where else to take her, so that's where we went. I didn't try to explain how her life was about to change, I figured Carmen could take care of that. Instead, I spent my last day with my beautiful raven-haired daughter with her riding on my shoulders and seeing the world through her eyes.

I wouldn't have made the same decision today as I did then. I would have stayed and fought and bought and bribed whoever stood in the way. Christina wasn't better off not knowing me. Wisdom gained in hindsight exacts a cruel toll.

With that same bitter hindsight, I know now I should never have let Elizabeth refuse to see me either. I should have parked myself on her doorstep until she had me arrested and gone back when I got out on bail. We could have worked it out. I'm sure of it now. Eventually, she would have forgiven me for Frank. She might even have helped me forgive myself.

I was right to let Ginger go. So was Barbara. Life taught me love doesn't always come wrapped with a pretty bow. As often as not it hurts one or the other of the people giving and taking, sometimes both. I think that's what happened to Rachel. Anna should have let her go the way Barbara let Ginger go, but she held on because she loved her daughter more than she loved herself.

Elizabeth looked at Christina. "Do you ever wonder what your life would have been like if he'd found a way to keep you?"

She shook her head. "I don't have to wonder, I know." She gave Elizabeth a smile and a wink through her tears. "It is what it is," she said softly. "For both of us."

Fifty-one

Christina

Christina leaned back in her chair and rubbed her eyes. Seven non-stop hours at the editing desk and she was only halfway through the training film River City Studio was doing for the Sacramento County Sheriff's Department. She was hungry, she had a head-ache, and she had shooting pains racing from her shoulders to her neck. She rocked her head back and forth, trying to work out the kink, and spotted Dexter trying to sneak past the door.

Digging her heels into the floor, she shot her chair across the room and swung through the doorway and into the hall. "Dexter—how much notice do you want before I quit?"

He tucked the folder he was carrying under his arm and looked at her over the top of his half-glasses. "All right—you can have a break."

"I don't want a break, I want to quit. One more month and I'm on my way to L.A."

"Shit." He came down the hall, grabbed the back of her chair, and hauled her into his office. "Let's talk about this."

She scooted closer to his desk and put her feet up. "There's nothing to talk about."

"What if I were to make you an offer?"

"This better be clean." They'd been working together six months, and Dexter had never come on to her. Not that she would have minded. He was kinda cute with his shaved head and dark red beard, but he wasn't her type. Way too nice. The guys who usually caught her eye had a bit of a bastard in them. Like Randy.

"You're not my type, Christina."

She laughed. "Amazing—you popped the thought right out of my head. So, what's the offer?"

"What would you say if I told you Ian Grayson has signed on for *After the Lightning*?"

"Signed on?" she said skeptically. After last year's Oscar-winning performance in *The Forest*, Ian Grayson had moved to the top of the A list in Hollywood. He was the movies' latest bad boy wanted by everyone from Spielberg to Howard. "Or you talked his agent into sending him the script?"

"I sent him the script myself. He's my cousin."

She put her feet back on the floor and sat up straight. He had her attention. "So what's the offer?"

"I don't want to go to any of the usual sources for money. With a star like Ian, I'm not big enough to keep control of the project if a problem develops. Which means we do everything on the cheap."

"And I'm cheap."

"More important, you're good."

She'd found the script on Dexter's desk a couple of months ago and asked if she could read it. The story was gripping, but chancy. For the first three-quarters of the movie Ian would play a seemingly unredeemable antihero. It would take a hell of a director to make the transformation believable. "So, how do I get paid?"

"Scale, plus producer credit, plus front-end cut."

"And for this I do . . . what?"

"Everything I can't."

She could go to L.A., meet all the right people, hook up with the perfect script, do everything right, and never get the chance to work with an actor like Ian. She smiled. "I want everything spelled out in a contract."

"You pay for the lawyer and it's yours."

Bemused, she shook her head. "I'm never going to get to L.A."

He spun her chair around and scooted her back into the hallway. "Yes, you will—unless you want me to pick up your Oscar for you. Now go back to work."

"I haven't said yes."

He gave her a knowing grin. "But you didn't say no."

"If you're going to strong-arm me you could at least do it over dinner."

"You're on. Eva's Roost tonight."

"That better not be some hamburger joint."

"Would I do that? Never mind, don't answer." He put his hand to his heart. "Eva's Roost isn't the biggest restaurant in this area, but it's the best. I'll give you another five percent if you don't think so, too."

She liked the odds. "You're on."

Christina didn't get home until two-thirty the next morning. She was an hour into her second wind and unable to sleep, so got up and went into the kitchen for a snack. As usual, Rhona had the refrigerator fully stocked, everything from pudding cups to lunch meat. She settled on strawberry yogurt.

She shuffled down the hallway to Jessie's study, her ragged stuffed bear tucked under her arm. Standing at the door eating her yogurt, she looked inside. A full moon and the neighbor's outdoor lighting cast the room in off-white ghostly light and deep shadows. With just a little imagination she could picture her father sitting at the antique desk, looking back at her.

"I loved you, Daddy," she said softly. "How could you convince yourself I would be better off without you?" She understood now that no one had told her he'd died. It was something she'd made up when he left and never came back. He had to be dead—otherwise he would have come for her.

"Was it really just easier to walk away than to fight for me?" Christina snaked her hand around the corner and flipped the light switch. Decorator lighting recessed in the ceiling and tucked over and in the bookshelves lit the room in a soft glow.

Christina put her half-finished yogurt on the table next to a wingback chair and went around the desk. She'd been in this room a dozen times, looked at the books, at Frank's Purple Heart, at the things on Jessie's desk, at the pen propped in a mounted block of gold quartz. She'd never felt free to do more than look at the arrowheads or spent bullets or to take down one of the books or open a drawer or look inside the battered, leather-covered box on the corner of the desk. To do so felt like an invasion of privacy.

Now, driven by a need to better understand the man who had willingly abandoned her, Christina propped her bear against the lamp, sat in his chair, and reached for the box. She lifted the top, looked inside, and pulled out a woman's watch, the face narrow, the band delicate. Next she found a man's pocket watch, a pair of screw-back earrings with a matching necklace, and a pair of old wire-rim eyeglasses. There were yellowed letters, a page from a family Bible listing births, deaths, and marriages of relatives dating back to 1820, and old black-and-white photographs curling at the corners.

Christina set the letters aside and studied the photographs. Even as a young boy, Jessie was easy to identify. Standing with his arms stiff at his sides, posed in front of an unpainted farmhouse, he had the same hungry, faraway look in his eyes that she remembered as a child. The others she named by elimination. The thin girl with braids over her shoulders and a toothless grin would be her aunt, the boy in overalls and a cap pulled low on his forehead, her uncle. Her grandparents had been captured in the kitchen, her grandmother standing near the stove, a spoon in her hand, a calico apron covering her dress. Her grandfather leaned against the counter, a smile of mischief and joy directed toward the woman he clearly loved.

Christina stared at the picture. She could almost feel their happiness. Her grandmother must have been an extraordinary woman to survive what awaited her. "How did you do it, Grandma?" she said softly. "How did you have your heart broken so many times and still go on?"

There were other pictures, including a baby picture with Jessie's name on the back. He was bare-skinned on a bearskin rug and plainly unhappy to be there. Most of the photographs had been taken on the farm, but there were a couple of mountain scenes where whoever took the picture stood back so far, she would need a magnifying glass to tell who the people were.

She couldn't see herself in these people, but then she'd never been able to see herself in any of her family. She looked pale compared to her half-brother and -sister in Mexico and dark compared to her sisters here. She'd never said so out loud, but there were times when she felt as if she didn't belong anywhere or to anyone.

She picked up a picture of Jessie standing on a pillared porch, his face in profile, staring at a cloud of dust on the horizon. He looked isolated and solitary, a boy not yet a man, a child unaware that sorrow would shadow his footsteps throughout his entire life.

Was she his surrender, his acknowledgment that he had won battles but lost the war for personal happiness? Was it possible that he really had believed he was doing her a favor by walking away?

She held the photograph closer, and when her vision clouded

with tears she held her father's image against her chest. "I love you, Daddy," she said again. "I always have. I always will. I wish you had given me the chance to tell you."

Moments later she reached for her bear and automatically tucked it under her arm, the perch it had ridden for over twenty years since the day it came home with her from the zoo. As she moved to leave, the empty shelf where Frank's medal had been kept caught her eye. On impulse, she crossed the room and put her bear on the shelf, adjusting his legs, centering him, then tilting his head just so. "Looks as if you have a new home," she said, smiling through her tears. "Looks as if we both do."

Fifty-two

Elizabeth

"We need to talk," Stephanie said.

Elizabeth's hand froze, the angel she was holding suspended beneath an already overloaded branch on the Christmas tree. She'd sensed a change in Stephanie since Thanksgiving, nothing tangible, just a confidence in her day-to-day decisions and an interest about things that didn't affect her directly. She was insatiably curious about her new aunts and fixated on her cousins, Cassidy and John, even including the two of them in her Christmas shopping. As casually as possible considering her heart was blocking her throat, Elizabeth asked, "About what?"

"Me—the baby. I've done some things I need to tell you about."

Elizabeth hooked the angel over a branch and watched it swing backward. "You want some tea?"

"Yeah, I guess. Just not that new herb stuff you got at the health food store last week." She followed Elizabeth into the kitchen.

"How about the old herb stuff?"

"The peach isn't bad." Stephanie filled the teakettle with water and put it on the stove while Elizabeth got the tea bags and mugs.

Elizabeth leaned against the counter as she waited for the water to boil; Stephanie sat at the table. "I didn't tell you the truth about my baby's father," she said.

Not even close to what Elizabeth had expected. "Oh?"

Stephanie flushed, her neck and cheeks turning a spotted pink. "His name is David Christopher, by the way. And I wasn't high, he was. He wasn't interested in me even though I'd been making a play for him on and off since our freshman year. I guess you could say I took advantage of him." She nervously twisted her hair into a knot on top of her head and then let it fall free. "He found me the day after the party and apologized. God, Mom—can you imagine a guy apologizing for something like that? In case you haven't figured it out by now, he's kind of a nerd. I was so embarrassed when I found out I was pregnant that I couldn't stay in school and chance him finding out. I knew if my friends knew it would get back to him eventually."

"Why?" Elizabeth asked, managing with effort to keep the question nonjudgmental.

"Why what?"

"Why put yourself through this now?"

"When we were at Rachel and Jeff's for Thanksgiving I tried to imagine that I was Cassidy's mother and wondered what I would tell her when she asked about her father."

The sentence was like a complex word game filled with intriguing clues. Why Cassidy and not John? Why speculate about a child you would never see grow to that age? Again, Elizabeth held her questions.

"Oh—I guess I forgot to tell you. The ultrasound I had when you were at Rachel's was pretty conclusive. I'm going to have a girl." She thought a minute. "No, I didn't forget," she admitted. "I just didn't want you bonding with this baby any more than you already have."

"I haven't bonded," Elizabeth protested. She thought she'd

been so careful not to let it show, to the point of purposely not asking about the ultrasound.

"Oh, Mom, I see the way you look at the babies in the doctor's office. You're like some deranged stalker."

"I'm sorry. That's my problem, not yours."

"Why are you and Dad so damn good to me?" The teakettle punctuated the question with a loud whistle. She got up to turn off the flame and pour the water into their mugs.

"You're our daughter. We love you."

"That's what it's like to be a parent? Your kid comes home and turns your life upside down and you just roll with it?"

"We're keeping a diary of all this so we can blackmail you when we're old and we need someone to take care of us."

"I'm serious, Mom. Is this really what it's like?"

"You're focusing on one difficult time and missing all the good things that come with being a parent. Your father and I love being your parents. There isn't anyone I'd rather share things with. There isn't anyone I have more fun with when we spend a day together."

"You had the whole summer planned." She turned from Elizabeth and concentrated on dunking her tea bag, avoiding the look in her mother's eyes. "Dad told me how disappointed you were that I didn't want to come home."

"He shouldn't have done that."

"No, but you should have."

"Would it have made a difference?" Elizabeth asked, knowing the answer.

"No. But I didn't know then what I do now."

"It's a lesson I wish you could have learned another way."

"See? There you go again, putting me first. What about all the shit you've had happen to you this year? You even dropped out of school because of me. After you become a mother does it mean your kids always come first no matter what?"

Elizabeth added a spoonful of sugar to her tea and joined Stephanie at the table. "Why are you asking me that? Really?"

"I've decided to keep the baby."

An emotional dam burst in Elizabeth. "I'm so . . . glad."

"Don't cry," Stephanie said, reaching for the box of tissues Elizabeth kept on the counter. She took one and handed it to her mother and then another to wipe her own tears.

Elizabeth wiped her eyes and blew her nose. "What made you change your mind?"

"Lots of things. Whenever I called my friends at school it was obvious I didn't fit in anymore. At first I was scared and then I was mad. Then I didn't care." She grinned sheepishly. "You think I might be growing up a little?"

"What about this David Christopher?"

"I told him I wasn't coming after him for money or anything, and that I'd understand if he wanted to do the DNA thing when she was born. I just needed to know more about him so I could tell our daughter when she asked."

"And what did he say?"

"Not a lot at first. He hadn't heard that I was pregnant. He must have thought about it a lot, though, because he called me back a couple of days later and said he wanted to see the baby when she was born. He's going to bring pictures of his family that I can give her when she's older."

"He sounds like a nice young man." Elizabeth could feel herself moving down a road she had no business traveling.

"I went after him because he was the only guy who played hard to get. The more he resisted, the more I convinced myself I wanted him."

"So what's he like? Other than being a nerd."

"He's really smart—tall, dark hair, on the skinny side. Incredible eyes. Oh, Mom, his eyes. . . . There is one thing. He has these huge Dumbo ears. If my baby looks like him I'm going to have to start saving to have her ears fixed when she gets older."

"What are you going to do about school?"

"That's what I need to talk to you and Dad about. I've looked into transferring to Fresno State and finishing up here, but I'd need help. I could work part-time, but I'll need someone to take care of the baby. I don't want to put her in day care until she's older and can tell me what's going on with the people taking care of her."

It was everything Elizabeth could do to keep from jumping in with suggestions. This was Stephanie's show. "What other kind of help did you have in mind?"

"If I could live here until I was through school and only work weekends, then you and I could arrange our schedules so that one of us would be available to watch the baby while the other one was in class." She peered at Elizabeth over the top of her steaming mug. "I don't want you to wait to go back to school because of me, I just want you to help me so I can go back, too."

"And Dad?"

She grinned. "He gets to pay for it. I'll earn enough working weekends to pay for clothes and stuff for me and the baby, and maybe a little gas money, but that's about it. I don't see how people live on this minimum wage crap. I have to work four hours just to pay for a movie and popcorn and a Coke."

Elizabeth laughed. "Welcome to the real world."

But it wasn't the real world that existed for any of them anymore. In less than a month she would deposit a check for ten million dollars into an account she'd had Sam set up at the bank, their first hint at the ways their lives would change. She'd had no idea interest rates were negotiable until local banks began bidding for their account. As Sam had said, them that has money, makes money.

If she could, she would leave the money untouched until Stephanie was through school, giving her the sense of accomplishment that would come from doing what she could on her own. But it was bound to come out. Christina or Ginger or Rachel would let something slip and—

The thought stopped her cold. When had she made the transition from wondering if the four of them would ever be sisters in the true sense to automatically assuming they would be a part of her life?

"What do you think of Christina and—of your aunts?"

"What brought that up?"

"Family."

"They're okay." Stephanie shrugged. "When I first saw Ginger I didn't think I would like her, but I do. It shouldn't be legal to be that old and look that good. I really like Rachel and Jeff. I can't imagine going through what they did and not feeling sorry for myself, but they don't. And the kids are cool. I hope my little girl is like Cassidy."

"And Christina?"

"I don't know about her. She's like . . . I can't describe it. It's like she's always pissed off about something."

"It's a show. She's actually a pushover."

"I'll have to take your word for it."

Elizabeth sipped her tea, thoughtful again. "You're not keeping the baby because you think it's what I want, are you?"

"Isn't it? What you want, I mean."

"Yes—but it has to be your decision."

"I can't go back, and I can't go forward always looking back wondering if I made the right decision. This isn't anywhere on the radar for what I'd planned to do with my life. Sharon and I were going to share a loft in New York and live 'Sex and the City' until we were bored, and then we were going to find the perfect men and get married."

"And now?"

"The only thing I know for sure is that I'm going to be a mother and I'm going to graduate. I'm going to let the rest surprise me."

"I'm so proud of you," Elizabeth said.

"I'm kinda proud of me, too. At least I feel good about what I'm doing."

Elizabeth smiled. "Want to go shopping?"

"What about the tree?"

"We can do it later when Dad's home to help."

"Christmas or baby?"

"Christmas today. I want to get something for my sisters."

They'd gathered their coats and purses and were on their way out when Elizabeth stopped to touch her fingers to her lips and then to the heart-shaped medal she'd framed and hung by the front door. It was as much acknowledgment of Jessie as Frank.

Family.

Fifty-three

Rachel

Her battery on her new phone dead, Rachel used Ginger's phone to call home midway on the trip to Sacramento and told Jeff she would call again when she arrived. It was the first time she'd been away since he'd come home from the hospital, and despite having a nurse for him and a sitter for the kids, she was nervous about leaving. But he'd insisted she go. He wanted to get back to a normal life, or one as normal as possible. Christina and Elizabeth and Ginger had called individually and suggested their last official meeting be held at her house, but Jeff insisted that they finish where they started, in Sacramento. Finally, not convinced, but unwilling to argue, she'd agreed.

"Would you look at that," Rachel said as they neared Jessie's house. The place was festooned with Christmas lights, wreaths, and garland. "I didn't figure Christina for the decorating type."

"Every time I think I have Christina figured out," Ginger said, "she does something that surprises me."

"Did you get her a present?"

"I thought we agreed we weren't going to do that."

"Uh huh." Rachel sent her a knowing look. "You did, didn't you?"

"I wasn't, but I saw something that was so perfect I couldn't resist."

"Me, too," Rachel admitted.

"And you didn't tell me? What if I hadn't found something myself?"

She pulled into the driveway and parked next to Elizabeth's car. "I knew you would. But just in case, I signed the card from both of us."

"What about Elizabeth?"

Rachel smiled. "Same thing."

"Me, too. Do you think they got something for us?"

"Elizabeth, yes. Christina, no."

Christina met them at the door wearing a sweater with a grinning black cat sitting in the middle of a box of broken ornaments. "Merry Christmas."

"The house looks beautiful," Ginger said.

"Wait till you see the tree. It's incredible. I found this amazing Christmas shop and went nuts buying ornaments. Rhona helped, of course. There's no way I could have done it without her. I've never had a tree over two feet tall that took me more than five minutes to decorate. And all I ever used were those glass balls you get at the drugstore for a couple of bucks. I threw them out with the tree every year, but there's no way I could throw any of this stuff out." Christina moved toward the living room. "Rhona did the outside while I was at work, and it looked so cool I said we just had to have a tree—so we did."

"How many cups of coffee have you had today?" Rachel asked.

"Why?"

"You seem a little . . . wired," Ginger answered.

Christina laughed. "I know. I've been this way for days."

Elizabeth came out of the kitchen carrying a tray with coffee and mugs. "Did you tell them?"

"Not yet," Christina said, leading the way into the living room.

Rachel stopped in the doorway to look at the tree. It was indeed spectacular, covered in lights and ornaments and filling the room with a dense, fragrant pine scent. There were three elegantly wrapped presents sitting on the red velvet cloth circling the base. "Wow."

"You wouldn't believe how long it took us to put it up," Christina said.

"Well, it's spectacular," Ginger said. "But I want to know what Elizabeth's talking about. What haven't you told us?"

Christina couldn't contain the grin that split her face. "I'm back in the moviemaking business."

"Here?" Rachel asked. "I thought you said you had to move to L.A. for that to happen."

Christina told them about her partnership with Dexter. "We start principal photography in Vancouver on February tenth."

"I *love* Ian Grayson," Ginger said. "I have never been as turned on by a guy in a movie as I was by him in *Another Harvest*."

Elizabeth laughed. "You and a hundred million other women."

"Have you met him yet?" Ginger asked.

"Once."

"*And?*"

"He's nice."

"That's it? That's the best you can do?"

Christina's grin broadened. "All right—he's a hunk. Spoiled but not obnoxiously so—he ate the whole bowl of M&Ms and didn't discriminate. He's really funny and self-deprecating but serious about the business. The reason he took this role and agreed to work for scale is he's terrified of being typecast and having his career end at thirty." She paused. "Before I forget—on a completely different subject—I have something I want to talk to all of you about. Since I'm going to be based in Sacramento for the foreseeable future, I was wondering if anyone would object if I bought this house."

"I think it's a great idea," Elizabeth said after taking a couple of seconds to absorb the news.

"I do, too," Ginger added enthusiastically. "I love knowing this house is staying in the family."

Rachel nodded and mentally stepped away from the discussion that followed. She surreptitiously looked at the women who had gone from adversaries to reluctant friends to sisters. They were all like blocks on a quilt, Jessie's slowly unfolding story the thread that bound them together. In ways that were both painful and comforting she'd grown to love the flawed, caring man who was their father and to envy Elizabeth and Christina the time they'd had with him.

"Let's not wait until after lunch to start the tapes," Rachel said impulsively.

"I was thinking the same thing," Elizabeth said.

Ginger took her usual seat, and Christina picked up the manila envelope Lucy had dropped by earlier. She opened it and reached inside. "There's only one," she said with obvious disappointment.

Rachel warmed her hands on the coffee mug while Christina dropped the tape into the player and hit play.

Jessie's Story

That's it, Lucy. You know the rest of the story because you were there for it. As usual, you outsmarted me. I couldn't see the sense to telling you my life story when I made that deal with you over lunch, but I think I understand what you were after now that I've reached the end. I was afraid of what I'd find if I let myself look back, but it wasn't near as bad as I'd thought. I made a lot of mistakes, none of them intentional, but that didn't stop them hurting people I never meant to hurt. If saying I'm sorry would change anything I'd put it on a billboard. My girls had a right to expect more than they got. I just didn't know how to give it to them.

They're fine women. I'd tell them how proud I was of the way they turned out, but I have a feeling it's not something they'd welcome coming from me. It's too soon. Maybe one day when you think they're ready, you could tell them for me.

Take care of yourself, Lucy . . . and, if it's not asking too much, take care of my girls.

The tape ended. A stunned silence followed. Rachel couldn't believe what she'd heard and considered asking Christina to play it again. "These tapes weren't meant for us," she murmured, not realizing she said it aloud until Elizabeth looked at her.

"You think Lucy did this on her own?" Ginger said. "That it wasn't in the will?"

Elizabeth shook her head, disbelieving. "Do you know what the consequences are for something like that?"

"What?" Christina asked.

"Disbarment for sure," Rachel said. "Possibly jail." She recoiled at the idea. "This can't be what it seems. Why would Lucy take that kind of risk just to get us to listen to these tapes?"

"That's obvious," Christina was the first to answer. "She was in love with Jessie."

That was the key, one Rachel would have recognized in the beginning if she hadn't been so blinded by hatred and anger. "Lucy could manipulate us, but she couldn't lie to us. That's why she gave us this final tape. Now the question is, what are we going to do about it?"

Christina looked at each of them in turn. "My vote is that we send her flowers—the biggest bouquet we can find."

"No," Elizabeth said softly. "It should be four roses, one from each of us."

"Yellow ones," said Ginger. "I have a feeling it's what Jessie would have chosen."

"Roses it is," Rachel said.

Epilogue

Caught up in her musings about time travelers and butterflies, Elizabeth missed seeing Christina enter the cemetery. Moving carefully between the headstones to avoid stepping on a grave, Christina didn't look up until she was within the canopy of the massive heritage oak shading Jessie's grave. The hug she gave Elizabeth lasted longer than their usual greeting, a silent acknowledgment of the reason they were there.

"Where's your car?" Elizabeth asked.

"I decided to walk. I've been trapped in that editing room for over a week and needed some exercise."

"How's it coming?" Christina and Dexter had trouble letting go of a film, often tinkering with it until the studio threatened legal action to get it into theaters by the announced release date. The result was an ever-growing number of awards crowding the photographs on the fireplace mantel.

"Another week and we should be there."

"And how's the back?"

Christina put a protective hand on her softly rounded belly.

"Better. I saw the doctor yesterday, and she said that we're both fine." She gave Elizabeth an unexpected, excited grin. "I was going to wait until everyone was here. . . ."

"But?" Even guessing what was coming, Elizabeth drew the word out, filling it with expectation.

"Do you have any idea how hard it is for me to keep a secret from you?" Not waiting for an answer, she took a deep breath and blurted, "It's a girl."

Elizabeth let out a squeal of delight and hugged her again, this time with joy. "Dexter must be in the clouds." After two boys Christina had been ready to call it quits. Then, as a joke, Dexter gave her a statue of a South American fertility goddess guaranteed to produce girls. She put the unbelievably ugly statue in their bedroom and forgot about it. Four months later they were in the middle of their current movie, in contract negotiations for another, and she was inconveniently and ecstatically pregnant.

"Not only in the clouds, he's started a campaign to get me to marry him."

"And this is a bad thing?" Elizabeth asked, repeating a phrase she'd been using with Christina ever since she and Dexter got pregnant the first time seven years earlier. It wasn't a moral judgment, it was a legal one, the same one she'd used when, at Stephanie's graduation, she and David announced they were moving in together and would postpone marriage until they were financially ready—or pregnant with their second child.

"I don't know. . . . In a way it's like saying what we have now isn't good enough or that this baby is more important somehow."

"You're kidding—who would think something that dumb?"

"Dexter's mother."

"Yet another reason not to like that woman."

A white Prius nosed through the heavy iron gates that guarded the entrance. "Here comes Rachel and Ginger," Christina said.

"Are you going to tell them about the baby?" Elizabeth asked.

"Later, when we're all back at the house." She glanced at the brass marker on her father's grave. "This is Lucy's time. And Dad's."

Another strong flash of guilt came over Elizabeth as she thought about the potential consequences to her sisters if they were caught. But they all insisted they owed this to Lucy. All she'd ever asked of them was to be reunited with their father when she died—any way they could arrange it.

"I'd understand if you didn't want to be here," Elizabeth said. "Dexter must have had a fit when you told him what you were going to do, especially now with the baby."

"It's not as if we're talking actual prison time," Christina said. "Besides, he doesn't know."

"Well, that's one way to handle it."

"What about Sam?"

Elizabeth smiled. "He doesn't know either."

"Wanna bet Jeff and Logan are just as clueless?"

"Yeah, can you imagine Jeff doing damage control with headlines like 'President of the Anna Kaplan Foundation Arrested for Criminal Trespass'?"

"Is that what we're doing? Criminal trespass? Shouldn't it have a more beefy sound to it—something like 'Malicious Mischief with Malice Aforethought'?"

"Too wordy. They'll go for something short and pithy when they file charges."

"Lucy would never agree to this."

"Maybe," Elizabeth said. "But only for our benefit. I have a feeling she'd be secretly pleased with the irony of her and Jessie's story coming full circle this way."

Christina's eyes pooled with unshed tears. "I'm going to miss her."

Elizabeth nodded. "I know," she said softly, reaching for Christina's hand. "Me, too." When Ginger got out of the car Elizabeth saw that she'd brought flowers. Yellow roses.

"Do you think Logan knows?" Elizabeth asked Christina. She wished she knew Logan and the boys better, but with two sets of twins born less than two years apart, their conversations, when they did all get together, rarely moved beyond teething or terrible twos or preschool. Sam knew him better from the times they golfed together and liked him a lot, saying Logan was the stereotypical firefighter, the epitome of the quiet, self-effacing hero. Ginger plainly adored him and Logan plainly adored her—for now it was all Elizabeth really needed to know.

"If he did, he'd be here." Christina opened her arms to her sisters. They exchanged hugs and kisses and quick updates about airport delays and traffic. The ordinary, the fabric of their daily lives, they exchanged in phone calls and email and text messages.

Ginger looked around, and let out a quick, nervous sigh. "Are we ready?"

"She's been hyperventilating since I picked her up at the airport," Rachel said.

Ginger didn't even try to deny it. "You have to remember I'm from the Midwest. We walk a pretty straight and narrow path out there."

Elizabeth reached in her purse and brought out four plastic bags, gently, reverently distributing them. "I thought we could try to cover this whole area—the tree and the grass. Just be as subtle as you can. The last thing we want to do is draw attention."

Rachel cupped her hands around her bag. "I hate having to do this. We should be—" Her breath caught in a sob and she couldn't finish. Finally, she managed to say, "It would have been so simple just to open the grave and let us scatter Lucy's ashes over Dad's casket," Rachel said.

"Policy," Elizabeth said to a question she'd fielded a dozen times. "Very, very rigid policy enforced by people with sticks up—" She reconsidered the crudity. "People with no imagination and an icy lack of compassion."

Rachel put her arm around Ginger's shoulder. "The more I thought about what we're doing, the more right it felt. Lucy knew what she was doing when she asked us to take care of her." She purposely looked at Ginger and then Elizabeth and Christina. "She knew no matter what, we'd find a way." Now she smiled. "After all—we're Jessie Reed's daughters."

Saying she would catch up with them at the house, Elizabeth lingered to say a final, private farewell.

She glanced around the area where they had scattered Lucy's ashes and saw only faint traces of color. The sprinklers would come on in a couple of hours and finish the work they'd begun.

In death Lucy would nurture and shelter and envelop her beloved Jessie the way she had in life. She would become a part of the grass that covered him, and the heritage oak that provided shade in the sweltering summers. She would be integrated into new branches where finches and doves perched to celebrate spring with song. Eventually new roots would reach down and embrace Jessie's casket, and he and Lucy would be together again.

Forever.

Acknowledgments

As always, John Morelli, M.D., is there for me when I have medical questions. Though reality doesn't always fit the way I'd envisioned the story going, I'm incredibly grateful for the number of times he's saved me from writing something that would frustrate anyone in the profession. If mistakes still managed to make it into the book, it's my fault. Thanks, John. You're the best!

Sadly, my knowledge of schizophrenia is intimate and ongoing, and didn't need research. I have a brother who has suffered from this illness since he was a young man. While I accept and take care of the man he has become, I will forever miss the big brother I knew as a child. I wish you peace and gentle roads, Fred.

A+

AUTHOR INSIGHTS, EXTRAS, & MORE...

FROM

GEORGIA BOCKOVEN

AND

Wm

WILLIAM MORROW

Author's Note

There were three children in my family, two boys and one girl—me. While I never had to share a bedroom or wear hand-me-down clothes, I would have given up all the privileges that came with being the only girl for a sister. Older or younger, didn't matter. A twin would have been perfect. My imagination ran wild with ways to fit that scenario into our family. Plainly, I've been spinning tall tales for a long, long time.

In that light, *The Year Everything Changed* was even more fun to write than usual. I was able to answer every "what if" sister question I'd ever imagined. While it was a challenge to come up with background stories for these women and to create the father who could bring them all together, the hardest part by far was letting go when I finished the book. I came to love these characters and wanted to know what happened to them after the last chapter. Thanks to my wonderfully understanding editor, Lucia Macro, I was able to add an epilogue that answered my questions and what I believed would be readers' questions, too. (Yes, writers really do become this invested in their characters—at least this writer does!)

Although I never got the biological sister I yearned for, I've been blessed with women in my life who are like sisters to me. We share important and inconsequential moments together; we laugh at the same silly situations, cry obnoxiously during sad movies, listen when it's important to hear, and hug each other when a touch is what's needed most. We celebrate accomplishments and feel profound sadness over loss. Thank you Karol, Kathy, Lu, and Susan. My life is infinitely richer because of you.

And there's another woman who makes my life richer every day and who has become the daughter I never had, my daughter-in-law. Thank you, Patty.

Questions for Discussion

1. In *The Year Everything Changed*, Jessie's story covers more than six decades of significant change in moral and social attitudes. In particular, a father's role in the family and in his children's lives has been completely rewritten. Did you find it difficult to judge Jessie's behavior by those previous standards?

2. Is being a sister always a blood bond or can it be a state of mind? If you were suddenly presented with previously unknown adult siblings, how do you think you would react? Do you believe it's possible to develop a true familial bond without a shared history? Would the genetic link be enough encouragement to make you want to try?

3. Should Jessie have tried to bring his daughters together sooner? Would it have worked under less dramatic circumstances?

4. Christina and Elizabeth are the only sisters who spent any time with Jessie as children. Why do you think their reactions at seeing him again are so different? Why was Christina so quick to forgive Jessie while it was almost impossible for Elizabeth to do the same?

5. We sometimes form opinions of people by looking at their other relationships. Did Lucy's passionate loyalty to Jessie and her willingness to risk her law practice to help him ac-

complish something in death that he couldn't in life change your feelings about him in any way?

6. Do you believe extreme beauty can be a burden? If so, how do you think it influenced Ginger's behavior?

7. Of the four sisters, Rachel had the most difficult childhood. For her, betrayal and abandonment are bitter fruits from the same tree. How do you think Rachel would have reacted if Ginger had told her that she was involved with a married man? Should Ginger have told Rachel after the affair ended? Would it have changed their relationship?

8. Did you understand or sympathize with Elizabeth's mother in any way? Was her behavior justifiable? Was she, like Jessie, a victim of the time that she lived in, when a woman's role and social resources were limited by society's expectations?

9. Grandparents raising grandchildren is not an oddity anymore. How do you feel about Elizabeth's reaction to the possibility of raising Stephanie's child? Do you feel she was being selfish or reasonable in her decision? How do you think you would react if faced with the same choices?

10. Which daughter do you feel was the most like her father? Which was the least?

11. It's left to the reader's imagination whether Ginger ever contacts her biological mother's family. Do you think she does? And if so, how do you think it went?

12. By the end of the tapes did your opinion of Jessie change? Given another chance, what kind of father do you think he would make today?

© John Bockoven

GEORGIA BOCKOVEN is an award-winning author who began writing fiction after a successful career as a freelance journalist and photographer. Her books have sold the world over. The mother of two, she resides in Northern California with her husband, John.

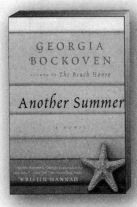